ISBN Paperback 978-1951653-01-9

Printed in the United States of America

PR Media Solutions LLC
413 20th Ave. West Palmetto, FL 34221

INVISIBLE ISLAND

COLLEEN BAUSMAN

Chapter One

The incredible story of the invisible island starts on the return flight from a training session that I had conducted in China. With the trip being a once in a lifetime opportunity and one I wanted to share with my youngest daughter, I was able to bring her along with me for the experience. With never traveling so far to provide training before I cannot fib, I appreciated her company and support.

In hindsight I am not sure if that was the right thing to do given the timing of global events however when thinking the end was near having my daughter with me was a comfort and a weight of guilt. If she had not come with me…

As we flew home and looked out the window on our voyage we could see was water below us and with it being a thirteen-hour flight I had no idea where we were when the sky turned almost black and the weather all of a sudden became absolutely, violent.

Just prior to the weather change, I was in the washroom, which if I looked back out of the door could see my daughter in the first seat. In hindsight, it is odd that when I went into the washroom I had taken my purse, which is not typical for me to do, and somehow I became a tangled mess in the tiny space and all I could think to do was get Amanda's attention and get her to help me. Luckily, when I opened the door she was looking right at it. I gestured for her to come help me and for some reason she grabbed her purse and walked up to the washroom to help. As soon as she got to the washroom door that I had open just a sliver, the plane started bouncing like wild. The flight attendants did not have time to react, when the captain came over the intercom to announce the devastating situation that we had just flown into, the seatbelt lights came on but with the suddenness and severity of the situation, our flight attendant slam us back into bathroom and yelled for us to lock it. There was no way that we could have made it the six feet to our chairs as the plane was within seconds of breaking apart.

With both Amanda and squished into the washroom and freaking out as we could hear the others screams and could feel the plane coming apart. The washroom cubicle broke away from the rest of the plane with Amanda and me in it. As we thrashed about and panicking we must have hit our heads and lost consciousness. In my thoughts at some point of our falling from the sky, I seem to recall the sound that a parachute makes when it opens.

In a haze and realizing that, I was not dead and that I was still stuffed in the tiny washroom with Amanda and with that thought … I remember being shocked conscious and quickly, gently started shaking her making sure she was alive. She let out a big gasp and she started crying which for an instant was the best feeling in the world. Until we realize that, we are trapped, in what feels like a floating cocoon but were the sealed washroom cubicle.

Although there was no light we could see the space we were in and we could feel that we were gently rocking back and forth like we were in a canoe. We had no idea if we were going to be able to open the door, and or what we might find once we do. Will we be floating in the middle of the ocean somewhere?

Once we calmed ourselves down enough and realized nothing was broken we decided, we had to open the door and face our terrifying unknown situation. With being admittedly the two biggest adult babies, we knew that whatever we were going to open up the door to, was going to be more than either of us was prepared or equipped for.
As we pushed on the door with our shoulders, we could see that something orange was holding the corner of the door closed so with our backs against the wall using our feet, we were able to push the door open.

As we lay on our backs and our feet pointing to the sky we can see the blackness of the clouds and the background looked muddy. Getting braver, we lift our heads up and look over the edge of the cubicle and to our amazement and surprise; we had floated and drifted onto a very small beach.

Wow, we survived a plane crash and ended up on a beach, it was like we had just won the lottery so we felt at that instant. Then reality sets in that there is no one else around or other signs of the plan or other wreckage there is just us that drifted on this tiny beach. As we gain the use of our legs we get out of the cubicle and pull it up further on the beach so it would not float away. That is when it became clear that the only reason that we survived the crash was that when the plane blew apart the emergency floatable ramp must have deployed and wrapped around our cubicle and acted as a parachute for the fall into the ocean and acted as the floating device once we hit.

The weather was so nasty with the sky black and turbulent and instead of rain, it seemed like thick black snow was coming down. Being terribly shaken and in shock but through it all the one thing we both had with us was our smokes in our purses, which like us, they survived. That meant everything to us at that moment.

As we are freaking out and leaning against our only source of protection from the elements, to have our smoke we try to comfort each other knowing our situation is grave. As we try to get our bearings, we can see that we are in a little cove of sorts on an island that has sheer cliffs around us. It appeared that this little area of beach was all there was between the water and the rock wall. We were definitely in trouble if we were going to be on the island for long because there was no wood to burn or water to drink.

We had no idea of what day or time it was with neither of us having a watch and oddly our cell phones that did not get wet and were safe in or purses would not even turn on.

As were having our smoke and acting historical, it seemed as though I could see a gleam of light that was coming right out of the rock wall. I bravely started to walk closer to the wall and if I stood just right, I was sure I was seeing a sliver of light that felt like it was coming from inside the island. I walked right up to the wall and by running my hand along the wall I felt a depression and void in the rock that could not be seen and was what I would call an invisible entrance. The only way you could tell there was an opening into the rock was by running your hand physically along the wall to feel the hidden opening.

From what I have been told, it was only a miracle that allowed me to see that sliver of light in the rock. As terrified as we were to venture in, staying on the tiny little unprotected beach was not an option. We had no idea if it was day or night because the sky was so hazy and blackened. We gathered are stuff lit another smoke and slowly went in and around the opening edge holding each other so tight that we could barley move when we thought we could faintly hear birds and flowing water.

The atmosphere was a humid but the air was clean and fresh compared to the heavy thick air on the beach. As we took a few more steps it was almost like we were dropped into an Indiana Jones movie with the path being light up with ground lights and scenic tropical plants on both sides of carved out and constructed path. Each step we took on the path would light up in front of us another twenty feet or so and we walked on that eliminating path for what seemed a mile when all of a sudden, the rock tunnel opened and against all odds, we had entered into a hidden internal tropical island world.

Chapter Two

As we got to the opening archway there was a beautiful bench and tropical trees and the inside was lit up and felt like we were on a tropical island, which we were but strangely enough, we were on the inside. We were in shock and could not comprehend what we were seeing and decided we had better sit down and try to take in what we thought we were seeing.

Being comfortable and feeling safe sitting there, we both must have passed out from exhaustion not even realizing that we had not even seen a glimmer of what we had been stranded on and walked into.

It seems that I was only out minutes before I heard concerned voices coming from both men and women and they were speaking English or so I thought and as the voices came closer I was sure I heard someone say "how the hell did they get here and not Sire" Or maybe I was dreaming.

There was a team of people that came to help us using golf carts and driving on small paved roads to get around the interior of the island. As we were being driven through the island we were in shock of what we were seeing. The place was like a small tropical town with modern homes gardens crops and livestock along with a small lake and fresh water stream. This place was paradise with entertainment and excessive everything included. And that was what we saw in the first hour of our inner island rescue.

Amanda and I were taken to the most elaborate state of the art home built into a mountain you could ever imagine. We were taken to a large open patio that had an infinity pool that overlooked the whole interior of the island. The patio had a twelve-foot bar that was fully stocked and outdoor seating for a lot of people.

We were first introduced to the head technical engineer Paul Kundrup, who informed us that all the residence were of a medical, agricultural or of a scientific background and are here to maintain and sustain the island indefinitely.

Paul had their head medical person Henrietta, Henry for short check Amanda and I over to make sure that we were okay. After our check up and in fear of being offensive we hesitated to asked if we could have a smoke but with how overwhelmed we were both feeling I clenched my face as I was about to ask … when all the sudden another fellow came onto the patio to see what all the commotion was and he was smoking a cigarette. Seeing him come in made excusing ourselves from the table to have a smoke that much easier. Then to our delight we were even told that there was no need to excuse ourselves when smoking. We were also told that they maintain a small tobacco production in the island to ensure there is no shortage.

Once we had started to settle into this amazing place and being introduced to the residence we were offered food and drinks which we immediately accepted and dove into. The food was amazing and even prepared by the Sires resident house keeper and chef, Rosie.

As we had our drinks and ate like we had not eaten for days, while Paul continued to introduce us to the residence of the island as they joined the patio gathering that was about to become more than just a social meet and greet event.

At about the time Paul finished the introductions of the twelve residences, all the sudden and out of the blue just as if I woke from a dream, I blurted out and startled everyone what day and time is it?

Chapter Three

In a heartbeat all I felt was panic I scared the hell out of Amanda as she got on the same page of realizing we have family that have no idea what has happened to us. Henry and Paul rushed over to me to settle me down as I grasped Amanda so tight I am sure she could not breathe. I let go of Amanda who was processing and quietly sobbing, I sat back in my chair and lit a smoke.

By the way I was taking in the cigarette smoke the fellow in charge of the agriculture and tobacco production Kevin, could tell that something a bit stronger may be in order and quickly offer a joint! We were shocked, and pleased at the same time thinking what kind of space aged place has cigarettes and pot! Really this can't be real, we must be dreaming. Whoever this Sire dude is that built this self contained invisible island is sure a cool guy.

After sharing the joint the conversation started getting very serious and real as Paul told us the day and time and had estimated that our families have known that our flight went down for approximately sixteen hours ago. Paul new that we were exhausted and told us that the team would gather again in the morning on the patio and give a presentation on the island workings and of our current situation and circumstance to not further overwhelm us.

Although there were three master bedrooms in the mansion Amanda and I chose to stay together so we were taken to the Sires king suite. The king room was like none other I have ever seen in any magazine or rich and famous homes or retreat show. The room was breathtaking and was equipped with every modern and technical convince you could imagine.

With being so tired and not understanding our feelings of anxiety and fears, as we were in awe of the room we could feel our wined and dined exhausted bodies that were topped off with a hoot were done and as we cuddled on the big soft bed we both crashed and fell asleep.

We awoke to Rosie the Sires resident house keeper coming through the doors with a tray of coffee with an aroma so amazing that we both sat right up tried to gather our thoughts. Rosie announced that our patio gathering was starting in an hour and said that breakfast would be served then. The room was so large that Rosie had to show us where the washroom was that had two of everything in, other than just the one sauna like really who has a sauna in their bathroom?

After showing us the massive washroom with all the amenities she took us to another room that was filled with ladies cloths of all configurations and colors. There was also a shoe rack that was as long as the room about ten feet and various sizes as well? Why would someone do that we asked and Rosie's response was … you will understand once we have the gathering, so get ready ladies, you have fifty minutes.

As Rosie left the room we stood there and just looked at each other and never said a word as we were in awe of the room that we were too exhausted to fully appreciate the night before. The first thing we said was we need a coffee and a smoke to get this day started. As we cleaned up all we could talk about was our family not knowing that we were okay, they must be going through hell right now. It took everything we had for both of us to not break down in hysterical tears.

We rummaged through the closet that was as big as an average clothing store and were flabbergasted to find Lulu Lemon in our sizes… sweet! All top names and styles that would be acceptable for this island paradise.

Chapter Four

When we emerge from our room to the patio we find that all of the people we were introduced to are there with the seating set up so everyone could see the twelve foot viewer that rose up from the patio floor.

Paul and Henry came up to great us and check and see how our sleep was and how well we were holding up. Then they asked that we grab some breakfast from the buffet that was bigger than the average hotel would have and take a seat so the presentation could begin.

It is that point that Amanda and I noticed that the mood was down and conversations seemed concerning. We filled our plates and sat right up front in our big comfy chairs. It was a bright day and birds were signing and we could hear the water fall in the background. From where we were sitting we could see almost the whole interior of the island.

Then Paul started to speak and everyone was eerily quiet, he wanted Amanda and I to know that what we are about to hear is a whole bunch bigger then we could have ever imagined in our wildest dreams. Paul also noted that for us to be on this island at all, was nothing short of a miracle! As the whole place was planned, calculated, engineered and created for this very situation to "not" happen… and yet her you both are?

The island project was a commission from a gentleman we refer to as Sire. By the sheer magnitude of this project it is clear that money is no object, to say the least. This stately palace was designed solely by Sire whom is a very secret person. The rest of the island designs are a combined effort of the people living in it. Paul talks more about him later but goes on to say about our presence....

That the situation is graver then what we are aware. Paul put up on the screen a global image that was showing all sorts of activity and you could see the blackness in parts of the world. As Paul zoomed in on certain areas of the glob he started to explain that. The reason our plan was hit so hard so fast was that the world experienced two catastrophic events concurrently.

The first was Old Faithful which blew an hour and a half into your flight then there was an eight point five earthquake off the coast of Miami. These two events happening at the same time caused huge shock waves throughout most of the globe and blew the smoke and ash so hard that it devastated the skies for thousands of miles. Taking planes out of the sky around the world. Paul continued to show real time footage of what was being reported globally and the pictures being sent back from Sires own space and satellite systems. When he had said that Amanda and I looked at each other in amazement of what was going on outside the serenity of the island.

Paul continued with the idiosyncrasy and odds of old faithful having a major blow out causing southern global devastation and the smoke and ash barely making it to the Canadian border is incalculable. So the up side to the mass devastation is that your families are safe from the toxic ash and smoke and are okay. They are also aware that your plan was only one of many that went down and that rescue efforts are being prioritized.

Paul directed his look towards Amanda and me, and said that with so much world devastation at this time for you two to be here and Canada specifically Alberta to not be devastated by the otherwise global environmental events is frankly freaking us all out! Paul did smile and give a little chuckle when he said that to help lighten the mood and prepare us for the next bit of reality that we are not ready for.

Rosie started going around with the coffee and gave us a wink as she filled our cups knowing that what was coming next was going to be hard to process and is a genuine voice, said that it might be time for a hoot. Rosie does not smoke but supports the benefits of the herb. Although this was not the time to be funny when Amanda and I looked at each other all we could do was smile and said that sounded like a good plan. There were a few others of the group that casually agreed and Rosie opened what looked like a cigarette case that was sitting on the main table and it was filled with pre rolled joints. We certainly needed something to take the edge off of the overwhelming information we were receiving.

Chapter Five

After our smoke break a young fellow named Dustin who was the island and satellite technical guru took over the projector and started to let us know more about the intricacies of the island and the creator.

At this point we had very few questions to ask as we were mostly trying to absorb the information and outside devastation that we only just learned.

Dustin starts his presentation off letting us know that all the residence of the island are all scientist of the highest degree in varying fields and that is why we were chosen to create this place so that life will go on. The decision and commitment to become part of this project was life altering. We have all had to leave all of our families and lives behind and know that we will never see them again as long as we live.

When you commit to Sires "invisible" island project it is a little like signing up to go to Mars, you may not come home but you will carry on to ensure the survival of the human race. At that pause, I remember my stomach feeling queasy but I did pipe up and ask what he meant by an invisible island because no one had made reference to the island like that before.

Dustin proceeded with explaining that the location of the island is one that was strategically picked first by scanning all the shipping voyage logs to cross reference and find a point in the seas of no less than ten miles square, where no one has traveled through in the last hundred years.

That was the first criteria the second was that a force field could be generated that would ultimately cloche ten miles around the island rendering it invisible. The island cannot be seen by satellite or seen from the air or water. If a ship did get close the force field would nudge the ship around the field ever so slightly that the navigation systems would not register and set the ship back on course once around the perimeter.

Having Sires satellite sent up to space five years ago was the start to realizing that the invisible island was going to become a reality for the very fortunate twelve people that the island was being designed to support. Amanda then asked with all these high tech systems why can we not communicate out?

The secret to the success of the invisibility of the island is that the only data that comes in is from our own satellite and as long as no data leaves the island there is no finger print for it to be found. We have massive servers to retain all the worldly information that we will need going forward and if we have to educate our future children here we can do that to the highest standards.

All the sudden I could feel by insides tense up and I said that all this stuff was real interesting but what does it all have to do with us I asked?

Paul got up and said that there was no more need to beat around the bush about the facts. The island was designed that when global catastrophic events occur the island will close up all on its own and will not allow any intrusions or exits until it is environmentally safe to do so. Bottom line until the island knows that it is safe outside and opens, you are both living here.

For us, Paul said proudly, this is what we have all been working towards, preparing to carry on life inside the island indefinitely if a catastrophic global event was to happen. You ladies will be taking the place of Sire and can live in his house and enjoy all the luxuries that he commissioned. At that time I am not sure that Amanda and I fully comprehended that this island may be where we die and without our families ever knowing what actually had happened to us.

For an instant seeing the tip of the luxuries and the beauty of the place, the home we were being offered some would say we won the lottery and for a blink of an eye it felt that way, but just a quick it became a reality that all the serenity, riches and comforts in the world do not get us back to the rest of our family or let them know that we are alive.

That was a sad and somber moment for Amanda and I so of course we began to sob as our situation was becoming clearer. It was then that Dustin proceeded to inform the whole group that although there was mass devastation thorough the world with little effects in the mid western provinces of Canada. The island protections system has calculated that at the current rate of reduction in environmental contaminants and time line to regain world satellite communications and air and water travel to start to rebuild the countries' economies, will be… Dustin points to the projector screen showing a blank year month, day and hour's template and then we hear a drum roll the screen went black and then popped right back with the blanks filled in.

The island was not going to open up for six months two weeks and thirty seven hours at the current rate. This was unexpected news for the people that have committed their lives and futures to this project. For the residence, this was a very short time to be secured in the island as it is designed to accommodate these twelve people and growing families for ten years to indefinitely, if conceivable.

Henry the head medical resident joined in by saying that they are to be the teachers of the new world, with the knowledge of eco life balance and eccentricity of being human. Whatever that means, she was passionate about her purpose for being here.

At that point I stood put lit a smoke and walked toward the infinity pool where you really could see the interior of the island or so I thought. Amanda joined me as we filled our coffee cups and just looked at each other and quietly babbled, wow, OMG, and wow! Is this really happening?

By this time we had spent the whole morning in the gathering and the residence did have things that they needed to do so Paul and Rosie suggested that they could reconvene after dinner. Paul had it set up that our agriculture dude and Dustin would take us on a golf cart tour of the island to give us some time to adjust and have this entire situation sink in more.

Here we are presumed dead, at a time in the world where there is nothing but mass devastation living life like we are in paradise with all the luxuries and extravagance money has to offer.

Rosie filled up travel mugs for us with a nice chilled white wine and handed us the cigarette case off the table. As we leave the drive way of the mansion you start to drive into the community that the residents live. The whole area is build like a little town with a park and instead of stores there are small buildings that the residents do their work out of. There is even a self serve coffee shop that has a patio with umbrellas and a wine fountain no less. Rosie provides daily fresh baking and creates amazing fruit platters for the little tropical road side self serve cafe.

As we have been driving and enjoying our scenic tour of the gardens, livestock and even small crops the question is how this is all possible? We were told the island even has seasons, periodically rains and automatically follows actual day and night light for the seasons.

As Dustin explained in laymen terms … the island is a totally encapsulated and self contained colony with the construction, equipment and expertise making it impenetrable other then total world explosion.

To maintain a proper eco balance it sometimes rains here but most vegetation is underground water fed. The island environmental balancing computer programming is equal or better than anything NASA currently has for their Mars project.

When you look up into the skies inside the island at night you will see the moon and the stars exactly as they are in the sky, space and time.

During the day you see the sun and the sky lit up with corresponding simulated holographic clouds that will form in relation to the brightness of the sun and temperature. The sun rises and set as it naturally does and we even have street lights on all our cart paths.

The crest of the island and where the main power source derives is a half mile thick man made crystal that too is impermeable. The crystal was formed in layers to form a dome over the mountain island. Even a small to midsized meteor grazing the island would not weaken its defenses. The island is designed built and programmed to survive at all costs and with the current world conditions the system is now directing us in our daily actions to ensure we maintain life essential balances as Sire designed and to continue to make progress in our learning and teachings in our fields of science.

At that time Dustin said for us to get back into the cart and he would take us to the islands fun place. We did not get very far from the café when we could see the area open up to a beautiful beach complete with water park paddle boats and an 18 whole mini golf course designed to scale and in every detail of the Las Vegas strip only miniature. That was incredible to see and there was even an area set up for a fire on the beach and BBQ and eating area. We sat at the beach for a bit and drank the last of our wine and had a herbal smoke to complete the tour.

We were starting to see why these people would choose this life of confinement over an otherwise most certain death! This Sire did not miss a thing and has constructed a modern day Noah's arch so to speak.

It was time to get back as we will want to freshen up and get ready for dinner and our reconvened gathering. Dustin said that Paul and other residence will have more information to ensure that we have a complete understanding of our surroundings and limitations. Dustin said that it will take a few days of instruction and question asking before we will settle into the life we have no choice but to thrive in for at least the next six months.

Trying to make us laugh Kevin did comment that we get to stay in the nicest house of the island and that once we do settle into life here we will only all see each other once a week for a huge dinner that Rosie and the other ladies put on. We will soon be left on our own with Rosie of course, she comes with the house, Dustin and Kevin laugh she manages the palace and caters to the occupants of the mansion in the mountain. He did also say with a smile that we will be expected to fill our days productively and we will find our thing as time goes on.

On that note, we all jumped back into the golf cart and started back, passing beautiful flowers and fruit trees of every kind all the way up the hill to the palace and the most amazing place you could ever imagine. The afternoon was a great distraction and helped take away our thoughts of what is going on the outside with our family when we are in this safe haven.

Chapter Six

As we pulled up to the grand entrance that lead up to the large open patio Rosie had a large decanter of fruit filled punch and she filled our glasses and said that the room was ready for us to freshen up and that she had our cloths laid out for the evening gathering.

We had a few sips of the fruit and win punch and then headed to our master suite to rest a bit and get ready for the evening. As we walked into the large room, we were curious as to see what Rosie had laid out for us to wear. To our surprise, Rosie had actually made us matching dresses out of the finest silk that just flowed when we walked. This is not what we would have picked but we did not want to upset her and we are not sure of the rules around here so we freshened up and put her dresses on.

We could already feel the glow from the large glass of punch that we had and we could feel that we were actually hungry. For us being hungry is a big deal, we are very light and selective eaters. In addition, we are not the healthy eaters we look like we should be, based on our small size.

As we come out to the patio the residence are starting to gather and feeling a little more comfortable we were gazing and walked around the bar where we came up to a huge pool table dart board on the wall and three operating slot machines. There was a large rustic stone fireplace and big leather chairs to sit in. Just past the pool table, there was a ranch style fence and behind that, was a two lane-bowling alley. This was the sports lounge portion of the patio. It seemed every time we focused in on something we could not believe our eyes.

As we finished our smoke and our glass of punch, and looked around to notice that Rosie had us dressed like royalty when everyone else coming onto the patio was wearing tea-shirts and shorts? About that time, Rosie came over to us and asked that we get our plates ready and have a seat so that Paul and Dustin could get started. The evening's presentation was going to be a continuation of the morning's session.

Paul thanked everyone for coming back and Rosie for once again putting an awesome meal together. Then Paul had the screen come from the patio floor and preceded with the technical information and screen shots of the islands daily systems up date and log. To us all the information showing did not mean much and Paul could see the blank look on both our faces and told us and the group that if we are going to be here for the next six months that we are to be orientated and instructed in the islands operations.

Dustin did confirm that the lockdown clock was still indicating the same amount of time before the world environment will stabilize and the island will open up again. The positive and expected news is that the outside conditions are having no effect or affecting the operating systems. The islands operating and environmental systems are handling the crisis as planned … so far!

Amanda and I can see and tell that the residents are all pumped and happy for this time because they have been working so long and hard preparing for it. We being here was certainly not anticipated in any scenario they had considered. Moreover, our feelings of being contained in the island for six months are not so festive. Although we are extremely grateful that we are safe inside the island instead of the definite dead we would be, not being able to let our families know is weighing very heavy on both of us.

Paul was saying that everyone on the island has an expertise that is off the charts and is their purpose for them being here. Amanda leaned over and quietly whispered so what is our contribution, I wonder if there is an opening for a safety person and a warehouse technician, then she smiled and that warmed my heart to see her face brighten for a bit.

Then the conversation took a turn that was unexpected when Dustin started talking about the founder and his dream and that it is ill fated that he did not make it here. The last scripted message that came in from the satellite has lead Dustin to believe that Sire is alive and safe may be somewhere in the Himalayan mountains? Again, that meant nothing to us but it had the residents whispering among themselves and we could see that was an important tad of information to them.

Paul could see the perplexed look on our faces, then came right out, and said that, the message could mean there could be a second sanctuary built. The group starts speculating that a second safe place in the world would make complete sense for a man with an unlimited bank account and the will and foresight to survive. That realization did make the residents feel a little betrayed or disappointed by their Sire thinking they were the only ones. However, these are all smart people and when taking into consideration the travel time in getting to the invisible island depending on where the Sire was in the world it only stands to reason that there was a backup plan or secondary safe haven.

Paul asked everyone to focus on the now and that we will need to carrying out our daily lives just as planned with the exception of taking some time to bring Colleen and Amanda up to speed on what we can and cannot do in the island and how our food sources are managed and reserves contained.

The inner island is a balancing of all systems that are monitored closely to ensure that while here we do not upset the balance and tip the scales. Kevin trying to lighten the mood said with a chuckle that we are lucky that Sires was an extreme person on all counts because, with Sires own personal treasury we can eat, drink and smoke ourselves silly for 10 years without shortage … so in six months will not even make a dent in our reserves.

As Rosie was fussing around the table she jokingly said that with the way Keith and Dustin eat, if we run short it will their doing. Then she said that we should be okay because other then Sunday dinner they have to cook for themselves and they may be brilliant young men but their culinary skills are less than stellar. You boys probably starve yourselves all week waiting for Rosie's Sunday dinner.

Paul brought the focus back to the screen and opened a file that indicated the coming week's schedule that had everyone's name on it and his or her additional responsibilities. Everyone has their field of work that they continue their studies on but everyone also has to support the island and all the work is shared.

We could see that most of our week was going to be spent with Rosie who we were most comfortable with and there were many blocked out times during the days that were listed as free time. We both looked over at Rosie and with a very reassuring smile; she said I will teach you ladies everything you need to know and then looked over at Paul and winked cutely at him.

All the residents were familiar with the schedules and changing routines and did not need to see this file and new that it was Paul starting to show us how they work and live together as part of our introduction to systems and the twelve residents names positions and functions on the island.
The next screen shot Paul showed us was a 3-D picture of the outside of the island and we could even see out floating cubicle on the tiny beach. Paul did say that this was one of the last exterior pictures on the system. Paul explained that once the island locked up it no longer needed to see. All of the systems information is now only data and through design. The people inside did not need to see the devastation on the outside. The only visual data that the system allows now is the global view that shows each countries level of exposure and what contaminates they are being effected by showing in varying colors.

Of course, the operating systems and the information being processed are more sophisticated however, I know that Paul is trying to make sure that they do not speak to far over our heads making us feel uncomfortable or inferior, which we were for sure.

It was at that time Paul directed the conversation directly to the residents saying that all their hard work and dedication has paid off with the island operating at one hundred percent efficiency and that he is confident, and comfortable with them all knowing what they are to for the islands sustainability. Paul went on to say, with a smile and with the addition, of our welcome guests.

Rosie's roll and position is affected the most by Sires not being here as it was her position to manage a caged extremist's home and lifestyle indefinitely if that were the situation. Paul made Rosie blush when he reminded the group that she has her masters in psychology and a couple other achievements that only meant that she was very smart.

At this time, I found my mind drift, noticing the setting of the sun in the background, and started thinking of time and that we have been away from our families for more than two weeks. For the residents they have willingly been here for a long time and only locked in for the past thirty-six hours.

I think Paul noticed that everyone was finished their dinner and with the signal of Rosie serving coffee, he began to wrap up the information session by thanking everyone for coming and reminded the group that we will all meet up again on Sunday.

With Paul lowering the screen and people getting up to mingle before leaving Keith opened the fancy cigarette case and lit two joints and started passing them around. Keith passed one of the joints to Paul who laughed and said you know that I do not smoke that wacky tobacco. Keith only offered to Paul to get a rise out of him and to show us how Paul always responds.

As the residents were all leaving Dustin and Keith being the last, Rosie piped up and suggested that a soak in the hot tub might be just what we need to relax and help us sleep. Rosie said she had our swim suites and towels laid out in our suite.

With that, Amanda and I were feeling awkward and a bit weird that she has cloths to fit us and that she is calling it our suite. Rosie could see with everyone gone we were not feeling comfortable in our new home. Rosie called us over to the huge beautifully carved oak twelve foot bar and said let us talk girls. She filled up our coffees and we both lit a smoke. Here I was trying to maintain composure to help Amanda stay strong when it was I that broke down and started crying. Once I started, Amanda leaned over and hugged me tight and she cried right along with me. Rosie came from behind the bar, gave us both a huge bear hug, and said there there, ladies, given the extreme situation you have survived and thrown into … this will not be your last tears while we are here, she said.

Once we had calmed down and whipped the tears away, Rosie reassured us that we are going to be fine and that we will be reconnecting with our families. Not that she wanted to put any more weight on our emotions but she went on to say that the real miracle is that Canada was the least affected by the catastrophic events and that we will have a home to go back to once the island establishes that it is safe to leave.

Until then ladies this house and everything it has to offer is yours. I will show you everything you need to know about the house and the many amenities and extravagances that it has to offer. As Rosie smiled wide and said with me being the best part of the home. I will take care of you ladies, and trust me when I say it will be easier for me then having Sire here. I love the man and would do anything for him but frankly he is a bit of a slob, eccentric and acts erratically at times … So you two being here taking his place is a nice surprise for me.

There are nine women on the island, we all interact regularly however in my position I am a superior to them, and that does have an impact on our relationships. Having you ladies here as our houseguests has brightened my life by bringing me two new girlfriends and companionship. And no… I am not gay! She said with a chuckle.

You girls go get your suites on, I will get the hot tub ready, and we can chat more while you relax. By this time, as we were heading to change looking out over our large open patio it was almost dark and the many paths were all lit offering a better look at the web of roadways around the island and below our palace. Looking to the sky, we see the stars above us and it was a full moon. The lighting and view was so spectacular there was nothing to indicate that it was not real or that we were capsulated.

We open the huge double doors to our suite and just as Rosie had said, there were bathing suits laid out on the bed. Not only two suits there were four to choose from along with two of the biggest and softest beach towels I have ever seen. The freaky part of that was, the towels were monogrammed with our names on them.

Amanda and I were not really talking too much about anything serious besides doing what Rosie asks. As e come out of our suite and onto the patio we were in awe of the hot tub area that is past the infinity pool and a couple steps down. The hot tub was surrounded by tropical plants a padded and a bench that had a fire table in front and a swinging chair. Rosie then proceeded to showed us the hot tub operating panel, because as she said … I will not be there to hold your hands all the time. The panel had toggles switches for the lights, music, hot tub jets and the pop up bar? Yes there was a huge pop up bar that seemed to come out of the tropical garden and of course Rosie pointed out another shinny cigarette. That is when I had to ask… what is up with all the pot? We are fans but this seems a little unexpected for a state of the age eco and environmentally friendly survival place.

Rosie began to laugh and said I was wondering when you were going to get up enough nerve to start asking about the things you do not understand. I am so happy you ladies are here. Then for a second reality set in as to why we were there but that soon passed when Rosie turned everything on and the music started playing "Will you Love me tonight" by Elvis. We all looked at each other and cringed and Amanda quickly said is there another station? Rosie showed her the display on the panel where you just enter the artist name, song or general type of music you want to listen to and the system plays.

And about the pot on the island, well She is an extreme person and dabbles in all forms of extracurricular activities which some would not be tolerable if here for an extended period. To compromise was to have a safer alternative to his otherwise mind and mood-altering forms of entertainment, hence the pot and we do grow some of the best mushrooms on the planet, from what Kevin and Dustin tell me. We can chat more about this later she said.

With the lighting and mood set around the hot tub Rosie pored us all a glass of wine and Amanda and I got into the hot tub, while Rosie sat on the padded bench by the fire table and gazed out to the stars like they were real. We were all quiet for a while absorbing the day and in awe of our surroundings.

We had our smokes, finished our glass of wine, and then got out of the tub. By then we were exhausted and finished for the day. We grabbed our towels, gave Rosie a hug, thanked her again for everything and headed to our room. On our way, we could hear her say that she was going to let us sleep in and not to worry about her barging in. Good night, ladies sleep well.

When we got to the room we barley had the energy to get up onto the huge bed. We both took our wet bathing suits off and wrapped up in our big beach towels climbed onto the bed and as we were hugging, with no words spoken only I love you and big tears in our eyes, we fell fast as sleep.

Chapter Seven

I was awaken by the sun peaking through the rod Iron and carved rock balcony that was just past the sitting area in our suit. As my eyes opened, I see Amanda sleeping like a baby and as I gazed around the room, I see two beautiful silk housecoats one a mint green and the other was a soft baby pink.

The green housecoat had a monogram with a C and the pink one had and A on the lapel. I knew that our names or initials being put on the clothing we were given was going to be one of my first questions for Rosie this morning. When I sat up, I could also see that there was a fresh pot of coffee and some strawberries on the table in our sitting area. As I wiggled, my way off the bed Amanda started to move and was waking up. I walked over to the housecoats and put mine on. The design of the housecoats was like something I have seen in the old movies. They flowed when you walked and went to the floor.

I looked over at Amanda and asked her if she wanted a coffee and pointed over to her housecoat and then the sitting area. Once she was up, I pulled back the balcony blinds to light up our room and sat down for a coffee and a smoke. I asked Amanda how she was doing and was there anything I needed to be doing to help her through her pain. She came right over to me to me and said, mom I have you here with me mom and that is the only Band-Aid for this situation. I could feel a rush of emotion come over me but was able to hold back the tears and gave her the biggest hug ever. Amanda put her housecoat on, then twirled around and sat down

That is when we heard Rosie knock on the door and say good morning ladies may I come in. Come in Rosie we are up she said I know, I could smell the smoke, then she smiled.

As Rosie started fixing the bed and grabbing our still damp towels she let us know that today we will learn more about our palace. If we thought that the hot tub set up with pop up bar was cool she said you have not seen anything yet. The palace is filled with secrets and surprises. Hearing that did peak our interest for sure.

I then began to thank Rosie for the housecoats and coffee and then had the nerve to ask about the clothing fitting and monograms … what is up with that? Amanda asked Rosie to sit down, have a coffee with us, and chat for a bit.

Rosie hesitated as if she was intruding but she did sit down and I poured her a coffee. Rosie started to say, about the cloths. Well Sire has some odd likes and dislikes and one of them is that as his keeper she was to ensure that, his cloths were all of the best quality and has included a sewing room to ensure that everything he wore fit perfect and monogrammed.

Do you girls want to see your whole suite? Huh we were confused, we had not spent much time in the suit but thought we had seen all of the huge space when Rosie said oh no, there is much more then the eye can see to this suite. Rosie went over to the rock wall on the one side of the massive closet that we were shown, and put her hand on the wall, which then like magic a portion of the wall slide back into the rock.

Amanda and I both stood up and slowly came around the bed to see what was behind the wall. The first thing we see is a treasure trove of shinny things, in glass gasses. Men's and ladies jewelry encased with a large selection of watches, cufflinks and sunglasses. Above the glass cases was an etched merrier that spanned the length of the room. The room was large and well lit, we could see the section for Sires suit coats, at least two hundreds shirts, pants and shoes along with several tuxedos? Rosie explained that as part of the formation of expectation of life in the island, there were to be several formal occasions.
Then we do not see a sewing room rather a mini sewing factory, with all the necessary sewing equipment and of course an embroidery machine. The hidden room has a back exit that comes out behind the bar and sports lounge

area. That is why we have not seen Rosie while she has been sewing for us.

Then Rosie said look at the time, girls you get ready and I will have some brunch for you when you come out. Brunch … what time is it, I said. Rosie replied it was almost noon and then said, you girls need a watch, go pick one out and I will see you shortly.

Wearing our amazing flowing housecoats and gazing through the jewelry cases, we did feel like the rich and famous. Feeling a little lighthearted and reassured, that it was okay, we both picked out the most ridiculously and rudely expensive watches we seen. Then I said well sweetie, a smoke and another coffee and we will get ready, Amanda agreed with a smile.
Walking into the washroom was like walking into a spa with two separate showers, Jacuzzi tubs and massage tables. When we were done, we planned to get something out of the closet but when we look on the made bed we see that cloths have been picked for us again.

Rosie was taking the stress of us girls having to figuring out what to wear, right away. It was like Rosie new figuring out what to wear is sometimes a big deal that for Amanda and I. When we were home, there were things we might not do because figuring out what to wear was too much bother.

When we come out of the room Rosie looked to see what watches we picked and she chuckled saying we missed the most expensive one. There was a smaller table on the patio that she had set for our brunch we all sat down and began to nibble and thank her for the outfits she picked out. Amanda asked Rosie how they had anything our size here. Rosie replied with I find stuff in the closet and just take them in. There is no Miss Sire however, I do not think he intended to be here alone but had no idea of who it might be so he planned for every occasion and sizes. Rosie said that she had eight wedding gowns of various styles and if that was not good enough she has a C can full of material she could make anything.

Sire is not here, you are our gusts, and you will receive the same care and attention I would have provided for him. That is my position here and if you ladies were not here, I would be the one person on the island that is not carrying out my position, as the others would have had to. I am glad to be of service and I am very thankful that you two ladies washed up on our shore.

Just then, we see Paul driving up the driveway with two crates in the back of his cart and a bunch of fresh flowers. As he came up onto the patio, he said with a chipper tone good day ladies, and handed Rosie the big bunch of flowers. Rosie thanked him for the flowers and took them over to the bar area where she laid them out and then disappeared behind the bar.

Paul complemented us on our attire for the day then noticed the baling on our wrists, and smiled, when Amanda said that Rosie allowed us to wear them because we were struggling with time and there are no clocks in the house. Yes, the only time keeping is in the operations facility, which is the main structure that houses all data systems, you will see that later, Paul said. Then he repeated what Rosie had said earlier, you did not grab the most expensive watch! We looked at each other and said we better go back and check out them cases again jokingly because Rosie said the exact same thing.

We asked if he needed help with the crates and he responded with a quick no, you girls are our guests and all you have to do at this time is get along with Rosie!
We both looked at each other with eyes wide open then realized he was joking and only said it as Rosie was coming back and in ear shot, and made sure that she heard that part. At least everyone was keeping a good sense of humor.

As Rosie came over, she gave Paul a tap on the shoulder acknowledging his comment and said to him do you not have work to do old man! Paul chuckled, rolled his eyes, and went to get the crates.

Rosie said that after she was done with the flowers and unpacking the crates that we would take the rest of the house tour. Of course we offered to help but we were told to go have a smoke she we would be ready in a bit. Paul brought the crates up to Rosie at the bar and then said good-bye for now if we need anything just dingle.

Amanda and I go back to our outdoor patio paradise and sat back by the infinity pool that overlooked the main interior. Then we opened the shinny cigarette case poured another coffee and have a hoot to pass the time.

About the time we finish Rosie pops out from behind the bar, came, sat down for a bit, and asked if we were ready for the rest of our tour of the house. We had not seen the kitchen or the other bedrooms in the house.

First Rosie says lets go have a look at the kitchen first, you girls will be amazed and once we went through the swinging doors, it was like we walked into a room of stainless steel. This kitchen could accommodate cooking for a hundred people with eight separate cooking stations or so it looked.

We could tell that this was Rosie's jewel of the house. There were six walk in freezers and three large sliding glass door coolers it was like walking into a grocery store and top an elite restaurant at the same time. All the appliances were industrial grade, floor mounted dough mixers, meat cutters, deep-fry station and pizza with more equipment we did not even know what you do with.

The kitchen was behind the bar and was as wide as the bar and the sports lounge area put together. With our jaws, still open Rosie assures us that other then getting a snake or fruit out of the fridge we will not need to do anything in there. Mater a fact, I would prefer you do not she laughed but meant it.

As we come back out of the kitchen, we take a sharp turn and down a rock wall hallway decorated with paintings, well lit, and had a twelve foot arched ceiling. The haul was as long as the kitchen and then went further back to the other bedrooms. The first room we come to has the same big wooden double doors and Rosie says this is where I stay, in the palace. When she opened the doors, the room was shockingly white and very delicately decorated. Rosie's furniture was all white wicker with white eyelet lace linens she had a huge puffy bed and a sitting area with a Jacuzzi tub off to the side. Her washroom had all the same amenities as the washroom in our suite but only one of everything. Rosie's closet was half the size of ours and did not look like a department store like the one in our room.

There were no windows in her room however with the mural surrounding the room it made you believe that there was. The Sires suite is the only room with a view of the interior.

As we came out of Rosie's room and went, back further to the last room Rosie opens the big doors and we walked into a log home-style suite. The room had a big stone fireplace with leather and plaid incorporated into the furniture, decorations and linens. The Jacuzzi and sitting area were somewhat inset into the rock and log walls with another mural that had you feeling like you were in the mountains.

This room was very rustic and had the same size of washroom as Rosie. At that point, we thought we had seen it all when Rosie implied there was more. More, what more could this place need? That is when she took has back to the front of the house and showed us the last door that had a big monogrammed W on the front and when that door opened is was a gymnasium. Rosie called it the workout room but I have been to schools that have smaller gyms and less equipment.

Rosie said that once we are more comfortable that for more interaction we may choose to use the community open air exorcize facility. With that ending our tour, Rosie said, there are still many things you girls do not know about our palace, and that we can take our time getting to know it.

Smoke break I say, as we head back over to the patio table. Rosie was only seconds behind us bringing a fresh pot of coffee and a jug of water with lemon slices in it. Wow you are amazing Rosie, Amanda says.

Rosie then says after you ladies have your smoke you can go relax in your room or take a walk around if you would like. The walk sounded like the best idea for sure, we needed to move around and do something. Once we decided on the walk, Rosie went behind the bar filled two travel mugs with coffee and handed us the shinny cigarette case and sent us on our way down the hill.

She would have dinner ready for us when we got back. We looked at our expensive watches and figured we had a couple hours to have a look around on our own.

Chapter Eight

As we started down the hill, there were palm trees and hibiscus flowers and vines hugging the pathway on both sides. We could not tell if all the foliage was all real or not but it sure felt real. We could here all kinds of birds and it was as if we could feel the sun hitting us as we walked.

Looking up the rock walls, we could see openings that looked like caves and water coming out of the rock like a waterfall in some places. When we saw that water coming out from the wall I said I sure hope it is supposed to be doing that or we have sprung a leak. I let out a big laugh that no one had heard before that startled the birds. My laugh is my signature, and can be so hearty that it can set people back in their chairs the first time they hear my bistouries laugh. It felt good to laugh aloud again.

As we continued down the path we started getting closer to the community center and could see some of the people that we had been introduced heading to the little open area self serve restaurant. Still feeling a bit shy, we were going to avoid the area and little gathering until Dustin sees us and calls us over. We had no reason to say no and we are going to be with these people for a while so we do not want to be rude at all. Therefore, we smiled and waved then headed in his direction.

As we get closer, the people there were welcoming us to what they call happy hour, when Dustin beams and says that he is the island resident mixologist and could make us any kind of drink we could think of.

I looked Amanda and it was as we could read each other's minds and thinking... really is this for real! When my mouth opened, I asked for white wine where Amanda was more creative and challenging asked for a strawberry daiquiri.

While Dustin was mixing drinks Janette, the biologist came over to chat with us. She is here with her husband Jim who is a physicist and they are from Sweden. In chatting, she was so genuine in letting us know that if there is anything we need, do not hesitate to ask. Although she said with a grin, with Rosie looking after you ladies you will have no material wants or needs while you are here.

Janice boosted that Rosie was the most resourceful person on the island and Dustin jumped in by saying that she could make a silk purse out of a pig's ear! We were already witness to that, she has everything picked out for us and it all fits like a glove and most of the clothing is even monogrammed which is cool.

As we continued the conversation, Janette pointed over in the direction of their home that was about a city block away and then pointed across the main path and a few suites down to show us the semi open hut style building where her and her husband work out of.

Dustin sat down with us and said that he lived at the furthest end of the island at worked on the opposite so that he had a better sense of distance and would not feel so closed in. At conception of the plans, we were able to pick our lots and location of our work facilities. It was always to be as much a community and that included a tropical small town main street with restaurant, working facilities, market and park.

By this time I looked at my watch and in a break in conversation, I said that we had better start back up the hill because Rosie was expecting us back for dinner. With the little glow, we had on and looking back and up towards the palace it was going to take a bit to get back up the hill. We all laughed and Dustin said no worries ladies I will give you a lift home. Dustin lit up a hoot for the road, we said our good buys for now and jumped into his cart and away we went back to the palace.

By the time, we got back Rosie was setting up the table and we could tell that the lighting was different with soft music playing in the background. Dustin dropped us off and said have a great evening ladies we will see you later. He did not want to stay only because he had something cooking in the crock-pot all day that he has been waiting for.

As we come up the patio stairs Rosie greats us and asks if we had a nice walk. We told her that we made it to town center and talked with Janette and we were there for happy hour. Dustin was kind enough to give us a ride back we smiled. Rosie then said that we will have our own cart to get around in and that Paul was getting it ready for us. This place was all so amazing to us and yet so normal to the people here.

Rosie gestured that we go and freshen up for dinner and that it will be ready right away. When we enter our suit of course, there are two new tropical print casual long dresses for us to change into. Seeing the two amazing dresses as bad as it sounded, even to me, I told Amanda I could get used to this. She smiled and gently shook her head and said I love you mom.

We came out and walked as though we were on the catwalk to show off our dresses to Rosie when we noticed that the table there was seating for four and just then, Paul drove up.

Rosie poured us all a glass of wine and Paul said that he heard we had a good day and we got out and visited. That is great for you to get familiar and comfortable with the ways and people.

I started to let Paul and Rosie know that we were finding it particularly hard because, we feel we are being treated like royalty when we know that and others out there in the world are suffering. Amanda added that all of you amazing people have a purpose and are contributing and we are eating the food drinking your alcohol, and smoking your pot and have little to offer.

Paul responded by saying we will find your contribution in time and remember ladies there is no kidding yourselves you are here for six months. There is an expectation that you do stay fit and healthy and that you learn how to live in the island. Remember we are all here because we want to be and you are here by some miracle.

To us here, we actually believe that if you two ladies are here by some miracle then you have a deeper purpose in this life and that it is our job now, to make sure that when you leave you are both in better shape and wiser than when you came in. In addition, no matter how well you tell the story we will never be found. The world will know you stayed alive somehow and although your story will be outrageous, no one else will be able to place you anywhere for the past six months. Paul laughed jokingly saying that being here will really be a walk in the park compared to the media frenzy that will take place when resurfacing from presumed dead in six months. Rosie piped up with enough of that talk Paul let us eat.

Rosie rolled over a serving cart that had a pot of chili, fresh warm buns and a salad with everything in it. We smiled when we saw that it was chili and Rosie said what… it was that or spaghetti; I know those to be Canadian favorites.

As we started, Paul said that he would bring our golf cart up in the morning and that we need to check out the virtual reality facility. If we need any excitement, Paul explained that if we see Dustin he will show us all the high tech toys and equipment to keep us occupied and fulfilled. Rosie said that we will need the extra curricular activities to keep our spirits up. She went onto say that while we are here you will be taken care of and that is just the way it is, and you are not to feel bad about it.

We wanted to know understand more about whey we could not communicate but they could receive information. Paul said I am not the best person to ask about that however the way I understand it the only way we can remain invisible is that no information every is leaked off the island. Our satellite only transmits to the island and continuously monitors all outside conditions. Dustin is the guy to see; his satellite monitoring facility called the birdcage and it is by the waterfall and the area you ladies came in at. Why the birdcage we asked? Rosie said I am surprised you did not notice it earlier but you will see how it got its name, when you go visit.

At the end of dinner, Rosie brought out the coffee pot and we all went over to sit by the pool and look out over the island. As Amanda and I had, our smokes and coffee Paul got up, thanked Rosie for the great meal and our company, and said that he would see us tomorrow. I then asked him so where is your house? Paul replied as he walked down the steps and jumped into his golf cart that my place is the one closest to the beach as he saluted and drove away.

Rosie then got up and was going to start cleaning up the table and putting the food away. Amanda and I got up and gestured to help when she said if you want to help open the hot tub pop up bar and grab the Baileys so we can have a night cap once I finish here.

We headed to the hot tub and there was the shinny cigarette case so we lit one up while we waited for Rosie. Although we did not do much we could feel that we were both tired and were soon ready for bed. Rosie came over, plunked herself down, and poured a good shot of Baileys in her coffee.

Well ladies she said this is officially day three for you and you have done great so far. This is serious and you ladies hanging onto your sanity is vital. We can cure almost anything here but if either of you go off the deep end mentally we will feel we have failed you.

Do not worry girls I will have you working before you know it so you better take advantage of the hospitality while you can she laughed. Then she chugged back her coffee and motioned for us to rise and head to our room for the evening. She gives both of us a big hug and we head to our room

As we enter the room, we see our night cloths placed on the bed so nicely and there is a small platter of fruit and pastries on the table in the sitting area along with a fresh pot of coffee. We could not figure out how she could do as much without us seeing her. There is not even enough time in her absence to do like this, what she had done. Something about Rosie just feels magical to us.

As we sit, together on the big comfortable sitting area, I asked Amanda how she was holding up and she smiled and said better now that I know that I cannot feel guilty for being here. Knowing that we are going to be able to leave this island in six months and reunite with our families. I am starting to be okay with living the lavish life and do well here… whatever that is? She laughed. We cuddled for a bit and then had a coffee and smoke before we went to the big puffy bed.

While we lay there, Amanda says it would be fun to stay in the log cabin room and we could feel like we were in the mountains instead of the tropics for a few days. Yes, that sounds perfect sweetie, we will ask Rosie in the morning. Good night, sweetie I love you, then softly heard … love you more mom.

Chapter Nine

We woke the next morning to the smell of fresh coffee and new matching outfits this time but with the outfits being casual shorts with different color tank tops we were okay with it. We both woke up feeling less burdened and more comfortable with our amazing surroundings and the comforts extended to us.

Getting off the bed put our monogrammed housecoats on had a quick pee and then we both moved to the sitting area for a coffee and a smoke? We could see that the sun was shining and we felt a slight warm breeze coming through our balcony opening. At that moment, I recall feeling as if we were on vacation and staying in a fancy resort.

After our coffee and smoke, we hope in our showers and proceed to get ready for a new day. We really were not paying attention to time at all and when we emerged from our suite Rosie was sitting at the bar having her coffee.

She looked over at us, with a big smile said good morning ladies, and asked how we slept. We had a great sleep and thanked her for the morning coffee and the cloths, again. She took our hands and leaded us to a nicely set small patio table and said you must be hungry come have a seat and I will bring you some food. Rosie poured our juice and coffee gave us a wink and headed towards the kitchen.

Amanda looked at me with a grin and said so what do we do today or what first? With a blank look on my face, I knew I had no idea and responded back with I do not know for sure. We chuckled at bit and then we see Paul and Kevin coming up the path with two carts. The one Keith was driving was Pink with beautiful tropical decaling.

As they came up the steps, Rosie rolled out of the kitchen with a cart full of food and said I thought you would show when the food was ready so I made extra as she looked at Kevin with a smile.

We got up to look at the pink cart and were so impressed with the work wow we said is this ours to drive. Paul said of course it is, who else would drive it? ... certainly not me he replied and laughed. Kevin said that we wanted to give your wheels a special touch and that is why we did not have a cart for you yesterday, we were giving it a paint job for our special ladies.

Well thank you so much wow again, it looks like a Barbie car Amanda said, Kevin said yes, and we will all see you coming. Only kidding, but we do have a driving in the island training and road test that you have to pass. We do have road and driving rules so we want to make sure that you know them.

Rosie said lets all eat and you ladies can start your driver training after. While eating we were giving a mini update on outside conditions and that they had not really changed much. There were still a lot of termers being felt creating further damage to structures but the casualties are down with people moving away from the hazardous areas. It appeared that the world leaders were all communicating and working on a united front and that all world fighting has seceded.

However, limited mobility people are being moved to the safe locations of the world and Canada will soon be bursting at the seams with being one of the lucky few safe zones in the world. We are not going to sugar coat it; the world structure is broken and chaotic out there and for today the one thing we can assure you of, is that your part of the world is safe. Paul ended with that is your news updates for today and continued with now let us go learn to drive the island laughingly.

As we were finishing the news and eating Rosie started clearing the table. Paul and Kevin stood up and went over to the floor projector and Amanda and I went off to the side to have our smoke and get ready for our in class-driving lesson. We were excited to do something and learn more about the island.

We sat down and Kevin opened I file called "Island driving 101" that made us smile. When the file opened shockingly, the title page of the power point presentation was of a young girl picture with her new driver's license that was pictured from the 50-60's bobby sox and all. They were definitely keeping their sense of humor throughout this mega invisible project.

The next slide was a road map of the interior of the island that included road names and addresses for each building. Wow, they did not miss any detail in recreating a tropical community.

As we were reviewing the road map, we could see that there were paths we had not seen yet. The drawing showed more paths that were not visible from looking down from the palace. Behind the housing area there was a drive path cut out from the wall and went up a steep hill to the bunkers. The bunkers are filled storage containers. The chosen bunker area was because the island walls are thicker on that side of the island and we could burrow further back for more storage space. Getting back on topic, Kevin said…

Our golf carts are a little special in that they do have headlights, back up lights and signal lights, which are required to be used, as you would driving any car. There are no seat belts in the carts because there is no need to speed Kevin chuckled. Paul added but you do want to make sure you have a good hold on when driving up the winding hill to the bunkers.

Then we heard Rosie say from behind the bar that we have to remember that drinking and driving is quite a frequent occurrence and something to keep your eye on. We put a ten-foot field flag on Dustin's cart, because sometimes after happy hour he forgets that he is not on a buggy off road track and you can see him coming through the bush. We all laughed and then Paul said how about we take you on drive tour and Kevin and I will show you the paths to get to each sector of the inland and how the paths intersect.

Great, Amanda and I were eager to see more of the island so as we were gathering our selves Rosie brings us to travel mugs filled with fresh coffee and a little leather purse for our smokes and shinny case. I will see you all later Rosie said a we were getting into the carts and are you staying for dinner? Both Paul and Kevin replied if you are cooking Rosie for sure. If Dustin has nothing in the Crockpot can I ask him along if we see him in our travels, Kevin asked so sweetly? Rosie responded with a big sigh, of course, we could not have the young man starve, and away she went back into the kitchen.

Amanda jumped in the cart with Paul and I got in our pink cart with Kevin and when leaving the grand entrance Instead of taking right and down the long road into the valley Paul turned left and we went up and back around to what is called the mountain look out picnic area. Paul wanted to show this area because this is where we were when we walked into the island and collapsed.

This landscaped area had a lookout point, picnic table, outdoor camp stoves and swinging chairs. This is a place that some of the residence come for a wiener or marshmallow roast and look out over the whole valley. Walking from the other end of the island, that is quit a hick and good exercise said Kevin.

From here, we had a good view of the waterfall and the lake and beach below. Then what seemed to be right under the lookout point and the rock ledge we were standing on was a structure that resembled a very large white rod iron birdcage and I laughed and said that is where Dustin works isn't it?
Paul said yes that is the technical head quarters and Dustin is the man in charge for sure. He has help with our other highly qualified people however Dustin is our systems and programming guru here.
As we turned to go back to the carts I asked Paul where exactly we came through I do not see any opening. Paul replied with the island closing up that the single opening sealed behind us almost as we were walking through it. That is how exact it is that you are here.

Looking back out into the valley and at then back at the wall I had to ask how did all of this get in here if that is the only entrance? It was too small of an opening to get this small community through one single tunnel. I said with a chuckle

Paul said we will take you down to Dustin and h
e will be able to help you girls visualize with a 3D perspective what we are showing you. Away we went back down the hill and when passing by our palace Paul and Kevin booth toot their horns for Rosie.

As we go down the hill and back around the path became windy and filled with tropical plants and flowers. We even seen a few small monkeys, they looked so cute. When Paul saw the look on my face when I saw that cute monkeys he said no, no, no we were told that we were not to interact with the animal life here, as we are not to upset their natural balance. Oaky, we get it.

As we get closer and can see through the trees better for sure ... what we are seeing is a house sized rod iron birdcage that as you enter looks more like a space ship command center. Then all the sudden, Dustin comes out of know where and startled us. He seen us coming down the hill he said, and who could miss that pink golfing machine.

Thank you for stopping by Dustin said and went on to ask what can I show you ladies first? Wow where do we start? Paul asked Dustin to bring up the 3D visuals of the island to show how the island is laid out. Colleen had asked about the single door that they came through, how we got everything through it. Dustin brought up an x-ray view of the island and the interior and went onto say that the island was a small bump in the ocean and we have built it up from a mile under the water. We did not have to bring things into the island to build it the island was built by using the world largest 3D printer for lack of better words. Everything that is here has been programmed and grown from layers and layers of computer programming. The volcanic rock around the island is the material that fed the system and built all the large components of the interior of the island.

Hard to believe, but even this birdcage, which was my design Dustin boasted, was created layer by layer and not by conventional construction means and is a dense rock mixture and not rod iron as it looks. As we get to building the crest and roof of the island, we used crystal for the layering, which supports our power sources. There is more than one of everything on this island and the bunkers are filled with supplies and materials to sustain life on the island for a very long time.

Looking at the island from this perspective brought a completely new light on the magnitude of this project. Dustin then brought up a visual of the world globe and showed us the darkened areas where the ash and smoke are hazardous with the colors changing as conditions improve, as he rotates our view of the globe we see Canada and there is no darkness. We could see something different when we looked at the BC coast but is was not the same darkness it was fuzzy and blue. Dustin did say that with earthquake the BC coast did suffer and reasonably small tsunami and the fuzzy blue is showing the affected areas. Not to worry the tsunami did not affect Alberta at all.

On that note, it was time for a smoke and a few sips of coffee as my head was overwhelmed with information. As I step out, I hear Kevin letting Dustin know that Rosie has invited them for dinner.
Amanda was right behind me as we light our smokes we see the guys looking over other files on the computer and saying how they were looking forward to dinner. As we chatted, we discern that Dustin and
Kevin are treated like Paul and Rosie's sons but that is the furthest thing from the truth. Although we do agree that Rosie and Paul may be smitten with each other, they are not a couple and Kevin and Dustin are the two younger of the residences single men. Paul does take on the father figure of the community for sure.

By the time, we had a few sips of coffee and finished our smoke the fellows came out and said that it is the cocktail hour and Rosie is ready to receive us. Amanda and I at the same time looked right at each other in sheer disbelief, really is this what life is going to be for the next six months? If we could read each other's minds that would have been it. Then we realize that Dustin and Kevin were planning on going for a swim in the infinity pool as soon as they got there. It was as if they were carefree kids.

Just before we got into the carts, Paul leaned into us and said there is plenty of time for you girls to learn the island and as you have questions please make sure you ask. In the carts, we were and away we went down the windy road and back up the hill to the palace for what will sure to be a wonderful evening.

As we, got to the stairs to the patio Rosie was there to greet us. She had this very impressive bar cart pulled over to the pool with the water wall we had not seen before operating and the lighting in and around the pool so relaxing. You could hear soft music playing in the background but nothing we recognized.

Rosie comes right up between us and loops her arms through ours and said ladies you might want to freshen up first and go for a swim or you can freshen up and change into your evening attire before dinner. She swooped us up as if she was excited to show us our outfit for this evening. When we got into the room, she had both our evening dresses hanging there that were wow, the embodiment of comfort, tropical style and elegance all at the same time, compete with pockets. All we could say was Wow! In addition to a big hug, we said we are not going swimming and laughed.

What would you ladies like to drink she asked as she strutted out of the room, and we replied, wine please. We quickly got changed while we listened to Kevin and Dustin slashing around in the pool. When we came out of our suite to join them the fellows all complimented us on our dresses.

As Dustin and Kevin got out of the pool, Rosie said you have time for your smokes before dinner so we all sat and relaxed around the pool sipped on our drinks, had our puffs and commented on the view, our interesting day and joked about our pink cart. Paul gave Kevin a little tap on the shoulder and said to him, you know you never did tell the girls the one main rule when driving the paths. Kevin wiggled his eyebrows and whispered oop's and Dustin said way to go bro and chuckled. Paul continued with saying that if we had not noticed while we drove around a bit today, everyone is to stop at all intersecting paths and then precede we treated them all as a four or three way stops.

Amanda gently waved her hand at the groups and said no worries here; we will never go fast and with the color of our baling wheels everyone will see us coming ... we all laughed. When Rosie jumped up and said dinner is ready people, we grabbed our glasses and headed over to the larger dining table on the patio. By the table, she had a buffet style four-station hot server that had pork chops, rice, mixed veggies and scalloped potatoes. At the one end of the table, there was a big bowl of Cesar salad and a fruit and cheese platter. Although there was a good verity of food it was, apparent that portion control was being followed for the pork chops that were thick and of a good size because there was only one each. The fellows thanked Rosie again for having them for dinner and we all started on filling our plates.
Once every one had their plates filled and were sitting back down I had to say that I am shocked and cannot believe how so much of this place feel normal and Canadian to me. Everyone speaks perfect English and Rosie; you cook our comfort foods even better than we do. I am amazed and feel like we here are the luckiest people on earth, and then Amanda raised her glass and we had glass clinking around the table in cheers!
Kevin said that tomorrow we should take a drive up to the bunkers, to the back of the island where the great agriculturist hangs out, you know the person that grows the best tobacco, and weed... ever! He laughed and Dustin agreed on the weed growing but Dustin did not smoke cigarettes.

Then Paul directed the conversation to us getting to know the last few people of the island better because he knows that we have met most of them but we have not really spent any time with the Chin twins Ryan and Jessie, or Henrietta's partner Elsie.

Dustin pulled a paper out of his pocket and was a map of the interior of the island with all the houses marked with who lives there and who works in what main street buildings to make you more comfortable in your first travels.

Amanda and I came close and were looking over the path map and address information complete with legend depicting the landmarks, homes, business and who belongs where. This was great we said thanks!

The island occupants totaled ten but we have always planned for twelve believing that Sire and his selected partner would be here.

We were all done our dinner and Rosie who had been enjoying and taking in the conversation went to bring over the big urn of coffee that was already sitting on a serving cart along with some light pastries. As she drove right past us with the coffee cart, we knew that was our cue to get up and move over to the hot tub sitting area. She hit some switches on the panel that she showed us the night before. The bar popped up, the fire table lit the area lights and water wall turned on. The impressions and view was spectacular and being able to look out and down into a tropical valley made this place feel endless.

As Rosie was making sure we had what we needed, Paul looked up at Rosie said, thank you a quick nightcap would be just what I need and home for us young fellows. Which Dustin and Kevin both looked at each other smiled and agreed yes for sure, we young fellows need our sleep. Paul is probably old enough to be their father so there was a chuckle there.
As we were sipping our coffee Dustin lit an after dinner hoot that we shared and then it was time for the fellows to leave once they had all finished their scotch and coffee … it made Amanda and I shiver to see them slug back a snifter of scotch. We ladies had had baileys with our coffee.

Like a shot, they got up and jumped into Paul's cart leaving our pink machine behind, and right up front ready for tomorrows adventure.

Rosie remained seated with us for a bit and finished her coffee before getting up to start clean up after our dinner. This time when she got up, we were more persistent in letting us help her but the only help she would let us give was to clear the table and put it all in the serving cart. Once the table was cleared, she told us girls to just sit down, have another coffee, and take a load off.

As we sat there we started looking over the map that Dustin had given us and were seeing structures and paths we had not seen or been on yet and were excited to get out tomorrow.

The list was important to us because we really, only new a few names and barely knew what their unique qualities are and the spreadsheet on the back of the map listed everyone's names and profession or fields of expertise. The map on the front showed their homes and where they were located when working.

Sire (Partner)	1 Palace	None	Guest
Rosie	1 Palace	1 Palace	Palace Master, Physiologist
Paul	2 Beach Cove	Whole island	Director of Island Operations
Dustin	3 Birdcage Ally	3 Birdcage	Director of Technical Operations
Henrietta	4 Haven Crest	1 lab Main St.	Director of Medical
Elsie	4 Haven Crest	1 lab Main St.	Surgeon, Scientist,
Jim	5 Hidden Acers	2 lab Main St.	Island Maintenance, Controller
Janette	5 Hidden Acers	2 lab Main St.	Systems, inventory Management
Ryan	6 Uptown Street	3 lab Main St.	Sustainability Systems Controller
Jessie	6 Uptown Street	3 lab Main St.	Systems, Design, Analysis
Kevin	7 Lucky Farms	7 Lucky Farms	Agriculture and Environment

With just sitting there not having much to say and not quite ready for bed we thought we would get our suits on and go in the hot tub for a bit and have another nightcap smoke. We waited for Rosie to pop out of the kitchen and told her of our plan. She looked over at us and said that was a good idea, your suits and towels are on the bed, and I will come sit with you in just a bit.

As we walked towards our suite to change I mumbled and smiled to Amanda … Man that Rosie does not miss anything and it is as if she reads our minds before we even think of it.

When we come back out Rosie was refreshing the coffee and pastries tray she looked up at us and said that once we were done our smoke and sitting in the hot tub for a bit these pastries will be gone she said with a big smile as she sat down and we climbed into the hot tub.

Another day gone by and we are still feeling as though this place and the treatment we are receiving is all a dream. Rosie said do you want me to get up, come over there, and pinch you to see if this is a dream. Oh no that is fine we believe this is all real we just may be cannot believe that we are the lucky ones to be here and taken care of by you Rosie.

Don't' get all sappy on me she said enjoy your smoke and the tub and if it feels better just think of me as your guardian angel that cooks and sews Rosie laughed as she poured a healthy glass of baileys to go with her coffee. After only being in the hot tub a few minutes we had to get out we were both feeling the drink, smoke food and the day come to a fast close, I am pooped Amanda agreed and Rosie finished her Baileys she stood up to give us a hug and said sweet dreams to us both. Hum! I am usually the one that says that, I thought to myself and off to bed we went.

Chapter Ten

Waking up the next day it was al was starting to feel normal with new outfits and fresh coffee every morning. We had our show and came out for breakfast and Rosie had a huge smile when she saw us because we somewhat were dressed in the theme and matching of our new pink driving machine. We thought we looked great too as we walked together to the table. Between our driving machine and these awesome outfits, the residents should see us coming and see us touring about the island Amanda said to Rosie, that's for sure.

Having been able to digest and process better, I feel I do have an improved and broader understanding of the island concept and fundamental expectations of being here on the island. With curiosity getting the better of me when Rosie sat down with us for breakfast, I had to ask so.... What was the plan for the human race survival if locked in for the ten years as Dustin had mentioned of longer.

Surprisingly Rosie's response was very candid and there was nothing shy about her answers. By design, we have women here like Jessie and Elsie and now in Sires partners place Amanda that are in their child barring years. Depending on the situation

Jessie and Ryan will become pregnant naturally, as they are young couple and planning a family any way. Then we have Elsie who has an older female partner Henry that would like to have children so her seed would be fertilized using sperm we have in our banks. Sire no matter what age was to ensure that the partner that he brought to the island was of child baring years so that she could help the future of human survival. Now with Sire not here with his partner there would be an expectation for Amanda to assist in the evolution process. No worries though, it's not as if you have to sleep with anyone, just that we will fertilize your seed.

That is huge Amanda replied, Rosie said that the up side to having children here is that you are not solely responsible to bring them up. When signing on all residence of the island know that if the task to continue the existence of the human race is left to the island residence, to grow and evolve humanity that it is equally their job to help raise and educate all the children born here.

It is typical for a family to have one or two children but if our situation requires more then what is deemed typical, these women may be encouraged to have multiple children and it would be unreasonable to think that they each what to raise more than the typical one or two. I am the childcare provider for the island and it is my position to ensure that when babies are a priority that everything is put into motion to make them happen. There are no worries on the baby front though, with only being in lock down for six months Jessie who is planning a baby soon will not even be pregnant yet she laughed.

Rosie then looked up at me and said that was a heavy topic you chose for breakfast, hum what brought that on she asked. Rosie holds nothing back and I had to think hard as to why I thought that was important to ask, and the only thing that came to me was. I guess I was thinking of everyone here being prepared to stay for so long and that having babies is a huge part of carrying on and I felt there must be a master plan for that two. Along with being amused, by watching Amanda's face and body language while you were explaining and talking about child baring years.

Then I asked Rosie there seems to be no secrets from us, are you not afraid that when we are off the island that we will tell all of them. The world will want to know what happened to us for so long and we will have to say something and that could lead the snoopy right to the source of location. Rosie said you don't' have to worry your pretty head about the world find us, because they never will.
Amanda then asked her if they would stay once we leave and Rosie responded with a firm yes. We have committed our lives to this island world with some of us being part of this project for twenty years.

For the younger ones they will have the decision to reconsider their options of leaving but as it stands now, even when the island opens in six months no one is asking to leave. Rosie laughed and said by then we may have to kick you both off the island because you will love it here so much.

Rosie got up and went over to fill our travel mugs as we got up and lit a smoke and had a good look at our pink driving machine and ourselves then headed to the stairs where Rosie gave us or coffee and our little restocked purse and said have a great day ladies, try and stay out of trouble. Remember if you need a refill, you can always stop at the café on Main Street and that happy hour is at three. See you later and have fun.

Amanda shot a quick look at me and said I am driving! Which was no surprise considering that even at home she always coiffures her mommy? We jump into our pink golf cart and see the Rosie has put a netted duffel bag in the back of our cart that has our big towels and bathing suites in it. We both look at each other and say wow as Amanda pushes on the gas and we are off.

The first place we wanted to check out was the bunkers. Although we know that, the bunkers are there, by design and construction they are quite hidden as well as the road that is hidden by the tropical growth. As we are making our way down the hill, we see Paul driving in the distance up the lane to Kevin place. We come to our first intersection and Amanda stops to look both ways, which felt funny knowing there, was no one else on the road but we were not about to get caught breaking the rules.

We smiled at each other and as we continued on our path, we could see the area on our left where the houses were. The only house that we have seen so far was Paul's house and that he pointed out to us when we went to the beach. As we, start up the other side of the island the path is similar to the one leading to the palace with a bit of a steep hill with a few curves.

Once we do get to the top of bunkers road we drove onto a parking lot with painted lines. Just to the front of the lots there was a rest stop area that had a washroom and picnic area that and over looked the valley and the palace looked amazing from where we stood.

Then coming out of the shadows is Jim who greeted us so sweetly and asked us if we were going shopping today. Shopping, no one said anything about shopping before. Jim replied they all probably wanted to see the shock on your faces when you actually start to understand what an extreme, eccentric rich person would want on an island if trapped.

I know you girls were taken back with the tolerance for smoking cigarettes and weed and to consider first is our medical. We can fix anything that is broken and smoking causes no more disease than any other bad element. It is in our body make up and jeans that predetermine our tolerances and if pushed past balance people get ill. Here we have the technologies and resources to fix that. Do not get me wrong Jim said, people will not live forever here but they will not die of horrific and painful or early deaths.

We are learning so much from everyone it is so amazing then wanting to get off the ill and death topic I lifted my eyebrows and being a typical female … I said so now what were you saying about the shopping?

Jim smiled as he was turning towards the big rock wall and said follow me girls and be prepared to be impressed. As Jim passed under the thirty-foot archway, the lights started coming on row-by-row and the sequence of lights went back the length football field, and was the width of one to. The train cars or "C" cans were stacked two high and laid out row by row. The containers were all numbered and the containers on the ground all have clear Plexiglas fronts so you can see what is inside.
At the bunker entrance, a couple computers are set up there to search the bunker inventory for items or the shopper can look through the catalogues. Amanda and I just looked at each other in pure amazement and could not help but gasp and spout out, really! This is over the top crazy!

Jim walked us up to these, what he called self-driving shopping carts. He explained that once you have your order entered into the system you get on your cart and it maps out the shortest shopping rout. Jim said let me take you around a bit and then this will make more sense.

He jumped in a larger drive cart and said for us to take a seat in one of the shopping carts and he would tow us around the bunker to show us how the inventory has been stored and managed. Jim stopped at one C-can and the front window lit to show that this container was the sunglass hut. Jim said everyone needs a pair of cool sunglasses and I noticed you do not have any. Therefore, I thought this was a good first shopping stop. We got off our shopping cart and as we get closer to the front the container the door slide open and the inside lights up. Once we were in and the container it is set up just like a store would be with cases filled with sunglasses of the big name brands. As we look around in amazement Jim made sure that we knew that we were to find a pare we liked and they were ours to keep.

I have always like a pair of Ray Bands that Amanda had at home but they were too rich for my blood and after looking for a few minutes low and behold there they were, the exact folding pair she has so that was my pick. It was not long and Amanda found herself a pair of Ray Band aviator glasses she liked. We looked in the mirrors to make sure we looked great and then we laughed and said so … how do we pay, we have no cash and I do not see a debt machine we all chuckled.

Jim said there is no paying for anything but we do inventory everything so that our systems can monitor depletion of our resources. There are some items in our inventory that we can reproduce and replenish using our many 3D printers. Then there are others items that once they are gone they are gone. We could reproduce the sunglasses but with over a thousand pares in here we should not need to have to her smiled.

We got back into our shopping cart and Jim drove further back to show us that the C-cans area arranged is sections like in a large department store would be set up. Then Jim looked at his watch and said it is time for lunch are you girls coming with, we are having lunch at the main street café today and I am meeting Janette, Jessie and Ryan there. Come joint us. Other then still being a little shy we had no good reason to say no so we said for sure acting all confident with our selves. We got in our carts and drove down the hill and into the Main Street area for lunch.

As were pulling up to the café we can smell something very familiar and a home favorite, tacos. There was even a blackboard sandwich sign that said today's special was beef or fish tacos. Included with the meal lemonade and there was a big punch bowl of that sitting on the counter.

Of course, Rosie is there making sure that everyone was getting their plates full and that there were enough condiments for the tacos. Rosie did let us guests know that the lemonade had a bit of a snap so not too many she laughed. Then she looked over at us and said nice sunglasses, I see you went shopping, so where is the rest she chuckled.

As Amanda and I sat with Jim and Janette while Ryan and Jessie were still filling their plates. Jim replied that we only had a bit of time up at the bunkers and that he is sure we will do better next time. Jessie and Ryan sat down and then Janette being the sensitive one asked how we were holding up. Knowing that being restricted to the island was not part of your life plan she said, being here no matter how nice will be hard on us at times. Janette wanted us to know that we can come visit them any time. Ryan and Jessie did not say much but offered whatever support we needed that they will be there for us.
To change the subject to a lighter topic and more comfortable Amanda asked Jessie what her role was in all of this as her position and title indicate to us that you do computer stuff. Amanda smiled knowing that calling her work computer stuff would get Jessie to explain better.

Jessie proceeded with her role being an extension of the work that Dustin is in control of, and that if there are any outside or inside environmental changes that the island has to compensate or adapt to, between Dustin and I, we monitor, analyze alter and write code as needed to keep everything in check. I have other skills that we draw on as need like the rest of the residents we all have to be exceptional in more than one field to be here.

Then I said … well Amanda, I think we are the exception to the rule here and then laughed with the rest chuckling along with us. Janette said you ladies bring something else special to the island besides brains and that is company for Rosie who winked back at Janette and a breath of innocence that we all find fun and amusing.

Then all the sudden we can see the field flag from Kevin's cart racing down the lane with Paul right behind him, coming for lunch. Rosie was restocking the food platters getting ready for the eaters of the group to get there. We noticed that Dustin was not there and when Paul was getting out of his cart, he said that Dustin was working on something and that he would be by for leftovers later.

Paul was letting Rosie know that he and Kevin were moving livestock around this morning for better grazing. Elsie was there for a bit to give them all their weekly check up and all the animals are doing well and are very healthy.

We could see Henry and Elsie across Main Street in their lab working away and Rosie walked over to their lab, knocked on the glass front, and waved them over for lunch. Rosie opened the door and was talking to Henry and then turned and came back to the café saying that Henry and Elsie were going for a picnic at the beach and going on the roller coaster where were done so there were not coming for tacos.

Roller coaster Amanda blurted out, I do not see any roller coaster here, and you have to be kidding, right? Yes and no Paul answered back, now what do you mean by that. Paul said that Dustin is the best person to show us but asked if we have ever been in one of the amusement park pods where you do not go anywhere but you watch a screen and you think you are falling from the Grand Canyon. Dustin and Jessie have created the old pod style and the virtual reality headsets that intensify the chosen amusement experience. You pick the theme, sky diving going on a safari or any roller coaster or water slide you dream it and we can make it so you can experience it.

Kevin did lift his face from his plate long enough to say that these entertainment toys have a dual purpose because we also use them for cross training we do regularly. I said wow; we have to give that a go! Jim and Janette said that their favorite pod ride is the eye of London Ferris wheel, Ryan and Jessie like river rafting in the Rockies and Kevin likes snowboarding. Which one is your favorite Rosie, Paul Amanda asked. Rosie said I am not that adventurous and like floating along the canals in Venus, with a glass of wine and nice music playing in the background. Paul had to think a moment but came out with riding a horse on a mountain trail. It can do that, Paul replied these machines could do more than the imagination can ask for and with Jessie and Dustin, if you can dream they can write it and build it in a virtual form of some kind.

By this time, everyone had finished and I could feel the snap in the lemonade, it was gin and lots of it. Kevin finished his lunch, belched stood up and then like a gentleman thanked Rosie for a great lunch and said abruptly and turned Smoke time!
Moreover, waved Amanda and me over and once the hoot was lit I was a taken back as Jim sauntered over for a puff. He said with a big smile … what? It is good for you! We really laughed then because to look at Jim, he was just not the guy to have a puff.

As we were finishing our smokes, Jessie and Ryan headed off walking to their house not far behind the café. Jim and Janette put some containers from the café into the back of their cart and Rosie jumped in with them and said take me home James. See you later ladies have a great afternoon.

Kevin asked if we were coming, his way next seeing as we had spent the morning at the boring bunkers come spend the afternoon at the pride of the island, my Lucky Farms. Kevin wiggled his eyebrows up and down and Paul chuckled and said watch him girls he will have you doing all of his work for him as he jumped into his cart and headed towards the birdcage. Rosie filled a large plate of food for Dustin along with a thermos of lemonade that Paul was taking to him.

I guess we are going to Lucky Farms and with a big grin on my face turned and I asked Amanda …are you okay to drive, I could feel the booze and she is twenty pounds lighter and two inches taller than I am so I was thinking she must have been feeling it too. She replied I am fine I'm fine and then plunked her new aviators onto her nose and said jump into my mean pink machine mom, were going to Lucky Farms.

Kevin's place was the furthest away from the rest of the residents and took up the last quarter of the interior of the island. Agriculture and livestock were vital to the project and considered sustainable. It was all most a straight path to Lucky Farms from Main Street so Amanda's driving was perfect.

As we pull up to the circle driveway, we can see right up into the open home. The front of the house was all open and it was made of bamboo and had a straw like roof. This was Kevin's home and man cave for sure. For a guy who did not cook much he had an amazing kitchen and his sitting area had big leather couches a stone fireplace and sports memorabilia everywhere. He also had a pool table and shuffleboard in his large sitting area. It was a ranch style, bamboo home. Kevin took us to the back of the house to show us the rest of the rooms when we noticed that just off Kevin's bedroom patio he had a hot tub and outdoor fire pit off to the side surrounded by tropical plants. The hot tub had grapevines growing around and on top of a slate wood frame. Kevin smiled yes that is where I sit relax have my hoots and eat grapes right off the vine, it is my little piece of heaven!

Kevin went to the fridge and grabbed us each a bottle of water and said come with me girls, I will give you the guided tour. One the one side of the lane is our vegetable gardens and we maintain small harvest of tobacco, weed, grains and rice's. The island operating systems nutrition projections is what determines the planting. What is grown at each cycle and the volume to be planted is based on depletion of resources, and at times, we may put in larger crops of a specific item.

The garden rows are all so perfect and there are no weeds, I chuckled. No, there are no weeds or chemicals used because all growing stock is pure and only insects or bugs brought into the environment were the ones help sustain a balance. As we saunter along, we go to the other side of the lane where we see a few cows two beautiful horses fenced off in the front of the property and as we walked along the side of the road and as we came behind the house there were pens for pigs, chickens and goats.
The back yard looked like a small hobby farmyard and we could see that Kevin was beaming with pride of his accomplishments and roll on the island.

We wondered around the mini farm for a while and I asked him if he managed all the work himself and he replied I like to think I do, he said but everyone comes to work on the farm as needed.
The schedule that the system generates and Paul puts out every week has us all doing various jobs around the island and has us working in different teams to keep it interesting. When it is harvest time, or when we are meat processing Paul and Jim help me out the most. Ryan and Dustin are squeamish when it comes to the meat processing work and prefer to help more with anything plant like. Kevin let out a hardy laugh and brought us ladies back to the front patio where we sat down and had a smoke before we headed back to the palace.

We let Kevin know how impressed we were with his Lucky Farms and that if he ever needs our help we will do our best. Amanda did let Kevin know that she did not think she would do very well at the meat processing either so please keep her in the garden she smiled.

Well Amanda I said, it's time for us to saddle up and head on up the hill to see what Rosie is doing. We stood up and Kevin looked at our bright pink cart in his driveway and laughed. What you laughing at Amanda said as she jumped into the driver's seat, this is our mean pink operating machine and it is baling. She pretends as if she is a daemon driver crunching herself into the steering wheel and revs the engine. We wave and thank Kevin again and away we go on our way to the palace.

As we come to the Main Street intersection, we thought we would take a quick drive to the beach and see what was going on there. As we drove past the Main Street buildings, the path becomes more over grown with tropical plants and flowers and then as you come around a curve the whole area opens up exposing the lake and beach. No matter where you are on the island, you can see and hear the large waterfall that feeds the lake. The waterfall is the first source of constant background noise that never shuts off with the second being the birds but at least they take a break at night the waterfall does not.

As we parked, we could see Paul's house off to the right and we could see Henry and Elsie at their picnic area across the lake. They looked like they were enjoying their afternoon, snuggled together on the picnic blanket where we could see a couple of bottles of wine beside them. They saw our pink cart pull up and gave us a big wave, clinked their wine glasses together and went back to their chatting.

We then lit a smoke and with travel mug in hand, we walked on the perfect sandy beach and into the bluest water. The water temperature was just right for swimming with the fish living a stream that entwines at different depths and temperatures with separating pools throughout the island to accommodate many types of fish, I remember Dustin telling me that when we first got here. Amanda looked over at me and with a big smile said now are you just not the leading authority and we both laughed.

Well that was enough for us so we turned around walked out of the water to the aground driers that when you stand on the twelve in by twelve inch square felt platform warm air is blown up as you shuffle your feet over the felt surface. This removes the sand and dries the feet at the same time too cool!

We got into our pink machine and headed back up the hill to the palace where Rosie was mulling about working on setting out dinner. Rosie welcomed us back home and asked how our day went and before we could say anything, Rosie interrupted and pointed to our room and said you ladies freshen up and change for dinner, and then you can tell me all about your day.

Of course, as we enter our room, we can see two new gowns hanging their ready and, as we get closer to the beautiful dresses we also noticed the added extra of diamond necklace's to match. Really, Wow!

We proceeded to clean and freshen up put our dresses on and our new baling

round our necks and came out to show Rosie. When she sees us come out she says awe you ladies look just stunning.
Only because of you Rosie, it is all you, we said with huge smiles as we went over to the sitting area where we saw that Rosie had set up cocktails for us.

Rosie came over and sat with us and said that if we are good we can keep the shinny things when we leave she smirked. I noticed that Kevin and you missed happy hour at the café she said the tour must have been a good one. The whole Lucky Farm set up was so interesting and Kevin went on so much even he forgot about the time.

The bunkers, Rosie you have to come to the bunkers with us sometime. We would feel much better going up there with you with us. For sure, I will take you girls shopping next week sometime. We will see where it fits into the schedule she laughed and then said only kidding.

We had our glass of wine and then Rosie got up and said dinner is served ladies, and I believe it will be just us this evening unless you are expecting company? Us we looked at each other surprised like not thinking that we may have been rude because we had not even thought to invite anyone here. We looked at Rosie with her replying you will become more comfortable here soon, and this is your home for now and you can invite whomever you like to it. You do not need my permission only my approval she laughed as we squirreled up our faces thinking aren't permission and approval pretty much the same thing. We took note that she meant, ask before invite.

As we walked over to the nicely set table on the patio, Rosie opened the serving tray to show us a colorful salad, and a casserole dish filled with Sheppard's pie. Wow! How do you keep doing this excellent chef and seem to know what everyone in the island likes to eat, you are a tailor and seem to do it all without being seen whipping everything up. Amazing we concurred and raised our glasses to Rosie. She replied with well then you are really going to think that tomorrow morning is cool too. I have invited Janette and Jessie here for a many-Pedy morning. Henry and Elsie were busy and were not able to come but they will meet us later in the day for tea. Rosie passed a quirky look at both of us and said I do not really mean tea she smiled; they will be here for cocktails!

We were eating better there then we had in months or even years and the conversations were always so wild that we would forget why we were there.

Finishing our dinner Rosie wanted to remind us that we would be having another group meeting potluck this time, with all the residence and we all thought it would be nice if you ladies told us about yourselves. We have not wanted to pry but it will do you both some good to tell us who you are.

Paul will have his new schedule, Dustin will give us further updates on the world conditions, and Henry and Elsie wanted to explain their new breakthrough. That sounded good, for sure we can however our stories are not as amazing as any of your. Rosie explained that we all really do want to get to know you and make you feel as comfortable and as home as possible.

As we got up from the table and were moving over to have our smoke and coffee. I looked over at both Amanda and Rosie and said I am tired this evening; I will not last long tonight. No hot, tub for me I would pass out in it. Amanda agreed with being pooped. Even though it was early once we finished our coffee and smokes I said think it is time to for me to pack it in. Amanda stood up and took my hand and we thanked Rosie for everything and asked what time Janette and Jessie would be arriving in the morning, Rosie said that they would be here around ten and that she would have everything set up on the patio. We said our good nights and went into our room.

On the table was a carafe of coffee and cut up fruit for snaking. We noticed that when we got into the room the closet door was partially open and the lights were on so we went inside to have a look. Right away, we could see that the closet had been reorganized and restocked with cloths sized and styled more to Amanda and my taste and age. The cloths are even separated by size right down to the underwear. There is no Victoria Secrete here all the under cloths are of good quality but are but for function not looks. We noticed that with only seeing the stacks of white bootie short panties. Nothing sexy going on here I said with a grin, as I held up the stark white full bum bootie panties.

Now we had a closet of cloths that we can pick from with so many items that caught our eyes we could not wait to wear them. After snooping through our new larger than life closet, we went to our seating area to have a coffee and hoot before bed. There is no real TV but we could search and request any programming or movies to see. Like having unlimited Netflix so once we were done the hoot Amanda crawled onto the bed and said let see what's on TV. The dresser on the wall in front of the bed had a built in scene so that when you turned on the huge TV the scene rose up from the back of the dresser.

Amanda started searching for something to watch and the first show she thought to search for was the Big Bang. This show always brings a smile on, and low and behold, the information on the screen showed that we could watch every episode back to back with no commercials if we wanted. She hit the okay button and then there we were watching one of our favorite TV shows having a smoke and coffee while we unwind. It wasn't long before I crawled on the bed too and gave Amanda a big hug and kiss and stuffed my head in the pillow while she watched for a bit longer.

Chapter Eleven

When we woke up the sun was shining and we could hear the birds and this time we could even smell breakfast, Rosie was cooking bacon. This morning there was coffee on the table in our sitting area but there were no cloths set out for us this time. I said to Amanda that I think we are on our own for picking out our own outfits today. She looked over and said crap! I will never find anything to wear.

We had a quick coffee and smoke and headed into the shower knowing that we had to pick out our own cloths it was going to take longer to get ready. Sure enough, we must have tried on four outfits each before settled on and outfit and we walked out of the room. Rosie said I was going to come check on you ladies what's up she asked. We were honest and told her that it was because we had to pick out our own cloths and that took a while whit so much to choose from.

Come lets have our breakfast and get this day started, we have our guests coming soon and we want to be all set up. By the time, we were done our bacon and scrambled egg breakfast Paul drove up. As he approached the table, he dug into the bacon that was left. I'm here to help set up your foot party.

Rosie then pointed Paul in the direction of her sewing and supply room; we followed to see if we could help and because we were curious as to what they were going to get. Sure enough, two big lounge massage chairs that had the water tubs under them for soaking the feet and big armrests so you can relax your hands while getting a manicure. The chairs were on casters and not hard to move but Paul had to put the two tote containers of supplies on a little push cart because they were was so heavy.

Rosie directed us to an area away from the entrance and closer to the bar where she wanted the chairs; lock the wheels she said we don't need Janette rolling off the patio … again! Paul and Rosie were having a privet chuckle when Amanda said… again? Yes Paul had to tell the story and he said we may be smart people but the last time we did this we forgot to lock the wheels on the chairs and Rosie accidently tickled Janettes foot and she pushed back sending the chair down only a couple of steps. Janette was fine but we were all so startled that we forgot to do something so fundamentally simple that we laughed our asses off while we helped her back up.

Rosie was opening the totes, which looked as if she was unpacking a beauty salon. Paul was the only one that could lift the two different totes. One of the totes opened up like a large fishing tackle box and the other looked like a mechanics tool chest with all the drawers. All the drawers and compartments of the totes were labeled and even had inventory numbers for restocking. (Incredible)

By the time our little beauty salon is set up, Paul says that is my cue ladies, I am out of here as he sees Janette and Jessie walk up the path. Rosie was beaming when she say Janette and Jessie and welcomed them up to the sitting area by the hot tub for champagne and orange juice before we get started. So how does this work Amanda said, I only get manicures I have never given one, she chuckled but mom on the other hand is good at them.

Rosie said no this is our treat and Janette and I will give you yours first and Jessie will sit and chat and drink until you are done. Then I will work on Janette and Jessie at the same time because that is what I do … and none of you are touching my feet she laughed but meant it. Janette agreed that Rosie could give two better than most could give one then had a big swig of her orange juice.

Then Janette said let's get party started. Jessie went over and turned some music on as we got ourselves comfortable in the big comfortable messaging chairs. Wow what a way to start a day I said as our feet were being put into the bubs of warm water.
We were saying that with Rosie getting our cloths picked out for us the first

few days we had no problem getting out of our room in the morning but now that there are cloths to pick from it took forever to pick an outfit this morning. Rosie looked up at me and said if it is easier for you girls, I will continue picking out your cloths, she added I actually love doing it. I even missed having to have them ready for this morning. Right away, I said you can pick mine and Amanda nodded for sure me to please. Right on, she said if you know what you might be doing, the next day let me know and I will have the right cloths for the day. Thank you ladies I know it may be a bit weird but I do enjoy picking out and creating your cloths.

Jessie commented that Rosie had made most of her cloths and when we have special gatherings, we all get a new dress for the occasion. The men all have cloths for every occasion including tuxedos; I just have to alter them as they grow. Referring to Paul, whom she said has gained a little weight over the past while. We chatted a bit more about cloths and beauty tips and It was not long and we were done then Rosie said break time, I will get more mix for our orange juice as she wisped behind the bar.

Janette then looked at us both and asked how we were doing Jessie leaned in showing support with Rosie refilling our drinks. I sat up and looked at Amanda and then over to the ladies and I without too much thought I blurted out for myself, I am doing great so great that I am starting to feel overwhelming guilty. When I said that, I knew Amanda was feeling the same but in her own personal way and she understood what I meant.

Here we were treated very special; I am relaxed, eating the best I have in a long time and sleeping well. Not to mention dressing better than I could afford to at home and having all this luxury readily available is captivating, so the guilt is starting to set in for me. There was a bit of a pause and Amanda followed up with I love being here and knowing it is not forever or even a year I am good with it all, she had a big smile shrugged her shoulders and said I am all good. She added knowing that family was all-good and that six months was not enough time for Aaron to fall in love with another woman, because there is no one that could replace this Amanda and felt confident in her welcoming home in six months.

Janette being the realist she wanted to make sure that we were not trying to hid our feelings or fears and that we had no delusions of our time here. I think that cleared that up the thought that we would be hiding our feeling for Janette, other than me having to get over our fortunate situation.

Rosie said look at the time it was getting close to cocktails on Main Street. We had better start heading down. You ladies go ahead and I will be right behind you so we gather our stuff and jump into our pink golf cart and head down. Jessie was laughing as she had a good look at the interior and the little touches that were added. She said I do not know what the fellow's infatuation with the color pink is but they wasn't to paint my five thousand dollar Bicycle pink! What's up with that!

As we pull up to the café, we see that everyone else is already there and that the only one missing is Rosie. With us already, having orange juice the drink for today was creasers and the snake was a platter of nachos. Dustin and Kevin were mixing the drinks as Henry and Elsie came up to say high and that they were sorry they have not been around much. Oh my goodness no worries we know you have your work to focus on.

Then Rosie pulls up and within seconds of getting out of her cart she asks Kevin what is taking so long for my drink I am parched don't you know. Paul jumped with saying one of the island rules is that you don't make Rosie wait when she wants a drink, which made everyone chuckle. I believe he meant it.

Once we all had our drinks, Paul offered cheers for another great day. Kevin and Dustin sat right in front of the patter of nachos with us all sharing in general conversation about our day.

After a bit Rosie piped up and said that she had talked to us girls about sharing some of their history with us at our next gathering and that we were looking forward to it. Amanda smiled oh yes I do look forward to mom doing all the talking. I looked over at her and for the most part agreed.

We will have a good dinner and get together this week Rosie said and she looked at Paul to let everyone know that there were some positive updates and we will all get to review then. Nothing is said until all information is confirmed; we cannot afford to play with any ones emotions not only our visitors.

Refill anyone, we hear Dustin behind the bar Jim was ready for a second and we moved over for a hoot and finish our drink with Kevin. Gradually people were getting up and ready to head home.

Then I hear Rosie asking everyone as they were leaving, what they were having for dinner. I thought that to be a bit snoopy, but being Rosie I believe she just wanted to make sure that everyone was eating good or to help her decide what she may cook tomorrow either way she like to know what people were cooking that was cute.

After Amanda's creaser, a few nachos and hoot she said that she was ready to go, so we helped tidy up a bit, said our good buys and Amanda let me drive home. I can't deny that was fun and I knew no matter how long we were in the island this might be one of the only times she lets me drive. I winked at her, and up the hill, we went.

Once we parked and walked up the stairs onto the patios we could see that the big mess we had left from our beauty morning was all cleaned up, the chairs and totes were all gone everything was put away. We looked at each other in amazement, how is that possible she was not five minutes behind us?

We no sooner got past that thought and there she is pulling up the driveway. We were chuckling as she came up the steps, when Rosie says, what are you girls up to, what is so funny? Nothing … it is just that you seem to do everything with hyperactive speed.

All the stuff from the morning beauty session is all put away and considering the time it took too bring it all out and set up we do not know how you cleaned it up so fast and were down at the café within what seemed to be just minutes of us getting there. Rosie just looked up at us and pretended to wiggle her nose as if it was magic.

We went over to the hot tub area for a sit and Rosie brought over the coffee pot and sat down with us. We were all quiet for a bit sipping our coffee while Amanda and I were sharing a hoot when Rosie says how about grilled cheese sandwiches for dinner tonight? We look over at Rosie and agree that is a great idea, I was not feeling all the hungry and grilled cheese is one of Amanda's all time favorites so I knew that would be good with her too.

We had finished our smokes and when Rosie got up to go to the kitchen, I motioned to Amanda lets follow. She knew that we were following her and I think because it was only grilled cheese she would let us in the kitchen with her. Once we were in the shinny stainless steel massive kitchen all we could do was watch her in action. With all the cupboards, fridges walk in coolers and freezers she knew exactly where everything was and I am sure she could have done, it all with her eyes. We stood behind the stove area as she was answering all of our silly questions, like Amanda's one about being afraid of getting locked in one of the freezers? It might be a while before anyone found you. Rosie replied with that could not happen here because all walk in compartments have sensors and will detect a human occupant being inside and would not lock. That was actually not a bad question. Then she went onto say something intriguing which was that Dustin knows where we all are at all times because of our heat signatures which are like finger prints, we all have a unique print so he can see who is where. Really, Amanda said, he can see me in the shower? Rosie smiled at Amanda while she flipped the sandwiches we can see a smug of colors within the island. The livestock are also monitored this way and the system studies their health based on the temperature of the animals.

Rosie put our sandwiches and a fruit plate on a serving cart and said lets go enjoy our dinner on the patios ladies. Once we were settled and started on the sandwiches that were grilled to perfection! I had a nagging question and this seemed a good time to ask. Rosie, you seem to know so much about everything on the island and other then Paul you seem to be in charge around here what is that all about.

Finishing her bit and reaching for her coffee she replied, it's complicated. Paul and I are the main keepers of the island and part of our positions required that we had to essentially know everything about the island from cradle to grave and we have to fundamentally know all our residence backgrounds to be able to know and utilize all our resources as needed. Paul and I can operate this island on our own however, we cannot repopulate, or educate in all facets. The full intent of the island is survival of the human race so after twenty-two years of working and being together we can almost read each other's thoughts it seems.

If you don't mind me asking, are you and Paul an item? You could see her blush almost before I finished asking the question. We all smiled when she said no, we have never gotten together in that way. Not even now when you know this is the rest of your life. You have both committed your lives to this island I am sure you getting together now would have no affect on the balance of life here and you would both be happier inside and then completely fulfilled with all of your other accomplishments.

You girls are just talking silly now Rosie fidgeted, we said no, no, no we can see the sparkle in his eye when you are around there is something more than just a long time working relationship here. You will see how he acts when they all come for our dinner. We shared a bit of a laugh as the redness was starting to come out of Rosie's cheeks.

When we finish and get up from the table Rosie asked if we were in for a hot tub this evening and I was not feeling it but Amanda decided she was going to go for a swim. The sun was setting and the lighting looked amazing dancing off the warm water in the infinity pool. While Amanda went to changed, Rosie cleared the table and pushed the serving cart into the kitchen. As Rosie came back out she passed by the hot tub panel she the switch the bar popped up she grabbed the bottle of Baileys and came and sat beside me and said lets have us a Baileys and coffee. We smiled at each other as I lifted my cup. Then out of the blue, I asked so, how much of this do you have here? I have gone on vacation and drank a resort out of Baileys how much can you possibly have here, I asked. Rosie said I believe that we have one hundred cases of Baileys in stock for one reason it is one of Sires favorites and the other, because it is one of mine, she really chuckled and tapped my knee, they do take up precious space.

The stuff only lasts so long I said, yes but we have temperature control lockers and by managing the temperature we can extend and preserve products for years past shelf life. Not only that with our expertise we can make our and even print the same labels. So once our hundred cases run out we will just make our own. We and we clinked out coffee mugs together just as Amanda was coming out of the room so she asked what's up what did I miss. I replied to her, take a guess at how many cases of Baileys are stored here. I have no clue she said, there is one hundred cases, and I think we will make it I said. Amanda got in the pool and was swimming around when she said how beautiful it was and that we should come in for a swim. Nope I am done for today I said and Rosie followed I am good for this evening, you enjoy.

In a quiet voice, Rosie commented that we were almost at a week being here and I know that you had said earlier about feeling guilt and I want to reassure you that there is no reason for that. The extra special treatment that you are experiencing and feeling is there only as a faced to help mask the ugly truths of our fractured world. The concept of the island was to survive, respecting all mankind with wealth to share, sustain world knowledge and intelligence needed to reestablish ourselves with even greater intelligence and higher standards for our futures. Rosie had a somber look on her face that just made me say Wow, that's deep. Then her face brightened up as she went on to say … and to accomplish that you build an island that has extreme riches, put extremely devoted and smart people on it and give them everything they could ask for. You should be comfortable with and enjoy everything the island and people have to offer. We love you being here and knowing that it is for a short time and that you will be going home, we want to make sure you enjoy your time and experience with us. Rosie patted my hand and then got up to go get a fresh pot of coffee as Amanda was coming out of the pool.

While Amanda was drying off she said so what were you chatting about, I looked up at her and said I think Rosie has made it her mission for me to get rid of my guilt feelings, I chuckled. Amanda so how are you doing with that, she grabbed my shoulder and I said with a smile, better now.

Smoke, coffee and bed what do you think sweetie, sounds good to me … me too Rosie said as she came from out behind the bar, minus the smoke I will have my baileys. As she poured our coffees and sat back down, we quietly gazed out at the stars.

We finished our coffees and got up to say our good nights and give hugs. When we walk in our room, the fireplace was going and the lights were flickering around our balcony it was so warm and comfortable feeling, you could not ask for better. I was popped and my head was still processing the day so I put my housecoat on and climbed onto bed. Amanda was not far behind me, I remember saying I love you sweetie and I was asleep!

Chapter Twelve

I wake up to the smell of smoke and as I open my eye's I see Amanda sitting all comfy at the sunny sitting area having a coffee. When I said good morning sweetie how was your sleep? She replied real good mom, I slept well, how about you? All good I sleep awesome in this bed, we got to get one of these when we get home, Amanda just laughed as I crawled out of bed and headed her way. As I was walking towards her, I could see her pointing in the direction of the dresser stand where I see the cutes golfing outfits I have ever seen I beamed and Amanda said really, what are these. Amanda is not an avid golfer but I sure am and I knew exactly what we were looking at. I said we are going to play mini golf today as I sat down and poured my coffee and lit my smoke with a big smile.

After our smoke and coffee, we headed into get ready for another day. Once Amanda had her little outfit on, I stopped putting on my shoes and came over to her and gave a hug, and whispered in her ear that she should be on a magazine cover. Even though the outfit was nothing she would have ever picked out for herself, she looked so cute and I believe she could see it.

When we come out of the room there was Rosie whizzing about the patio fixing flowers and then bring over the coffee pot and a jug of fresh juice. Good morning, ladies you look fantastic, I said I gather from the outfits that we are going to play mini golf today. Rosie gave me a big smile and said is it that obvious? Amanda said there couldn't be anywhere else you would wear these and laughed. Rosie and I looked at each other and smiled we knew they were a bit over the top and more then what would be worn at home to go mini golfing nevertheless she did look so cute and she did know it.

Rosie said that after breakfast we could take a drive down and try our hand at it. The layout of the course is so fun to play. You are not coming with us we asked she said no not today girls but next time I will for sure.

As we nibbled on bagel bits, fruit and yogurt Amanda noticed I was wearing the diamond necklace with my mini golf outfit and commented that may be the necklace was a bit too much for the day and I replied with, shinny things go with everything Rosie chuckled and said oh so you are one of those are you. I could not deny it I love my shinny things. Why do you call gems shinny things she asked and I replied, it makes them sound less expensive. She looked at us both with a smile and gave her head a shake and said as she got up, I think you are so awesome.

Away she went to fill our travel mugs and gather our smokes for us. You girls go and set yourselves up in the lounging area by the course, have your smokes and enjoy your game. For some reason it felt like she was rushing us away, but we did not question her so out to our pink driving machine and because it was such a short distance, we did not have a smoke we figured we would wait until we got there so we started down the hill.

As we come around the u curve in the area of the birdcage and where the trees open up we could see the entrance to the course and we see Henry and Elsie just getting out of their cart. We pull up park and they came right over. It is great to see you here the course is a blast we come here usually every day about this time, to start our day off. We said our good mornings and brought our stuff over to one of the lounge tables where Henry and Elsie joined us.

They commented on the outfits being just perfect for the day and said Rosie must be at her handy work. If you cannot find it in the bunkers Rosie can make anything even without a pattern, describe the garment style and give her a day and like magic, you have a nicer item then you could have even dreamt.

Well girls we will get started on our game and you can follow behind us and we will see how well you do at this, your first time. Henry winked and turned to Elsie and put her arm around her to escort her to hole number one. Amanda and hung back and had a hoot and a smoke before we tackled eighteen holes of mini golf. This was going to be fun and we were in no hurry.

Once we were ready to start, we grabbed a club from the wrack and away we went. With the flashy theme, being the Las Vegas strip I said to Amanda just before we started that I thought my shinny necklace was just right for the occasion. Amanda chuckled and started, she did great on the first hole, we both were doing really well and then when we got to the ninth hole we could see across the course to Paul's beach house and that he was working out front. Amanda could tell I was about to yell out and she grabbed my arm and said mom please don't do it, what I said she said you know what I mean… you were going to yell. That would have echoed everywhere. Amanda hates when I embrace her, I laughed and went back to hitting my ball.

May be when we are done here we can head over to see what he is up to. Amanda said that sounds good we have not really seen his place yet. We could hear that Henry and Elsie were getting ready to leave so we look over towards the lounge and seen them waved and Elsie said have a great game girls; we will catch up with you later.

We were having a great time and laughing almost all the way through the game although we thought we were good, thinking back we did suck but we had fun. When we were done, we agreed that we would do better next time. Amanda said we better; Rosie will be with us she smiled. We sat in the lounge and had our smokes and then thought it was a good time to venture over to Paul's to see what he was up to.

Gathering up our stuff, we jump into our driving machine and go back to the palace road and turn left towards the beach and Paul's place. As we pull up Paul is having a drink of water and sitting on a long bench. Good day ladies he says I seen you coming from across the lake. How was your first golf game he asked? Awesome even though we are not that great we sure had a lot of fun the course is well laid out. Paul said that they could change the layout and theme of the course any time. The ground under the course has in-ground rollers and coasters that can be manipulated to change ground elevations and hole locations. If we were to be here for a long time, you do not want to play the same thing.

For verity in activities you go see Dustin, he has the gadgets and trinkets to amuse. We all have our favorite tech toys and activities so there is no pleasures in life that we would miss out on and using computer-generated distractions can fill a void.

Paul stood up and asked us if we would like anything, I have just made a fresh pot of coffee and mine is better than Rosie's but don't tell her I said that he smiled and gestured us to follow him in. Wow Paul this place is amazing, even from just walking in the front open area of the house we could see the house was manly and had all the luxuries. The wall behind the fireplace had the largest TV I have ever seen in a home and he said he needed a large TV so they could see it from the outdoor patio.

As we walk into the kitchen area, he pours us a coffee as we gaze around at all the woodwork and cabinetry that has all been beautifully carved. There was a floor to ceiling wine rack that was full and a humidor beside the wine wall with a lot of cigars in it and I did recognize the one kind with the yellow, black and white dot wrapping as being the Cuban Cahaba cigars. Paul was surprised I was familiar with cigars and even more interested that I had been to a cigar factory when I was on vacation there once.

Paul said I have done many things and have gone many places and going to a Cuban cigar factory would have been one I would have enjoyed the experience of. Would you like one he asked? No, no, not for me thank you. We all chuckled when I said I would go green if I was to smoke one of them, and yet you smoke weed he says, yes but that is different both Amanda I quickly responded with a big smile and Paul shook his head and grinned, you girls. What brings you girls here is there anything I can do for you. We saw you from the golf course and just thought you looked like you needed company I grinned and said only kidding we just thought we would drop by and see what you were up to.

I am meeting Rosie and Kevin at the café in a bit; she wants to re-arrange some equipment or furniture before cocktail hour she really did not say what she was doing only that she wanted our help around two this afternoon and it is getting close to that now. Let's have a refill and we will head over there. Sounds good, your coffee is great, I nudged Paul as we walked out to the front patio.

Paul actually had a cigar with him so when we sat down outside Amanda I lit a hoot and Paul laughed and took a bug puff off his cigar. Amanda said we have not seen much of Dustin I hope that he is not having any issues with his work. Paul looked over and with a positive voice, he said everything is fine and that there are times when he has to monitor island conditions closely and this is just one of those times and he is one dedicated smart guy, let me tell you.

There was a bit of small talk about our golf game and then Paul said well… at least one of you dressed for the occasion. Amanda and I looked at each other up and down when Paul commented on me wearing my shinny necklace to the Las Vegas strip he chuckled and by then, we finished our hoot and Paul butted out his cigar and said time to go girls.

As we walk up to our carts Paul dropped his sunglasses on his nose and said that is just way to bright and sand shot out from the back of his tires as he sped away. When Amanda saw Paul wipe the cart around she had a huge grin on her face gripped the steering wheal and was right on his tail. It was a single file race all the way, no passing! We were laughing all the way and the people already at the café could hear us coming and were looking our way as we arrived.

Rosie said to Paul what you up to old man, one of these times you are going to dump you ass right out of the cart farting around like that. You are a bad influence Paul, he said what me, how about Dustin and Kevin they are animals when they drive around and that is when she told the fellows that they were all bad drivers, but not you Jim you are a good example. Jim puffed out his chest and said did you hear that boys I am a good example. Kevin belted out with a smile that is because she just does not see you, driving like a maniac. Jim said well … that's all that matters isn't it? The group had a laugh and then Paul asked Rosie so what is it you need done anyway.

We are having a fondue festival and I wanted the tables rearranged so that we can put on the turntable so we can all reach the pots and cut up morsels. That is it; you called all of us here to help for that, no not really, I was board and ready for happy hour a bit early she laughed.

We all then worked together to set the tables and turntable up and putting the cooking oil in the twelve fondue pots. The Rosie, Janette and Jessie started bring the trays of cut meat, fish, cheese, vegetables and fruit. This is the largest fondue set up I have seen we could be here all night eating away. That is the plan Rosie said. Saddle up to the bar people we have lime or strawberry margaritas on tap today.

We got our drinks and then moved back out of the way to have a smoke when we looked at each other having another I can't believe this place, moment. Just way to cool all the time. It is like we are anticipating a down side to being here but so far nothing negative how is that even possible?

Amanda listened to me babble as we noticed the group drifting over in our direction as Elsie points out to the trees behind us whipping around and then we see the florescent field flag of the golf cart going back and forth, Paul blurted out at Rosie see … I am a good driver compared to that. Then Dustin pops onto the road, slows right down, and acts like nothing is up as everyone is staring at him with Paul pointing and looking right at Rosie. Her only reply, that's okay it's Dustin and he is cute.

She winked at Paul and then wiggled her hips as she walked back to the bar. You could tell we were all enjoying the banter. With everyone there now and the fondue pots all hot we sat down and started to feast on all the food that the ladies had cut up. Eating fondue takes a long time, this is not fast food dinning and with twelve people, it was already getting dark by the time we had finished.

We talked about all of us getting together for what will be a potluck gathering on the seventh day of our encapsulation. Dustin was tight lipped although positive about giving his updates and Henry and Elsie had a win they will tell us about. Rosie reminded Amanda and I that are going to share our story so we can all get to know you better Then Paul let us know with a big smile that we made it onto the schedule and that there are many meaningful things that us girls can do around here. Jim and I have been working on mechanical systems improvements so that when it does come time for the girls to leave we can maintain all system. We will update and talk about it all at the gathering for now let's have another drink he said. Then Jim jumped in with now that is what I call a long happy hour. We all laughed.

By this time after having a couple margaritas and getting a little more chatty, I leaned over to Jessie and pointed at Ryan and said he does not say much does he. Jessie and Ryan laughed when surprised me by saying with this group you can hardly get a word in edge wise. Kevin, who likes to talk himself, agreed however if you give Ryan, a chance to talk you couldn't shut him off he said as he smiled and nudged Ryan as he walked by him. Rosie said everyone gets their turn just some more than others she lowered her eyes and giggled knowing that she can at times; dominate a lot of the conversation.

When looking around at how everyone was interacting you could see Henry and Elsie right into each other and that, they were quite happy to pay their attentions to each other and really only jumped into the conversation so they did not come across as being rude, so it seemed. Jim and Janette were just a match made in heaven if there ever was one. With not being able to express them accurately, to Amanda and I, Jim and Janette together, they could stop global suffering. A bit extreme but as a couple they swell and strum every human's heartstring and is a kind of super power.

Watching and listening we realized that Jessie is Jim and Janettes daughter. They were not introduced that way. Although deeply committed to the project, with Jessie was always being part of the equation. Ryan came into their lives as an only child from a small family whose parents were lost in an avalanche while skiing. Ryan had the motivation Jessie, the education and expertise to be here. They were happy and talked a bit about their few recent off island occasions or vacations with the most recent vacation being with Jim and Janette on a European excursion. The year before that it was for their wedding that was held in Lake Como Italy. The mood was good and the chatting went on back and forth.

Feeling no pain, I leaned to my side and looked at Amanda and said smoke! That is our cute to get up from the table and move away. As we stood up we could smell the fresh coffee and it smelled inviting. Waking over to the bar, Rosie poured us a cup and we lit our smoke. Paul had his cigar butt that he lit and Kevin and Dustin sparked a joint. The sun setting and café lights twinkling against the background gave the dusk a glimmer it was so serial through our cloud of smoke. We all started pitching in to clean up, which was surprisingly easy, the oil was poured into a recycling container and the pots went into a conveyer belt dishwasher.
All the leftover food is poured into one feed shout and you do not have to separate the food groups. In no time, the place was all cleaned up and everyone was ready to call it a night.

As everyone was saying their good nights and heading off, Amanda took a few steps towards Rosie and I heard her say quietly so do you need a lift baby, I think we are going your way! Rosie snuggled right up to her and replied thanks but no, I have my ride and gave Amanda a little nudge to get out of here. We could take a hint we knew that meant that Paul was giving her a lift.

We climb into our pink machine and give a big wave and away we went, slowly until we were out of site. Once you get to the hill to the palace, they can see you again so Amanda behaved herself driving up the hill.

When we get to the patio, Amanda turned to me and said you know we did not change for the evening I think that is the first time since we got here. As I walked over to the hot tub area, I turned the lights on and made the bar go up, I was so proud of myself. Out of curiosity, Amanda went into our room just to check and then I hear mom, come here you got to see this.

I was instantly excited so I walked quickly to our room and seen Amanda holding up two cotton pajama gowns. The smaller one was pink with Cinderella designs and a white one for me with mini mouse designs. They looked so comfortable and flowing we were all giddy as we went to get freshened up as Rosie says and changed. The pajamas were perfect and of course, I kept my shinny necklace on. Amanda smiled at me and gave me a peck on the cheek as we headed for the door.

When we get out to the patio we are shocked, no Rosie. That was unusual she hasn't left us alone up here before. It did feel weird but we knew how the coffee worked I got the bar open and the lights on we were doing just fine. As we pretended to float around the patio getting coffee and fixings, Amanda looked at me with a sly smile with her eyebrow raised and said … hoot? Perfect I replied and we settled in waiting for Rosie to come back.

As time was, passing and we were enjoying our surroundings I asked Amanda what she thought about Paul not showing us much of his house. She said I would not read too much into that he is a guy. That is not what he would be thinking. Not that he has anything to hide and if we would have asked, I am sure he would have shown us around more but Paul is just not the mad to take two girls on a house tour she laughs. I thought about what she said and yes, he is a man's man with a hint of cowboy. What makes you think cowboy? We only ever see him wearing those square towed brown cowboy boots and his pants always go on the outside of the boot and wrinkle at the bottom just right. Amanda let out a laugh and said I don't know about you sometimes mom, you say the dandiest things.

If you want to wonder about something, how come with all the amazing clothes and the "drive in" closet she smirked do we have such a small selection of shoes? Amanda knew that would get me thinking knowing that for me, it is always a tossup on favorite's shoes or jewelry. Shoes are more affordable!

Just like magic, Rosie appeared at the steps and kind of startled us because we did not hear her coming at all. As she headed in our direction and looked at the coffee pot, she asked if it was fresh and yes we shook our heads and I even opened the bar all by myself I smiled.

So … how was the date, we both stared her right in the face knowing she was going to blush when she said oh no, no, Paul and I just had some work to catch up on, really I said did you have a glass of wine while you were so called working. Oh, don't be silly girls she said, we just enjoy each other's company Okay that is good enough for us we agreed, not wanting to press her or piss her off.

So … what was I hearing you girls talking about shoes as I came in? We were noticing that with all the amazing clothing from play to red carpet that there is not many types of shoes in the closet? That is an easy one Rosie replied you probably noticed that for the most part we wear flip-flops or Ugs.

When I get your cloths ready usually put with them a pair of the pink lather ballerina slippers because they form to the foot and are comfortable or a flip0flop to match your outfits. We have more styles of shoes then you can imagine in the bunkers, I believe Sire had a foot faddish because there are a lot of impractical shoes being stored. In addition, the beauty of our technology is that we can make any kind of shoe you can dream and in any colors. Having said that, I am not sure, why we have so many shoes in inventory she shrugged her shoulders and poured herself a healthy Baileys and coffee.

When we go shopping at the bunkers next week, I will take you to shoe lane as I call it and you will see what I am talking about. Hum, that sounded like we were going to enjoy our next rip up there.

After having, a couple of sips of her coffee Rosie said will have a lazy morning and then we will get ready for our potluck dinner with everyone here. The group should start arriving about three in the afternoon and our up-date meeting is at five. Rosie let us know that she is looking forward to tomorrow with it being the pot luck, everyone puts their hearts into their dishes and it

is a different kind of get together then at the café or the beach. You girls will love it, we end up with a buffet table that most resort hotels would envy, and she laughed.
Yes, I guess we should put some thought into our sharing with the group tomorrow, and with that being said Amanda, may be that is our signal to head to bed and think on that. Tomorrow will be another great day however, a long one I am thinking. Rosie stayed seated and lifted her coffee cup and said you ladies sleep well and I will see you bright and early tomorrow she smiled. When we stood up and gathered our stuff we modeled her dresses and twirled around as we said good night Rosie, thank you.

We headed to our room and although tired we thought we would sit by the balcony and have a smoke before going to bed. As we sat and looked down to the valley we were reflecting on our lives when Amanda looked at me with big tears in her eyes and said mom, without you I would have not made it as far as I have in life. Moreover, I would have never survived to this point if you had not always been there for me. I felt a big lump in my throat, my eyes tear up then we both leaned into each other and gave big hugs and were both softly crying. I whispered in her ear sweetie, you are my precious.

Then to lighten our thoughts I said yes you are right I have bailed you out of some of the unpredictable situations in your past and got you working in the right directions. Yup it is all me I said smiling! Well we better get our beauty sleep we are having company and I think we will hear a lot more stuff about what is going on and what we have been signed up for on the schedule. As we, head to the bed I stopped turned to Amanda who was right on my-heals and said we did not ask Rosie what we are cooking for tomorrow's potluck? Amanda lifted her eyebrows and replied Rosie, is not going to let us do any cooking in her kitchen I am sure that we are set up and cleanup crew at best. Will see, will see, as we were cuddling into our big soft bed we were fast asleep in no time.

Chapter Thirteen

I think we both must have woken about the same time, and it was because Rosie had just wisped into the room brought coffee and had out comfy three-quarter length leggings and tank top and lightweight mesh running shoes. When we sat up and had a good look across the room at the clothes Rosie had laid out, I looked over at Amanda and said now those outfits have Amanda written all over them. For sure, this will be a good cloths day as she headed over for a coffee. I love the shoes they are so cute and mine fit perfectly. I love this place I said with a big grin, as I joined Amanda in the sitting area.

On this particular morning when we were finished getting ready felt great and we sat and down and had a hoot before going out to start this day. There was a lot about this day that was making us both feel excited and anxious all at the same time and we did not know what it was.

When we get out of our room to greet Rosie we did not see her but we did see a table set with two steaming cups of coffee and a tray of bagels and a verity of cream cheese. There was even a vase with fresh flowers in it on the table. We headed towards the table when we hear behind us Rosie saying loudly coming through, meaning get out of the way of the kitchen doors. She had a serving cart with four beautiful pies that looked so good as she pushed them past us and said that they need to set and she likes to leave them out in the open for about a half hour the kitchen is too closed for them to set properly. Man those look good Amanda said to Rosie.

Have some breakfast girls Rosie said as she was heading back to the kitchen when I remember to ask what we were cooking for the potluck dinner. Rosie stopped in her tracks, and turned to say with a huge smile oh dear, the cooking is already done. Amanda laughed I knew she would have it done before we even got up. Rosie winked back at Amanda and you start girls and I will join you for coffee in a minute.

We had a few sips of coffee and just had our beagles fixed when Rosie came out to join us. Once she gets seated, she fixed herself a beagle and asked how we slept. With us both nodding good, she proceeded with I believe Paul, Jim and Dustin will be here a bit earlier than the others to set the tables and projection area. The rest will arrive when they have finished with their culinary masterpieces.

So what are we supposed to do to help with, Rosie grinned and said you girls just being around is good, after we are done breakfast you girls can go have a game of pool or darts in the lounge, you have not spent any time back in the sports lounge yet and it is a neat place. There is also the slot machines that are a lot of fun and will help to pass time. My face lit up when she reminded us of the machines we do play them at home for fun and not much money. My husband and I enjoy playing them together when we go to our local pub.

No worries ladies when I need your help you will know it and I will call don't you worry. Amanda yes I believe you, however I do not see you ever needing our help with anything, we chuckled.

Rosie finished her coffee and said well girls go give your luck a try. Just push the start button and enter your name and your new game will start with two hundred thousand credits with the lowest bet bring five thousand credits. Don't worry if you lose it all you just start a new game. Rosie says my game has been going on for two years and I am currently at a three and half million credits. Then she jokingly voiced like the impossible challenge, beat that, she said as we got up and headed over to the machines Rosie must have got up as soon as our back were turned because by the time we looked back she had the table cleared and was pushing the serving cart into the kitchen.

There were three machines and we each picked an end machine, sat down and touched the start button. Our screens lit up and using the key pad, you enter your handle. Amanda signed herself in as Princess and I signed in as CB. Then the screen showed a rolling list of games to choose from and to my excitement, I find a version of the game that I love to play at home. Amanda also seen some games that she was familiar with and chose one with fish.

I thought this was going to be so fun so I got myself more comfortable pulled the ashtray up and before I could set my hand on the button for my first try, Rosie came right up behind us with a fresh coffee and said … winning yet! I hit the button and all the sudden I was overwhelmed with missing home and my eyes filled up so I kept looking straight at the scene and let out huff when I did not win on my first spin. Rosie smiled and said keep trying and patted me on the back as she was going to the front.

Amanda looked over at me and seen a drop from my face so she asked is that a tear drop or drool mom? She knew it was a tear and was only trying to make me feel better. I just replied, I miss LB and that was all that was said and we both continued playing and all of the sudden winning and winning good. After a bit we were having so much fun playing, having our coffee's and smokes. For us this was the perfect great escape and was very relaxing because we were not playing for real money.

We were not paying attention to the time at all and only sometimes heard Rosie moving about on the patio when Amanda caught from the corner of her eye, that we had visitors. I looked at Amanda and said there is no way it is three, she looked at her watch and said no they are early and went back to her game. At that time, I had one million credits so I thought that was a good place to stop for now so I saved my game and lit a smoke to see how Amanda was going. I could see Paul and Jim were here but there was no sign of Dustin yet. Amanda said he would be the guy that shows up at three like he was asked to. And for what he really can help with or needs to do will only take thirteen minutes but leaving nothing to chance Rosie and Paul would have him arrive at least an hour early. We chuckled away for a bit and then she hit a big jackpot clapped her hands and said I'm cashing out! She saved her game and we gathered our cups and smokes up and headed back out to the patio.

Good day ladies Paul and Jim said when they seen us coming out of the lounge. Jim asked how we did on the machines. Our faces were beaming so they knew we did good but we soon realized that we were only as good as our low expectations once we heard the credits they were up to we knew we had a long way to go and that they just burst our bubble. They both laughed, as our disbelief showed on our faces when Rosie confirmed they were not kidding.

So … What is the plan what can we do I said, like I was stepping up for assignment, when Paul leaned and tilted his head in Rosie's direction and said I have no idea with a smile. Rosie went back into the kitchen so we stood there and waited a minute for her to come out, still joking about the machines.

Rosie came out and looked at us all just standing around waiting when she said you all look so lost, honestly, this place would crumble if it weren't for me she boasted and with chuckles, we all quickly agreed. She probably really was right.

Then Rosie sweetly asked the fellows if they could please pull out the buffet table and let them know that she has sent Dustin to bring up the large hot serving caddy from the cafe. I think Kevin was going to see if he needed any help.

What can we do, believe it or not, I actually do have something you can do for me and that is drive down Henrys office she has the table covers and napkins there. Is it open Amanda asked and she yes Elsie is doing the cooking this time and Henry is finishing her work for this evenings meeting.
Okay we will go and pick them up is there anything else, nothing I can think of right now, Jim asked seeing as you are going down anyway can you stop by the house and pick up the large flower arrangement that Janette made for the buffet table. With all the food she has been preparing that will be one less thing to bring when I go pick her up.

For sure, no problem so we headed to our pink driving machine and feeling useful we went on our way. It was a good that that we did have our map because we had never been to Jim and Janettes house and it is tucked back and in behind the café. We went to Main Street first and met with Henry who was working on her computer when we arrived. She greeted us so nicely and showed us the two bags of tablecloths and napkins and said that she was excited for this evening. We agreed like we knew what this meant to them but were clueless. This was a potluck dinner with a few people, what is all the hype.

We thanked Henry and let her know that we are also have been asked to pick up a flower arrangement from Janette. When Henry looked over at our cart and said I am not sure it is big enough to carry the flowers chuckling into her hand and when seeing my eyes open wide, only kidding girls. You will see what Janette can do with some flowers and a vase when you get there. See you in a bit we said, now curious were eager to find the house.

We come around the bend and drive down the lane when Jim and Janettes house appears through an opening in the trees. As soon as we seen the house you just know it is them. We did not think that she knew that we were coming and were a bit surprised when she came right out to greet us even before we had a chance to get out of our cart. She said it is no nice that you have come to pick up the flowers; Jim let me know to be expecting you. Come on in as she motioned for us to go up the stairs into the large open living space that was all in one kitchen, dining and living room. The fire was circular with dobby Arizona and Mexican look about it. The fireplace-chiming stack was visible all the way going up through the middle of the fifteen-foot ceiling. We walked by all the entertainment gadgets and then Janette showed us the man cave behind the open living area that has a bowling lane, never mind the small stuff like a shuffle board.

Both Amanda and I complement her on the house it is pristine and comfortable then she takes us to the back of the house where the bedrooms were and not so surprisingly, their bedroom looked like a haven with some burgundy blue green tartan with a tan contrast and was filled with pictures and memorabilia.

Off their bedroom that also has a fireplace is a small patio with a hot tub and pool. Off to the side of the patio, there was a short path to Janettes green house, where she does the flowers. It was humid in there so when Janette said as she went to pick up the bouquet, oh dear look at the time, I better let you girls get back up their if Rosie is waiting on the tablecloths and flowers. We complemented her on the huge arrangement of stargazer lilies that smelt amazing, a little over powering however; it was a very familiar and one of my favorite floral aromas.

Janette carried the arrangement back through the house and out to the cart I got in my seat and then she gave it to me to hang onto while Amanda drove us back. The arrangement was tall and top heavy so I could not really see out the front and I had to pay attention and hang on. Dumping the flowers would be just too embracing so I made sure that Amanda took it easy getting back. We were both in awe of the size and the smell it was overpowering sitting right in it.

As we pull up Jim was there to greet us and grab the flowers from me so I could get out of the cart and Amanda took the two bags over to Rosie. Perfect timing she said to Amanda we just got the tables set up and we have the buffet server ready for the food. Wow, this looks fantastic is what I said when I came onto the patio and seen the set up of the buffet hot-serving caddy off to the side and the circle of tables set with name placards.

The patio looked more prepared for a white glove event not like any potluck I have gone to I chuckled to Paul who was standing beside me. He gave me a nod letting me know that he agreed, and said under his breath yup, this is not like the potlucks I remember having growing up, he said with a smile. Rosie new that Paul was only trying to rattle her a little and tug at her obsession with anything worth doing is worth doing with taste, class and right the first time philosophy.

Rosie not shaken at all by what Paul said followed up with well that is the way they are done here at the palace she chuckled especially with having our guests here this time, this is a special occasion.

I helped Rosie put the napkins out on the table and noticed the names on the plates and that Rosie had put herself sitting between Amanda and at our table. I thought that was interesting but not worth mentioning, Rosie has to have seen that Amanda and I always sat beside or across from each other.

All the sudden we hear Kevin say its break time as we hear him crack a beer open. Just then, we see the rest of the gang start to pull up bring their yummy smelling contributions to the dinner.

Just then, Rosie grabbed our hands and said I have something in your room for you ladies if you would like to freshen up before dinner. Amanda was comfortable in what she was wearing but seeing the lay out and the way the rest of the ladies were dressed she was excited to see what Rosie had pick for us.

When we look at what she has in this case made for us was we could not believe our eyes. For me there was a tan crop top and matching high waist full-length slim line skirt with slits up both sides. Amanda's was a soft pink and the same style of crop top with her skirt being also full length but low waist with one slit up the left leg. They were amazing and fit like a glove.

This time our ballerina slippers were sparkly.

When we come out, we can see that everyone has arrived and dressed for the occasion. Henry saw us first and called over to us to come to the bar saying there you girls are, you both look amazing oh my goodness Rosie you have out done yourself this time. We both nodded at Rosie and gave the thumbs up as we headed over with the group at the bar

We both asked for a glass of white wine and moved over to have a smoke while the others were getting their drinks and chatting about the meeting order. Kevin came over to join us because other then progress on the my side of the fence he was not concerned and was more concerned with making sure we knew that the only thing that we were going to want to eat was his secret gourmet dish.

Hum and then pause … I sense in your tone and by the way, you came over, saying the only thing we are going to want to eat makes me think there a little friendly culinary competition going on around here. I replied to Kevin in a louder voice so of course, the others heard what I had said. Then to my amusement, Jessie quickly responded with friendly! … There is nothing friendly, when it comes to culinary competitions, around here. Everyone laughed while looking over in Rosie's direction. Rosie made no bones when verbalizing she was the best chef even with the other ladies standing right there. No one was insulted as Jessie continued, because Rosie did not just think she was the best chef on the island, she means the world! No sad feelings if you do not quite measure up to Rosie's standards in the kitchen, Rosie blushed and the group howled.

Everyone looked so nice and relaxed we all had our cocktails and were settled around the infinity pool when just as we put our smokes out , Rosie rang a little dinner bell letting us all know that we can come be seated and get comfortable. She motioned for us to head over to the buffet and dinner table area.

With we were sitting down in our selected seats Rosie stood right by the buffet table and with a big smile and proudly welcomed us to a new eating experience and this evening we have on our menu for your taste buds to tantalize over, as she drew out her introduction we could see Kevin fidgeting.

Then she started listing off the dishes and started with Looking over at

Elsie and said from Haven Crest we have an iceberg sundried tomato and cucumber chunked salad with a cheese and pickle platter. Then she looked over at Janette and announced and, from Hidden Acres we have a dish of roulade and sauerkraut with fresh dinner buns. As Rosie pointed to each tray, she could angle the above mirror top so that the people sitting down could see into the dishes. Next, we have from our young Uptown Street couple, a four-inch thick backed lasagna. Lucky farms have brought us a creamy Tuna Neptune pasta casserole with a pastry bottom. Kevin stood and took a bow and said to the group and you are welcome. Rosie said silly man sit down; he said you are taking so long I won't be hungry by the time you are done. She says hush now I am almost done. She cleared her through and pointed back at the table and continued and From Beach Cove Paul has brought his famous BBQ ribs. The palace has complimented the assortment and has made porgies and cabbage rolls. Dustin brought the buffet table so that excused him from having to cook Rosie looked over at him as he shrugged his shoulders with a smile and said my skills are not in the kitchen and he wiggled his eye brows and sat up straight. Paul let out a big high laugh and said yes, Dustin we all know where your skills are at. It's the Birdcage and not the bedroom if that is what you were trying to imply. The group chuckled then Rosie said come and get it people, dig in.

After all, of the food introductions it did not take long for people to get up and start filling their plates. The selections were all things I was familiar with and liked and having a small scope of everything my plate was full. Amanda did not try all of the dishes but filled up on the ones she knew she liked.

Once everyone had their plates full and sitting it was real quiet and all we could hear was the soft music that Rosie had playing in the background and the birds singing in the distance. I was so worried about getting BBQ sauce on my outfit that I put my napkin in the neck of my top to protect myself. I saw Paul glance over at me and smiled and gave his head a little shake but you could tell he loved my napkin move because he could see I was really enjoying his ribs and I was making a mess eating them. Rosie also smiled and giggled under her breath when she saw my make shift bib too.

I could see around Rosie and that Amanda was doing real good herself; I have not seen her eat this well in a long time. Kevin and Dustin were already going up for seconds by the time, I had half my plate done and when looking up at the buffet mirrors I could see that all that food that was there to start with was almost gone.

Rosie was the first to finish and get up and started fixing the desert tray and brought up the coffee pots. As she was cleaning the area up a bit then Janette and Henry joined into to help. Amanda and I finally finish with Kevin and Dustin left eating until all the food was almost gone. Wow, man you fellows can eat a lot, I said as we got up from the table, we were so full we had to move around.

With us off to the side, we watched as the group cleaned up the buffet table and started getting things ready for the presentation. Rosie had a beautifully set table with coffee tea and deserts on it that was being left out for our meeting.

While we were standing out of the way and just about to have our smoke, we heard, Paul say that we would be starting in about fifteen minutes. Dustin and Kevin came over to join us for a smoke when Dustin started saying that we are going to enjoy this meeting because we understand the island better then when we first got here. We are excited to present this evening. Kevin looked at Dustin and jokingly said hey bud; I only came for the food and new company! They laughed as we stood there listening to them banter back and forth. Then like scolding children, we hear Rosie say to Dustin and Kevin I cannot believe you two are as smart as they say you are as she chuckled, you could tell she liked picking on the young fellows and that they enjoyed her mother attention.

All right everyone with a commanding voice we hear Paul please take your seats we do have a bit to get through and depending on how many questions ours guest have we … he looked up and then gasped well we could be hear all night and chuckled then quickly followed with only kidding ladies. Amanda and I had a perplexed look on our faces, as everyone was looking at us. I smiled big as I could feel my cheeks warm up with all eyes on us.

Okay gang this is where we are at and what we know Paul said as the projector screen emerged with the first picture being of the glob that was turning slowly, on the side bar we could see numbers scrolling by lightning fast and without spaces just a mass of data whipping through.

Paul looked right at Amanda and I and said where to start and he paused. Let's recap what you know so far about the situation and if you have any questions jump in ladies. You landed here the end of October and you have now been here a week. When the island locked down all outside, indicators were saying that it would be safe to leave this island in six months and change.

You know that the island is invisible however; we know that you do not understand how or where you are in the ocean Paul smiled and Rosie who was sitting right beside looked at me smiled at me grabbed my hand and patted it gently. We sat there looking so naïve and innocent, Amanda batted her eyelashes around the room so cutely and I with raised eyebrows and I had a sheepish grin, they were all right, we had no idea where we were. Carrying on Paul enlarged the world globe and rotated the view first showing us Canada and then turned the glob showing the invisible halfway around the world from home.

Both our eyes opened wide when we seen how far we were away and that there seemed to be nothing around. How do we get home from here I asked. Then Dustin stood up stuffed the rest of his donut into his mouth, whipped his hands on his shorts. I could see Rosie rolling her eyes beside me and I smiled. I am sure that Amanda see her reaction to. Paul smiled at Dustin as he casually walks up and put his hand out for Paul to hand over the controller.

Okay leaving this to the pro he said confidently, standing straight, he said we would get to how you are leaving further on. First the cool news and what Henry, Elsie and I have been working on is a few days ago we had a thread of data that is easiest described in laymen terms as a thread and like a hair on a world internet blanket. The hair we found was imbedded in data filtering through our hidden satellite. The hair was an anomaly that got through and we had to figure out. It took three of us three days to decode the information that was hidden in public untraceable data streams.

Dustin took a big breath and looked at all the group and hit the button on the controller. To the group's delight the start of the video was of a very majestic looking gentleman, almost prince like, sitting in a grand chair who started his greeting with I am sure that my people are smart enough to be watching this message and I hope you are all doing well. Dustin paused the video and looked at Amanda and I and said now that is our founder Sire. Dustin took the video off pause and the gentleman continued boisterously with Rosie may lady, I love you I hope you are doing well and I miss your cooking. He spoke with a bit of an accent but I could not pinpoint the origin. I looked over at Rosie and she was blushing with pride that he had addressed her personally and first.

Then this stately man says and you Paul, you old dog how are you doing these days. I hope that Rosie is not over feeding you in my absence he smiled and winked. Then quite casually, carries on with yes, speaking of my absence. The good news is I and my family are all alive safe and doing well. With all of the intelligence and advanced information, we were able to retreat to an alternative safe haven. Dustin paused the video knowing this meant something to the residence and looked at the group who concurred that this was not the only place that Sire created. The group had a bit of discussion around them always wondering if there was another place and other super people running it. By the Sires own admission implied there was.

Dustin took it off pause and Sire continued his transmission. We understand that everything is operational however; we are picking up two unaccounted for human signatures. It will be a few days before we receive your transmission back so we are surmising that with two unexplained human signatures that through some miracle, out of the forty-nine planes that went down two survivors found their way in. As impossible as that was supposed to be we have not come up with any other expiation.

If we do have guests on the island please make sure that they are well taken care of and made to feel at home and comfortable as this all must be extremely overwhelming for them. We are having system problems here and have not been able to receive an accurate atmospheric reading and are not able to update. Dustin paused the screen again, and said to the group with a bit of a tone, so how are they able to see us and extra heat signatures when we did not even know they existed and, by the way he looked at Paul, who are they? Paul replied with we are obviously sharing the satellite with at least one other entity which must have been designed in segregated secured in sections. Paul said that is interesting and something we did not know before and told Dustin to keep rolling.

To Amanda and I there being another place on this earth built similar to this at this point did not surprise us, although we could see that for some not knowing that there was another secret place was a deception they were not happy with but knew that Sire must have had his reasons for keeping a secret from them.

Sire went onto say that from all the intelligence and inside government transmissions, he is happy that all countries are all coming together to pick of the pieces of the world and rebuild. Our scientists have concluded this will be a short duration lockdown and a test of our systems with the most important being maintaining our umbrella that keeps us hidden from the rest of the world. I hope this message finds you all well and that the island is operating as designed.

As Sire was closing his message, he tipped his hand as a salute and said Kevin my good sir, I miss the quality of your herb, and then to Dustin I know you have new gadgets for me to try and I will soon. Then addressing Jim, Janette, Jessie and Ryan the island would not be complete without the family values you bring and Henry and Elsie you are an intricate part of the plan and I love you all for your dedication and devotion to a project that has proven its importance.

I bid you all a farewell for now and will be looking for your needle in a haystack replay over the next few days. Please provide us with detailed systems up date and any information regarding your guests and start the island opening preparations in accordance to atmospheric timeline. If assistance is needed for guest departure, we will coordinate over the next few months to master a plan. He blew everyone a kiss and cut off transmission. Amanda sat back in her chair and said quietly that was an abrupt good bye as we smirked at each other. Dustin heard what I had said and he looked at me with a perplexed look and said no, I think that is was cut short because of time. The less time spent transmitting means the harder it is to find.

After that, the group was a bit quiet and all the sudden then Jim piped up and said I need a refill and looked over at Rosie and continued with and I do not mean coffee he smiled. Yes she I agree put both hands on her knees and stood up walk behind the bar and rolled out a restocked serving cart with rum, vodka, red and white wine and bottle of baileys of course. Rosie was prepared as always so we stopped to get our drinks and have a smoke.

As we were standing with our wine and having a smoke, I said so that is Sire hey, he looks sharp, rich and important. Ryan commented that yes, he is all of that and more then Henry said and he smells as good as he looks, she glanced at Elsie and they both laughed.

Dustin still had the remote control and asked us girls if we wanted to see something cool of course, we replied and he flipped through a couple screens and all the sudden the birds stop singing as loudly and the interior lighting change so dramatically it started to freak us out. We could actually see the interior of the island as it really was without all the special effects, which beautified the jagged rock walls and the changing of setting skyline that was there seconds ago was gone. The background sounds of the tropics could hardly be heard. This was crazy, Amanda and I looked at each other with eyes wide and together we walk out to an opening looking down into the valley and across to the bunkers to have a better look at what things really looked like. The dramatic change felt like we went from being inside paradise to being inside a hollowed our rock. The most amazing transformation was seeing what appeared to be a natural skyline disappear to reveal the high surrounding jagged rock walls. Looking up the jagged rock wall you can see where the milky white crystal dome seamlessly starts which looks like a cut and carved block of salt instead of shinny crystal. I remember Dustin or Paul saying earlier that the crystal dome also supports the islands power so in my mind I was thinking shiny crystals and was suppressed to see the milky white dome plugging the opening. The island did not look or sound the same at all, and as we turned, we could see the group was looking on and waiting to see our reactions to the new reality.

Amanda said with a straight face trying to hold her emotions and be cool at the same time, said that is different. I smiled and said to Dustin jokingly, please turn the island back on this place is scary! As Dustin was readjusting the system and while still curious about the dome, I turned to Paul and asked. Was it you who had said earlier that the crystal dome helped to support the power systems? Paul answered by saying that it is because of the density and thickness of the dome we do not see it as a shiny object. The dome acts like a microscopic solar panel and can draw whatever light and energy from the atmosphere and sky and then trickles that energy back to our systems.

Paul, let us know that the waterfall can also be controlled and shut down when needed, and is something we will have to do when it is time to leave. It does take some rerouting of the water systems so knowing when you will be able to leave will mean that you allow the forty-five days to make that happen without blowing up the island he chuckled. That is what Sire was talking about in his message.

Paul said another piece of island trivia is that you know how we can see where the heat signatures are on the island. All of our carts and paths are dialed into our operating systems so that even a blind person can dive a cart

here and could never hit anyone or drive off the path.
The carts can go off the road; however, they have to be manually switched by turning the button clockwise on the dash that has a little picture of a tree on it. The off path button is located by the ashtray he smiled. Amanda said I wondered what that little tree meant and just never thought to ask.

With Dustin standing beside me and everything looking and sounding normal again I shifted and asked how significant is it that they, whoever they are, know of you and you don't know of them. I felt everyone's heads lift and eyes on me when Dustin replied, that can only mean that they are bigger then we are and just as well hidden. Oh! I took a puff off my smoke and a sip of my wine realizing that bothered Dustin more than the others.

Rosie motioned for us to all head back to our seats and said lets carry on or you will have us up all night. You could see the light bulb go on when Kevin blurted out we should go for an evening swim down at the lake when we are done. That sounds like the way to end this evening as he raised his glass to the group looking for support on the idea. Ryan raised his glass and Kevin said right on dude it's you and me later, Kevin looked at Jessie and winked.

Dustin was still holding the remote control and with everyone seated, he flipped to a new screen and said, although Sire indicated that their atmospheric systems were not operating accurately. Henry, Elsie and I have confirmed ours are working perfectly. We were saving this as your surprise ladies and remaining residence ... that with the initial environmental reporting of when the island would open was in April with the recent improvements to our global environment the island will be able to open in March and you will be able to go home.

Amanda and were so happy to hear the good news that things were better in the world we hugged and then Rosie put her arms around us and did not say anything. Although four months was, still a long time that did not put a damper on the good news. Paul said to Dustin while also looking at Henry and Elsie now how in the heck were you able to keep this secrete from me? He looked confused and continued with I over see all system and review them with a fine toothcomb and I did not see change. You people are good.

Shall we carry on Dustin faced the group and with the remote flipped computer screens to show off the new schedule that had our names on it this time and we were wondering what kind of tasks we were going to be assigned. When the spreadsheet popped up, we were glad to see that our assigned time was at Lucky farms that we felt we could manage without looking like fools but that was yet to be seen. It is not like Amanda I have spent a time living the farm life that is for sure.

Kevin clapped right on I have help this week; you could see Elsie and Jessie roll their eyes because they spend a lot of their spare time in the gardens and working with the small animals. We hear Henry say, Kevin you always have help and looked over to see that she had a big smile. Kevin continued his big smile rolled his eyes and shrugged what can I say it's my charisma.

The group gowned and mumbled as Kevin looked at Amanda and I and said, we will start you off simple with picking tomatoes and pulling weeds and not the ones we smoke either he laughed. I can learn you the farm life ladies. Then Rosie broke in with I will be watching you Mr. Kevin, you better not have them doing all of your chores while you are sitting around smoking the weed. The group laughed at Rosie had said knowing that Kevin would not do that anyway. He was a fun matriculate person that was very devoted to his farm and hard working.

While Amanda was looking the schedule over better, she noticed that we were only listed at the farm for three hours a day and only on day two, three and four. Amanda asked first, why the schedule does not use the words for the days of the week and only use numbers? Good question, Dustin was quick to answer by saying that the island is made up of data and programming and using numbers instead of words is easier when writing code. Her second question was why are we only working three hours per day? Dustin shrugged his shoulders knowing that was not his question to answer and jokingly said that is above my pay grade and snickered as he sat back down. Rosie was quick to jump in and say now, now, girls you are our still our guests not our work force she smiled and then said this is a good start.

Well that raps it up my presentation for this evening Dustin said and I am glad that we were able to report positive news today. Dustin then handed the remote back to Paul and went to his seat.

Once sitting Dustin looking for some parse from the group he deliberately took a big drink of his rum and coke and huffed like he was exhausted after giving his exasperating presentation. We were watching his over acted motions and Ryan looks over at Dustin lifted both his hands in the air and says in a high pitch voice, really was it that hard? Dustin looks over very sly like and lifted his eyebrow at the group and says no with a pause … it was just that dam good as he leaned back into his chair proudly, the whole groups burst out laughing.

Paul had the remote in one hand and his drink in the other and when he seen that his glass was almost empty he called out to the groups and said recess kids. Kevin jumped up and headed over to the pool area where he had a hoot lit within a few seconds of Paul calling the break. Amanda and I well we were right behind him of course with Dustin and Ryan following us. With the five of us standing there Dustin sparked another hoot snickering in a quiet voice we don't have much time, it does not take Paul long to mix a drink. Paul figured that we are chuckling about him and Paul looked at Kevin and said take your time I have all night. Then Paul, Jim and Henry were talking amongst themselves and Rosie, Janette and Elsie were fussing around the bar and food carts.

While we were having our smokes, I commented that without all of the effects the island looks so different Dustin said that that component of building the island was one of the most intricate and difficult features we created. The volume and sounds of the birds and some aromas are artificially enhanced and are still being perfected daily. Wow, it is hard to conceive that a lot of what we are seeing and hearing is real projection however not physically here. Too cool, Amanda bumped my elbow and winked like I sounded as though I actually understood science and depth of what I was saying.

Then we see across the patio calling us back to our seats once again when Jim picked up the remote control this time and once we were all back in our seats proceed with saying that now the girls have gone to the bunkers we thought it might be a good idea to explain them better for you.

I know the rest of the group love the bunkers and secretly are frequent shoppers he says as he raises his eyebrows at the group. Amanda and I look around the table and could that everyone else was trying to avoiding eye contact with Jim and looking around so innocent taking a sip of wine or shuffling the napkin around to avoid acknowledgement. That was funny to watch and was a good introduction!

After the cute pause, using the remote Jim flipped the screen over to show the x-ray look at the island, which showed that in the thickest area of the island, was used and carved out to house the bunkers. We had told you that the island was constructed in the same fashion you would think of a 3D printer operating however only stationary objects were constructing as the island was being built layer by layer. We are sitting on a sunken island as our base to start our construction a mile under the water.

As the construction rose above the water, our hidden satellite provided us the digital coverage and with being in a remote area of the ocean far from shipping corridors and we even took into consideration parrot hunting grounds. Jim noticed us looking up at him like we were questioning what he had just said so he repeated yes parrots! They generally operate broken ships with failed navigation systems that could disable our ability to navigate them around the island.

Getting back to the bunkers Jim says, as most of you know the bunkers are set up like a mega department store with containers for all facets of living. These C-cans as they are called were all stocked on land and brought onto the island full. To shop at the bunkers you can go on the computer put in your order and when you get there put in your name and the cart will automatically take you to the areas of shopping you want and in the shorted order. On the other hand, you can also choose, so you ladies are aware, the order in which you want to do your shopping. If you think of something else, in the midst of your shopping, you enter the department or item you are looking for and it will add to the drive program.

The bunkers are so well equipped that anyone of us could can remodel our homes and wardrobes as time passes. Being able to change things is the way people stay healthy when in captivity, Jim said with honestly. Jim directed his attention back to Amanda and I and said well so far all you have is a pair of sunglasses each I am sure the ladies will help with that.

Oh yes and to ensure that we all do not become hoarders he smiled we have a great return policy. You can take anything back when done enjoying the purchase. Purchase, I said a bit loud, grasping my shiny necklace, and with a serious face, I glanced at everyone around the table and quipped and you mean I have to pay for this? Everyone howled at what I had just said and how devastated my face looked when the thought of having to pay for the necklace crossed my mind, when Rosie who was laughing into her hand looking at the shocked look on my face, of course not Rosie she replied. That is just the term used there is no money here and you can keep the necklace she nodded giving her approval.

It was getting late and Paul and Rosie could see that people were getting restless so Paul stood up and said how about we call it a night and Colleen and Amanda can give us their story at our next cocktail hour. We are learning a little bit you girls all the time but we do all want to hear the story and get to know you with the same frame of reference. It also saves having to all of us the same story over and over he chuckled.

By this time, Rosie was pouring coffee and had pastries out to snake on while the meeting was ending. I took Amanda's hand and headed over to where Paul, Jim and Rosie were now mingling and I asked there is more I want to know like how we are getting off the island, and with Sire asking about extra people will you tell them it is us. No one had left yet and all were in earshot, just mulling about chatting. When they heard me ask my questions to Paul, they all moved in closer to hear what Paul was going to tell us.

Paul looked at me and said I am sure you have many questions yet to be asked and to address your first question as far as the plan to get you ladies off the island. It will not be simple to have you rescued and us undetected so we have a couple of options that we are studying. We will all have a roll in your departure and once all the facts are together we will meet again to go through the information as a group. We should have our profiles complete in the next few days. I can tell you that your departure will be more luxuries then your arrival, he smiled trying to make light of the question.

For question number two yes, for sure we will let Sire know in our returning message who you ladies are and where you come from. However to be honest there is little he will be able to do with that information as far as communicating to your families that you are alive and coming home soon.

Pail satisfied my curiosity and provided insight as to timeline. Knowing the information was coming was good enough for me because even with environmental improvements we are going to be her for three months, so we have time.

With Paul winding the meeting down and answering my questions, Jim, Janette, Jessie and Ryan, gave their salutes and salutations for a wonderful dinner and evening then gave a round of hugs and handshakes then got in their carts for home.

Henry and Elsie were right behind them thanking Rosie for everything again and giving Amanda and I hugs and wishing us a good night on their way to their cart.

Kevin and Dustin moved themselves over to the hot tub area and were about to lit a hoot. While Rosie and Paul started talking about dinner, we headed towards Kevin and Dustin for a smoke and a Baileys.
By the time, we reach the bar Kevin was passing the hoot around. Dustin asked us what we thought of all the information we heard? I said that the one word that comes to mind first is … positive. I was left feeling positive even though I know I do not understand I have complete trust and belief in all of the people here. Amanda raised her coffee looked at both of them and said here, here agreeing with me.

Rosie and Paul came over to join us for a nightcap and once Rosie had her big shot of Baileys poured she sat down beside Paul and looked across at Amanda and I and began to tell us that everyone thought that we are doing amazing here. We understand and get that you may be smitten with some of the highlights of being here however we have never heard you complain or become overly emotion regarding things you have no control. You are making it a lot easier for us … to like you girls. Rosie said it with such a straight face and dry wit that Amanda looked right up at her with puppy dog eyes and with a slight pause, we all laughed. In reply, looking at Rosie and Paul I thanked the little group for their help in making our unplanned stay an amazing experience and joking said no worries on the emotional rollercoaster, Amanda and I only turn into emotional messes when we don't have weed and or when watch chick flicks. Kevin and Dustin thought that was pretty funny and Kevin said then you landed in just the right spot we have the weed, and Dustin added and over a thousand chick flicks for you to choose from, when you need a good cry, that is.

Although Dustin and Kevin looked like they were comfortable, Kevin looked at Dustin and said time to bud. With that being said they both stood up, Kevin had a big stretch then Rosie and Paul stood up motioning them to move themselves along. Then Amanda and I got up to give them a hug before they left. Dustin did not have his wheels with him so Kevin was giving Dustin a ride home. As they pulled away, we could all hear Dustin tell Kevin to keep it on the road this time, and away they went laughing down the hill.

Paul then came over to us and put one arm around Amanda and the other around me and gave us both a big squeeze and said you girls are great, we a glade that you are here safe with us for now and we will get you home to your families as soon as we can. For now, I suggest you take advantage of what the island has to offer and keep Rosie busy he smirked looking at Rosie and gave us both a peck on the forehead before loosening his consoling embrace. Rosie then walked Paul to his cart where we did see Paul give Rosie a kiss on the cheek before he left.

When Rosie turned around, she should see that we were looking right at her and she immediately started to blush, it is not what you think she said, Really Amanda replied with a big smile, as Rosie was walking towards so what are we thinking she asked? There is nothing smooshy going on between Paul and I, when Amanda followed with …Yet! You are silly girls we have known each other for years we are close friends she paused and lifted her head and said right to Amanda with a grin and no benefits! We had a good chuckle when she said that. Well girls it is time to get my beauty rest and we agreed we were tired. This was an eventful day with fantastic food and information. As I nudged Rosie's elbow I said at least now I do not have to worry about Amanda's driving and her running anyone over. We all snickered a bit. Rosie asked us how our coffee was and did we need a top up before bed. We were good but Rosie went for a refill before heading to her room, so we gave her hugs and always thank yours and wished her a good night as we headed to our room.

When we got into our room, we both headed right for the balcony sitting area, were we both collapsed in the comfy chairs, and we were exhausted. Now that we were alone a flood of questions rushed through my head with the first words out of my mouth being, what did you think of Sires? Once I said that, Amanda seemed to come back to life and bounced back with, he does not look anything like what I would have imagined. That is for sure! The gentleman we were seeing looked so well groomed prim and proper. Like that, guy looks like he smokes weed she snickered. He must be into something bad because Kevin said the weed was a compromise, so may be that means he is a cokehead. I thought about it for a second and smirked at Amanda and said yes, that's all you need, is to be stuck inside an island with a strung out cokehead leader and we both laughed.

It is obvious that he is somewhere in the world he got the message through I said and that I noticed that Dustin was uncomfortable thinking that there was another safe have that they were unaware of. May be the other safe haven is not on the earth? If he has an island why not have a baling spaceship and took off in it, when the shit hit the fan on earth. When she said that I looked at her with opened eye's wow what a profound thought where did that come from? You have to mention that to at least Dustin tomorrow.

We sat back into our chairs and then Amanda said I know that I should feel and be happy about not having to be here the six months we were first told, but even three months in paradise feels like a lifetime. I am a big baby who can't be away from home for long she was looking down but no tears when she said that so to lighten her feelings I responded with, then prison would not be a good place for you I smiled at her as she lifted her head. I feel the same about how long we are going to be here but when they were talking about it taking forty-five days of preparation that made me feel better because that means in only a few weeks they will be starting to get us ready to leave. Moreover, if things have improved that much already may be we will even be able to get to go home sooner. Amanda looked at me and said mom you are always the best in making things feel better even when they may not be. I love you, I love you sweetie I replied as we reached over and held hands.

What's the plan for tomorrow Amanda said, well we're not on the schedule for tomorrow so I was thinking that we could go spend some time with Dustin after this evenings presentation he is the guy in the know and we can snoop around more. He also has all the virtual reality toys and rides and I want to try some, I winked. Sounds like a plan, then we both motioned to get up and jump into bed.

We were popped that was an exhausting day, as we lay there and both discuss knowing that the exhaustion was from the interacting with people that is hard for us. We are all good with the work environment interactions because they are essential to promotions and a paycheck; otherwise, we are actually shy and reclusive people. We kid that we mask it well when in social settings and most people would see us as both being open friendly, thoughtful, kind positive personalities, and that character takes a lot of work to maintain, like today.

Night mom, night sweetie as we snuggled in, and then said I wonder what we are wearing tomorrow? Amanda could tell I was excited and just oh mom, you are so silly, I love you.

Chapter Fourteen

Waking up to another perfect sunny day of course, I smelled fresh coffee and was excited to open my eyes to see what was picked out for us to wear today. The bed is so big and soft that to climb out takes some doing, which seems to wake Amanda up and looking over seeing that she was still sleeping, I just laid there for a bit thinking of home and hoping that everyone was doing okay. It is hard not to cry when we start thinking about our families and home that I think we avoid it but laying there I could not make the thoughts stop so I figured it was best that I get up before I breakdown and start crying.

I wiggled my way off the bed with Amanda still asleep and seen our cloths for the day. I love everything Rosie has ready for us and this time was no exception. The cutest shorts with pockets and tank top style T-shirts with matching flip-flops of course. I even heard myself say perfect out loud I love this part of where we are so much, I thought as I walked over to the fresh pot of coffee in the sitting area.

I was may be being a tad rude but while Amanda was still sleeping I lit my smoke, so it was not long before she was awake. I think I lit my smoke on purpose because I did not want to sit there alone, what a mean mom I am I was thinking to myself when I took another puff and snickered under my breath.

When Amanda hauls herself out of bed and comes back from having a pee, she see the outfits Rosie has picked and said awe aren't they cute then walked over to where I was sitting and plunked herself down.

We had our coffee and a smoke then started getting ready. Having a shower is like standing under a warm waterfall with spray nozzles coming from everywhere and it takes a bit to adjust them all to your height and where you like to stand and sit in our personal, doublewide showers. Amazing!

We get dressed and come out to the patio where Rosie is there to greet us with her big smile and good morning's. We show off our outfits to her as we are walking because we know she likes when we do. She gets a good look at her handy work and it does show our enjoyment of them and appreciation. As she guides us to the table, she has set for us she asked how we were doing today?

Amanda and I looked at each other shook our heads a little and with a smile and almost simultaneously said, all good with me. We had a great sleep and we enjoyed the get together yesterday and the news that things are better than thought. Rosie gave a bit of a sigh and yes it was a good day and the food was one of the best they have put on. I believe they were all trying to impress you she snickered and I must say they did do a dam fine job this time, but don't let them know that I thought it was that good, we cannot have them thinking they are really good, she snickered a bit more this time.

Rosie poured us coffee then put some jam on a slice of toast then she sat back with toast in hand and asked what was the plan for the day, girls. Amanda replied while I was having a sip of coffee that mom wants to try out some of the tech toys that Dustin has and that we have heard do much about. I think that is where we are going first. Without giving time for us to respond further out of the blue, Rosie asked if we had any questions about what we seen and heard yesterday. Like she felt there may be an ulterior motive to seeing Dustin this morning. Her intuition was bang on!

Well yes, were interested in what is happening and the message we will send back out and we wanted to pass on a thought that Amanda had last night that may not have been considered yet. Rosie sat up in her chair and looked at Amanda and spit out girl what is it she pressed. Then Amanda almost felt silly in repeating her theory that Sire could be in a space ship, instead of tucked away on earth somewhere. We could see Rosie's face light up and she said you could be onto something, that would be something he could do, as well no doubt she replied.

I noticed that Rosie did not seem personally concerned about where Sire was and asked her why it seemed to bother Dustin more than the others knowing that there is another safe place. Rosie said I think it is a pride thing; Dustin is one of the world leaders in his field and Sires having an unknown safe haven means that he has found an equal to Dustin and that Sire did not include or share that with Dustin whom was thought to be one of Sires closest confidants. Oh!

What else about yesterday, going home earlier than expected has got to make you feel better and you made it on the schedule she smiled at us both. We are doing fine Rosie, my light bulb went on and I come out with, and we will even better when you take us shopping because you know Rosie, shopping heals everything.

Rosie changing the subject asked so what kind of things do you want to try out down at the birdcage? I did not have to think long to say that I had been on a ride at our West Edmonton Mall, Oh Rosie said I have actually heard of that place, that is all, I have hear of it she smiled and said carry on. I explain the ride as a stationary one that you go into a pod that had six chairs that have a slight movement to them a bit the same as the pod but the movement was minor on the body. The ride was fun because of what you were seeing on the screen that made you feel like the floor was falling out or you were driving a fast car, there were a few different themes you could choose from I said excitedly. I took a breath and Rosie calmly said like it was no big deal oh yes we have that and much better sweetie, you just wait and see you will love and be amazed at where you can take yourself and not even leave the island.

We finished up our breakfast and as we got up to have our smoke Rosie says I will get you girls your traveling mugs ready and put a care package together for you to take to Dustin. We moved over to the pool to have our smoke while we waited for Rosie to come back. With not being in any hurry to go anywhere we decided to have another coffee and a little hoot before we set off for the day. Besides, Rosie was taking longer than normal in the kitchen so this was a good way to pass the time we were smiling, at each other knowing we will make any excuse to have a hoot.

As Rosie comes out of the kitchen Amanda says to her we were worried about you, you were in there for quite a while. Then we just laughed as we see that Rosie is pushing a large cooler that has wheels and a telescopic handle like a suite case. That is here care package for Dustin, are you feeding for a week Amanda asked as she was still chuckling. Rosie replies he is a growing boy and he needs his sustenance she just gave us a big smile knowing that was a bit overboard and to play down the quantity, she added it is so he can share with you. Ya, right we say nudging and smirking at each other so she could see we were not a hundred percent convinced we were her motivation.

We load the rolling cool into our pink driving machine and Rosie hands us our coffees and smokes. As we were standing there, I asked Rosie what she was doing today and she said she was going to stop in and see Henry and Elsie for a bit and thought that Paul and her had some work to finish and that she would catch up with us later. By the way, girls I almost forgot to tell you, we are having cocktails on the beach later and we are having a big wiener roast. After all the food, we had last night we thought a simple and easy snake would be good today and fun.

Amanda took her seat behind the wheel then I jumped in and as we said our good buys, Rosie headed back towards the table and we were on our way down the hill. With what we thought could be a care package that could feed a small town, we joked about that on our drive to the birdcage to see Dustin.

Driving along we are seeing things a little different today knowing that some of what we are looking at is not there but we pay little attention to that because to not know, and looking around this place all you see is a tropical paradise and it was very easy to make the mind believe it.
Pulling up to the birdcage, we pay more attention to the over emphasized size and design of cage like building and the beautiful grounds around it. As we get closer to the entrance, we can already see Dustin outside waiting for us to arrive and rubbing his belly, like he is starving. I looked at Amanda and said I know that our driving machine is bright but how is it that they always seem to know when we are coming, I never see them talk on a phone or anything, and how do they do that! Amanda stopped right in front of Dustin who did not even budge as she pulled up.

Before we get out of the cart Dustin is already in the back, taking out the rolling cooler and says I understand you have a care package for me, Amanda chuckled and said care package, we were wondering if you were trying to feed a small village on the side. He looked up at her and said I am a growing young man and Rosie always says that I have brains, good looks and two hollow legs. If you have not noticed, Rosie loves to feed people and she knows us fellow's lover cooking and the attention.

As he rolls in his small fridge on wheels into the entrance, he said welcome to my world ladies, the first thing that catches your eye when you walk in is the fantastic rod iron spiral staircase to the second floor. Taking the cooler to a counter that was off to the side, and unpacking the container he could see us admiring the staircase and said that he lives upstairs and the main floor is his working facility.

The birdcage is the place that has it all and is the hub of the islands operating systems and information mainframe with a string of servers hidden in the rock walls to insulate them and further aid in avoiding detection. Amanda and I went over to where he was unpacking the food and noticed that behind the counter the area looked like a mini lounge with sink, fridge, wet bar and microwave. The furniture in the lounge was unique in color as the furniture was a bright blue leather couch and large armchair with oversized autumn. Wow, that is so cool Amanda said when she came around the corner and saw the bright blue leather. When we saw, the bright blue leather at we had to go over, sit on the big couch and chair, and have a good look around. The lounge area is of the same rod iron construction in the shape of a half circle filled with flowers and greenery.

When Dustin lifted his head from the containers chewing on a BBQ rib he asked us what we wanted to see first. He headed over to us to sit down and I asked him, how do all communicate, I do not see anyone phones and us coming here today was not planned and yet you knew we were bringing you a care package. Dustin looked up at us both surprised smiled and let out a ha! Sound then said with BBQ sauce on his face, which I motioned for him to wipe as he carried on saying I guess we just never thought to mention it but it is a real good question.

Phones are so yesterday he said if you notice we all wear glasses but not all of the time. All our inter island communications are done through wearing the glasses. If you have heard of the Google glasses before, which we both nodded our heads yes, he continued saying that our island glasses were designed to specifically meet our limited needs. With this being a small place we have found that we enjoy one on one communications however, to relay simple messages like… the girls are on their way and bringing food is a quick commend that is simply done through the glasses. Dustin went onto say that learning to communicate through the glasses was not easy because for some functions you just think of what you want done and in others you have to look at a spot in the frame of the glasses to change screens or read messages.

Paul and Jim would rather come see you then communicate through the glasses. Coming from the tech guy, people spend way too much time on their person devices, it is just not necessary. We use the glasses more now that you ladies are here then we had been.

By communicating through the glasses we can keep, everyone informed as to what you ladies are doing and where you are, he said jokingly. With making the comment of keeping track of us so casually, Amanda said really, and drew out her… so what is up with keeping track of us. Dustin smiled knowing that the comment of close watch disturbed her thinking our every move was being watched. Dustin laughed it is not as if you are being watched like criminals it is all for your good and because it is our job to take care of you.

Dustin looked at us and said that he could not say it enough, that us two have survived against all odds and for that we feel responsible to get you back home. Without any other reasonable answer, we all believe that there must be something very important that you still have to do in your lifetimes. Nothing else could possible explain you surviving two catastrophic events with millions of lives lost, half the world contaminated and you smack dab in the middle of it all to survive an ocean plane crash, and find the one and only opening into an invisible island and safe haven. He had an intense look on his face, finished with mind blowing, and put his hands to his temples and made the hand opening motion. Dustin had a big smile on his face and as he was getting up to fill his glass with lemonade, he asked if we would like some. I apologize for not asking sooner but I see you have your go cups and we started talking and I totally forgot. Amanda lifted her go cup and said Rosie won't let us leave home without them, we both smiled. The lemonade looks refreshing and I think I have had enough coffee for now she replied; Dustin looked at me, and asked how about you Colleen would you like a glass. With a nod, yes we both headed towards the bar where he had the ice machine and a huge clear glass urn of lemonade.

As we are getting our drinks, Dustin being very genuine said he thought it was important for us to know that the residence, we all feel special and chosen to take care of you. Then he went onto say… having said all that, Paul and Rosie always know what everyone is doing all the time he laughed.

Well it must be time for a smoke break Dustin said as he took a joint out of a wooden box he had on the bar. Once poured our lemonade Dustin lit the hoot and we headed to sit back down on the blue couch, and Dustin sat in the big blue leather chair that could have fit two of him in. As I was looking around, I said with a smirk, good thing it does not rain much around here. We all look up and then back at each other after looking up through the open fancy rod iron dome of the oversized birdcage room.

When Dustin smiled took a hoot and passed it on and started coughing out that it does rain on the island then sitting up straight, proudly announcing and I am the higher power that controls the rain around where. Lowering his voice and leaning into us a bit, he says, I had it pour on Paul's house for about fifteen minutes one time and Kevin and I laughed our asses off watching him. From the birdcage loft, we could see across the lake and watch Paul go to all the work of battening down all the hatches of his beach house and then the rain just stopped. Paul had to open it all back up again, man that was funny. I had to admit envisioning Paul standing on his beach house porch getting his boots soaked is what made me chuckle.

What happened Amanda asked Paul and Rosie must have been upset. Well Paul was a little miffed however; they did know that the system needed to release water back into the lake they just did not know how. We all laughed then and I have not laughed like that since I got here. People have said I have a laugh that cannot be forgotten and the nickname cackles has always followed me. My laugh surprised Dustin who then sat back in his chair laughing, which made Amanda laugh more.

Then all of a sudden I remembered what Amanda had said the night before about Sire and the space ship so I nudged her while she was having a sip of her lemonade and said let Dustin know about your epiphany, my what she says with a smile, you know the spaceship!

Epiphany now where did that come from she looked at me with her head tilted. Shrugging my shoulders smiling, it must be from spending all this time with the smart people and looked at Dustin, to take the heat off knowing she was thinking I was using words she would not normally hear me use.

So anyway, what about a spaceship Dustin looked at Amanda? Well I had the thought that if Sire was in a safe place but you do not know of any other place on earth that could be. Maybe with the time he had he got in a space ship and that is why he was able to communicate, because he is not doing it from the ground but from space. Dustin had a flabbergasted look on his face and it was as if the light bulb went on. He jumped up from his chair and said now why did I not think of that and started walking towards his operating panels waving his arms forward. Amanda and I looked at each other, as he walked not saying anything, waving his arms, to mean we were to follow.

Amanda not only are you beautiful you are brilliant Dustin says as we get to his semi circle wall of screens and panels. Surprisingly his main computer chair that Dustin moved out of the way when he came in was on an in-floor rail that glided to move from one screen to another with ease. While Dustin was hammering away at the keys at the one end of the station, I had to check out his chair while Amanda went over to see what he was doing. Numbers were scrolling by on the one screen when a message popped up from ALL, that they are following the new data. What does that mean Amanda asked as she pointed to the pop up message? He took his hands off the keyboard and replied with a grin that means that the alternative code to have our systems reorganize exploration has been accepted, and that all the residents are aware of your theory. This is great; we will have a lot to chat about on the beach at cocktails and wiener roast later yum, I cannot wait he says as he rubs his stomach.

Great job Amanda anything else you have to share he smiles. With me still sitting in his chair he looks at us and says so what, can I show you or tell you about the island that you are curious. Dustin offers to help fill in some blanks on things we had not had a chance to ask or check out. With the offer, made the only obvious question I had was ... what is the plane to get us off the island when it is time? I looked at Amanda and then Dustin thinking that was a good question when Dustin looked back at us and said now that is probably the only question I cannot help you with right now. Dustin said it is not that we are keeping secrets from you girls it is that without all of our information compiled we do not have the best-case plane and are still working on ideas. There is nothing concrete to tell you at this point, other than you are either sailing or flying out of here. I never thought that there were any secrets and we do trust that when it is time, you will let us know and you will have a perfect plan. Dustin agreed and said you bet we are going to have the best well laid out plan to get you home that you could imagine ladies.

For now how about a tour of the rest of the birdcage and we can chat as we go.

Then I will show you some of the virtual theme rides that we have. Dustin says come with me girls and I will show you my home, I think it will blow your minds. I have a water slide from my bedroom that takes me right in to the lake. No way really, Amanda says Dustin motions for us to follow him. As we climb the spiral staircase once, we got to the landing we come out to a large round living room with windows three quarters away around the room with the one-quarter wall being a solid with fireplace and large TV above the mantel. Off to our right we noticed a smaller kitchen that had a breakfast nook with padded benches that was beside the opening to the balcony with rod iron sliding door. Dustin took us past the living room down hall past another massive bathroom that had two TV screens mounted so you could see them from where ever you were in the bathroom including his exercise equipment that was also in there.

When we get to his bedroom he opened the double doors and what a shock. From the outside of the birdcage, structure it looks like one very large birdcage joined with a smaller one.
Once you get into his bedroom, you see that half of the room goes back into the rock like parts of the palace and the bunkers. The second floor actually goes back into the rock another fifty feet Dustin said when he seen the stunned looks on our faces. As we walked in further, what is the floor to ceiling mirror in the bathroom is actually a revolving door to the bedroom. Dustin did not show us that the floor to ceiling mirror was a door until we got into his room he was proud of that design feature as it was his own. Underneath the half-open dome was the oversized bed with a sitting spot by the Jacuzzi tub and then we see past all the plants to reveal his theater, all done in red velvet. Then on the other side of the theater is the hot tub area where the water slide starts that Dustin told us gives a ride all the way to the picnic area on the beach, where we are going later. The walk path around the hot tub leads back to the kitchen balcony is all connected and that we had seen the entrance to when we came in.

Amanda and I both had our mouths wide open as he was showing us all his extra features of his home. The room had a bright tropical theme with all the furniture being heavy brown wicker, other than the red velvet theater, of course.

Amanda spoke first and said how amazing she thought it all was while I was still gazing around asked why the red velvet theater. Dustin said with a smile that he was feeling nostalgic when he designed the theater although saying proudly that the virtual surround sound and big padded reclining chairs are special. The highly developed special features of the theater surpass current world technologies. He said his favorite feature of the theater was the old fashion popcorn maker and soda machine on the fully stocked bar.

As we moved over to have a seat by the hot tub with the amazing tropical back ground and sun shining in Dustin pointing to the full sized old fashion popcorn maker. Dustin chuckled and said that it drives Rosie crazy when I make pop corn because she can smell it as it wafts through the open dome up to the palace. Rosie told him one time that if she smells popcorn she has to make popcorn. We were all having a lazy day a while back and I thought I would watch some old movies to pass the time and of course, I had to make popcorn. It was not ten minutes and Rosie was at my door giving me heck because she could smell the popcorn and she did not have any more in her fridge. Instead of going all the way to the bunkers, she figured she would come here and get her fill. It really was a great day Dustin said, we spent the rest of the afternoon and evening watching old movies getting tipsy and eating popcorn. Dustin chuckled more come to think of it, that was the one and only time she has ever got on and rode the waterslide, man we could all hear her yelping and laughing until she shot into the lake. I heard the splash and then a second of silence before we could all hear her yelling my name out so loud.

After having a few wobbly pops, Rosie had dismissed the intenseness of the water slide ride that tunnels through the rock. The slide is a fantastic one-minute ride that it designed with several twists, turns and drops and when she got her head out of the water she knew, I was up here laughing my ass off and that everyone else was having a good laugh too. Rosie was all-good with being the one to give the group a good laugh and Paul was right there to help her when she popped out. Paul made sure that Rosie was okay and he took her home, and then Dustin winked at us as if he knows there is something going on between them but he never said another word.

Dustin glanced at the modern looking rod iron grandfather clock by Jacuzzi sitting area of the bedroom and said lets carry in the tour shall we, the time has been flying by today, I am so glad you came for a visit today. I complemented him again on his home with Amanda agreeing right alone with me when we all stood up and went back to the main part of the house through the kitchen balcony, completing the full circle tour. Back in the living room that had couches in a U shape with large autumns and coffee tables facing the terracotta fireplace. Looking at Dustin with a big smile, I gave him the two thumbs up as we headed down the spiral staircase. We could tell that Dustin was proud of his home and it was amazing. Thinking that all the homes we had seen so far have been unique and over the top in their own way, never mind the palace design of a tropical paradise resort.

Once downstairs Dustin says how about we finish our hoot that we left due to someone's epiphany he looked over at me and grind, and then I will show you girls the pod ride that we were all talking about. Dustin stopped to refill his lemonade and we had our smoke and a smoke still chatting a bit more about his house. Then all the sudden Dustin says let us go check the pod out and then we should be heading to the beach for our wiener roast it is getting to be that time he said rubbing his stomach.

You are going to love the experience he said as we all got up and followed Dustin who took us behind the staircase and to the right of the operations area to see a bunch of high tech stuff that for the most part we had no idea of what we were looking at. Other then the pod and arcade style racecar-driving simulators we did not recognize much. Dustin went to the computer and opened a file that he said he thought we would enjoy because it was like being on a rollercoaster but it takes you on a two-minute tour of many backgrounds that are just the coolest. Dustin opens the door where there are two chairs, which almost surround you once you get in them. The pod has many speakers and sensors that will send out a mist if you are in water and a puff of smoke when you are in hot zones, it is just too cool he said once we were seated and as he was closing the door we hear him say, enjoy the ride. At first it was pitch dark, excited more than afraid Amanda, I grab for each other's hand, and then the screen lit up showing the forward view from the front seats of a rollercoaster. With the second, we had to see it before we took off the digitally enhanced ride look massive and insane. At first, the speeding scenery was of an amusement and then it was as if we came off the tracks and were unexpectedly dropping into the Grand Canyon, my stomach felt like it went into my feet at that point and I could feel Amanda squeezing my hand tighter. The view seemed so real as the venue and background was changing, we felt the water during the speedboat segment and when sipping through what was like a volcano theme we did smell the smoke. We had and all the physical emotions of flying and descending at great speeds just as much. The ride was so extreme and fun and our two minutes went by fast.

When Dustin opened the door we were, just beaming that was fantastic we were both saying as were getting out of the pod although I was quick to say that once was enough for me, for a day and laughed. As Amanda and I were settling down Dustin said well girls I believe that it is time for us to gather up our stuff and head to the beach. I am sure that Rosie is there and already set up by now he smirked.

Amanda went back to grab our stuff from the sitting room and we headed to our carts. As we were jumping into our pink driving machine Dustin looked at both of us and smiled, I love your cart it looks good on you girls. Then he took off saying try and keep up Amanda, laughing as he sped away.

It did not take long for us to get to the picnic are on the beach and we were not the first ones there but we were not the last so we knew that Rosie would be pleased. As we walk up to the group there are hugs and handshakes all around when Rosie asked Dustin if he had a chance to get into his care package, which he relied I sure did and thanked her again. Amanda commented under her breath to me, did you noticed that he did not let her know that he went for Paul's ribs first and not one of her dishes. We chuckled a bit as we mossy up to the huge punch bowl where Rosie says to the group today's drink is a tropical rum punch, it goes good with roasted wieners she said with a smile. Then we hear Ryan say who was standing behind Rosie that tropical rum punch goes with everything silly. Rosie winked at Ryan and said I agree with a big smile.

Paul comes over to Amanda and I and asks how our day was going and did we get the full tour of the birdcage. We sure did and looking back from the beach at the tops of the two birdcages you would never know that is all that it is, I said and Amanda said she could not wait to try the water slide.
As we, all started to draw towards the food table, there is three different kinds of wieners and a big pot of baked beans, coleslaw, potato and creaser salad. At the end of the buffet of food, a fruit and cheese platter finished the line.

Jim had the open pit fire stoked and was ready for the roasting to begin. Rosie had the roasting sticks all standing there ready with Kevin and Dustin their first roasting two wieners each at a time. Ryan was right there as well however he only had the one wiener on his stick. All the ladies and Paul, were the last to start roasting because we prepared our plates first. It was Paul that said to the fellows roasting that we thought It was probably best that we fill our plates with our favorites before you fellows get over hear he laughed with us all implying that we agree with the comment. Then we see Jim playing on what Paul had just said by hustling right over to the table and grabbed a plate and stood right behind me in line. That made Janette and Jessie laugh with the expression Jim had on his face the action was perfect because it also included Ryan who has also known habits of being a big eater when it comes to his favorites.

We all sat at the boardroom-sized picnic that had a miniature railroad that ran around the inside of the table just past our placemats. Ryan could see we loved the train on the table and he began to explain that there was a couple engines and train cars that carry all the wiener roasting and picnic condiments you could want or need. That is so fun I said to the group and this is your doing I asked Ryan, he made the motion of tipping his hat and I thought this was a Dustin thing. Dustin lifted his head from his plate and so no I can't take credit for this one this is Ryan's creation as he hits the button in front of him smiling at everyone and he grabs the hot sauce out of a train car as it pulls up to his setting.

When the train came around to what you want you could pull it from the train car as it goes by or push the button at the track base in front of each setting and the train will stop. If you want the train to come your way you push the button twice and from its current position it will calculate the travel either way forward or backwards to get to the person, taking the shortest amount of time. Amanda and I were so impressed with what we were seeing because from a distance, you do not tell there were train tracks on the table and we must have assumed that the large table had a design. Ryan said that he stores the trains in the maintenance room attached to the beach washrooms. He was pointing in the direction of the stone path that lead to the beach washrooms. The straw hut style structure was almost hidden by all of the flowers and greenery around them.

The table was quiet for a minute while everyone dug in and as Henry put her hot dog down, she looked over at Amanda and said good job on thinking that Sires could be in space. While Amanda looked up to acknowledge her pleasure with a graceful nod and smile, Elsie jumped in saying that the new data should have results for us later tonight or in the morning. It would be great to know however, that changes nothing here on the island so not to get anyone's hopes up as she looked at us and continued saying to the group that this will mean we will be able to communicate easier with Sire once we can connect the threads. Once Elsie finished she looked over at Henry and softly patted her hand then apologized for intruding on her comment. Don't you be silly girl, you followed up nicely as they cozy into each other.

Rosie stood up with her glass of punch and said after dinner lets go out on the water boards, that is one thing I can do that I do not have to get all wet and I can paddle with my glass with me so we can just float around for a bit as the sun sets. Everyone reached for their glass so we did to and gave a big sheers and clinked glasses all around. Then we all went back to finishing our dinner and drink the fruit punch.

Once I was finished my dinner and stood up to get more punch I said to the group that with the wallop the punch packs, I am not so sure I am balanced enough and smiled. While Amanda followed me to the punch bowl, Paul said you are fine girls, the water is so calm and we just float around, then he lifts his forehead and says I am sensing that you have never been on a water board. I was not surprised that he dialed into my uneasiness considering I had only had the one glass of punch. Amanda was all ready to get out there when I had to admit that no, I have not ever been on a water board before and then I looked over at Rosie and said well it's too bad that we did not bring our bathing suits. Rosie was quick to respond and everyone heard her, saying of course, I brought our stuff. The group looked at us and chuckled, what were you thinking; of course, she brought your stuff. Kevin and Dustin rolled their eyes like how silly could we be to think that she would not have us taken care of. Janette was saying to us not to worry girls, I go in whatever I am wearing, its only water she smiled.

Moving out of the way of the food area with us both having a full glass of punch it was time for a smoke or two before this chick gets on a water board I said to Amanda with a chuckle. Mom you will love it, I know you will Amanda smiled and bat her eye lashes at me. Dustin, Kevin and Ryan came over to join us for what Kevin said was a special smoke. So, what is so special about this hoot I asked Kevin he held up the joint and said this is part of a unique blend of weed that originates out of the Congo, I believe the exact region was the Kendo area. Wow that all sounds interesting and special but knowing her mother as well as she does she told them no matter how wild this weed is it will not take her mom down and then began to laugh as she came and stood closer to me, like she was so proud. What a thing to be proud of your parent over I said, and then I thanked her very much and gave her a hug. Everyone first silenced by the shortfall implied and then all howled at response.

I proceeded to say that my philosophies are simple and that we should live our lives with humor while maintaining ethics and honesty. Be kind, respect our earth and all people and indulge with moderation. Of course there are a few more but they are all good and I believe in the positive and natural effects of smoking weed. I am double knuckles now and I have been smoking weed since I was a teenager. In my young adult years, we did all sorts of bad drugs and as I matured and working myself silly and raising two girls, weed helped me through it all. The kids nor or I have ever been a burden to any medical benefits or healthcare system and for me, I have had a successful career and I contribute that to the weed.

With me opening up a little and talking about myself, I could tell that everyone had moved over and listening with drinks in hand. With Amanda and I not talking about our personal lives, Jim saw this as an opportunity to ask the simple question of what we do for a living. After just saying what I had about the weed, I knew it was going to blindside them when I told them that I am a certified health, safety and environment professional working in the commercial and industrial sectors and have been for more than twenty years, or I guess I used to be. Paul and I were the first to burst out laughing and then the group joined in as they all realize the potential conflict. Amanda was laughing so hard because she was waiting for me to tell them what I did for a living; she knew it was going to make them all howl.

Once Rosie caught her breath she said to me you little thing, you are in construction and oil and gas, I would have never thought that of you and then Rosie looked right at Amanda who finally stopped laughing and, so what do you do for work? Amanda said proudly that she is a senior warehouse technician and that she has to fly into her to work where she stays seven days and then they fly her home and she gets seven days off. That floored them just as much because Amanda looks more like a model and visualizing her wearing coveralls and driving equipment just did not fit the person they were standing in front of or talking with at all.

Henry was very interested in hearing more about us and said how about we take the story telling into the lake the sun is starting to go down, it will be wonderful, and the girls can tell us more about themselves floating out on the lake. The suggestion had everyone instantly pumped to get out on the water.

Jim and Ryan went to get the boards that are all standing in a sand sled that they pulled over from under the trees by the parking area. Everyone had their own unique boards and to our delight, Jim and Ryan held up our boards up to show us that they had our initials on them so even we had our own.

With the boards in the water, and everyone with their cloths pushed the boards out to where the water was passed the knees, and sat down on the board and started paddling. Henry, and Elsie were first to push off with Jessie and Ryan were right behind them. Rosie, Kevin and Dustin were fussing around the bar while Amanda sticking by mom who knew I just really did not want to embrace myself never having been on a water board before.

Jim and Janette were waiting for Amanda and I to get on our boards and they were going to go out with us. Once I got my feet in the warm water, I was fine, the board was wide enough for me to sit on and it was calm. This was good, I could do this I sat on the board my feet barley touching the sand and I gave a little push and it took very little paddling to glide the board through the still water. As I look back, I can see Paul pulling off his big leather boots and Kevin and Dustin bringing another board on the water that looked a bit odd from my position and I was quick to realize I am good with straight but turning no so much so I could not see what they were doing. With Amanda floating right along with me and loving every moment of being out on the water, I asked her what they are doing back there.

When Amanda looked back Jim and Janette could see the look on her face and started laughing when Amanda turned back at me and said you are not going to believe it. What I said and bravely turned my body around to see, coming up behind us was Dustin pulling a floating water board bar, complete with punch bowl. Not only was this a floating bar, it had music coming from it and LED lighting that danced on the water in sync with the beat of the music. We could not believe what we were seeing and Dustin made sure he pulled the floating bar right past us to show off. Kevin was right behind him and passing everyone there punch filled Sippy cups that sat in the cut out cup holder at the front of the board.

Coming up from behind was Rosie and Paul who were taking their time and chatting away as they reached what formed into a circle of boards with the glowing bar in the middle. Amanda was looking all around and said to the group this is just amazing, I looked at Amanda and added there are not enough words to express this experience. Amanda and I still looking around and awe we had forgot that we were going to be carrying on our conversation and telling the group more about us.

As I go to take a sip of my punch, I sense a weird silence and as I look up, Jessie did not hold back and said so… tell us more, about Colleen and Amanda we really do want to know more about you. We know all of our life stories so to hear yours will be refreshing and help us understand you both better.

For sure, I replied not that we have a huge story to tell and I will try not to bore you I chuckled a bit feeling all the sudden a little shy. I know what she needs Kevin said with a huge smile as he proceeded to light a joint which broke the silence as we all laughed as the hoot was being passed around.

Then I began by saying the short version is that I come a messed up family with multiple divorce and a wacked out mother and two sisters that I have not seen in years. I have not had anything to do with my mothers or fathers families in years. You have all shown more compassion for us as human beings in this short time then my own family has in my lifetime.

I was not a school scholar by any means and with leaving home at fifteen I worked many jobs, when I was younger like waitressing and then into the printing business for a bit. I landed a job at a flower shop and stuck with the flower business for eight years, and did well.

In that time, I married and had my daughter Jennifer, whom now has two daughters of her own, when I was twenty-one. The marriage lasted seven years and they were seven years of packed bull crap. The only good thing that came out of that relationship was Jennifer! Five years later, I had my precious Amanda with another fellow that was not husband material.

At that point, with having two kids I was supporting on my own I needed to change my line of work so that I could be a better provider for them. With a passion to survive, succeed, and prove I was better than my family ever gave me credit for. I did get a job that dealt with underground construction for a cable company and at a time when safety in the work place was becoming a thing. I jumped on the safety band wagon took all the training and before long I was the corporate safety officer for a midsized construction company. From there I took as much industrial safety training that I could which did get me to a comfortable income.

While the girls were young, I had a live in nanny named Kelly that also worked at the girl's day care so they always were well taken care of. Kelly's family met Amanda when she was only six months old and Kelly's mom became grams to Amanda. Kelly's family was now also Amanda's for life I said as I looked at Amanda and smiled. Jennifer did have her dad still in the picture so he did take care of her when I could not. He never paid child support but he was around to help sometimes.

The hard part of my success is that my girls suffered in not having much time with me and they did a lot of their growing while we talked over the phone. As the girls got older, they could always count on our two-week summer vacation away from home and that was always a very special time for us.

As I was having a puff, Amanda looked around the circle and added that she always thought that she was rich because she was able to do everything and go so many places. I have always felt spoiled and lucky, knowing that it was all because of what mom did and sacrificed for us girls. It never gets old hearing my girl's say, they loved their youth and they never felt deprived.

Before going on Rosie spoke up and said you were a florist? I look over at her and said yes at one time I was a florist. Rosie's face lit up as she looked at Janette and winked then said well I guess we know who is in charge of flowers from now on, we all chuckled and I relied no, no … the arrangement that Janette put together was perfect, mind you it had about five hundred dollars worth of flowers in it I smiled. Looking back at Rosie I nodded at her and said you know you do a wonderful job with the flowers, as well. Amanda added that I still do silk wedding flowers for small events and then takes a sip of her punch.

Paul confident after having a few glasses of punch and I thought I saw him even take puff of the hoot as it went around, boldly asks, so what up with the laugh? There was a slit second of silence, Amanda and I looked at each other, when Rosie shot Paul a scorned look, do not be rude old man she said. Just then, Amanda and burst out laughing and almost fell off our boards. My laugh is bigger than I am and has influenced my whole life, and not always in a positive way. I have been asked to leave outdoor venues, the racetrack of all places, because I am disturbing people around me. I never leave, and I chuckled. Amanda and I were wondering when my laugh would be the topic of conversation. Not astonishingly, my nickname for most of my career has been cackles and or red because of my auburn red hair.

Kevin, Dustin, Ryan and Jim were still quietly killing themselves laughing over Paul's abrupt approach to the question. We could see all the ladies thought the whole thing was rather funny too with Amanda and I chuckling right along with them and having a drink.

Paul tried to retract in a sense, by saying it is not that your laugh is a bad laugh, it is that it comes out of nowhere and I think the first time I heard it, I thought we had a sick monkey and I could swear that it echoed throughout the island. That started everyone just howling again because they all heard it at the same time and they did not know what they were hearing it stopped everyone in their tracks. Did they have a monkey on the island that was in pain, or was Dustin just screwing with us in the birdcage.

Listening and watching Paul as he refer to my laugh like a monkey in pain with such a straight face, the fellows all just lost it and all rolled off their boards. Once the laughter had settled and the fellows were getting back on their boards. I wanted to let them all know that I love my laugh and once you know what it is you are hearing, and that it is not a monkey in pain, you will find that it is very infectious. I bet once you realized what it was that made you all stop in your tracks, it made you smile.

With a big smile and my Sippy cup hoisted in the air, looking around at the circle of friends and proudly said and thank you, all for helping be able to screech out a good laugh again. Cheers!

Rosie piped up and let the group know that her hips were hurting and her feet were waterlogged it was time to go in. I was ready right with Amanda helping me get turned around and the other boards started shifting, the lights glistened off the water as we headed back to shore.

With Amanda and I paddling side by side, she looked over at me and said I had a great time and it felt real good to laugh like that again mom, I love you sweetie, this was great. Then I feel my toes go in the sand letting me know I can soon stand up. This was the part I was worried about the most that I fall over into the water getting off the board. Before I had time to think about it anymore both Elsie and Henry fell right back into the water with a big splash when they tried to stand up. Elsie lost her balance first and then grabbed

Henry and pulled right back in with her.

I was off my board and on shore like a pro and got out of the way while the fellows ran over laughing to help the ladies get out of the water. Once all the boards were in the rack Rosie says lets top up everyone's punch before heading home, we do not want to waist this she smiled. While we were gathering our stuff, Kevin came over and said it must be time to fill your shinny container with a wink, and then gave us each an interesting pack of smokes he says came from China. The package was so beautiful, the pack of Kevin gave me were a turquoise in color, and Amanda's were pink. They were a feminine looking smoke for sure; they were the long and slender kind. Thank you so much we both gave Kevin a little hug.

Jim gets the groups attention and asks if anyone needs a ride as he looked over at Elsie and Henry mockingly when Henry quick on her feet wisecracked back to Jim the carts always get us home safe, they almost drive themselves.

Janette and Jessie came over to say there good nights and wanted to thanks us for sharing with them it was so much fun. As they draw in for a hug I asked so how did everyone know that it was not Dustin messing with everyone? Janette and Jessie looked at each other and smiled back at us and Jessie said that it was actually Dustin, who sent out the alert through our glasses, because the sound startled him so much that he dropped his glass of juice on the floor. We laughed quietly and I smiled at Amanda as we gave our hugs. Jim and Ryan were already to go and once their ladies were in the carts they saluted as they drove away. Then Henry and Elsie came over to give us a big hug and thank us for the great time, we want to hear more now Henry said as she turned to head for their cart.

Kevin and Dustin were helping Rosie load her cart and Paul was putting his boots back on. Amanda and I headed over to help Rosie when she said smiling with her rosy cheeks, we are all good here girls you head on up to the palace and I will be right there.

Paul was covering the fire pit and Kevin and Dustin were done clean up and were going for a swim. Before we left, I went up to Paul and let him know that it was great that he asked about my laugh and gave him a hug good night. Then Amanda and I waved to them all thanked them for a wonderful evening and headed to the cart and as we were just pulling away we hear Rosie say, do not wait up girls we could hear her laughing as we drove away.

To the palace, I say to Amanda she smiles grabs the wheel tight and says up the hill we go.

When we get to the palace the lights are on so nice and the infinity pool was sparkling, this place is special I said to Amanda who was just as impressed. We were both wet and wanted to change, so we went in our room and put on our housecoats that Rosie made us when we first got here that we love so much. We came back out to the patio and seen that the coffee was ready so we went right over and poured a cup of coffee. Then I looked at a Amanda raised my eyebrows and asked if she wanted to go back and play our games on the machines. Brilliant idea she mom, we grabbed our coffee and smokes and headed over to the lounge with our flowing housecoats making our walk feel so graceful.

As we are settled in and starting our games, which we were both, so proud of our scores; we began talking about our day and I said that I was so impressed with Dustin and his home that was something hey! Something, his place is out of this world amazing and I cannot wait to go on the water slide, I quickly replied and that will be one you can do on your own sweetie that is more than this old doll can take. Even the ride today had my stomach wondering what was going on even though we barely moved so I am thinking it is best I stay away from that we both chuckled and Amanda said we will see and went back playing her game.

We must have played for at least a half hour without saying anything other than a yippy or right on, when we would win and a bit of a whine when we thought, we should have. Amanda hit a big win and while the count was taking place on the screen, she looked over at me and said with a smile… hoot! You bet, I said and stopped playing. I reached for my coffee while Amanda was lighting the extra special batch hoot that Kevin gave us earlier. I needed a refill and asked if Amanda wanted one and yes, I am so popped that no caffeine is going to keep me from sleeping. I commented that by the time we finish the hoot we will be done anyway and laughed. From the coffee bar I could see out into the valley and the sky was so beautifully lit, as I panned the lengthen of the island looking out to the farm and then Main Street and the houses. As I am looking out at the waterfall, lake and beach, I notice that Rosie's cart is at Paul's beach house with the headlights on so I thought she would be on her way soon. As I was walking back to Amanda she tells me to hurry she cannot smoke this all by herself. I smirked and said you could have put it down and grinned as I passed her cup and sat back down, I let Amanda know that Rosie's cart was at Paul's and her headlights were on so she must be coming home soon.

Amanda passed the hoot, and with her puff of smoke drawn up into the smoke exhaust systems, she said once we have finished hoot, have one of our pretty smokes, and drink my coffee. I am going to bed she looked at me and let out a big sigh and I agreed this has been another huge day for us and at least they got to get the shock of my laugh out of the way and now I won't feel like I even have to hold it in. The topic is now out in the open and they know to expect more, said proudly. We had a good laugh rethinking their expressions and reactions. Amanda and I loved that part it was so funny to watch.

We went back to playing the machines and had our colored smokes and then we were both done. We saved our games and gathered our stuff, then walked over to put our cups away when we noticed that Rosie's cart was still at Paul's with the headlights on. We were too tired to give it any thought and headed off to our room. We got ready for bed and both climbed in and before our heads could hit the pillows and we finished saying our I love you, we were asleep.

Chapter Fifteen

Waking up to a sunny room and the smell of fresh coffee is the best and we both started waking up about the same time. Amanda was all snuggled in the covers, I could not see her face, and then I hear the words muffled … do you smell that. Then Amanda sat right up the coffee smelt extra rich today and that drew us right out of bed. With first, seeing if there would be anything picked out for us to wear today because when we went to sleep, Rosie was still not home and may not have had time.

Does that woman even sleep? I looked at Amanda as we see in the mirrored dressing area two very nice shorter summer dresses with small random floral designs, with white leather flip-flops. Where does she find the time to do all this as we head for the coffee pot and a smoke.

After our coffee and smoke, we were not long getting ready. Although there is a wall cabinet filled with all the best make up in the washroom the only thing we have been using is the amazing face and body creams we have to choose from and mascara. Our skin is radiant and glowing so there is no need for anything else. With having close picked out and not wearing makeup, that cuts our get ready time in half.

While we were getting ready, we were chatting about Rosie and wondering when she did get home, and trying to figure out what was the plan today. With not being able to decide Amanda says let's just go for a drive after breakfast and see what we find. That sounds great I relied as we headed out to the patio.

Coming out to the patio, we see Rosie coming out of the kitchen who greeted us with a big smile and sounding so perky, with her good morning ladies how was your sleep. We both spoke up at the same time, Amanda said awesome and I fantastic. I did a little twirl showing off the cute little dress I was wearing that seemed to hold me in, in all the right places and give an hourglass figure. Amanda's dress did have a v-neck where mine was a round, we had different floral designs, although her dress, was a bit shorter than mine. Amanda just turn slightly to show off her cute bum and we all chuckled as Rosie gave it a little spank and said your are so cute, now let's have breakfast ladies.

We sat down and Rosie dished all our plats from the small hot serving cart she had by the table. Rosie said I hope you are up for scrambled eggs, sausages and toast with a side of fruit of course. We both were hungry and gestured yes and Amanda told her that her food is always so good, even when I am not hungry, I want to eat. That is good to hear she said, maybe we can get some meat on those bones of yours. Amanda and I looked at each other and just smiled, thinking the very same thing I am sure, like that is not the first time we have heard that before.

Once Rosie was sitting I told her that we had a great time playing the machines when we got home but then got so tired we went to bed, Rosie knowing where I was taking the conversation said I did not get home until late myself. Paul and I had a great time just chatting about the evening that we forgot that my cart was running with the headlights on and the battery went dead so I hung out at Paul's until the cart was recharged. Then she looked at us, winked, and went back to dunking her toast in her coffee.
We snickered while we continued then Rosie asked us what we are doing today because we are not scheduled at the Lucky Farms until tomorrow. Amanda replied that we did not have any plans for today, and so far, we were just thinking of taking a drive after breakfast, did you want to come with us Rosie, Amanda asked.

Well, I did promise you girls a shopping trip to the bunkers although I was planning on going there after your first days of helping out. That sounds great Rosie we will go when you are ready and following yesterday I am good for a leisurely day today, and shopping will be the complete opposite of that I laughed and looked at both of them with a gleam in my eyes.

We finished up and helped put a few things away before Rosie whisked us away and saying go have your coffee and smoke by the hot tub before you head out, I will be right with you she says as she is pushing the cart back to the kitchen. We move over and light up our smokes and gaze around, the view is always breathtaking. Here comes Rosie with our go cups and a covered basket. Who's the basket for Amanda asked as Rosie came towards us, it is for you girls just in case you want to have a picnic as she lifts the cover of the basket the first thing we see it two bottles of wine and several containers all neatly stacked and organized. That is so sweet I said and Amanda leaned into Rosie and gave her a hug you are just the best.

Before you go girls, Rosie linked her arms with ours and asked if we were okay with our sharing yesterday and all the stuff about your laugh, are you sure we did not upset you. Oh Rosie we had a great time and I loved everyone's reactions and comments. Like I said, my laugh is a part of me that can cause pain or pleasure and I love it, so we are all good on that for sure. I am so glad Rosie squeezed my arm, and said with a smile we all love your laugh.

Relieved and smiling, Rosie turned and started carrying our basket out to the pink driving machine. A few of us will be at the Main Street café later if you find yourself in the neighborhood. I let out a bit of a laugh and relied everywhere on the island is in the neighborhood of the cafe. Rosie waved and wished us a good day as she turned to go back to the patio where we see her have a seat with her coffee before we drove away.

Were we going first I asked Amanda and she said that at the bottom of the hill we always turn but the road does go straight it is just overgrown. I think the road goes around the perimeter of the farm but I wanted to check it out. I went to look at the island road map and could see the dotted line she was talking about. Once we get to the bottom of the hill we continued straight into the overgrown entrance we had to duck to avoid being slapped with branches and flowers as we entered. The path opened up once we got through the entrance.

Amanda drove slowly so we could have a good look around when we could hear the trickling of a stream on my side of the road. We stopped to walk in towards the rock wall and when pulling the underbrush back we could see there was a little stream with a little waterfall that went into a fishpond. We stuck our hands in the water and could tell that it was a lot cooler then the lake. Too cool, I look at Amanda and said as we turn around and headed back to the cart, to see what else was up the path.

We were joking around and pointing out all the pretty flowers we had never seen before and with the path covered with the greenery, we were feeling like we were being sneaky. It was not long and we could see were driving alongside the farm and chatting back and for the we were thinking that the path must end at the back of the farm. As we drove a bit further that path was leading away from the fence and not following it. We were more curious now, when all the sudden we see a dark tunnel so we stopped to have a look on the map to see what it had on it about this area. No one had said anything about a dark tunnel Amanda looked at me and I said no, no one has said anything to me about it. As we look on the map, the path shows as a dotted line that stops at a rock face. The map must be out of date because there sure is a tunnel there now Amanda said with a perplexed look on her face. May be we should not go in there I said to Amanda we should ask about it first. Amanda feeling all adventurous and replied no one said that there was any place we could not go or to stay away from so I am sure this is all good mom, let's check it out what can it hurt.

Okay I agree to go but, I let her know that if we get in trouble I am going to blame it all on you and I laughed as she turned on the headlights and proceeded slowly. The headlights of the cart lit up the space around us but we could not see very far in front of us. The tunnel was smooth with no jagged rocks and was a perfect circle as Amanda drove slowly the space became brighter and we could see we were coming to a curve in the road and once we got to the curve, the rock tunnel opened up to expose an airplane hangar with one small jet parked inside.

Our heads turned to look at each other and with faces of pure shock, we could not believe what we were seeing. And then we were questioning each other as to why have would not have mentioned or implied anything about the plane. Then I remembered Jim saying that we would be leaving in luxury and that we would be flying or sailing out of here. Ya, but Amanda followed they never said anything about having a plane right here.

Well now we are here do you want to go have a snoop around I said to her. For sure, I have never sat in a personal jet before, we both giggled and decided to walk in from where we were at the curve. As we walked towards the plane, I said to Amanda, I am sure they have a good reason for not saying anything and I am certain that they all know that we are here by now so if something was up, Paul or one of them will be here anytime.

There were all kinds of benches and tool chests and equipment along the sides of the hanger and was very well organized. The hanger was brighter now and we could see the whole space. We first walked around the streamlined or aerodynamic jet to get to the staircase leading up into the beautiful white jet.

Being excited to get inside when we were in, we just laughed in a wow moment this was incredible. All tan leather seating with fine crafted wood working throughout. Amanda let's stay on the plane one night and pretend, thinking of the luxurious interior. When Amanda said I could care less to fly again, ever, but this is nice. Her comment hit me like a bricks, wow your right I said back, we almost died because of a plane wreck. I cannot believe that did not even cross my mind when seeing the plane. Are you oaky sweetie I asked as we both sat down in the lounge chairs. I am fine she says with a reassuring voice. Although I know, I will not be working out of town when I get home. I will not be flying back and forth for work anymore. I was happy to hear her say that, she has put in her time she can do what she does in the city.

Well sweetie, this is nice but do you want to go, we will have a smoke and a coffee when we are out of the tunnel how does that sound, mom you read my mind, I love you. As we get down off the plane and start walking back to our cart we notice that the lights start to dim behind us.

Well, that was cool Amanda said as she got in the cart yes seeing a plane in there was unexpected but my question is, how do they fly it out of here? Amanda turned looked at me and said now that is the question of the day, we chuckled and both tried to come up with anything reasonable but we had nothing. We will have to ask Paul or Jim when we have a chance. As we come out of the tunnel, Amanda pulls over so we can have our smoke and coffee. It felt so secluded where we were surrounded by the plants and trees and flowers, it was nice sitting back in there. We had nowhere to be so we figured we might as well lay down the picnic blanket Rosie gave us and have a hoot. While we were, sitting there after lighting the hoot is was not two minutes, we could see a rustling in the bush, and it seemed to be coming right for us we started, getting freaked thinking it was some animal when we hear it's only me ladies, we finally can see that it is Kevin coming through the trees.

He came through just smiling saying I could smell my special blend even while cleaning out the barn, and thought this was a good time for a break and I would come join you. Hey, right on, come join us, Amanda said and then so how did you know it was us back here, I nudged Amanda with my elbow, said the glasses, and smiled. Kevin said hell no, I can smell my hoots anywhere. I pass Kevin the hoot he takes a couple good puffs and then tries to ask us what we are doing back here while holding his breath. We just went for a drive and thought we would check out this path that showed as a dotted line on the map. Kevin looks at us both with wide eyes, so … how impressed are you with the jet isn't she sweet.

I agreed with Kevin right away complementing on the sleek design and interior, she sure is but how do you get it off the island I squirreled my face at him, there is no runway I smile. Kevin proceeded to tell us that this jet does not need a runway only and opening, okay but there isn't one of those either. Kevin went onto say that, once our systems deem it safe to expose itself to the outside atmosphere the Island has a few openings can be opened up in four locations. Really, we thought there was only the one we came in through Amanda said with a surprised look.

There is so much to learn about the island that we could not possible tell you it all at once so as you discover new things and have questions we can all help to answer them. The plane is no secret and the map was never updated when the tunnel and hanger were completed that is why you followed a dotted line here. So are we getting off the island on the plane, I asked Kevin replied that has not yet been determined but we are working on the plan.

Amanda interrupted with, so where are these openings. When talking about openings through volcanic rock walls that are a quarter mile thick, it may take several months to open. As an island, nondestructive feature the opening for the plane requires water flowing like a raging river over the back end of the tunnel and hanger, which has been designed to fall away under the precise conditions that we create from inside the island. That opening process is estimated at taking eight months to complete.

Oh, is all I had to say with Amanda clear on this one she says and the others… Kevin could tell that our conversation was going to take a bit and he seen the wine bottles in the picnic basket when he came through the bush. Kevin went over and got the basket out of the cart and said, okay Rosie what do we have in here today he smiled, and looked at us both and said I love Rosie, as he opened the wine. Asking then, if we would join him in a glass. We all look at each other shrug our shoulders and Kevin hands us each a glass.

The suspense is killing me Amanda said where are the other openings. As we settle back in and Kevin, re-lights the hoot he proceeds. The next one is the entrance or tunnel that you ladies came through it seemed small it was only because of the vegetation that had grown up inside. All of the bunkers were brought in through that entrance and anything else that was not created by the digital imaging or 3D printing was for the most part brought in through there. Although this may be a bit deep, we utilize the powers and forces of kinetic2 energy and do not need a lot of heavy equipment to do our bull work. We also utilize sound waves and bands to do a lot of our work for us as well. It is all the science and physics behind this place that makes it so unique.

The entrance you came in, is the quickest and easiest to open Kevin says, as he takes a good drink of his wine then carrying on to say the tunnel was designed in fifty-foot sections that have six-foot thick slab walls to seal and separate each section. With the pressure created in each section, they draw upward, pulling, and sucking the base rock up from the foundation of the island filling each section as the island closes up, one section at time starting with the outer perimeter and working inwards. Astonishingly enough when you ladies were walking towards us the island was already closing behind you. You two being here, is incalculable and is a phenomenon, he lifted his wine glass and said cheers,

Amanda and I were enjoying listening to him tell us more about the island, paused and filled his glass and re-light the hoot, again. Although Amanda was listening intently, she was on a mission, and wanted to stay on track and knowing enough about what lies out the entrance we came in, she looked at Kevin and asked again, so where are the other two. Kevin looked at us and said you want to guess? Amanda not wanting to play said oh come on just tell us I am so curious.

Kevin sat up and with a stare, trying to look mysterious he replied where they are may not be half as interesting as what is in them, he winked and we had no idea of what he was talking about. Okay, oaky I am just pulling your legs. Kevin really had us thinking now so he proceeds to tell us that the third opening is behind the waterfall at the lake. No way, what is behind the waterfall Amanda asked immediately. That is the what, and there is one large catamaran and a very fine yacht, let me tell you Kevin says, she is sweeter then sweet and hands down nicer then the jet.

Now getting those babies out takes some doing and if we do open to let them out it will take three years to bring the roof thickness back to the what it is today. Why is that not a problem in the hanger, I asked and he side quite frankly, that once the jet leaves this place it cannot ever come back. We can only remain undetected if there is never a link and aircraft coming out of know where or dropping off radar these days, would draw to much attention. He continued saying that we would start a rebuild and fill of the whole that was created by the water to let the jet out but if there were looming eminent danger, we would implode the space sealing it off. Wow you really do have everything covered don't you I commented.

To let the boasts out we have to shut the waterfall off which provides pressure, combined with sonic waves and kinetic2 energies we will actually slice off the back end of the island giving enough room for either of the boats to sail out from. Replacing the cut out is what takes the time and if emanate danger was looming imploding could potentially damaging the water systems. We could create enough coverage in a few months to provide some protection however if the event was anything worse than this one the world has just suffered the island would have been at risk of exposure.

With a couple seconds of silence passing as we were absorbing everything that Kevin was telling us, Kevin reached over to gram the second wine bottle and really smiled and wiggled his eyebrows you will need a top up for the last one he said jokingly and poured more wine for us all. Then he says smoke, I was already grabbing for mine I was so intrigued to hear about the fourth opening. Amanda was right into Kevin talking about and opening up about the secrets of the island and not that they were holding back from us, it is just is what is here that you can't see.

Kevin said that we believe that as something is become conscious and questions are formed and asked, then we can explain and answer. To overwhelm you with information you might not care to know, is wasted. Checking out the dotted line and stopping for a hoot has brought us here to bring to light something new and I believe easier to take in, not that you have been here a while.

Both Amanda and I agreed with the information timing to much at first would have been too much and at least now we are not as shocked and taken back at all the new extremes of the island as we learn about them.
Well hang onto you hats ladies because the four entrance and exit is just behind the road that leads up the hill to the bunkers. The road will take you to the backside of the lake where there is a picnic area but the road to get to the loading dock is like this one a bit overgrown. The road is marked with a pictogram of a set of diver's air tanks, you can't miss it just look to right. Any way once you are there finally you will see a six-person submersible luxury submarine. There is a quarter mile of rock above the sub and we cored through a half that through the base so sub descends to the ocean floor and leaves from there. With the island closed of course, the bottom is sealed but when it is safe to do so, it would be the easiest, safest and quickest way off the island. With the added bonus of being able, to travel undetected. I am not saying for sure but I think that may be the way you will be leaving the island.

Few, I am all talked out now Kevin said as he finished the wine in his glass. You ladies all good here I have to get back now as he stands up and stretching a bit but leaned back over to pick up his half-smoked hoot and smiled at us as he put the butt in his lips. Maybe we will see you at that café later and you can ask Paul when you can have a tour of the sub.

We thanked Kevin very much for all the information it was great chatting with him and off he went rustling through the trees and underbrush.

Wow, Amanda and I were astonished and looked at each other like we were really dreaming so much so that I joking said to her, pinch me. The quickly retracted because she was actually making the motion too. We laughed as we noticed that Kevin drank most of two bottles of wine, oh well Amanda says that was great as she starts to try and get up after sitting there for what seemed a long time. We were both a little slow getting up.

Once we were mobile and packing up the picnic basket I asked Amanda while I was holding up both empty bottles of wine, do you think they are trying to turn us into alcoholics, Amanda, no I just think that alcohol and weed are just there way of dealing with an imperfect, perfect world. What do you mean by that I asked her. Well this place is what some people might says is heaven on earth but the reason this places exists is because of our imperfect world out there that these people have had to disconnect themselves from, with alcohol and weed in moderation being coping mechanisms. Now look at who is talking uptown, I said to Amanda that is some deep thinking I chuckled and we jumped in to the cart and headed back out and through the overgrown entrance and heading to the café.

We caught from what Kevin said as he left that we should talk to Paul before going to the sub and we know he will be there today, Paul is always there for the cocktail hour. As we were driving, Amanda could see I had a serious bewildered look on my face, and said what's up. I said looking forward how are we going to get home in a sub. We live in Alberta, the prairies … Amanda with a daft look, get's it, and we both blast out in laughter.

By the time we get to the café and pull up everyone there were laughing and said we could hear you coming from blocks away. At least I am easy to keep track of, as long as I am laughing that is. As we join the group, Paul let us know that Kevin was able to give us more island learning today, and he was wondering what we thought of the unique thought that when into the creation.

I looked at Amanda and then said speaking for myself, once you are able to put all though of money aside, nothing here is more than you would expect of a private save haven. The island is beyond comprehension and out of this world, high tech and learning more about the island all the time, is exhilarating. Amanda was with me and added that knowing more about where we are is making every day easier.

As we cozy on up to the bar, Rosie is right there and said well with you girls having wine earlier the drink for cocktail hour is gin and pink lemonade. They go together rather well she said. Amanda wanted Rosie to know that we did not polish the two bottles of wine off ourselves, so in a whispering but loud voice, for all to here she says Kevin drank most of the wine. Of course, he did you girls, would be in bed if you drank two bottles of wine she had a smirk on her face like we were newbie's we all started laughing, Rosie and the others knew we were not big drinkers.

With not wanting to draw attention back onto us, I posed the question to the group, so why have all these crafts if you really never intended on using them. We could see that they did like when we asked questions and there was always someone to step up to the plate to answer. In this case, it was Dustin who chimed in responding with saying that in the islands conception there was no scenario was left to chance. Although, he looked up at us and then took a breath and when exhaling he blurted we only seemed have missed you two out of them all. I did have a good hardy chuckle over that, which made everyone laugh even more. As we settled down and started, nibbling on the huge platter of nacho's that Rosie brought out and put on the two sided stand up bar in the front of the café.

Henry and Elsie came over after getting their drinks and asked Amanda and I, if we wanted to come for a visit after our morning at Lucky farms tomorrow. Elsie said we would love to show you our home and chat with you more. Absolutely we have loved seeing all the homes they are amazing and so special. We have not seen Jessie and Ryan's home yet but we will get there, Jessie looked around the group and said, yes, saving the best to last and she smiled and turned directly to Janette, knowing full well that we had already been to her mom's house and seen it.

Then Paul looked at Jim and said we can show the girls the sub the following afternoon how does that sound, Jim nodded back to Paul and a wink to us he seemed eager to show us. Amanda and I must have had a grin from ear to ear, seeing a submarine up close and going in one will be awesome.

Oh my goodness Amanda said as she pushed herself away from the nachos that were so good, I have had enough of them and got up to get another pink lemonade at the bar. She looked back and asked if anyone need a refill after a quick check the consciences was, no. She filled her glass and moved over to have a smoke.

I was still nibbling and then figured this was a good time to ask Kevin who had been sitting there so quiet, what is the plan for us tomorrow at the farm. Actually, ladies we have vegetable picking that you are going to be helping with. We do all the work by hand and we do grow enough to sustain the island so it is not your average garden that's for sure. We have several crops of varying fruits and vegetables that are ready for harvest. We also do all of the food processing and preserving at the farm and later you will be helping with some of that. We will keep you aware from the animals as you asked and now we know why it is best that we do so, Kevin face when red and he could hardly contain himself when he finishing by saying … no offence Colleen, but you scare them. At that point I think everyone was about to fall off their chairs giggling and I could see Amanda's face and her mouth drop, and let out a huge laugh. Oh, my goodness I could hardly catch my breath, I had to get up and go have a smoke with Amanda. Rosie loves when the topic is my laugh she gets a kick out of it.

As the smokers moved over, we looked kids at school in the smoke pit while the none smokers try to stay out of the wafts of smoke the conversation went back to the work we would be doing at the farm. Rosie made it clear as she wagged her finger at Kevin that the girls are not have to work ourselves silly either, we are only there to help out for a few hours.

Kevin was joking and mocking Rosie by acting out her actions and wagging his finger. The group laughed while Rosie's checks went red and she gave Kevin a tap on the shoulder.

As the cocktail hour was winding down the couples were first to head off home, with Henry say8ng before they left, see you girls tomorrow. We waved as they left and then asked if there was anything we could do to help with clean up and we received the usual sweet sounding no. Oaky then, I looked at Amanda and said, I guess we will head up to the palace thank you Paul, Kevin and Dustin for a great day and we will see you all tomorrow. Rosie we will see you later, everything was wonderful again.

Amanda took her place at the wheel and I jumped in and waved to the group as we drove away. It is early yet is there anything you wanted to do Amanda asked me and I had thought about it so she suggested that we go for a swim when we get to the palace and then we can go for a hot tub before bed. How does that sound she looked at me with a smile and even I was surprised that going for a swim sounded like a good idea.

As we pull up just like the evening before the large open, entrance onto the patio looks so grand that you find yourself walking slowly up to the patio taking in all the exquisite details. We put our cups and smokes on the table in the hot tub sitting are and go to our rooms to find our bathing suites. We walk through our suite doors and of course, our bathing suites and big beach towels are sitting there ready for us on the bed. I swear Rosie can read our minds before we even think the thoughts ourselves I said to Amanda as I started changing. All Amanda replied was, freaky and then proceeded to change.

By the time we come out of the room Rosie was parking and as she came up the stairs and seen us with our suites on she smiled at us and said, I wondered if you were going to want to go for a swim this evening, I guess I was right. Amanda followed up with you are prepared for things we haven't even thought of yet, how do you do that. Rosie looked at Amanda and winked at her, and said it's magic. Then she went back to fussing around the coffee bar as we slowly got in the pool.

The water was warm and as smooth as glass and we did not want to make waves. The ultimate feeling is swimming up to the edge and looking out over the whole interior of the island. From the edge of the infinity, pool is one of the best non-obstructed views of the valley. While looking over the edge we were looking for the signs of the waterfall entrance and the sub entrance. We could not see anything through the waterfall, and when we look on the other side of the lake, where Henry and Elsie were having their picnic, Amanda pointed to a small road sign that was about a quarter of the way up the path. We could not see if the sign was a picture of air tanks but we thought that must be where they were talking about.

When we looked, back to see what Rosie was up to she was pouring coffee and had the bottle of Baileys close at hand. She adjusted the lighting and turned on some quiet background music. We went for a couple laps in the pool and then I was ready to get out while Amanda was up for a few more laps before coming out. I wrapped myself up in my big soft towel and went to sit over with Rosie. What another great day I say to her as I was sitting down. This place is out of this world, I said to Rosie so positively when she replied yes it is, but who is going to believe you when you get home. That was the first negative I had heard Rosie utter and was taken aback by her comment and asked her to explain what she meant.

Rosie seemed solemn when she said I am not as concerned about getting you off the island and home as I am, about what will happen to you when you get there. We do not want you to become a media nightmare when you get home so we are putting a lot of thought into the plan. I have to be honest we have tossed some extreme suggestions around so what I am going to say to you now Colleen is…
When the ten of us say this is the plan, you are going to have to trust that our way is the only way no matter what. Wow, that sounds serous Rosie should I be concerned. If you put your trust in us, there is no reason to be concerned however if you struggle with part or parts of our final plan you could put yourselves in danger and it is important that you understand, we only have you and your families best interests at heart.

Amanda was coming out of the pool and walking towards us when Rosie motioned by zipping her lips that was all she was saying about the topic now. Amanda noticed it was quiet when she walked up so to break the silence I jumped in my seat and said hoot, Amanda smiled and sat down. You girls are so funny you drink coffee like pros you are light and respectful smokers smoke and you always light up when it is hoot time she giggled. Rosie have you smoked much Amanda asked politely. Yes, of course, and I still have a puff on occasion, sometime a hoot is just what the doctor orders, literally I am not kidding you, Henry has her weed concoctions that she creates for whatever ails you. It was definitely implied by Rosie's hands swirling around her head that Henry's concoctions can mess with the mind.

Too funny Amanda said, we might have to ask her about that tomorrow when we are over for our visit. I passed the hoot to Amanda , and a little flash of the past went through my mind and think her thought through I said maybe that is not a good idea for us sweetie. I smiled and continued by saying, there is no telling how disruptive we could be to the balance of life here, if we got wasted on something exotic. I think we are safest with the remarkable weed. I laughed with them and at my young adult years still flashing through my mind.

We all went for our coffee cups and sat back in our chairs when Rosie looked up and said yes, what a wonderful day and you girls are heading to the farm tomorrow, I know you will enjoy it. Yes the farm and then Henry and Elsie's it will be another good day of not being idle. You have kept us so occupied and we are learning more things about the island and the wonderful people in it. I batted my eyelashes at Rosie and Amanda made an awe, sound and saying that is so sweet.

Are you going into the hot tub I asked Amanda as we were still passing the hoot back and forth, Rosie Said go ahead you two and you can take that in the tub with you. Here let me fill your coffees and I will adjust the jets down so they don't beat on you while you are sitting in there. Oh, my goodness this feels right out of this world good, I said as I got into the tub, with hoot in one hand and coffee in the other. Amanda right behind be what a great way to end a great day she said to Rosie and I. After Rosie toped up her Baileys and coffee, she sat back in her chair, put her feet up and gazed into the night sky.

We all were relaxing and taking it all in, listening to the soft instrumental music in the background and just gazing around with the only thing breaking the peacefulness of the mood is me coughing after taking too big of a hoot, Amanda always laughs at me under her breath, when I did that.

While we were sitting in the tub relaxing I asked Rosie what her plans were for tomorrow, knowing full well that she would have her whole day planned out by now. Hum let me think she smiled, after breakfast I am going to Paul's house to make the boys a fish dish that none of us with any brains will eat so Paul, Jim, Ryan, Kevin and Dustin are having dinner there. I was thinking that with you spending the afternoon with Henry and Elsie who are scheduled to be in the lab sometime early evening that we have Janette and Jessie over for dinner. That sounds like a great idea Rosie, Amanda said, it would be nice to have dinner and spend time with them.

So you are going to cook two dinners tomorrow, I smiled with Rosie happily saying back, yes I do get to cook two dinners tomorrow. Well, our hoot is done and I feel like a prune, time to get out Amanda, stood up at the same time, and we were able to step out without splashing water and graceful. We wrapped our towels around us and went to give Rosie her hug good night. Big day tomorrow I said, time for this cat to hit the hey Amanda smiled and put her arm around me said yes it is time for you to go to bed and off we went to our room, leaving Rosie gazing into the night sky having her coffee and say sweet dreams girls.

Once we got to our room, and started getting ready for bed Amanda said out of the blue, could you engine us leaving here in a submarine. That does seem a little out there that is for sure I commented. Then Amanda came right out and asked what the weird silence was that she felt with Rosie and I earlier.

It was strange what she said, she wants to make sure that we know that whatever the plan is, that it will be our only option. And that there is concern not in how we get home but what will happen to us when we get there. She really did not say much more but I took from what she did say, how do we explain our existence for the time we will have been gone and who is going to believe this story. May be we will get more out of Paul and Jim when we get our tour of the sub. For now, we are a ways from going anywhere and I am sure that when they do have the Yreka moment, we will know. You are so right mom; I am not going to get myself into a dither over what is clearly out of my control to change.

We both take a big jump at the bed gave our hugs good night with our privet good nights to family at home we crawl up onto the big soft comfy bed, and under the extravagant sheets and comforter and drifted off to sleep in no time.

Chapter Sixteen

Waking up this morning did feel different because we were actually supposed to be somewhere. I think I was awake first with Amanda waking up once I moved the covers to see what we had out today. Secretly, the cloths being picked out and perfect every day was the high light of my every morning and was the first thing I looked for once my eyes opened. At first, I thought I was seeing double because there were two sets of blue jean overalls and two Lulu lemon outfits. I was wiping my eyes when Amanda sat up and said no way, we have overalls and straw hats she smiled. When I said so, what is the Lulu Lemon for then, she said that is what we wear under the overalls so when we are done our work at the farm we can take the overalls off before we go to Henrys and Elsie's. I looked at Amanda and said wow you are on the ball this morning, I am impressed I said while I was stretching and leaning to crawl out of bed.

We moved over to our sitting area for our coffee and smoke which has become our routine and give us some alone time because once we go out of our room doors, the day always begins with Rosie there to greet us and take care of our every need. From there the day is filled with intermittent conversations as we are learning something new, every day. We enjoy our bit of time in the morning and at the end of the day to have our one on one time.

As we were getting ready, Amanda who was dressed first looked so cute in her overalls with her hands stuffed deep in her pockets and her hat firmly on her head then rocking back and forth to emphasize her farm girl innocent look.

As we come out of our room with our straw hats on and overalls, Rosie looked over at us and smiled so big and clapped her hands a little and said bravo ladies, you look perfect for your day. Come have some breakfast you will need your energy for today. Amanda looked at her as she was sitting and said I thought we were going to be picking fruit and vegetables, well yes, you are Rosie said but you still need a good breakfast ladies and gave a wink.

While we were having our toast, fruit and yogurt breakfast, Rosie asked us what we thought of all the crafts we say yesterday. Our eyes opened wide and before either of us had a chance to say anything, Rosie said cool hey. Cool, Amanda replied, leaning forward what we saw yesterday and learned is over the top remarkable, cool is an understatement, smiling. I then asked Rosie if she had ever been on the jet or the boats or in the sub. Rosie began to explain her experience by saying as a matter of fact girls, all the residents had to learn to fly, sail, and operate strategic and key components and equipment of the island. I cannot envision you flying the jet Amanda said with a big smile that is so awesome you can fly the jet. Rosie chuckled at Amanda, and said let's hope that it is never me that has to. The whole in the roof would be bigger by the time I got out of it she laughed more, seriously implying that she is not good at it.

You know ladies, if you were going to be with us longer, that it would have been our responsibility to start your training to be able to do the same. There is no way to ever know, who could be the last person standing and if it is left to you to save people or evacuate the island , you need to be aware of what you have available and fundamental understanding of operations to help in making informed decisions in high demand situations. With all the training done through simulation, we are all masters at these different operations however it is base information that we can draw on if ever needed.

Although Amanda and I were into our conversation, and Rosie could see our faces go blank as we were envision ourselves in the pilot's chair of the jet. When she said well we better get you ladies on your way I am sure Kevin will be waiting for you. He is existed to have your help and show off his crops. As she was getting up, she said could I ask you girls to grab two baskets of strawberries before you leave the farm and give one to Henry when you see her and you can bring the other one home or I will get it from you if I see you later today.

Rosie had our to go cups ready but then headed back towards the kitchen, and as we stood and gathered our smokes up Rosie comes out of the swinging door with another care package, this time for Kevin. I chuckled at Rosie and commented that is why people like to see us drive up, because we are their food delivery. While Rosie was carrying the care package out to our cart, she said we couldn't have food go to waste now could we.

As we were getting in the cart, I said good luck with your fish dish, oh thank you, it is funny that I like to prepare and cook this dish when I will not eat it. Rosie then sent us on our way wishing us a wonderful day and implied she would may be see us later at the cafe.

We were excited to be doing something meaningful other than explore and relax that we did not even have our smoke after breakfast. We had our go cups filled with coffee so Amanda had us to the farm right away so we could have our smoke and coffee while Kevin lets us know what we will be doing first.

Like Rosie said, Kevin was sitting out on his front porch with coffee in hand waiting for us to arrive. As Amanda, parked Kevin came up to greet us and once again welcomed us to Lucky Farms. Kevin spots his care package and goes to get it from the cart to take it into the kitchen. He calls for us to sit on the porch we will have coffee before we get this show on the road he says as he is unpacking the care package. I love Rosie he says as he comes out to sit with us on the porch.

Amanda and I lit up our smokes and looking out towards the garden when Kevin says what a beautiful day, I think you are going to enjoy the first patch, it's easy and not messy. The first patch that needs to be thinned is the peas. Amanda looked at him and said right on that is perfect, I can do that. Kevin looking at the way we were dressed and said at least you look the part as he chuckled at us. I replied hey these are perfect for the farm and I especially like the added touch of the hat, as I gave him a huge smile. Kevin was pointing out the different gardens and fields, and explaining what is planted and where. Also, that they change up what they plant all the time. We eat what we can fresh, and then we freeze or can what we cannot. We even have our own island Lucky Farms labels and packaging he says proudly.

Once we were done our smoke, we walk out off the porch and Kevin heads us off through the rows and rows of vegetables, to almost the middle of the football field sized garden. When we get to our spot, we see there were two little stools one on each side of the first row of peas, for us and two pails to put our picked peas in ready to go. Kevin wanted to make sure that we knew what they were looking for in size and what to leave so he picked a few with us to start. Once he seen that we had the hang of it he said well ladies I have a few other things to check on but I will be back to see how you are making out. If you need me for anything, I will be out back repairing the pigpen. I swart they are the most destructive bunch of critters we have. Kevin smiled and began to turn around to leave and said check you later gals.

We looked at each other, thought this was pretty good, Amanda grind, and said at least we could not screw this up ... we can sit, smoke drink coffee and be productive all at the same time. We both squatted on our little stools and started picking away. There was a lot of peas and at different stages of growth so it took a bit of time before we could move our stools. As we are picking away not really saying much all the sudden we smell some of Kevin's special blend wafting our way, so we look up to see Kevin coming towards us and offering us a hoot. We stand up to share and as he lets out a puff of smoke he says I never thought to offer before we started how rude of me, I apologize ladies. I look at Kevin smiled, and said you know that is not soothing someone expects to do before they start working hey. We all chuckled as the hoot was passed around Kevin looked in our buckets and said good job, job, keep up the good work. Got to go he smiles and as he motions to leave, he hands me the hoot, turns around and says I will be back.

Now that is the way every none safety sensitive workday should start I laughed jokingly with Amanda adding and yes with the employer providing it, we really had a good laugh then. With having a little glow on, we got right into what we were doing and started picking up the pace. We were went stead for about an hour and then it was time for a sip of coffee and a smoke. We stood up to give our legs and back a stretch, lit our smokes, and grabbed our coffee cups. Out of the blue Amanda says to me can you imagine them teaching us to fly a jet or a submarine, I was worried we were going screw this up shrugging her shoulders and smiling at me. Now where did that come from I asked. They all had to learn and Rosie did not say how long the isolation would be before they would take the steps in training us. Why you want to learn to fly the jet before we leave? Sure why not, it is all done through simulation so I can't really crash a plane and it might help me with the yuck feeling I have towards flying now.

That would be something to learn, good for you for thinking of trying.

Myself, I am good with just being a passenger. We butt our smokes have a drink of coffee and sit back down on our little stools.
We were both quiet and in our own thoughts picking our peas and getting impressed with how full our buckets were. We ate a few as we went so we could have had more but they were so good we had to stop and eat some and stuffing the empty pods in our big overall pockets trying to conceal the evidence, like kids.

It did not seem long after our smoke that Kevin was heading back our way and as he gets closer, he started complimenting us on how much we did get done. I really want to thank you ladies for your help today and you are now free to go. We are done for the day I asked, yes for sure and tomorrow we have strawberries to pick. Oh yes, I just remembered we were supposed to get two baskets of strawberries and take one to Henry and Elsie's and bring one home for Rosie, thanks for reminding me I said. The baskets are already on the porch waiting for you. Amanda, there they go doing it again reading our minds before we even have the thought, Kevin smiled and said hey you have to get up real early around here if you want to keep up. No kidding, I said as we started heading towards the house. Once we got to the house I had to go to the washroom before we left, I was in awe of the ranch style home.

Kevin knowing that we were going to Henry's and Elsie's for a visit he did not want to hold us up and had the plump red baskets of strawberries in the cart for us. Before we were leaving Kevin asked how our smokes were holding up, we let him know that we were all good and thanked him for everything and said that we may see him later or tomorrow for sure. Amanda pulled through the big circle driveway, we headed up the path towards Main Street, and were to go past the café, and then needed to take another right and follow the path into Henry and Elsie's. During our short drive, we complemented each other on a job well done and that we were looking good doing it.
As we slowly pull up their driveway, we were overwhelmed with the smell of the white stargazer lilies that were everywhere. Amanda loved the flowers although at first she found the aroma overpowering I told her to give it a minute to desensitize a little which will reduce the intenseness of the smell.

We can see that Henry and Elsie are on their front porch sitting in two willow woven rocking chairs having a glass of wine. As Amanda, parked and I grab the basket of strawberries for them, they were welcoming us into their home. Elsie came to get the strawberries from me and Henry got between

Amanda and I and put her arms around us saying we are so glad you come for a visit girls and guided us to our willow woven seats on the porch. As I was getting seated, I commented that the furniture is beautifully designed and well built. I have seen willow work before but nothing of this quality of weave and wrap. Fantastic craftsmanship Amanda nodded as Elsie was coming back onto the porch, knowing I was impressed with the furniture she asked us if we wanted to take a guess at who built all of it.

Really, it is one of you that did this, Oh my goodness I am going to guess Rosie because there is nothing that woman cannot do Amanda replied. Hum, I had to think a second even to take a wild ass guess who would have done this, I know I guessed that it was Paul. Henry and Elsie looked at each other, laughed, and said at the same time, it was Jessie who built all of this. Now that floored both Amanda and I we were not expecting that as the answer. Wow, you guys can really do it all around here can't you. Henry said some of us do much better than others, I couldn't even weave a basket she giggled. Then right away began to ask us what we would like to drink. Amanda and I kind of fumbled a bit and pointed to the white wine they were having. Elsie piped up then and said you know, the reason I asked for the strawberries was because I make an delicious slushy drink using them, Elsie looked at Henry and asked if she would like a strawberry slushy. Henry gleamed at Elsie, that is one of my favorites you know of course I'll have a batch sweetie. Elsie was going to head back inside when Henry said come on girls lets show you around and we can helps Elsie by staying out of her way she says with a smile.

As we enter into what instantly hits you as being an old Louisiana styled living room and kitchen with jazz memorabilia on the walls and in the shelves. The living space went into a sunken living room with huge stone fireplace TV screen and music corner with piano and a brass instruments sitting in stands. So who is the musician here I asked and Henry replied, well we both dabble and play a little bit on all of them and we try and learn a new instruments as we go. Paul also plays a few instruments with the guitar being the instrument he plays, like a star. Elsie's says now don't forget Jim he will pick up the kazoo once in a while, we all laughed even Amanda who barely knew what a kazoo was.

We could hear Elsie blending up a storm in the kitchen so we went into see how she was making out when we walked into the kitchen that had one open wall with pillars holding the roof feels like you have stepped into a flower garden setting with dark wood features and breakfast nook area with a water wall. The appliances had wood covering so that even the double door fridge looked like a old fashion cooler. There was a long ceramic looking counter and bar with a triple sink and fancy chopping block in it. At the front of the kitchen is an antique looking heavy dining table that looks like it could seat twelve. Henry was pointing her favorite things out in the kitchen and dining area, which was very cozy, and not overly feminine for two ladies living together.

Elsie was done mixing her fancy drinks and even put little paper umbrellas and a fresh strawberry on top. While we were picking up our drinks, Henry and Elsie raised their glasses, we did the same, and we all gave a cheers.

Let's take our drinks and we will show you the rest of our humble home. As we pass the oversized living room, we come to what we would call almost a normal sized washroom that had an instrumental design and carried the jazz theme of the living room. Elsie did call the average sized bathroom the guest washroom and implied by pointing up that their washroom was up in their bedroom. Past the guest washroom, we walk into an open lounge and bar area with a wide woodblock staircase leading up to the master bead room. As we passed by the staircase there was a long stand up bar with pool table, pinball, and two slot machines around the room. Then you go through the high wood beam archway with palm trees on both sides as you walk towards the outdoor pool, hot tub and fire pit cove. The property was partly against the rock wall on the kitchen side of the house making the back pool area feel more closed in and privet. Henry pointed to a stone path that takes you to a little green house and tool shed.

Amanda finally had a chance to take a good sip of her slushy drink, and then complemented Elsie on her drink; while we were both parsing their home, it is outstanding. Elsie looked at Amanda with appreciation of the complement and then waved her hand and turned, indicating we were to follow, as she says, if you think this is nice wait until you see our room upstairs you will be just, blown away.

We start to climb the wide wood beam stairs with the wall to the high ceiling painted with a mural of peacocks and flowers that were almost three-dimensional and flowing as we climb the stairs. At the top of the landing we can see a massive log frame four-poster bed king sized bed with log nightstands. One half of the wall behind the bed was a portion of exposed island rock wall and at the end of the rock starts the log frame of the large second floor balcony with beautiful log furniture and fire tables.

The second floor balcony wraps around to the front of the house where you can see out towards Main Street, the lake and waterfall. Another quaint sitting area that had a unique feature was at the end of the balcony, where along with two loves seats and tables there was two bright red porcelain claw foot bath tubs that both faced towards the lake. Amanda spotted them and said now those are cool; I have never seen anything like them before. I replied oddly enough, I have actually seen a red claw foot tub before when I was young; I tilted my head and smiled back at them.

Going back in to the bedroom, we could see that the ceiling fans all operate off one gear and oversized rubber bands connecting the three fans. Those are neat to see I commented to Henry as I took another sip of my drink, with her replying they use no energy and they make no sound I love them.

There was a fireplace and sitting area around it and a large TV mounted on the wall. We were both trying to take it all in when, both Elsie and Henry started walk towards the exposed rock wall to the end of the one nightstand. Where there was smoothly carved out archway leading into the rock wall. This was what they really wanted to show us as the gem of the house. Walking through the high arched opening, we see to the left the large washroom with a floor to ceiling mirrored wall, white marble counter top, with a trough style sinks. There was a waterfall shower for two, Jacuzzi tub and cedar sauna dry. Past the half wall was a perfectly organized drive in closet with a octagon merrier at the end with chairs and coffee bar. We stopped to gaze around the room we could see they enjoyed. Henry said that sometime we come in here and have our morning coffee just taking our time deciding what to wear, it is so peaceful in here we find. Elsie had her own side of the closet even though they were very close to the same size; Henry had a larger chest and everything was made to fit her like a glove which was a tad different from Elsie who wore her cloths lose and comfortable looking.

In the drive in closet, you can go through a set of Tiffany glass French doors, and enter into a privet exercise room with a mirrored wall with hand railing along the one side. Part of the area looked like a dance studio that had a sliding Tiffany glass door leading back out to the second floor balcony.

Thank you for showing us your home I said, it is truly amazing, if the world could only see they would be jealous I smiled and raised my glass to the ladies. Amanda was still in awe of the space that she took a big drink and gave herself brain freeze. Amanda wobbled a bit and agreed their home was over the top beautiful.

We could have spent more time up there but Henry's drink was empty so she started for the stairs with Elsie right behind her saying to us it's time for a refill girls. Going back to the kitchen and toping up the drinks Henry wanted to sit in the breakfast nook area by the water wall. Elsie had a remote control that started the living room fireplace and soft jazz music in the background.

We all sat down and had another sip off our drinks when Henry pulled shocked us by pulling out a hoot from a little box on the table and asked if we would like a puff. Amanda and I were surprised because we had never seen her have a puff before. Elsie got up and went to the fridge to bring out a platter of cheese, crackers, pickles and pepperoni and more to snake on. Amanda or I did not want to be snoopy but I could not help myself from saying that we did not think she or they smoked because we had not seen them partake before, when we were around.

Henry smiled at us, and said do not be surprised girls, we all smoke weed here it is just that we all pick our times. Well then, than thank you Amanda replies we would love to have a puff, and then jokingly said we did work so hard today, then she looked at me and we chuckled a bit as I said, no she is only kidding we did enjoy our day and we were actually productive.

Henry lit the hoot and we started nibbling on Elsie's munchies platter when it came up in conversation the question as to how long Henry and Elsie had been together. We were, set back by their ten-year long relationship and congratulated them for the commitment to the island and each other. Elsie told us then that it was their ten-year anniversary today. About the same time, Elsie was telling us about it being their anniversary; we see Paul and Jim drive up with smoothing large in the back of the cart that took the two of them to bring into the house. We all got up to see what the package was and when Jim and Paul pulled off the tissue paper warping we could see a large fruit and flower basket arrangement that was so massive the fellows put on the large dining room table. Happy anniversary Paul and Jim said as they tipped their hats and said we had better get back. Elsie said you are not staying for a drink; I made my strawberry slushy's and it is our anniversary so it would be rude to say no. Okay, okay Paul said, we would stay for a quick one; we do not want to be rude he looked at Jim who nodded agreeing.

Great, Elsie went right over and poured Paul and Jim their drinks without the umbrellas, as the rest of us girls were looking over the arrangement, when Henry found the card and read aloud the message, which simply read, with love from us all. Elsie came over and Gave Henry a hug they were both moved by the gesture. Paul and Jim pulled up beside where we were sitting and clearly enjoying their drink. Henry asked Paul how the fish dish was going with Rosie at his place. Paul relied with a serious face; well we were glad to have to deliver your flowers, if that says anything and then he cracked a smile and said only kidding everything is fine. Jim looked relieved that Paul was not going to lead us on. Rosie is doing fantastic of course and she will be done soon.

Amanda and I had finished our drinks and knew that we were having Janette and Jessie over for dinner and that we should be on our way soon as well. Without feeling that we were cutting our visit short by congratulating on the anniversary, I let the group know that it was time for us to be heading back. Just then, I hear Paul and Jim take the last slurps out of their drink and we all motion to stand up all together.

As Amanda, Jim, Paul and I were heading for the door we thanked them, and congratulated them again and gave hugs all around before saying our good nights. Before we were driving away Amanda asked Jim when Janette and Jessie were coming up and he thought he heard them say in an about hour from now. Paul and Jim were heading back to Paul's place and we were on course to the palace. We waved to Henry and Elsie who were in a tight embrace as we were leaving. They look so cute Amanda leaned over and said to me. Home James, I said to Amanda as she pretended to step on the gas pedal.

With finally absorbing the house we just went through I turned to Amanda and said now is that not a house for two. Beyond words mom, that house is just beyond words. What was your favorite feature, I asked her, she paused and said I love the log four-poster bed. Oh yes for sure I agreed and then followed with I think my favorite was the sunken living room, that was cozy. We both were quiet for the rest of our short drive just going over all the unique things in their home.

Palace at last, Amanda parks the cart and as she is getting out of the cart says to me, you know we never did change out of our overalls. I thought of it when we got to Henry and Elsie's I replied but they were clean and it seemed like too much hassle. Any way we looked cute with them on I laughed as we walk up on the patio.

Assuming that Rosie was still working on her fish dish at Paul's we were a bit surprised when Rosie was there to greet us on the patio with a glass of wine. Wow where did you come from Amanda asked with a surprised tone, Rosie smiled and said I was dine down there a while ago but I cannot have them thinking it was easy she laughed. Oh, my goodness, look at the table you have set, china, silverware candles this looks so nice I commented. Rosie looked at us still in our over alls and says how about you girls go freshen up and I will check on dinner. Before Rosie turned, Amanda said with such fancy settings what are we having for dinner. We are having a surprise, now go get changed Janette and Jessie will be here soon.

Changed I said with a higher pitched voice, then looked at Amanda and wiggled my eyebrows, excited because that meant Rosie had something nice picked out for us. We took our glass of wine in our room and went to see what she had out for us. We can see the reflection in the mirrors of wide band halter dresses one with a small collar and double breast brass buttons down the front. The other wide band halter dresses had no collar or buttons although had a slit up the side. The one for me was navy blue and Amanda's was burgundy. Once we had the dresses on and shiny accessories, looked in the mirror, we could not believe how Fifth Avenue we looked. Were did not hear any commotion out on the patio so we thought we would hang back and have a smoke before Janette and Jessie arrived.

We at there so proper like and drank our wine and puffing on our smokes when I looked at Amanda when this day is done I am going to be pooped but I am looking forward to our sub tour tomorrow afternoon. Me to Amanda replied, that almost slipped my mind I was just thinking about going back out to the farm tomorrow. Finishing our smokes, we figured we better get out to the patio, and chat with Rosie while we wait.

We no sooner got out were Rosie was standing when we see Janette and Jessie pull up. We all go out to greet them when we see Janette carrying two bottles of wine. Rosie right away, say's to Janette you should not have, knowing the wine is coming out of their personal stock that they brought back from their last vacation. Janette replies wine is meant to be drank with friends and family and you are both, so what better time to drink the wine. We all laughed with Jessie commenting with a smile, that someone already had a glass before she came. Once on the patio we could see that both Janette and Jessie were wearing fifties styled dresses that looked so classy and they even had the little white gloves on. You ladies look fantastic Amanda and I gushed. We were chatting about all our outfits when Rosie brings us all up to a rolling serving table that has been set up with an assortment of seafood and veggie appetizers and wine chilling. Rosie always wears perfectly fitting scrubs. The cloths a person would see a nurse or dental assistant wear. However, she always looked different because she always wore different colors and variations of the classic clinical style.

Rosie was beaming you all look so wonderful and thanked Janette and Jessie for coming. I then thought to ask Janette if she arranged the fruit and flower basket for Henry and Elsie today and she nodded yes and proceeded to say that it took her most of the day to do it. We were there when they received it and without a doubt Rosie, it took Paul and Jim to carry the basket into the house it was massive and beautiful. Janette graciously thanked us for our parse.

Amanda looking at Jessie said speaking of Henry and Elsie they told us that you Jessie made the woven willow furniture on the front porch, that was fantastic and must have taken hours of work. Jessie was please that we liked her furniture and looked at Rosie and Janette and said very positively that sometimes that is all we have around here is time, and for me that just suites me perfect.

While Janette was holding her wine and picking out some shrimp, she said to us that after a time of being in such a relaxed environment she suggested that we find that we require less sleep. When it is unwind time but not sleep time, we like to keep our minds and ourselves occupied in many different facets to balance our lives with the inclusion of staying mind or body active an additional four hours a day over the average adult. That explains it then, I looked at Amanda that is how Rosie does as much as she does she does not sleep. I turned to Rosie and I blurted out a laugh, which made everyone laugh as I gave Rosie a hug while we all chuckled.

Okay, I am hungry I said, to the ladies and by the looks of the table Rosie is ready for us. Yes, for sure girls you fine a seat and I will bring the cart out. Janette offered to help even though she knew it was futile, Jessie, Amanda and I looked at Janette and she said, what I had to offer and we all smiled.

Rosie came through the kitchen doors with a large hot serving cart that was even had the hood lit up. My goodness that smells good Rosie what are we having Jessie asked, as Rosie proceeds to open each of the hot trays there was prime rib, garlic mashed potatoes, asparagus, Yorkshire pudding and in the last tray was lobster tails the tray was filled with lobster. I was so going to bust out of my dress by the time this dinner is over I said aloud. Amanda asked how you could make all of this when you spent most of your day at Paul's cooking. Rosie looked at Amanda winked and said … it's magic. Let us get started ladies the fellows have no idea what they are missing Rosie said as started filling her plate.
I understand you did well at the farm today girls, Janette commented. The farm is remarkable and we did enjoyed picking the peas today. Tomorrow we will be picking in another area and we definitely could have worked more than the three hours I replied.

Amanda added that we are looking forward to seeing the sub tomorrow and learning more about it. We understand that we cannot see the watercrafts yet because the waterfall is blocking access. With seeing the jet and the hanger I can only engine what a mini sub looks like. Rosie looked up at us and said, who said anything about it being a mini, sub that vessel sleeps six comfortable and has a galley five star restaurants would envy she spoke proudly of the submarine. Janette and Jessie both agreed that we would be impressed when we see it. My favorite Jessie said, is the yacht, it is so lavish, white leather and purple accents you definitely feel royal on that.

Rosie had a look around the table and made sure that all our wine glasses were full and then said to us all with her glass raised, cheers to wonderful company and conversations. Jessie and I said at the same time, cheers to the food. Amanda was enjoying her dinner but skipped on the lobster, which was fine by me because that meant I could eat her share. While everyone was still working on their first plate I got up for more lobster when Rosie said take as many as you want, I have more. More I said, that was all I needed to hear and I plunked three tails on my plate. Amanda looked me and smirked and then the rest of them saw my pate when I sat down and started to laugh. What, she said I could take as many as I wanted and I stopped at three just to be polite, there are only three left in the tray. That had us all chuckling as we continued to enjoy our dinner.

I began to ask about the work that Janette and Jessie do when Jessie said that the work they do is all about supporting the island and monitoring all systems and writing instructions when needed. Right now a lot of our attention is on your departure which we are making headway on. That is good to hear Amanda remarked, when we are going to more about Sires message and the plan for leaving.

Rosie proceeded with answering the question by saying that we are planning a get together here not tomorrow but the next day. Jessie followed up with yes, Elsie, Dustin and I believe we will have all the information complied and ready to present by then. With that said, our faces light up and Janette wanted to make sure that we were not going to be disappointed in the update and emphasized that we may not have all the answers by then but it will be the most current she smiled confidently.

I spoke up on both our behalf's and said to the ladies in the most sincerest manner, letting them know we trust them and that we will do exactly as we are instructed. We are secure in whatever plan is devised and we want to reassure you all that we comprehend how important it is that whatever needs to be secret remains' secret.

You ladies are taking this all very well and every day in stride, I know that the luxuries do help, however there is no filling the void of not being able to let your family know that you are okay and we all feel for your families as well.

Rosie then jumped in and had to comment on my, eating the four-lobster tail. Oh, my goodness, you are not going to have room for desert Rosie said, and chuckle turning the conversation on me. Yes, I ate them all as I pointed to my plate and wiping the butter off my hands. Rosie had a glass-warming dish on the table that had moist rolled up cloths. I puffed out my cheeks with all eyes on my plate I admitted to even being able to eat some of the prime rib and I had one asparagus I smiled proudly.

As we were all finishing, and still parsing the food and moaning over how full we were, Rosie got up to bring the coffee over to the table and remove the dishes off the table. The serving carts are easy to load and within minutes of being finished eating our dinner, Rosie and Janette cleared away the dishes and Rosie rolled the cart over to the kitchen. When Rosie came back from the kitchen, she made sure to make extra noise so we would all look her way, when she came through the door, with the tallest angel food cake I had ever seen, and it was pink.

Amanda and Jessie could not believe what Rosie was bring out because angel food cake is both these two girls absolute favorites, right down to the color of the cake and icing being pink. Even Amanda and Jessie did not know that they shared the favorite. The girls were so delighted but had no room for cake right now; I need to relax for a minute before I am putting anything else in me. Amanda was still sipping on her wine, wanted a smoke so she excused herself from the table, and moved over to the hot tub area. I had my coffee and was right behind her to get out of the way of the ladies, as they were all none cigarette smokers.

Jessie did come over to join us while Rosie was cutting up the cake and Janette was helping her serve up the eight-inch angel food cake slices. Rosie was beaming she was so proud of her cake and then called out to us saying ready when you are. Jessie and Amanda where laughing when they looked at the table and seen the huge slices of cake that were sitting there waiting for them. My eyes opened wide when I saw the cake and looked at Rosie, I started rubbing my full tummy when she said come on girl, just one bit. The cake is so light and airy; you will not even know you are eating more. Before we moved, back to the table Jessie was telling us that if we need our hair done she has the island beauty salon at her house and that she cuts and styles everyone's hair on the island. Right on Amanda says to Jessie my mom has not had her hair cut in five years may be we can get her in the chair here. Jessie looked surprised that I had gone so long without a hair cut that she said to us well she can't hide from me here she laughed and we all joined in knowing that she was not kidding.

Amanda and I finished our smokes and with Jessie, walked back to the table to see if we could eat any more. As we sat down Rosie wanted to let us know how much she enjoyed our company. Jessie looked over to Amanda and asked how she like the seven day in and seven day out work schedule. I was curious as to how Amanda was going to answer because typically she suffers very mixed emotions. Amanda did pause before responding and said that there is a lot about the schedule that is great, like when you take one week's vacation you are actually getting three weeks off. However, she believes that her personality is a go home at the end of the day and work the regular Monday to Friday shift.

Once my sweetie gets his journeyman electrical, he will be the one going out of town and I will be the work from home chick. Amanda smiled and sounded confident in the plan until, she hesitated and said well I guess that was the plan anyway and slightly lowered her head. I was quick to respond that is still the plan and by the time we get home you will not have to worry about working. What makes you say that mom, I really was trying to make her laugh by saying with being gone so long, all your debts will have been paid and I blurted out another hardy chuckle and then said we just won't tell them you are home and I chuckled some more. The ladies were laughing along knowing I was just making light of our situation and that we have to keep our chine up and reframe from assuming changes.

After our coffee and eating more than a few bits of the cake, we were all losing our steam and Janette indicated that it was time for them to be going home. Rosie got up, abruptly went to the kitchen, and said one minute I will be right back. We all got up for hugs and salutations when Rosie came out with two care packages for Jim and Ryan before walking we walked them to their cart.

Once they were out of sight, Amanda, I looked at each other, and both motioned to go to the room and change out of our dresses. We passed Rosie who was pouring herself a coffee, all I said was housecoat on the way to the room. It did not take long for us to come back out and sit with Rosie to finish off our wonderful evening off in comfort.

We noticed that Rosie did look like she had a full day and was ready to pack it in, as we were sitting and digesting our dinner. Amanda and I were having our coffee and were going to have a hoot and smoke before bed. Rosie asked us if we were all good for the night, with Amanda swiftly saying perfect Rosie. Then to our surprise Rosie says to us, I am done for today girls I will see you both in the morning. She grabbed the bottle of Baileys on the table and stood up to give us hugs and then said as she was walking away that the lights will turn off on their own and down the hall she went with her coffee and baileys.

Amanda and I went to relax around the hot tub and have our smokes before bed. Wow that was a heck of a lot of socializing for one day, Amanda commented. I agreed as I lit the hoot, yes they do not know that we do not do people well. We laughed to ourselves quietly, knowing we were both very introverted even though we are not seen as being that way. Even our own families do not realize how difficult it can be at times for us in social gatherings.

While finishing our smokes and coffee we gazing around when I said to Amanda I think that we should prepare ourselves for some reality when we all meet next. I get a feeling from Janette that there are some unease of our departure but I am not sure what they are exactly dwelling on. They all seem confident in our getting off the island however; I sense hesitation with some part of us going home.

Amanda was being very adult when she reassured me that she realizes that us going home will not be without some snags and may be a lot more involved then what we care to think about right now. We were both high and calm, helping to making any conversation of going home less stressful. I let her know by reaching for her hand and giving it a little squeeze, how much her demonstration of strength in what she had just said, meant to me.

Well sweetie I looked at Amanda and said it is bedtime as I motioned to get up and out of my chair but then acted like I ate too much and could not. Amanda grabbed my hand, and helps pull me out of the comfortable loveseat we were sitting in. When we get to our room although we were both tired, we wanted to have a shower before bed. Our washroom is amazing, two people can be in there, and no one has to wait for anything because there is two of everything. We love it.

When done our showers we thought we would have a tea and a smoke before we went to bed. We had a hot water urn in the sitting lounge area so we could always make tea in our room. Being comfortable and having our smoke before bed we chatted more about Henry and Elsie's house and jokingly as we put our smokes out and took our last sip of tea, Amanda reminded me that I could finally get my hair cut.

We pull ourselves up into bed, give each other a big hug, and say our good nights when Amanda said quietly you know mom, even though I could have my own suite I only want to be with you. Me too sweetie me too, I love you sweet dreams. We snuggled in and had our thoughts of home as we always do with the faint sound of the waterfall we were asleep.

Chapter Seventeen

Waking up today meant seeing the submarine and that was my first thought as I awoke. Amanda was awake before me and was sitting up in bed stretching and putting her hair in a messy bun when I looked over at her and gave her bright and cheery good morning sunshine. She smiled and gestured to me with a forward nod, to have a look at what we had to wear for today. I sat up right away to have a look and I had a big smile, oh, my goodness we have a different style of blue jean overalls and a picnic table design (red and white checkers) sleeveless shirts. Although that was not the funny part, we each had a pair of Uge boots with bows in the back of them.

We laughed when we seen that this time we did match there was no differences at all. I said to Amanda, as we were going through our getting ready routine I will find out if she did this to be funny or not. Otherwise, dressing us like twins borders on creepy. We were both laughing as we come out of the room with Rosie there to greet us who also started laughing when she seen us. So what is up with the twins outfit I asked Rosie she said that she did do it on purpose and because Kevin was saying how much we looked alike and kept on about looking like twins I thought that seeing as you were going there today, I would mess with his brain. I hope you do not mind girls, I figured that you would be okay with the funny, and I promise I will never do it again. We looked at each other and shrugged our shoulders and smiling we had no problem with the match and she did sound sincere about not doing it again. We did our modeling of our outfits as we walked towards the little table Rosie had set for breakfast.

When I seen the light breakfast of toast, fruit, cheese and yogurt I said to

Rosie that she must have known that we were still full from last night and I complemented her again saying her food was the best ever and smiled. The compliment made Rosie blush. While Amanda was nibbling on her breakfast, I asked how Rosie slept last night; she winked and replied, like a baby and pointed to the empty bottle of baileys sitting on the bar.

I love the boots Amanda says to Rosie and she let her know that she has several pare of these but none with the bows they are so cute. Knowing that Amanda likes the boot was not the reason that she picked them for today. Rosie started to explain that with sitting on the small stools in a crouched position, the soft boots are more flexible and they stay on the feet when walking through the garden. I have a practical reason for picking them over fashion sense today. In addition, they are a soft sole boot, which is required on the sub, and when you take your tour of the sub this afternoon.

Rosie went on to tell us that the plan for today was when we were finished working at the farm we were to meet Paul and Jim at the café. She then said that we are all so excited for you to see it that some of us may come with you on the tour, if nothing else but to see your faces when your do. We all laughed when she said that because I am sure the expressions on our faces seeing everything we have has been quite humorous to them.

You are a wealth of information Rosie, I do not know what we would do without you here Amanda said again as she has on many occasions. Well it is time to get on our way I said to Amanda we have work to do you know, sounding like this is routine on day two.

There was Rosie with our go cups ready and our smokes all gathered up as she walked us to the cart and handed us a care package for Kevin and it was a big piece of cake. Rosie said I have a piece left for Dustin and Paul I will take them theirs in a bit.

As we get in the cart, Rosie reminds us to go to the café when we are done at the farm. She waves as we drive off and head down the hill. What a great day I said to Amanda as I lit her and myself a smoke while she drove to the farm.

Pulling up into the parking area Kevin is there to greet us so we thought, but when he got close enough all we heard him say was cake! He was just pulling our leg and then gave us a big good morning and said oh my goodness I am seeing double, as he looked at our matching outfits. Tell Rosie ha! ha! for me he said. Then with a funny smirk asked us to come sit on the porch and finish our smokes and he paused, watch me devour this cake he laughed as he was opening the container that had a plastic fork and napkin taped to the lid, of course.

How was your dinner last night I asked Kevin, who's face lit up as he was going to explain how great their dinner was and that the guys all played poker until dawn, so… I will be napping later he chuckled.

Are you not going to come to the sub with us later Amanda asked then he shook his head and said we will have to see if I catch my second wind. In the short time we had been talking Kevin was done his cake and wiped off his mouth and said speaking, of second winds, let us have a hoot to get this day kick started. Kevin had one sitting there ready to spark and started passing it around and said as he puffed out some smoke, you girls will enjoy your tour this afternoon and pay attention it is not just the sub but also the containment and access that is amazing and I am sure you will enjoy hearing all about them.

I have you girls set up just a few rows over from where you were yesterday, you will see the buckets and stools waiting there for you he said. The hoot went around again when Kevin said he was going to be starting canning tomatoes out back in the processing area and to come get him when we are done. Kevin jumped up and said see that was all I needed cake and hoot, I am recharged; he tipped his hat and turned to walk to the back of the house.

Well I guess that is our cue to get to work sweetie and up we got heading towards the pea patch we were in yesterday. When we get to our station, we get our selves comfy and have a few sips of coffee before we get started. As I looked at Amanda, I said it really does feel good to believe we are being useful, we chuckled with Amanda saying back so how useful does, our three hours a day for two days out of seven feel, to you, mom. We chatted back and forth, about how beautiful it was and getting excited for our tour and then realizing that Paul and Jim were going to laugh at us when they see us dressed the same but oh well, Rosie will be there to and we can blame her. We picked away without paying attention to the time when all the sudden Kevin comes out of nowhere and scares us by letting us know that it is time for us to on our way. Once we got over the scare I said already, wow that went by fast. Amanda stood up and stretched her legs agreeing that we had no idea what time it had gotten to be.

Kevin walks us back to our cart and thanking us for our help, we did a great job today we will have you operating the farm before long he joked. Oh no, Amanda was quick to reply we are only the help and we are all good with that she smiled and shook her head no, letting him know she was serious.

We get in our pink driving machine and start pulling away and waving at Kevin as we leave. That was a good morning I said as Amanda smiled and said yes but I bet our afternoon is going to be better. We both went for a sip of our coffee.

When Amanda comes to the intersection, we can see ahead that Paul, Rosie, Jim, Jessie Elsie and Dustin are all hanging out at the cafe. We pull up in our matching out fits and everyone burst out laughing. Rosie had told them what she had done so they were all waiting to see what we really did look like. They were not disappointed that is for sure they thought the joke on Kevin was as funny as we looked. That is when Amanda told Rosie that Kevin told us to pass on a, ha! ha! from him.

Wow are we all going for the tour today I asked Paul who looked at the group and replied well I guess we have a few more then we thought that is for sure. Elsie moves over to Paul and says, I love going in the sub, Henry and I have spent a few evenings in there just enjoying the atmosphere. Jessie also let the group know that she and Ryan have spent some time in there; it is like staying in a fantasy hotel suite. Exactly, Elsie agreed that is how it feels.

Rosie then said, even I am getting excited I have only been in it the one time after passing my navigation simulation testing. Let us fill up our drinks and we can go have a look at this marvel. Everyone had their drinks and Rosie was dumping our coffee out cleaning our go cups and filling them with white wine for our tour.

We all get in our carts with the pink driving machine at the rear, which was good with us because we wanted a smoke and we did not really know where we were going. Amanda and I gestured a cheers with our go cups and had a sip of wine and barley a couple puffs of our smokes and we were stopping already. Well that did not take long Amanda looked over at me and smiled as she started getting out of the cart with smoke in hand.

Where we had stopped was only twenty-five feet onto the road the led to the backside of lake, picnic area. All we could see in front of us was a wall of jagged rock covered in lush vegetation and the little sign with the air tanks. Paul looked at Amanda and I who were right beside him and then the group and said follow me people. At first, it looked like Paul was going to walk right into the rock wall when he stepped on a big flat stone that was level with the ground and the wall slid open. The opening was about twelve feet high and eight feet wide and opened like a patio sliding door.

As the wall slid away, the lights started to flicker on exposing the huge excavated cave that has been, cored through to the ocean. Jim let us know that in addition to the bunkers above us that you have seen girls, this area is also referred to as a bunker however; this one houses and protects the huge floating vessel. The construction is much the same as the jet hanger only this one has a sub in it and not a jet. I could feel that Amanda and I were being watched to see our reactions as we were starting to get a better look as we walked further in to the hanger.

The lights all lit and Amanda and I waking close together being hyped about where we were. Once we were all the way through the entrance and in the massive cave we could see there was a walk path around the bobbing vessel that was in a pool of perfect size. Jim proceeded as the tour guide speaker and said that the sub is an eighty-foot fat belly luxury vessel. Not all submarines built or designed are for the navy, there are many rich people that own their own submarines, and then he looked up at us all and said joking, granted they are mostly drug dealers but hey, they know luxury when they see it.

Paul bumped my shoulder smirked and said see safety lady, we even have hand rails around the pool so no one falls in, he chuckles and winks at Amanda. We all start following Jim as he led us to the ramp taking us to the top entry where there was a small deck and when Jim hit what looked to be a doorbell a cylinder rose up from the sub that was the access to the narrow spiral staircase. Already impressive was the shiny brass hand railing and the dark rosewood lacquered stairs. As we descend in the sub we are first in a lounge area with all padded and molded tan leather love seats and bench seats with bar and TV and brass framed portholes. There was a round coffee table in the middle of the lounge, which illuminated and gave a three-dimensional view as if it were a fire table with no heat.
There was room for all of us in the lounge area that Amanda and had to take some time to soak up the plush surroundings. Our moths were open as we

gazed around the handcrafted interior.

Rosie, Elsie and Jessie found themselves a comfortable chair to sit in while Jim took the rest of us to the front of the sub where the operating controls were. When we walked through the man way opening the fellows all had to duck with Amanda and I walking straight in. There were gages, toggles and panels throughout the cabin. Paul lowered a brass periscope so we could have a look through while Dustin went and sate in the captains chair. The oversized steering wheel was also shiny brass, rosewood and handcrafted, and set in the middle of the cabin.

Amanda pointed to the glass top table behind the captain's chair and said now that looks like it does something she said to Paul. Dustin smiled at Amanda from his captain's chair and complimented her on being so observant. Dustin then pushed a button on the side of the table, which then lit up showing grid lines and ocean floor elevations. Dustin went onto to show us the glass top table was managed the a vast amount of information for navigation and mapping along with being able to show real time visuals of all around the sub. When Dustin went to show us the camera action all we saw was darkness below and the light above, he smiled, well I guess there is not much to see when only floating in a big black pool of sorts, we could not see anything but the light above and the yellow hand rail around the pool.

With this system, Jim said with confidence, they could thread this submersible through a needle in the blind if they had to. This baby is state of the art and can go deeper than any other vessel in the world. This vessel can stay under water longer then the food could sustain even one person and trust me, when I say, this place is well stocked. The pantry is nutritionally equipped to feed six people for nine months comfortably.

Wow, wow, crazy Amanda I again, just blown away by what we were seeing and hearing. We could tell that Paul, Jim and Dustin enjoyed showing us all this stuff even if we did not understand it all, they knew we got the significance of some of the features we were seeing. Let's take you back to the rest of the underwater resort Jim chuckled with Paul smiling, implying this is no regular sub. Single file, we all exit the cabin where we see the ladies were chatting and having a good laugh themselves. Paul looked at Rosie and jokingly said you are not talking sass about me again are you. She quipped back at him saying we have much better things to talk about then you old

man.
Jessie was standing and ready to venture through the rest of the vessel with Amanda and I right behind her wanting to see what was behind the purple toughed and brass button and framed swinging doors.

What we first see as Jessie holds the door open for us is an amazing Victorian designed dining area with built in china cabinets around the room and chandelier over the table. The royal purple and brass button padded armchairs that were round the heavily carved table, all had brass claw feet.

Off to the side of the dining table was a sitting area with plants discreetly cordoning off two white wicker chairs with a small table between them with and ashtray on it? Above the chairs was a ring of colored lights Dustin pointed to the two chairs under the ring of tube lighting, and said that is the only smoking area in the sub. Then he went onto explain that the lighting system acts as an exchange and it's real purpose is to remove all the smoke of two people smoking, he winked at Amanda and showed us the humidor filled with cigars, cigarettes and even a stock of special smokes. I guess it is a good thing for you girls that Sire was an avid smoker, of the finest quality I might add.

There were statues, paintings carvings around the room and in the cabinets, that all looked very expensive and antique. Very lavish I said as I looked around the room again and had a big sip of wine this time. Amanda had sat in one of the big dinning armchairs taking it all in.

Lets carry on Rosie says as we head to the next section that was the galley, which Rosie said she did remembering as being impressed with. As we enter and all file in it is as if we walked into a five star restaurant kitchen with all stainless steel cooler doors and appliances, with all the cooking utensils you could possible need. Opposite to the food preparation, area of the galley was a wonderful breakfast nook that was bright with tropical flower designed padded cushions on the benches. There were hanging pots above a large wood chopping block at the end of the counter.

Jim walked over to the large etched glass door and opened it showing off the selection of wines in the cooler. At the top of the cooler door, there was a small keypad and small screen. This was a feature of the kitchen, that Jim liked and he wanted to show it off to us. Wine selection starts by entering the name of a wine or type in your wine preference like, medium dry white and watch the racking system rotate until it finds the name of the wine or the closest to the description of the request. The system finds the match or closest too wine and brings it to the front of the case and opens the door.

That is amazing I said with Amanda responding with just how much wine is in there. Jim answered by saying there are exactly twelve hundred and thirty three. I guess you do not sneak anything out of there Amanda chuckled when Jessie went up to the door and put in her selection and we watched the interior bottles shift around until it stopped with her bottle right in front. Thanks she said to Paul as she hung onto the bottle and said to the group, this will go nice with dinner this evening.

Rosie called Amanda and I over to the computer that is built into the kitchen where she was showing that all the food and drinks are inventoried and that there is food stashed in any void space available. If you see that, you are low on rice for example the system will let you know exactly where it has been stored and that there may be more than one storage location outside of the large kitchen pantries. See what I mean Rosie said and pointing at the screen, the inventory page showed that there is three hundred pounds of rice under the kitchen nook benches. Monitoring food is vital in this vessel and the inventory adjusts in the system when you put in the three-day menu. The system will also only allow distribution based on number of occupants and duration of being submerged.

Rosie gave the computer a tap and said this kitchen does everything but prepare the food for you. It was Elsie leading the way to the sleeping quarters with Amanda at the rear, and speechless. Following the group the first room we come to is the king room that was a little over, the top with the leopard pints. At the one end of the room, it was all bed with nightstands with bookshelves up the walls. The dressers and closets were along the interior with the TV screen was suspended from the ceiling and positioned flat up against the ceiling keeping it out of the way. There was a small sitting area in the open design deluxe washroom with Jacuzzi tub and steam shower, all the luxuries Elsie boosts.

I commented on all of the beautiful woodwork and seeing so much brass, every porthole was brass, along with fixtures and features like the claw feet on the dinning furniture. Paul was telling us that Sire is very nostalgic and he is somewhat like you Colleen... he likes his shiny things. Paul and I started laughing and then we all had a good chuckle with Dustin putting in his two bits and saying so where is your shiny necklace today, I went to touch my neck and realized I was not wearing it and jokingly replied, it did not match my outfit today so it is back at the palace. The group laughed, had a drink and carried on. Further, up the hall and on the other side of the vessel were two other bed rooms that looked like cruise ship suites as well and had the same brass fixtures and dark rosewood inlay.

The second bedroom was so inviting with a puffy comforter, designed following the purple theme, and had a queen bed, TV and a full washroom with tub and shower. With the third bedroom was navy blue and white and had twin-sized bunk beds that also had a full washroom with tub and shower.

Past the bedrooms was a sliding glass door that took us out onto a deck that had exercise equipment set up on it that overlooked part of the engine room. Amanda asked about noise, would you be out here on a machine when the sub is in motion. Dustin was quick to say that this vessel makes no noise, the people inside would be detected before the vessel ever would he thought he was being smart.

Rosie gave him a tap on the shoulder and chuckled, you and your gadgets, making this out to be nothing special. Once we got to that point Paul pointed to the staircase and said that the belly of the sub is operating systems and storage not much down there for you girls to see. Jim hoisted his cup in the air and said and that ends our tour people.

Amanda and I just look at each other in disbelief before turning to walk back through the sub to the spiral staircase where we came in. As we start up the stairs and get to the landing at the top Paul at the end of the line asks us to hold up there, because there was one last thing he wanted to show before debarking. When he got to the small landing, there was another button, besides the staircase lowering one that slid back a twelve foot long by twelve foot wide, twelve inch slice steel off the vessel top that as it pulled back we could see a lounging deck with bar, fire pit and outdoor BBQ.

We all took the few steps into the outdoor lounge and took a seat in the sectional couches as Paul was telling us that this is quite the feature when depending on the situation, may not ever be able to be used. Dustin agreed with Paul that other than being open in here there was little chance it will be used.

Sire did not want to, and was not going to miss any opportunity because of poor planning.

Jim shook his cup letting Rosie know that he was empty and new that she would get the group moving. She took from his cue and said there are people waiting for us at the café and we do not want to make them wait. Let us go, and chat about the tour more, I am sure Amanda and Colleen have more questions we can help answer them, better with some food, she laughed.

Rosie, Jessie and Elsie were out of the bunker first and were going right to the café with me and Amanda needed a smoke so we held back. While Paul, Jim and Dustin taking their time we thanked them for the fantastic tour, and we let them know that we would be right behind then as we got in our cart and lit our smokes. We were still speechless other then Amanda saying as she took off, now that was incredible, my reply, no shit!

It only took a couple minutes before we were pulling up in front of the café and everyone was there some were mulling around the bar and filling their glasses and others were surrounding the three platters of snakes that Janette and Henry put together for today's cocktail hour.

We put our smokes out with Rosie calling us over to the bar for a refill. At the bar Rosie asked us if we wanted to stay with the wine or would we like something else. I noticed that the fellows were drinking beer so to be funny I asked her for my favorite Canadian beer and I almost dropped to the floor when she pulled a bottle of what I had asked for, right out of one of the coolers of ice. Really you have to be kidding who drinks this here, I asked her while Amanda was still giggling over my reaction of having my brand of beer that I asked for jokingly, why do you have this here. Kevin piped up said it is Sire and myself that fancy Budweiser, as he moved away from the snacks. He continued saying, and we are enjoying it while it lasts.

Although we can extend the shelf life here, that is all. It did not make sense to waste storage space on beer when we can make our own here, having said that we did manage to find room for a small stash Kevin smiled and then finished his beer in one gulp.

Amanda had a refill on her wine and then Rosie came out from behind the bar with her drink and Henry and Janette came over to ask what we thought of our tour while the fellows were still talking about beer.

The one thing that I noticed was that the sub did not feel like a confined space. All the sections seemed spacious and roomy. Certainly not what I had anticipated, Amanda agreed that she did not know what to expect and knew it was going to something, she just had no idea how big that something was. I gushed more on the technologies of the submarine and capabilities with more than the luxuries of home I chuckled and looked around the ladies with a huge smile, I was impressed.

Suddenly Amanda made a little turn, with her nose in the air, and smelt that someone had lit a hoot she looks over to see Kevin and Dustin both holding up a hoot and were waving us over for a puff. After everything of the day, a puff was just what I needed. As Amanda and I moved over to the fellows the rest of the ladies joined the group, no one bothered about the hoot because they all just wanted to be in the conversations.

With us all standing around the long, tall narrow center table that had varying height foot rests. Paul gets everyone's attention here, here everyone, now that the girls have seen the sub; we wanted to let you know today, that the submarine is the way you are getting off the island. Our statistical analysis for that portion of the plan has been determined. Paul and the rest of them were pleased that the system did what it was programmed to do, and then Henry said to Amanda and I that tomorrow we will be able to print out the plotted navigation for the journey. Dustin and Elsie gave high fives and Jim complemented both of them for the work they have done.

Dustin added that we will have Sires message completely decoded and with the mapping and navigation plans, we can start talking about what we will be doing over the next while to prepare. They were all so positive; I did not want to be the party pooper so I jokingly said with a confused looked on my face … so where would a sub come up in the prairies. There was a split second of silence, when they all started laughing and Rosie said the sub is your way off the island silly girl, we know we are not getting you to your doorstep using it she chuckled. When Elsie spoke up, to reassure us that by tomorrow, the plan for our voyage home will all be laid out and plotted and relayed to everyone.

Amanda lifted her glass and said as long as I do not have to drive the sub, I am good with any plan the system or you all have, then she put her hand on her hip and foot down. Then seriously saying we were not leaving here alone, then looked around the group and the Paul … so who is going with us. Amanda played that perfectly and everyone roared. Kevin shouted short straw, which made the group carry on more. Really, I spoke up I had not thought of who would be going with us before and I was instantly curious, how that was going to be decided. Once we had settled, Dustin said looked at Amanda and I and went onto say that they know that there will be three people going with us however, we will not know who until tomorrow. The system will consider the entire plotted journey and match up our skills to coincide with the expertise needed to get you all the way home.

That is amazing I said, and then looked over at Rosie and said I hope that you come with us, Amanda put her hand on Rosie's, and said me too, it will be scary without you. Thank you girls she replied sincerely then looked at us and said now don't be going and getting all sappy, we have a long ways to go.

With the chatting and nibbling, we all were in need of a refill, with Rosie first to the bar who went to grab more beer, and filling the wine glasses. Jessie and Ryan were ready to go home for the evening so with their full glasses and bottle of wine Jessie got off the sub they were saying their good nights and headed home.

While Jessie and Ryan were leaving, Kevin and Dustin were talking about playing a game of virtual golf. Once set on that plan they decided they better get going too, if they were going to play the full eighteen holes. Like two gentlemen they motioned as though they were tipping their hats to us ladies and then saluted to Paul and Jim, jumped in their carts and on their way to the birdcage for a round of golf.

Once Kevin and Dustin were blazing the trail, Henry and Elsie came over to give us hugs and say their good evenings and letting us all know that there were a couple red tubs calling our names. The evening was ending with Janette and Rosie cleaning up the dishes, food and bar. Paul and Jim were hanging with us and Amanda spoke up to thank them for showing us everything today, and now knowing that is how we are leaving is one less thing to think about for me. Today was amazing for sure and we are excited to hear more tomorrow.

Janette gave Rosie a hug and then came to give us hugs and her good nights then took Jim by the hand as they walked to their cart and waved as they drove away. We had our stuff ready and gave Rosie, Paul their hugs, then for fun I asked Amanda if I could drive the pink driving machine back to the palace, when she shot a look at me with her eyes wide open, paused, and with an embellished laugh, she says no! We chuckled together knowing I was only kidding. Okay then, catch you later, I said and waved to Paul and Rosie as I got into the passenger's seat and away we went.

As she drove, I said my brain is on overload and I need to decompress. Amanda agreed and replied that for her some of this is so overwhelming, and we have no choice but to go with it, whatever it is. So true and I think tomorrow will be an information overload kind of day.

As Amanda pulls up to the palace, we can see it looking as wonderful as it always does. It was time for a hoot and of course, there was a pot of coffee ready for us when we came around to the hot tub area. Rosie had the coffee pot on a timer and we could hear it finishing its gurgling as we entered onto the patio. Not even bothering to change our matching outfits, we sat down for a fresh coffee and hoot. We just wanted to be quiet for a bit and again absorb the day.

We enjoyed the hoot and quiet time as we passed it back and forth not saying much, other than me commenting on how cute my feet looked in the fuzzy boots with the bows in the back we did not get into any deep conversation that is for sure. Once we were finished the hoot, we thought it would be nice to go to our room and use our privet balcony tub for two; we could have our smoke and coffee there before we go to bed. We filled our coffees and carefully walked to our room so we did not spill.

Getting into the room I said, I could smell fresh coffee. I looked over at our seating area and see that Rosie had put our room coffee pot on a timer as well, when I hear Amanda gasp no way, what, what, and I see that our privet tub has lit candles around and was filled with the jets lightly bubbling. Rosie even had our bathing suites, towels and housecoats ready. Holly crap that woman is incredible, she better be coming with us for the ride home I said. Amanda replied incredible, no she has to be super human, we giggled a bit over her comment because Rosie does make us wonder, especially at time likes this when we did not even think of it until we were already here.

It only took a couple minutes and we were changed, and into our bathing suites, with all our provisions with us, we were in the tub relaxing.
With the tub having the formed lounge seats, the beautiful lighting and not

feeling any pain, I could feel myself starting to drift and flash through all the stuff I had seen while Amanda was sipping on her coffee thinking to herself. Wow, this is wonderful I said to Amanda to break the silence. You bet momma-bear just what the doctor ordered she says as she lights her smoke. Then she looks over at me with half closed eyes and says after my smoke I am going to bed, I am right with you on that sweetie, I am done like dinner for today.

At least we can sleep in Amanda reminded me as she got up to get out of the warm bubbling water. Not realizing how exhausted we were, when we got out of the tub, we wrapped ourselves in our big fluffy towels crawled up on the bed. Amanda mumbled I will change in a bit, I just need to close my eyes for a minute, yam, me too sweetie was the last thing I remember saying and then it was lights out for both of us.

Chapter Eighteen

As I was awaking, I could feel a rush of anxiety come over me as my eyes opened I could feel my heart beating and sensed that something not good, I did not know what had me feeling that way, I just felt that something was not right. As I lay there I started thinking that the rush that had overcome me, may have something to do with our information we were going to be receiving today.

Amanda started waking up as I look over at her and see her eyes open, still wrapped in her towel and wearing her bathing suit. Aren't you a bit damp I asked her with a smile, I had gotten out of my suite in the middle of the night when I got up for a pee. She grinds and replied, actually no, I am completely dry and comfortable all warped up in the blanket sized towel and proceeds to roll herself off the bed. As she goes to get her housecoat, I was looking over to see what Rosie had out for us this morning.

Much better, I commented aloud when Amanda came over to see that we both had a pair of shorts with pockets and a tank top. Pointed out to Amanda that we can always tell whose is who's, because your stuff is always shorter than mine is, I chuckled. Rosie was very conscious of age appropriate looks.

Then we head over for our coffee and smoke to start our day. We poured our coffee, lit our smoke, and as I sat back in my chair and began to tell Amanda about the rush I felt when I woke up and that I sensed something heavy about the day. Oh, crap she replies, knowing that I have sensed bad news in the past call it woman's intuition. Or sweetie I said smiling and looking at her with a grin, it could have been just gas. No worries my little sunshine, today will be a great day.

We knew there were no plans for the day until later in the afternoon so we took our time getting ready chatting about the sub and joking about the leopard room, we would be staying. As we were finishing getting ready Amanda looked at me, with a curious look and said, I wonder how long it is going to take for us to get home, I am sure we will find that out today sweetie.

As we venture out of our room, and seeing Rosie with her back to us having her coffee, I came out and loudly said good morning Rosie. Who did not even flinch, as I thought I would have startled her and without turning around we could hear her say, wondered when you girls were going to get up.

We approach the table and then she looks with a big smile and looks us up and down to see how well our clothes fit and look. Amanda says you did it again lady, you are amazing and having the tub and coffee ready for us was, I don't mind saying was a little freaky but in a good way. Rosie replies with a grin to Amanda and says, it is no big deal, do not worry I cannot read your minds. I just felt that after the full day you had, that you could possible need some privet alone time.

Then Rosie wanted to let us in on the plan for the day and went on to say that with all the information that we hope to get through today we have decided that we will be starting at noon. Therefore, you do not have a lot of time if you were planning an activity. I replied that we did not have any plans for the morning other then helping you get ready. Rosie looked up at us, raised one eyebrow, and said jokingly, I was done before you girls even thought of opening your eyes and then chuckled.

Well we can at least help set the tables and bring the carts out Amanda said to her, well if you insist Rosie says. More than your help girls I love your company so we can hang out here this morning or we do have a couple hours we could go shopping. Our eyes lit up, shopping, hum that sounds sweet Amanda ads, as the thought ran through my mind for a second, I commented to Amanda, and looked at Rosie to say that may be only two hours of shopping with Rosie, will not be enough time. We all chuckled. I began to say that once Rosie shows us some favorite shopping spots two hours would not be enough when Amanda realized that waiting would be better. We could see that Rosie was glad that we did not choose the shopping for today.

How about we turn the ones on in the lounge and play the machines for a bit, unless anyone is up for a game of pool. Rosie and Amanda both thought that was a great idea, Rosie happy to be close to her kitchen. I could also feel that Rosie was glad that would be entertained and occupied, until the group started to show up. With now having a fun stay in plan, we quickly finished our toast and fruit breakfast.

Rosie being done first stood up to clear the table with Amanda and I helping to load the cart as we were done with our plates. Rosie filled our coffees and was going to take the cart to the kitchen when she said have your smokes girls I will be right back.

Smokes she said, hum I think this day needs to start with a hoot, as I looked over at Amanda with a big smile, who was just grabbing for her cigarette case and put it down as she agreed, I think we need to kick start this day it is going to be an interesting one. We spark the hoot and start passing it back and forth when Amanda said what happened to Rosie she never takes that long in the kitchen we giggled.

As we finish our hoot and half way through our smoke, Rosie emerges from the kitchen. When I say we thought you got lost back there, no, no, I was just putting the final touches on our dinner. Amanda says it is not even noon yet and you are putting the final touches on dinner, wow. Rosie smiled and waved us over to the lounge. All the lights went on and then Rosie asks what kind of music we would like to listen to and it was Amanda that blurted out some good old country and western music that would be good.

Rosie looked up at Amanda a little surprised at her request but found us some good old country music that started softly with Dolly Parton signing coat of many colors. As were getting our selves comfortable at the machines we hear Garth Brooks and a newer song that let us know we were listening to a mix of country music old and new, which was comforting to us.
With the music playing in the background and our games all up, I asked Rosie what kind of music does she listen to normally, and she answered with my music of choice is the sound of the big band. That music just takes me away as I feel the emotion in the music, I am not sure why I like it but I do she smiled.

Dirking coffee and pushing buttons with some wins and some not so big wins, we were having a great time pointing to each other's screens and gasping at what we almost had. Although it was Amanda, that did hit a jackpot on her machine and it would not stop ringing for about a full minute. I gave her a nudge and chuckled too bad, you don't get to take any of the that with you. Amanda gave Rosie and I the sad face but was thrilled with her big win despite not getting any money. Mind you, she was getting high in points and even Rosie commented on how well she was doing.

Before too long, Paul pulls up and comes over to see how we are all doing. We say our good mornings as he pours himself a coffee and props up against a beam beside us so he could watch for a bit. Paul seeing Amanda's score, he complemented her knowing that she had only been playing for such a short time. When Rosie asks him if everything is ready for the presentation and he told her that Elsie and Dustin were just finishing up and they would be here shortly. We did not realize how much time had passed playing the machines and bantering back and forth.

Once Rosie heard that people would be arriving soon she saved her game, looked at us, and said well that was fun girls I really did enjoy our morning but it is time for me to leave this for now. As she jumped down off the tall-padded chair, we asked if there was anything that we could help with yet and she, replied I will let you know when I am ready. As Rosie was leaving the lounge, area Paul said to us that he I like the tunes, as he followed Rosie. We could see them with their backs to us talking quietly together. Amanda and I looked at each other and she we said I hope everything is fine and that they are only talking about their secret affair. We giggled and decided that was enough for us too and started saving our games. Amanda talked to her machine and said I will be back for you later and I will take mine all in hundreds, we laugh and jumped out of our chairs.

Just as we are coming out of the lounge, we see Dustin, Elsie and Henry pull up with everyone smiling and greeting each other Amanda and I were a little more at ease. If doom and gloom was coming, they were not showing it. Then all the sudden Rosie comes out of the kitchen pushing one cart and pulling another Amanda went to help her get them into position and said, no kidding you are ready.

The bar was re- stocked and had a fresh pot of coffee and a large glass urn of punch sitting at the end of the bar. As we mingled with Elsie and Henry for a moment and asked how their tub's were last night they both gleamed with Elsie replying heavenly and Henry expressing that is one of the best feelings as she glances sweetly at Elsie.

Then we see the rest of them coming up the path with Kevin being the last one. With everyone on the patio exchanging friendly greetings and Rosie, making sure they got to the bar to get their drink of choice, Dustin looks over at us and nods to Kevin let us have a hoot before we get started. Sounds good to me as we get out of the way of Jim and Paul setting up the viewing area. Ryan shuffled over with his glass of punch to stand with us as he had nothing he was to be doing but staying out of the way. As we were standing there, Kevin asks in a chipper voice asked if we were pumped, for today and before Amanda or I could answer, Dustin with a huge smile, jumps in and says yes, I am jacked there is some real cool stuff we have learnt. We laughed amongst ourselves as we were passing the hoot around and watching everyone getting ready.

With the rest of the group, hovering and fussing around the food carts and bar while Rosie was telling them about Amanda's big win on the machine this morning. We finish the hoot and quickly had a smoke so we could join the rest of them while they were starting to find their seats.

As we were walking over Rosie pointed out the seats we were to sit in so that we could see the screen and be able to see the group at the same time. Rosie explained, as she pointed that with this group, you never know who is going to have the answer to a question. Even I am surprised by who responds to some of the more recent quires, she looks over the group and smiles acknowledging the talent.

Now that we are all settled, Paul stood up with remote control in hand and announced that Dustin was first up with Elsie and Henry assisting. Dustin thanked everyone for coming and said that he was excited for the presentation today. Dustin opened screen showing a picture of the Rocky Mountains, he looked at us and said I put that in for you. We both smiled and thanked him as he carried on with opening a file named Sires. When the file opened, we could see graphs, charts, and a bunch of writing that did not mean anything to Amanda, I, and looking over at Kevin he seemed confused as well so, I did not feel as bad.

Dustin then started to explain what we were looking at and what it meant to all of us. When Amanda thought of Sires being in space, we changed our searches and incredibly, we did not find him in space we found him in the ocean on the other side of the world from us. To our shock, we discovered that he had been working on an underwater community that he fled to instead of our island. Obviously, like this place, we are sworn to secrecy and if we do not know about something, we can never lie about it.

Elsie piped up and said jokingly; yes and it only took him a hoot and an espresso to calm down once discovering the secret underwater community. Everyone started to chuckle when Dustin said I am all over it now and I get it. Carrying on he says as he clears his throat, from what Elsie and Jessie have concluded to remain invisible the underwater community has limited communications can only transmit one message that is no longer then thirty three seconds at a time, and only every twelve hours. We have been collecting data and piecing all the encrypted messages and there are no more visuals from Sires only coded messages.

The breakdown of the messages are first, that he has confirmed that we from Alberta, Canada however, our names have not been released.

Second was that he was starting to receive our plotted travel plans and schedule and noted his above ground intentions to assist with the last leg of our journey home. Knowing that he is able to help with the above ground travel arrangements relieves a lot of pressure on us, as we have limited resources above ground and no longer connected to the outside world. Elsie was able to write the program so that Sire will start receiving the chart it in bits, over the next few weeks using their thirty-three second window every twelve hours.

Thirdly, Dustin said before looking down, Sire was quite adamant that for our guest's well being and safety that we be smuggled back into Canada. Hugh, I mumbled glancing over at Amanda. This is where it starts to get complicated. Amanda and I both sit up straight in our chairs and said smuggled, why smuggled, it sounds so bad. Looking around the table, we could see that the others were not surprised. Rosie stepping into the silence to smooth the suggestion by saying no worries girls, it will all make sense.
Dustin began again, we realized from the message, the reason we would smuggle you in was to get you there without turning your homecoming into a circus. I take no pleasure in saying this but the harsh reality girls is that by the time we do get you home, you will have most likely already be

presumed dead. This is where the politics comes in Dustin finished and Janette took over by saying with the government issuing a death, certificate your passports and no longer any good, and our names will come up in all systems as deceased. The fear then would be that you could be, accused of fraud. We could not get you through any international boarder without huge explanation and delays.

We can give you new identities with your history being mirror image just change your names. Amanda puts her hand up a bit and says to Janette, but the government will think we no longer exist. Oh, you will exist and have the exact same personal history; it is that you will only have different birthdates, and social insurance number, as you call them in Canada. We can do all of that remotely and without detection, in essence bring you back to life on paper. We will recreate your financial history and set you up for the rest of your lives she had a big grin and wiggled her eyebrows. Then I asked what about our partners, Janette, everything can stay the same with them, the only time you would need to use your new names is when dealing with anything government, financial or passports and with not having to work anymore, you can rebuild your relationships and redefine your lives together.

Then we hear from Paul who says if I may interject, getting you ladies home safe and sound is priority however bear in mind to us the secrecy of the island is paramount.

Getting you girls home is going to be easier then the elaborate story you are going to have to tell and maintain for the rest of your lives for the people of past. I will summarize for you all the script that has been generated as the easiest to maintain. You will have the script ingrained by the time you are home.

Remember this concocted story explaining your absence and arrival home is for your safety, if you try to tell anyone the truth about this place, they will think you are off your rocker crazy and being gone for so long, it would not take much for people to be convinced you are. You are not going to survive all of this to be ridiculed or locked up Paul chuckled, not on my watch. Awe that is so comforting I said, but what could ever explain three months away and presumed deceased. Hum, at least that is getting easier to think of, I said aloud. Amanda looked eager to hear the story we have to remember forever.

Paul then went onto say that our close family will hear the story of you surviving the plane crash as you did, and that you were left stranded on an island that incredibly did have a small village of people. The people on the island do not speak any English; there is no electricity or communications. The only thing that matters is that they took good care of you and treated you very well. When a container ship came by the leaders were able to bring it in close enough to put you on board the ship coasting a small fortune that meant nothing to the people of the island. Before we left, the people of the village gave us two bags of American money and put us on the ship. The crew did not speak any English and they kept a close eye on you while you were on the ship for four days. Although the crew was respectful, you did not do anything without first motioning your intent, like pointing up when wanting to go on deck. The container ship docked in Vancouver where you could have contacted your family but were afraid to. You take a limousine back to Edmonton where, Amanda will contact a trusted friend to arrange Aaron going to LBs that evening and wait for a package. Where you arrive together and connect them first.

There are only two people you can tell the real story to and that being LB and Aaron. They will have to understand the on paper, identity change. I hope that you follow through on the entire plan, which is that once home, you are to show them verification of the truth that cannot be told to your partners. The proof that you are not lying will be in the same form as a mission impossible instruction, once the message has been viewed it will self-destruct, destroying all evidence. You are then to higher, a privet jet and get the heck out of dodge. Then you can send for your other family members and only explain the fixed story to them. Being family, and using your real names, they will be so happy that you are vacationing and home safe and suddenly wealthy; the fixed story will satisfy them.

At that point, being out of the country if there is any media generated you will be wealthy enough to shield yourselves from publicity and the story will fade away. Well, that is a quick rundown of the little fib and secret we will all share. Does anyone have any questions Paul asks the group? As I stood up to get a glass of punch, still taking the in the story. Amanda asked so if that is the story we are going to tell anyone we have to explain it too, what then explains the changed identity.

It was Henry that spoke out to answer Amanda's question this time and she said that for the very few encounters you would have the changed identity, can simply be explained away as trying to keep a low profile. It will be because of your newfound riches that people may be more nosey then your identities, she chuckled. Rosie called out break time and the group was all quick to rise and move around.

As we were getting up I said to the group, I hope my memory is good enough to tell the exact same story the same over and over again, I laughed. Henry said we have that covered for you too I explain in a bit she winked as she headed for the punch.

A few of us moved over to have a smoke while Rosie, Jessie and Janette opened up a couple palters of sandwiches, with cheese and pickles on the side to snake on while we carry on.

Having our smoke, I looked at Amanda and smiled making the motion of the head exploding with my hands, which made her smile. The information was very interesting Amanda commented and we are listening so intently, that it will take just a little bit to absorb. I am all-good though, and I know there are a lot more questions to be asked and answered before the day is out so bring it on. Dustin was right with her and said okay lets carry on and as we approached the table Rosie made sure that we all got to the sandwich bar and had full glasses before we sat down again.

Once settled, I hear Dustin say to Jim my good man can you please explain to us how we are bring them home. Jim stood up and Dustin handed him the remote control where Jim filled the screen showing a world map. The world map had no names on any landmasses or water all we see is an X in the middle of an Ocean and a dark blue zigzag dotted line that travels half way around the world away from the X and stops in Alaska. Almost knowing the answer I asked why there were no names on the map he is showing us. Does it really matter he said jokingly, I thought for a second and nope, it really does not matter, I never knew my geography anyway I smiled. A solid green line on the map depicted the flight home.

When arriving at the pickup zone in the Alaska harbor, an icebreaker ship will set anchor at least fifty feet away from the sub to ensure there is no possible contact. The icebreaker will send out a jet boat to retrieve, Jessie Ryan Colleen and Amanda. Exposing Jessie and Ryan is the biggest risk we are taking however; we have to ensure that you get on that jet so the plan accepted Ryan and Jessie escorting you.

You will disembark onto a jet boat, then onto the icebreaker and into doc within forty-five minutes. The captain of the icebreaker will then drive you to the Alaska airport where Sire's very special privet jet will be waiting. Once the plane is off the ground the icebreaker captain will take Ryan and Jessie back to the sub and the journey home begins for the team. You will land at a privet airstrip just outside of Edmonton, Jim pointed to the solid green line on the map showing a direct rout home, and where he finished by saying and there will be a waiting limo to take you home.

Before you ask, Ryan chimed in and said that the submarine travel will take ninety-six hours; four days and the flight from Alaska to Edmonton will take a little over three hours before landing in Edmonton. The reason the sub will take so long is that the plotted rout is definite the longest rout however it will keep us out of all shipping lines, avoid sonar, radar and with the our kinetic2 electrical plus surrounding the vessel even be shielded from satellite imaging and just stay out of everyone's way to travel undetected. Elsie admitted that she was surprised when the plotted rout had us disembarking in Alaska instead of off the coast of Vancouver.

It was Ryan that realized Alaska was chosen because Sire can manipulate customs and flight manifests without being detected. To land in Vancouver that has suffered some repercussions from the tsunami would not be idea and put the plan at risk.

Amanda then asked the million-dollar question and looking around the table with a smile, so who drew the short straw and is coming with us. She looked at Kevin who was the one who indicated that the short straw was the way the crew was going to be determined. There was a chuckle around the table, when Paul sat up in his chair and said the selected crew, not by picking straws, rather chosen for their skills. You crew will be Jessie, Ryan, Rosie and myself. When Paul listed out the crew, both Amanda and I were taken back and pleasantly surprised because we would have never through that Ryan and Jessie would be part of our journey home. Both Ryan and Jessie gave the group the two thumbs up indicating they are excited and ready for the challenge. Amanda and I gestured back with our two thumbs up, with Amanda saying this will be awesome, Ryan nodded back.

Paul went onto say Jessie will work the intricate navigations and Ryan will manage vessel operations, So what is your job, I asked. Paul gave a big smile and said I am the captain. Rosie blurted out a laugh by title only girls; it is really Jessie and Ryan who will be sailing you home. I will be going along to make sure you are all fed and watered, and then said looking at Paul and I am the chief. With the expression of authority she had on her face when she gave her title, started the rest of the group laughing. It was clear that Rosie was boss.

I look over to see that Kevin is quiet and taking all of this in as he was not part of the island systems component, even though he understands this all he was hearing the departure information for the first time.

Next up Jim says, bring the group back into focus, we will not know the exact departure date. Jim flips to another screen that shows a calendar with the systems timer that is currently indicating that we have less than ninety days before the island will allow any part of the island to open. The island knows the exit rout chosen and will start the countdown of the bottom core implosion thirty-six hours before. Once the blasted core settles and clears away which could take up to twelve hours, then that is when the crew and passengers get on board, submerge and descend through the core and then out to the open ocean.

That is when Kevin did pipe up and says we will have one heck of a send off party for you while the core settles he looked at us girls and smiled big, as he went to get up. Paul then said to the group let's stop here for a refill and snakes. Rosie, and all the ladies agreed, and as we all started getting Amanda and I getting some punch when we seen that Dustin and Kevin had already filled their glasses and both had a hoot lit. We mossy right on over and noticed that so did everyone else, to stretch and mingle.

Amanda went over to Jessie and Ryan and said she was glad they were coming on the journey with us and they thanked her, because if it was not for us being here they would have never had the chance to prove their skills and be part of an adventure. I was standing Jim and Janette, with Janette asking how we were holding up and I looked at her and without giving the question any thought I replied, surprisingly well and chuckled, showing one hand holding a punch glass and the other a hoot. I just worried that I will not be able to keep the story straight. No worries Colleen and Henry can explain that part better than anyone can.
Breaks over Rosie called out to the group, we have a couple more things to go over and we can stop for the day. We all started back to our chairs with

Henry standing with remote this time.

I understand the concern about the difficulty in keeping secrets and in this case a story consistent for all time. I have created a filter she says as she opens the screen to show a simple round disc piece of filter paper, something like a paper coffee filter would look like under a microscope. What we were looking at was interwoven paper threads in a disc shape the size of the end of a cigarette and the thickness of paper. Henry showed us on the screen that the disc we were looking at had been magnified over a thousand times, and went onto say that the actual disc size is no larger than the head of a pin.

Amanda and I looked at each other and were starting to put what she was saying together and I reached for her hand knowing that what Henry was talking about was going to go in us. We look up and see that everyone has reassuring faces and Rosie waves her hand, and lips to us no worries.

Relax Henry says to the group the intent would be to implanted one of these microscopic filters into the left temple which is programmed to disallow the individual to tell any other story then what has been given. You will retain all of your memories however will only be able to speak of then together. I want you all to know that this device was created out of need but it will serve us all on the island as well. This will allow us to leave the island easier if we desire, because we can now block all secrets.

Dustin jumps in by saying that I know you have all seen the spy shows where they get their information out of people in all sorts of gruesome and nasty ways but with this device, drugs nor hypnotizing will not change the story. Henry has created a unique device that is undetectable, and would not even show up in an MRI. The sad part of the creation is that the rest of the world can never know he says to Henry.

Thank you Dustin for the reminder she smiled back at him, now ladies what do you think about the filter. The whole procedure of injecting the disc just under the skin in the left temple will only take ten minutes, with not even a band-aid required when done. I trusted Henry and Amanda trusted me, and knowing for certain that neither one of us wanted to skew this up for them in any way. I asked so when the disc would be implanted. Implying we were open to the plan and not resisting, we could sense Henry's appreciation in the trust we are bestowing her. The implanting of the disc would be done approximately three days before departing so that we can monitor and ensure all is good.

The program will activate once your partners have seen, and have had for them confirmed, the real story of living in an invisible island, and that is where the wealth and the new identities have come from. The program will assume the story of taking a limo from Vancouver once that has been. Your partner's confirmation is also acceptance of keeping the secret that will feel as though it is a dream and fade in their memories, as the fixed story is all that will be, spoken. The memories of your time here will only come to you when you are both alone and together. Upon the death of one of you, the memory will be totally blocked and no longer accessible to the one living. This place is only special to you, together.

In the fixed story, you will still have had wonderful experiences and face new challenges so the stories will still be good, just not as good as this one would be, she laughed then took a bow and clicked off the screen. We all clapped as she was sitting down, understanding better that what she had created was masterful.

Are we all good with the information of the departing, for now Dustin asked the group who all looked around at each other and thinking then nodding positively, we are good Kevin gave the final approval?

Then Paul stands up to address the group, and proudly says, last but not least is the schedule which he popped up onto the screen for everyone to see. Paul using his laser pointer showed us that our names were there more than previous schedule of three hours and only for two days. Which was fine for us and we were helping at the farm, which was all-good. Paul commented that it is harvest time and we can really use your help now. Rosie spoke up and said the work will help keep you two occupied as leaving grows nearer.

Then we hear Paul say with a pitched voice, hey who messed with the schedule he sees a blocked out day and when he opened, the message said Rosie, Colleen, Amanda shopping day. Really Rosie, Paul looks over her and gives a wink with Jim saying, yup, Rosie is the only one who would get away with that one and get's the group chuckling, making Rosie blush on purpose. As people were going for their drink and sitting back in their chairs, Dustin speaks up and said that in part of the message decoding that Elsie Jessie and I, realized the great wealth that Sire's is extending to the new identities to ensure you are able to carry on without restraint and live out your lives in style.

With not wanting to come across like there was any expectation, I did let the group know that frankly being wealthy when we get home does help make the identify change easier to accept and then looked at Amanda to observe if she was on the same page, which she was. I was as shocked as Amanda was, by the group's quick reaction making sure that we had no cause for question or any guilty about the money that is being given, that is who Sire is.

Kevin asked Dustin if there was anything else deciphered from the compiled messages. He answered that they only have segments and are continually threading them together, as we receive the transmissions. Dustin asked Elsie and Jessie if they had any updates from their end and they had not made any progress as of this morning, we are expecting another transmission come in shortly and we will see if that completes something for us.

Rosie stands up and asks the group, does anyone have any other questions there was silence, then one by one, Rosie pointed to each of us to make sure that we were all satisfied for now. Great Rosie said, the bar is open and dinner will be served in fifteen minutes. We all got up from the table and all of us ladies helped Rosie clear the tables and get them ready for dinner. As Rosie and Henry were going to the kitchen, Rosie calls back to Amanda and I says go have your smoke girls, before dinner she said. You don't have to twist our arms as we get out of the way and go stand over by all the fellows who were just doing the same and as we get closer we can hear them joking with Paul about him being the captain.

Amanda and I were talking quietly that this was getting us all excited for going home, when Kevin passed us a hoot before dinner and asked if we were pumped now. Yes, from both of us this place and all you amazing people will be very hard to leave.

Just then, Rosie and Henry come out of the kitchen pulling the two serving carts that they parked and opened the lids to show us that is was salad and past night. There were four different salads to choose and then spaghetti and meatballs, lasagna, chicken fettuccine. There was also, garlic and cheese toast.

It did not take long for everyone to dig in and fill their plates; we were all hungry after taking in so much information, sipping on punch and having the odd puff throughout the day. Even Amanda had a full plate and was sitting down and eating before me.

As we were eating, a odd question came to mind and I asked the group, what if when I get home LB has moved on and does not want me. Oh my sakes alive, do not think like that Janette says abruptly, you will only have been gone a few months LB will still be grieving.
With Kevin making a joke and light of my concern-saying lady, if there is another woman taking your place already, you jump back in that limo higher a privet jet and go anywhere in the world and enjoy your life. I am only kidding girl, Kevin says to me.
Your fellows are going to be so crazy, ecstatic when you get home, it will be a reunion to remember for sure.

I went onto say, that everything seems so well organized and you all are so sure and confident of every step, I want to thank you all from the bottom of our hearts and want you to all know, that we appreciate it all. We all raised our glasses with cheers. The group acknowledges that they valued our trust and that our situation has written a new chapter in their lives that otherwise would not have been, with choosing to live in an invisible island.

We went back to finishing our dinner that was incredible. Watching Kevin, Dustin and Ryan eat was almost painful, Amanda even commented to them that they were all going to burst; Paul got a chuckle out of her saying that to them, so matter a fact like. After eating too much Amanda and I both went to get up and grab another glass of punch, it was so good and you could not taste the alcohol making the drink more enjoyable but still potent. We moved over to sit in the hot tub lounge area to sit in the big reclining comfortable chairs do digest. It was not long before the rest of the group found themselves a spot by the hot tub and relaxing not saying anything, just listening to the water swirling and the soft music playing that Rosie turned on. The smokers were smoking and the rest just quietly moaned.

I think we all smelt the fresh coffee at the same time as we seem to come alive and started moving about, with Dustin and Kevin discussing the better brandy and Paul disagreeing with them both. They seemed very serious about the better one Ryan and Jim were chatting back and forth on which Scotch to have and us ladies had baileys of course and a cup of Rosie's fresh coffee. Sitting back in our seats, we were capping off the day talking about how cool the sub ride will be.

That is when Dustin and Kevin let Amanda and I know that neither one of them could do eight days in that vessel no matter how big it was. Henry confirmed that these two do not do well in confined spaces. I squarely up my face and reply but isn't this island a confined space. Henry laughed at my comment as her and Elsie were getting ready to leave. Before leaving Henry let all of us know that, they are both enjoying all of this very much and that they are glad we landed on their island and then said their good nights, with Rosie walking them out to their cart.

After Amanda and I had been chatting with and thanking Jim, Janette, Jessie and Ryan about our coming voyage, it was time for them to get going as well. As they were all leavening Paul, could see that Dustin and Kevin were fading and give them a shout saying come on you young fellows, it time to be getting you home. They both struggled to get out of their chairs but were fine once they got on their feet. Dustin and Kevin came over and gave Rosie, Amanda and me, a hug before leaving.

Well ladies this was a great day and Rosie fantastic food again, thank you for having us. Paul took Rosie's hand, gave it a kiss, and came to give us a hug and away he went. Once the headlights were gone, Rosie turned around, looked at us, and said with authority now you girls grab a coffee and you go to your room. Not able to hold back her smile any longer she said only kidding ladies, it is just that you both look beat and I think that if you go have a smoke and finish your coffee that bed will look real inviting.

Amanda answered before I could saying a word, that sounds like a perfect idea Rosie I am pooped, we had a group hug and then went to our room. Once in the room, we flopped down into the chairs and were going to have a smoke when I said I wanted to change first, good idea Amanda put her smoke down and we changed into our housecoats and then went back for our smoke and coffee.

We sat and I said to Amanda can you believe what this is going to happen, it seems so easy to say but we are really going to travel half way around the world in a sub and when we get home we are going to have new identities and we will be rich. We just looked at each other speechless for a minute and after a couple puffs of our smokes, Amanda looked up at me and said I am done mom, I have to go sleep. I am right with you sweetie, we butt our smokes out and both climb into bed. We had a big hug and sweet dreams and snuggled into the covers.

Chapter Twenty

When waking up on this particular day, knowing what we now know and being clear on timeline, our daily lives were about to become routine for a while, laying there thinking over our routine for the next while, I realized I totally felt at ease.

We got up that morning, loved our clothes as always, enjoyed our morning sit together, and getting ready and then we found ourselves whispering when we started talking about having money and what it will be like, feeling guilty or greedy for talking about it. We were not, owed anything; so we thought and if it was true, we did not want to jinx it. Why are we whispering Amanda said, I have no idea I replied to her, it is not like it is a bad thing, is it. We chuckled and went out to meet Rosie.

Rosie gave us a chipper good morning as we sat for coffee as she asked us if after our sleep we had any questions we had thought of from the summary we received yesterday. Amanda and I looked over at each other and I did not have anything specific in mind Amanda thought for a second and said nothing off the top of my head, but I sure am glad that you are coming with us. I think I would not feel as comfortable about all of this is you were not coming along.

While I was going to take a sip of coffee, I had the sad thought and looked at both of them before saying aloud, at the end of our journey to Alaska and once we get off the sub, we will never be in contact ever again. Yes, Rosie say's in a somber voice, that will be tear jerking however, we do not want to dwell on that now and Henry did say that if we want them to be able to track us for the rest of our lives, that can be done through tracking the filter. She was not going to activate the tracker if you ladies did not want us too.

A tracker Amanda asks, what would a tracker do? Rose answers that Henry is the expert but I got that it could see where you were in the world and follow your vitals and health as long as you live. We would know when you had a cold she laughed, but that is about it. We would not be able to communicate. Hum Amanda gave a half smile I think I like the idea of you being able to see me. I agreed, I would have no problem with that at all and might even be comforting in our subconscious, because we are going to forget about the implant are we not. When you are together, you will remember and can share the comfort thought of us here watching over you, but you are right alone it will not be a memory at all.

We went back to nibbling on breakfast, when I looked around and seen that everything was already cleaned up and then asked what Rosie was doing today. I remembered that there were no names or activities on the schedule for today but forgot to ask Paul why yesterday.

Rosie said that today is a holiday for us girls. With barley, being able to keep track of time in a day or what day it is, what is the Holiday name Amanda asked? No name Rosie responded, we just have it in our calendar that one day out of every thirty days is a down day for us all. No scheduled activities or responsibilities, however if we want to work we do. The only actual holiday we have all clung to is, Christmas, Rosie's face just lit up as she started saying that we love all the festivities of Christmas.
We celebrate for three days, you will see girls, and we will show you how to celebrate Christmas. We have a three-year tradition that has become the highlight of the year for us; until you girls came, alone she said and laughed. Even Christmas cannot top, us having guests this year though, Rosie gave a big smile and gushed and you will be here to see it all, that is fantastic. Rosie picked up her coffee, sat back in her chair, and reminded us that Christmas is not far off.

We were ready for a smoke and Rosie knew it and before we could get up to smoke away from the table She got up and brought over the ashtray and said let's just sit here for a while girls, we have nothing to do and nowhere to go for right now. I filled up my coffee and we lit our smokes and sat back. With Rosie looking like she had something on her mind Amanda asked slowly so, what you thinking. Rosie smiled and looked over at Amanda and said what I want for Christmas, she laughed. We were not expecting her to say that for sure and chuckled with her and did ask so what would you want for Christmas Rosie. All I want from you girls, is something you make yourselves and I can keep forever.

Rosie reminded us that they will always be able to look back at your time here but that she wanted something we make so I can feel your touch and you will be with me for all time. Her saying that brought tears to my eyes and I could see that Amanda was feeling the same. Awe Rosie we love you so much Amanda says as we lean over closer to her and smiling. Will we be able to take anything with us as a reminder of you, I asked. She looks over at me, I will make sure you do girls.

As we were sitting and chatting we see Paul come up the drive. Paul came up to the patio and said hey girls looks like you are enjoying your day of leisure. Dusting and Kevin were bugging me to make ribs again so we are going to BBQ ribs at my place this evening if we would like to join. We are not having a bunch of fixings but if you want to eat your fill of the best ribs in town, you need to be there. Rosie looks up at Paul and says that sounds good to me, I have not started dinner yet, what do you say ladies ribs for dinner. For sure that does sound good although I still fill full from yesterday Amanda replied

Paul was glad to hear we were going to come for his BBQ ribs so thanked us for accepting the invitation and as he turned to get back into his cart, remember ladies it is not about quantity it is all about the quality. He waves and says catch you later, as he takes off down the hill. As he was leaving, I asked why he did not just use the glasses to send the invitation; Rosie says oh Paul, no he is not a fan of them and prefers the personal touch.

Well ladies Rosie says, we lots of time to take it easy so how about you girls go have a relax at the hot tub and a hoot while I have just a couple things to do. I will back for a coffee in just a bit. We all get up and clear off the table together and then Rosie, thanks girls now go sit and take a load off and pushed the small serving cart into the kitchen.

We get ourselves comfortable and I go to grab us a hoot when I open it and see that our shiny container is getting low, I showed Amanda we only had two let, we will have to let a special somebody see later Amanda smiled. We passed the hoot back and forth when Amanda said I think I can smell the ribs cooking. She was right; I could smell them then too. I was getting up for coffee and brought over the pot when Amanda noticed that Rosie had been gone a while and we had not heard any noise coming out of the kitchen. I was filling Amanda's coffee when out popped Rosie from the kitchen looking ready.

Rosie had changed out of her light colored scrubs and was wearing a navy colored pare they fit her real well and had a casual look to them with her pants rolled up, ready for a beach party. Rosie comes over to us and says now I will have my coffee and baileys while you two change, you do not want to get BBQ sauce on what you are wearing.

Good idea, we will do that and be right back. We could sense that she was ready to go and we know that she usually liked to be the first one anywhere, so we got up and went to our room to see what she had out for us. When we got in our room Amanda, I burst out laughing, and I am sure everyone heard us when we saw that we had the matching scrubs to Rosie's. We could hear her laughing from inside our room. We quickly change still chuckling and making sure, we rolled our pants up just like hers and came out to show her that we were ready to eat ribs.

We were still seeing this as comical as we sat down, to gather our stuff and let Rosie finish her drink. Amanda pipes up and says I'll drive and like a shot Rosie says, shot gun. Amanda's face dropped and I sat up, that was so like home, when Amanda looks at me and says you snooze, you lose. We all started getting up and walking to the pink driving machine when I said to them both from the back, I feel naked I do not have my go cup. Rosie looked at me like I was serious, and was about to ask Amanda to hold on when I said no, no I am only kidding I am all good. I think that is the first time you have let us leave without them I said to Rosie, your right girl it is.

Amanda had us at Paul's beach house in no time flat and when we pull up the only ones there were Paul, Kevin and Dustin. As we are getting out of the cart Rosie says to Paul, the others are not coming are they, how did you guess Paul answers? Simple, today is a couple's day and I am sure they did not want to hurt your feels and they certainly knew there would be no waste. Paul was not at all upset or concerned because in the background he could hear Dustin and Kevin already talking about dividing the leftovers.

With us all out of the cart, the fellows all noticed that we were wearing the same thing, and did not know if we were being funny or if this was something chicks do so, Paul being the gentleman he says you all look great sounding a little unsure of himself. When Rosie looks around and says with attitude, we know we look great and these are our, BBQ rib eating outfits and without taking a breath she goes on to say and no one has offered us a beer yet. Rosie had us all chuckling as the fellows now realizing that no, this is not something chicks would normally do.

We had our beer in seconds and could see that the only things on the table were large plates, a basket of napkins and metal buckets to put the bones in. There were not even forks on the table, and when Amanda saw that she said to Paul, so all that we are having is BBQ ribs and beer and we are using our hands to eat, do I have that right. Paul, Dustin and Kevin thinking this was cool, Amanda cracked, and you wonder why the others could not make it. We all laughed; given where we were, it does sound a little primitive.

Amanda went right over to Paul, gave him a hug, and said I love the dinner I have smelled all afternoon, I was only joshing you. Then Kevin said loudly okay everyone take your seats Paul's famous BBQ ribs are ready for some serious attention. We all find a seat; Rosie asks if anyone would like another bear, with Dustin and Kevin asking her to bring one each. Paul put a full rack of ribs on each of our plats with Amanda's looking bigger then her; we looked at each other and whispered there is no way.

Well dig in people and enjoy, the napkins are wet and warm, you are going to need them he says proudly as he sits down to his plate. I look over at Dustin and see that he actually put on an oversized man bib and when he seen me looking at him he said aloud, what, this is how I eat ribs, and with a rib in his fist, he took a big bit and smiled trying to keep his lips shut with his mouth full.

There was no talking for about ten minutes straight other then Kevin asking Paul for another rack of ribs we were all hands in and elbow deep in BBQ sauce, they were tender, juicy and amazing.

Once we came up for air I was surprised at how much both Amanda and I were actually able to eat and, I think the rest of them also noticed that we did very well, for having a rack of ribs on our plates that looked like dinner at the Flintstones. I did not say that aloud, but I sure knew I was going to say that to Amanda when we are in our room, she would laugh her ass off when she envisions the appearance.

As we were finishing Dustin looked up from his plate and oh, yes what was to funny this afternoon that made me wound my jester in my game any way? Rosie smirked and said that was the girls when they seen that we had matching outfits, sorry about your jester dude, the rest of them thought that was funny and all I said was oop's I hope he will be okay. Dustin assured us that her would be fine, knowing that we were really only talking about a video game character.

We had our fill, and had to use at least one cloth to get all the sauce off and then got up from the table and moved to have our smokes and finish our beers. Amanda opens our shiny box, shows Kevin, revealing only two of his special smokes left. Thanks, for the reminder Amanda, hang on I have something for you. Kevin walks over to his cart and brings back a cigar box of a verity of cigarettes and very special cigarettes. That should hold you over for a while he says and winks at us. Dustin looks at Amanda holding the box and says, I know where I am going when I run out he chuckled.

We had stood around and were chatting about how beautiful the lake and the waterfall looked, when I asked the group if there was a chance that we were going to get to see the boats behind the waterfall before we leave. Paul spoke up and he said that there may be one window of opportunity to see them when we implode the core. That would be the only time we could manage the waterfall long enough for us to have a look. It will be a while yet, before we have detailed ocean movement information once the core is open, to know if it would be safe to suspend the waterfall. We will see ladies, they are a sight Rosie commented, I hope you get the chance as we see her try and hold back a yawn.

Seeing Rosie look tired, I spoke up and said I think I am ready to call it a night if that is okay with you girls, both Amanda and Rosie took the cue and started giving their hugs and thanking Paul for ribs and for inviting us, when all the sudden we hear Rosie yell out shotgun. They guy's just laughed when they saw our faces because we did not know that she calls it all the time, never misses.

We chuckled as we were getting in the cart, with Rosie whispering to us, yes they can clean up that BBQ sauce mess. Home girls, Rosie said, which sounded strange to us because we have only called it the palace and have never called it home. We both answering cheerily mumbling aha, when I said home James and tapped Amanda on the shoulder. As we were pulling up the driveway, I know Rosie sensed our awkwardness although she did not comment or question.

Walking onto the patio, Rosie gives us a big hug and says, ladies you are a dream to be with and I enjoy your company immensely, she said so sincerely. Then with a big grin, however I am going to bed I think the last few days have caught up with me, or it is the ribs, either way I will see you girls in the morning.

We were also done for the day so off to our room we followed right behind Rosie with Amanda carrying the big cigar box full of goodies we hear Rosie call back to us sweet dreams. Once in the room we go to our sitting area and see what goodies we had in the box. I look over to see that there is coffee waiting for us so we figured that we could stay awake long enough for a cup of coffee and a smoke.

When we settled into our seats and finished snooping through the box that had several packages of four rolled hoots in each package with strange names on them and a couple more packages of the pretty colored and designed cigarettes. Cool Amanda says and I said not as cool as what I thought you looked like sitting behind that rack of ribs on your plate. Wasn't that something, she paused as I could hardly contain myself, so what was it she asked as I had already started laughing and broke out saying you looked like you were having dinner at the Flintstones. I caught Amanda so off guard that she almost spit out her mouth full of coffee and I had to laugh into a pillow. The vision was priceless, we laughed about that for a few minutes trying to have our smokes and coffee. Once we settled it was time for bed, so we cleaned up a bit more and climbed into bed. Amanda rolled over close to me, and said I am so full, me to sweetie me to. Love you was that last thing whispered.

Chapter Twenty-One

Every morning was becoming more and routine, we were part of the daily life here now and having cloths, and meals taken care of, learning new things all the time without pressure, and where cocktail and happy hour with extraordinary people being always informative and a constant. We work and being around positive people, time was starting to pass by quicker. It is true that time flies when you are having fun. Having all the toys and activities, we have in our spare time, improved our golf game, playing virtual golf and I have gotten much better on the water board.

One morning we woke up and seen that our outfits for the day had bells and mistletoe on our shirts. Although Rosie was talking about Christmas a lot more, she was not countdown. When it came to time, Amanda and I chose not to keep track.

The schedule Paul creates is a three hundred and sixty five day spreadsheet with continuous blocks of one to seven days with only week numbers for the year was listed without the name of the month. We just never bothered to know the date base on which week it was in the year.

Although we knew, Christmas here would be like none we have ever experienced; this was going to be a tough time for us. Even thinking for a second that our partners lives are devastated while we sit in paradise, is too much to bear. There are definitely thoughts that we have to avoid and are sensitive to; Christmas will make it hard not to think of our family at home.

When we came out to great Rosie for Breakfast, her face was lit up as we gaze around in amazement, to see that the entire patio transposed into a winter wonderland. There were lights, garlands and Christmas flowers everywhere. Rosie asks us if we know what today was and with a pause, looking at each other and then looked back at her, we knew what day it was, we had not forgotten the blocked out day on the calendar. We did not want to be rude and ask because Rosie had not mentioned it the night before, which we were expecting her to do. When she did not bring it up we were too shy to.

Right on, we are going shopping I said and then asked Rosie, so how close are we to Christmas anyway, oh we have a few days she said calmly. Oh, my word, you have to be kidding me, I was shocked; I know that Amanda and I were intentionally not paying attention or talking much about the days and weeks passing to avoid getting anxious about our leaving. Then Rosie clarifies dates seeing on our faces that we were clueless of the date. We could see that she was happy to spend the day together.

The feeling of excitement did come over me, however it was not for shopping or that Christmas was coming it was, that I had a rush or flash come over me, of Amanda and I pulling up to the house in the limo. My body language indicated I was excited for the day; I just kept the fleeting sentiment that we are going home soon, to myself.

As we were chatting and Rosie says you have, your smokes and I will get our provisions for our shopping day. Paul pulls up with his cart, to drive us to the bunkers. We were having our smoke as Paul come onto the patio with a big smile and good morning, as he walks over to the coffee pot and pours himself a coffee. When he says dragging out his words, so where is she, knowing the answer, we look up with a smile and point to the kitchen at the same time Rosie comes through the swinging doors.
Paul comes and sits by us as Rosie walks closer with three go cups, and a full picnic basket. You girls are nuts making a day out shopping, I will never understand it Paul says shaking his head. Rosie was quick to remind him that she spent the day up there with him when he was looking for stuff to change one room in his house. Yes but that is not close shopping for the day he replied, if it helps Rosie comments I want new placemats chuckling at him. When Amanda says, shopping is just another amazing attribute, of the feminine side. Rosie liked Amanda's outlook.

While we were finishing our coffee and smoke, I asked Paul why he was driving us. He replied, with a smirk and looked over at Rosie and went onto to say, well I do not need to drive you there as much as I will need to drive you home, your cart won't hold a day's worth of shopping, especially if you get those placements. Paul winked at us and then said I figured I might as well drive you there and back.

Rosie pipes up are we ready girls, let's blow this popsicle stand she says, Paul grabbed the picnic basket and pretended that it was very heavy by walking slanted as we all chuckled, who says that any more Amanda gave Rosie a hug as we walked towards Paul's cart.

I thought Amanda traveled a little quick sometimes but we were down the palace hill and up the Bunker Hill in a blink of an eye. Us girls were hanging on tight and enjoying the quick ride. When we get to the parking and picnic area before the entrance of the bunkers, we see Jim and Janette just coming out looking like they had a cart full and fun.

We were excited now because this was our first time to see how this worked and what was available. We said our good mornings in passing and Rosie asked if we would see them later at the café as Paul help load them up; for sure we are taking advantage of the blocked out day too Janette smiled at us girls.

We wave as they take off down the hill, when Paul turns to Rosie and says just let me know when you have had enough of the shopping nonsense he laughs and jumps into his cart and waves as he takes off down the hill.

Okay now girls, let me show you how this is done and you let me know what you want to see Rosie walks us up to the large arched entrance. We walk up to the computer and she shows us that all our names are listed so we open our cart and pick the department, store or designer and the system will create a shopping path for us.

What is we all want to see different things I asked. Good question the system will compile all the shopping and create a path that lets us all see what we want in the shortest amount of time. The carts are uploaded the programmed with the travel rout and they drive themselves. Amanda says how about you do your shopping list and we will go from there.

Okay then Rosie says, the first place I want to go is the Christmas store, and then to the Kitchen corner. In honor of you ladies being here this Christmas

we have decided to make our Christmas Eve dinner a formal one. With the food we prepare we need comfortable clothing Christmas day. Last year Kevin and Dustin showed up wearing red and white sweats for dinner. Rosie giving a shy, they looked so cute.
With having a formal dinner, I thought we might go to gowns galore. Rosie said I have had no reason to go in there and if we do not find anything we like there, I will make us our dresses and we can pick out the material in fabritastic. Amanda and I noticed the list seemed rather long and that the bunkers were even give store like names.

Wow, I said looking at your list that sounds like a good shopping day for me. The only thing I see on the list that I would love to check out, as I was going to pint to the screen. I stopped dead in my tracks, put my head back a bit, they both look at me waiting to hear what was on my mind and said, what do we get to take home with us when we leave, we had never thought about that or asked before.

Hey now, that is a real good question Rosie exclaims, and was swift to answer you will be allowed one carry bag and one large suitcase each. We will ensure nothing you do take can be traced to anywhere. Rosie thought for a second and said how about we also go look at carryon bags. When it is time to start packing your suitcases, they will be brought to your room. Oh, okay Amanda said, that is cool and I am good with your shopping list too Amanda smiled at Rosie.

Let us have our coffee and I will unpack our basket and you girls can have a few minutes for a smoke before we check this out. We have a few puffs off our smoke and we were ready and waiting for Rosie to put the win in the chiller.

To the Christmas store, Rosie says loudly, we walk over to our carts with Rosie in the lead and as she, hits enter on her cart we take off like a train with carts that are not connected. As we were being pulled in further the lights were turning on. We must have been at least eighty feet back in to the cave When we turn right and going to the far corner of the cave when we see two bunkers light up like Christmas and as we got closer there was even holiday music being played. We pull up to the candy cane, and garland front when the doors opened the lights were all on and it was as if we were walking into an Christmas store. Ornaments, baskets, trees, lights, decorations of many themes and there were the placemats that Rosie was talking about. Amanda and I were wondering around the store in amazement.

It did not take long for Rosie to pick out what she came here for and I came across a box of nine glass and gold angles I fell in love with and to me symbolized all the girls in my world. I realized that these might not be something I can take home with me although I thought they would be nice in our room over the holidays. I showed Rosie what I had picked and she smiled. Amanda found herself a Christmas wish cup that changes colors intermittently and when the cup turns red, you are supposed to take a drink and make a wish.

The weird part of shopping here is that you do not pay for anything, you take what you want and you put in your waiting cart. With each of picking, something out and Rosie getting her gold, green and burgundy placemats, Rosie says onto the kitchen store girls.

As we are taking our last look at the brilliant overstuffed Christmas store, I asked Rosie what she wanted out of the kitchen place, don't you have everything a Kitchen could want already, I asked. She looked back with a grin and replied, I am not sure yet. I always find something when I visit, that I do not have.

Walking to our shopping carts we and thanked Rosie for the gifts when she said do not thank me girls; it is Sires and Dustin's supercomputing wizardry that considered verity and wealth of inventory putting all this here for the residence long-term comforts in mind. That is crazy Amanda says, and getting it all here concealed must have been something.

Rosie replies it was surprisingly not that difficult, and we even got the majority of what you see in this bunker cave, in one load. Wow how did they make that all happen, I asked Rosie with Amanda just as curious. Rosie explains that the way all theses bunkers got here was on one old cargo container ship, which unfortunately sunk in the middle of the ocean, the entire crew miraculously surviving. With of course the focus being on the surviving crew as forecast, unbelievably talk of the sunken ship and cargo almost went unreported and was not investigated Rosie tells us. Once the specially sealed containers were all sitting on the bottom of the ocean Paul, Jim and Ryan brought them here in order of cave storage layout. Now that sounds like something you would see in a movie, I said to Amanda as Rosie smiled at us as she got into her cart and as we moved ahead the Christmas

store lights were going out as we were leaving.
The lights were on in the kitchen store and doors open when we got there, which was only five bunkers up from the Christmas store we just came out of. We all get out of our carts with Rosie leading to get in the store. Amanda asks Rosie so what was it you wanted in here, as we start looking around to see the entire kitchen and cooking knick-knacks in the store that was two connecting bunkers. I said to Rosie for you this must be like a toy store for kids. She popped her head up from the shelves she was checking and smiled I love this place. When I find new recipes, I sometimes have to come here for the right utensil or container to do it right.

She waves us over to the computer screen, and says that all the stores have these and how they work is you type in what you are looking for, and it will let you know exactly where it is on the shelves. If there is, nothing coming up in inventory the system will notify our tech people who can see about creating the item through 3D printing or regeneration. Just because it is not stored here does not mean that we cannot create it she chuckled. As Rosie went towards the back of the shop, she told us to have a look around girls and if you see something, you think need, grab it.

I will only be a few minutes she says and then suggests that when we are done here that we go out have a bit of our picnic and then we can come back to the shoes, gowns and accessories. Rosie knowing that we were probably ready for a smoke, we both replied sounds good to me. We looked around a bit and saw some great stuff, everything from pasta makers to ice-cream scoops and everything in between but nothing we needed or could think Rosie did, until we came across an apron that had written on it world's greatest chef embroidered in gold. Amanda tucked it under her arm, went, and put it in her cart hoping Rosie would not see what we picked out for her. I went out to the cart with Amanda to wait for Rosie after having my snoop around.

As we waited for Rosie, Amanda I chatted about the inventory it is crazy how much stuff is here and jus as we were saying to each other that we were ready for a smoke, Rosie comes out of the store smiling. What did you finally decide on Amanda asks as she sees Rosie with a bag of small items. She whips out a funky new turkey-basting utensil and says, I scored jokingly.

As Rosie goes to get in her cart, she says come on girls I know you need a smoke, and I am ready for a glass of wine and away we went back out to the picnic area. Once out of the cart I walk past the picnic table and looking out I said back to Rosie and Amanda, the scenery from up here is gorgeous; you can see everything from this spot from the valley below, the houses lake waterfall, birdcage the palace and from this location is the best overhead view of the farm.

Amanda came up behind me and handed me a smoke when Rosie asked if we wanted wine of coffee. With Rosie having wine I figured what the heck, wine for me with the same for Amanda. Rosie was giving us our glass of wine when Amanda went to get what we found in the kitchen store for her. Coming back with the apron all open Rosie could read the message and said awe, thank you girls. I love the gold embroidery and the message, well frankly, that is just the truth, we chuckled agreeing with her. I will wear it Christmas eve she paused, over my fancy dress of course we giggle.

As we sat and had a few sips of wine and nibbled on the snakes that Rosie brought and were enjoying the view when Rosie says well if we plan on going to the café we had better get moving, this could take a bit. We finish our smoke, take a swig of wine, and get back on our carts.

Not comprehending what a gowns store would look like here, when we pulled up to the store we were all shocked even at the entrance we could already see the huge selection, styles and designs hanging all in clear plastic bags. Rosie told us that it did not matter what the size was because she could fit anything to us, so it is only a matter of picking out the dress. As Amanda and I walk deeper into the store, Amanda says back to Rosie, you say that as if it is going to be an easy thing to do. Amanda and I with wide eye's, like where do you start she says to me.

Rosie looks at us and says you girls are so funny; your hang up with picking out what to wear is interesting. Okay then, if it is that easy you find yours I say to Rosie as a challenge. We all start going through the racks of dresses from ball gowns to sexy sequin dresses and colors galore. After Rosie had looked through what must have been a dozen dresses, she looked over at us and said looking puzzled, you know girls, you may be right this could be harder than I thought.

Amanda and I looked at each other and smiled when she says I guess the best thing to do is just grab a few and try them on. Then I came across what I thought would be a perfect dress for Rosie and I held it up for them to see, they were both impressed with my choice from what they could see, through the bag. The dress was a high color, sleeveless white sequined gown, that a slit up the left side. The white dress accented with emerald green sequence borders, looked elegant and not to showy. Amanda found a couple splashy dresses to try on as well.

Being inundated with all the dresses, I thought about and had to ask Rosie, so who was to wear all these dresses and when anyway. Sire wanted to make sure that glamour and elegance remained a component of life and with not knowing whom he might be with, he wanted to have all the bases covered. There are even wedding dresses here Rosie said as she went into the change room. I had a couple dresses picked out but wanted to see what Rosie looked like in the one I found and Amanda went in the other change room to try her little dresses on. When Rosie flung the curtain open and came out of the change room, taking the stance of a model with her hand on her waist I gasped wow, and Amanda pushed back her curtains as we were both so impressed and complemented her on how amazing she made that dress look. Amanda looked down at her feet and said I would ditch the fuzzy boots though; she snickered and closed her curtain to finish changing.

I love it Rosie said, I love the way it fits and feels, and it will look awesome with my apron you gave me. Rosie was smiling looking at her in the three way mirrors, I could see she knew she looked good in the designer gown and wanted to see what it looked like without the fuzzy boots and even grabbed a pair of high heels off the display just so see. Rosie looked over at me, and said I am not even trying on another dress this is it, I absolutely love this gown. Thanks, she smiles does a slow twirl and then goes back to the change room to change.

Amanda came out wearing a unique and perfect little black sequin dress with gold accents that fit her like a glove. It was not too short, so she would be comfortable and the cut of the dress gave Amanda an hourglass figure and cleavage she did not she had. When she stepped out tears almost came to my eyes she looked breathtaking. Rosie came out of her change room, saw Amanda and went over to her to touch her shoulder, and made a sizzling noise saying, you rock that hot stuff.
For sure this one is for me Amanda says while she looks at herself in the mirrors and slips on the heals that Rosie left, to see how it looked. I am impressed Amanda commented I have never liked the first dress I have tried on I am shocked as she kept goggling at herself and checking out the three sixty view.

Okay my turn, I know I said as I kept filing through the dresses. With having gowns and worn them throughout my life I was looking for a design I have not had the pleasure of wearing before and I finally came across a deep red silk tuxedo gown. With the tuxedo gown being the first one to catch my eye, I figured I would go try it on, know that Rosie can make alterations if needed.

While I was changing, I can hear Rosie and Amanda talking about how impressed they are their dresses and how good they make them look. I needed help getting the zipper done up so I came out half done up with Rosie coming over to help I look up into the mirrors and I was surprised, Wow this looks good, this looks real good I repeated. Rosie came over, sifted the dress around the sides, and says I will take it in a smidge and it will fit like a glove. Amanda was very impressed too, mom you are beautiful that dress is stunning on you. That is incredible I looked at both of them for us to all love the first dress e try on even Dustin could not calculate those odds I let out a cackle and we all chuckled.

How about shoes Amanda asked Rosie, the display one do not fit any of us. Rosie nodded her head to go behind the first set of cloths racks and there you have shoes. I still had my dress on, followed them to see the selection, and was presently staggered by the selection and sizes. It was obvious that someone was not a fan of big feet because the largest size was an eight and started and five and a half which I found interesting and mentioned to Rosie she smiled at me and said you are very observant aren't you. Strangely enough, you are right; Sire would never be with any woman with a larger then size eight foot. Our Sire is blind to a woman's height, weight and facial features however if she has big feet she does not stand a chance. Fortunately, for all us ladies on the island we all have under size eight feet and concludes that may be us ladies would not have been picked for this project if our feet were bigger she chuckled and said I am only joking. Sires foot faddish, is real but only applies to the woman he would be with.

Amanda was first to find a perfect match to her dress and her size, that was a satin leather high pump with gold metal band around the ankle and the same gold metal on the toe and heal. Rosie says I never wear high shoes I do not want my feet to hurt. I let her know that for comfort a wedge heal sometimes helps. We are analyzing the wall of shoes when Amanda finds a pair of white leather, wedge heals with wide band open design that provided the little bit of extra height needed and would hold the foot. Rosie commented they look great as she looks for her size in the stack.

I found a sleek pair of black platform pumps that fit like a glove and finished the look of the dress off perfectly. This is the best sopping ever I beamed at Rosie as I was going back to change. Rosie and Amanda were getting the shoes and their dress packed up as I came out with my stuff in the cart we both went over to Rosie for a group hug. Amanda says first this was very special and I add we are going to all look like Hollywood Christmas eve. Rosie had a huge smile we were all excited now, to get all dolled up.

You girls ready to go she asks, knowing that we all had enough for one day; we nod and acknowledge that we are ready to leave. We get in our carts with our goodies for the day and were praising each other's outfits as were drove out of the cave. Rosie said to leave our stuff in the carts and Paul can get them for us when he comes to get us. We will have a seat at the picnic table and finish our wine while we wait for Paul to come. How will he know we are done Amanda asked as we are seated Rosie replied, once we parked the cart at the finish he was sent a message that we were done. We will be lucky to get in a couple sips of wine before he arrives, she giggles implying she has him wrapped.
Amanda and I just get our smokes lit and here comes Paul up the path right on cue, when Rosie said see what did I tell you, which made us all burst out laughing. As Paul get's closer he says what, what is so funny, he looks at Rosie who is still chuckling and replies, the girls did not know how you were going to know to come and get us and I barely finished explaining to them, and there you are. Shot Gun she yells and winks at Amanda.

Rosie began to pour Paul a glass of wine while he transferred our shopping into the back of his cart. Paul was holding up the dress bags and says well, I guess you found something after all. Amanda's face lit up when she was telling Paul how amazing Rosie looked in her dress, this will be a red carpet event and Rosie will out shin us all, looking for a reaction from Paul. He could not hide his expression of delight in seeing Rosie all dressed up. To make light of his obvious anticipation he replied well then I guess I will have to dust off the old tux if that is the case, I can't have her looking better than me he jokes as he gives Rosie a nudge and smile when she hands him his glass of wine.
Paul let Rosie know that the café was starting to smell very good. I looked over at Rosie and asked so what is on the menu and who is doing the cooking

with you spending the day with us. We are having Buffalo wings, cactus cut fries, and Jim is the man in charge today. Rosie leaned over towards us a bit and said in a quiet voice, that Jim was the only one she trusts with the deep fryer and then smiled.

How was your shopping today Paul asks us. It was fantastic and walking out without paying does take some getting used to I commented. With Amanda replying we did not get any Christmas presents though, she looked at Rosie and then me, other than the apron, we picked out for Rosie and already gave to her, and we are running out of time.

Rosie and Paul looked at each other and then Paul explained that we do not exchange actual gifts at Christmas on the island. With everything available to everyone, here there is no need for a gift exchange. Although, Paul went onto say, we do however exchange hand written cards. I looked at Rosie and asked, did you not imply that our presents for you were to be handmade. I thought that meant that we gift everyone something and that you preferred to have yours handcrafted. Oh dear I guess I should have said that better no, no, I was just being selfish and I want something from you girls as a keepsake, and if you make it I will feel you with me all the time. Awe that is so sweet Rosie I could feel the lump in my throat when I said with a sly look, careful for what you ask for. I am not very crafty however I can sure color I said proudly. Rosie and Paul looked at me with a puzzled glance and then looked over to Amanda, who let them know with her confident nod, that I was serious, then we all had a chuckle when Rosie said again, I love you two, as she started packing up the basket.

Well let us go see what Jim is up too and with any luck we will get there before Kevin, Dustin and Ryan eat it all on us. Amanda and I smiled and butt out our smokes and walked with Rosie to the cart where she took her rightful seat in the front passenger seat. We could tell Rosie liked when Paul chauffeured her around.

As we sat, back and hung on, Amanda and were chatting about the color of my dress and how unique it was when all the sudden we are parking at the café. That is one quick ride when you drive Paul, Amanda said as she passed by him walking towards the bar where Elsie was standing in charge. Rosie headed right over to see if Jim needed any help or really just take over, which seemed to be case with Jim suddenly standing close to the bar beside Janette.

We walked over to Jim as said wow that did not take long, Jim smiled, I knew my time was up when she arrived and he and Janette snickered, we can always count on her to take over they whispered.
As Amanda I Jim and Janette came up to the bar, Amanda asks while she is putting her elbow up on the rail with a drawn out so Elsie what is on tap today Amanda asked. Elsie beamed and replied with having Jim's hot food we are having my world famous slushy's to take the heat off.

As Elsie was getting our drinks and Rosie was setting out the food, here come Kevin Dustin and Ryan right on time Paul calls out to them, as they are getting out of their carts. I heard Dustin say to Paul that everything was ready and was going to light up in fifteen minutes. I looked over at Jim and Janette with Elsie looking excited, I was going to question what I heard when Rosie spoke out and said you just wait and see. Amanda and I looked at each other when we hear Dustin say hoot and waves everyone out to the front of the café. With us all drink in hand and two hoots going around, we were asked how our shopping went and I know that we beamed when we said we found our dresses for Christmas eve and that we are so excited. Amanda informs the group that Paul says he is even going to dust off his tuxedo.

Kevin blows a big puff of smoke out and laughing he says now this I have to see when Dustin and Kevin nudged each other jokingly. Rosie stared at the two with a serious l look and a smile and said I look forward to the same out of you two. This is a formal evening and I know you will do your best to dazzle us all providing Dustin and Kevin with a little positive reinforcement she felt they needed, with the group all loving the way Rosie the hold that Rosie has on them and how they carry on with them.

With a second of silence, the couples drew closer together with them all knowing what, the something was, that was to happen as Dustin starts his count down, five, four, three, two, and one. As the group all looked towards the lake, our jaws dropped as a massive holographic four dimensional image of a fully decorated Christmas tree appears with colored lights, bows and ornaments that looked like it is coming out of the lake and hovering. The first thing that came out of Amanda's lips was, that is without a doubt the largest Christmas tree I have ever seen, that is so freaking amazing and too cool I commented, still mesmerized by the dancing lights and sheer size of the image. I did not have the words to describe the comfort the image gave me. We were all in awe and captivated by the colors, lights and the size. We all clapped and the three young fellows took a bow.

Jessie got the groups attention and said she wanted to make a toast. Henry followed with a here, here and we all lifted our glasses as Jessie simply said, here is to being able to turn keeping our Christmas tree going another year. There was clinking of the glasses and a sense of tradition and unity amongst the group. When Rosie says to us all while taking her last look at the tree before heading back to the bar, Jims, hot munchies are ready when you all are. As Rosie walked by Ryan, Kevin Dustin she gave them a pat on the back. As Rosie was going to the bar, Paul explains to Amanda and I who were still gazing at the large tree with changing colors as you watch. That, we have the tree lit for a few days before the holiday and goes away New Years Day.

Ryan added that they could change the picture and background; it just seems that a decorated tree feels the warmest and most Christmassy to us. There is a fireplace in the background, if you watch you can see it come into focus off to the side of the tree that will be more prominent and visible as the sun goes down. We also pipe background Christmas music throughout the whole island on Christmas Eve and day only. Jessie with her arm around Ryan says yes, I love the music that keeps us in the spirit but two days is enough she chuckled looking at Ryan and then back at us.

Amanda and I understood how much that this holiday means to them and with us here, they were making sure we were every part of it. All the sudden a waft of buffalo hot sauce was in the air and us smokers now done were moving in on the food. I need a refill before I dig into those as I pointed to the chicken strips and wings that had an orange hue to them.
Amanda agreed; drink first she says as she is walking past Jim and pats him on the arm the chicken looks so inviting although, I am not wild for spicy food this is the exception for sure. I do like the cactus fries with the sour cream and chive dip, and I will have some chicken just because you made it. Jim says to the group that is you have not caught on yet there are three platters of chicken wings and strips and the colors of the plates indicate how hot the sauce is. The red platter is the hottest, yellow is medium and green is mild. As we notice the color of the platters, we see Dustin and Kevin who were not listening to Jim, both taking scoops of wings off the red platter that was closest to them.

Everyone but Kevin and Dustin were trying to act normal and carry on while holding in their laughter waiting for them to both dig in. Within seconds, they both had a wing done and another one in their hand to follow when

Dustin cleared his throat and looked up at Kevin and said jiminy cricket those are warm. Kevin had the second wing already in his mouth and just shrugs his shoulders at Dustin, as if he was not feeling the heat. Rosie was just waiting for the expressions with both Henry and Elsie cringing, watching them eat the hot wings, as the group commented and chuckle over Dustin's reference to Jim in his confirmation of the heat.

While we were nibbling on the chicken and chips and watching the huge tree in the background become more brilliant as the afternoon fades, Jessie looks over to Amanda and I and asks us to come to their house for dinner tomorrow. We have all been so busy, we have finally finished our renovations, we want you to come see the finished product and we can chat about our coming voyage. Amanda and I without hesitation of course we would love to come for dinner and see your house. Your house is the only one we have not seen yet and from what we have seen, all the houses on this island are the best in the world. Chatting with the group, I commented that all the individual designs are unique and it would be hard to put one against the other, when Amanda said I do not think I could even do that.

Then it is settled Jessie said with a smile, we will be seeing you tomorrow afternoon. Amanda and I were chugging on our drinks pretty good and were enjoying conversation and watching Kevin and Dustin still eating up a storm. Rosie pipes up and says you got to love them, as we all turn our heads and stare at them with their faces in their plates. You look like you are starving Rosie says to the fellows.

Dustin replied to Rosie the only way you do not feel the heat is if you keep eating, once you slow down you feel like you are on fire, he smiled at the bunch of us around the table and gave Jim a nod. Kevin looked over and realized we were all, focused on him, as he popped his last chicken strip in his mouth and sat back; holding up his orange fingers up indicating he was done. Rosie shook her head smiling at Kevin when she saw his fingers and got up to get them warm cloths, to clean up their hands. When she tossed them the warm cloths, she let them know the rest of us only needed napkins; she turns and smiles.

With everyone sitting back, comfortable and talking quietly amongst each other with Amanda and I finding ourselves drawn to gazing out to the tree. While sitting back enjoying the scenery and the company, we hear Henry thanking Elsie for reminding her of something. Which Henry wanted to share with us by letting us know that we are ready for the filters to be place, her expression was one of pride and joy however; the interpretation of what she said was we were getting a needle, sooner than we thought. I replied not wanting to sound concerned, I thought that was happening a few days before we are to leave. I was able to better define perimeters and have perfected the device.

This being a huge achievement in the scientific world and the group understanding the significance they all stood and gave Henry an ovation with some bravos. We stood up along with the rest of them although we truly did not comprehend her triumph.
Before anyone could sit, back down Kevin calls out that deserves a hoot kind of celebration Kevin says to Henry with a big smile as he wipes his hands one more time and gestures to Henry and Elsie along with Amanda and I to come have a puff.

As we were getting ready to move Rosie said no, no, sit, sit, you can have your puff here, we could tell that Rosie was interested in hearing how Henry has perfected the device that was going to be put in us to stop our remembering and to ensure we remain with the fabricated story while. Rosie, Janette, Jessie were cleaning off the table while the guy's all went for a refill before Henry starting to say as, Elsie says to her go one, tell them your breakthrough, everyone was ready.

Henry beamed as she began to say that the filter she created had more capabilities then we had first envisioned. The design of the filter was for our sole purpose of blocking specific memories and creating a new reality for that time for the girls. However, when Colleen asked if we would be monitoring them or could see them, and originally I had said we could see their physical location and monitor their vitals, here. Once I got back to my lab, I started thinking about possible potential, if we could monitor could we not help protect against natural ailments and make the rest of their lives as comfortable as possible. I realized that through the vitals we could send signals to their systems to avoid such conditions like diabetes and other naturally occurring ailments that can come with age. While the system monitors their vitals on a regular base if there are changes in the reading that indicate a decline, we can send a signal to the brain that will hammer out the problem. In simple terms, if the system were to detect white blood cell count to low or two high the system would send an automatic message to the body to create the antibodies needed to put the system back into balance.

Then Henry looks at us and says there is also another upside with having the filter, Amanda was quick to ask, what that is when Henry replied, neither of you will ever get Alzheimer's. We all laughed with the irony of having an implant for forgetting, that ensures we will not lose our memories. She continued with saying to ensure that as you age your story stays true the filter will not allow any mind-altering decease to take hold, we cannot have you out there babbling and sounding crazy when you are a hundred she chuckled.

To summarize, we can do more than just monitor their vitals we can help to ensure that you have long healthy lives, she looked over at us proudly when I said oh my goodness that is simply amazing. Amanda and I both went over to give Henry and Elsie, who was a big part of the work, a hug. It was an emotional rush thinking that we were going to have our own guardian angels looking out for us.

Rosie brought Henry a refill on her drink and we could see that Rosie gave Henry a wink and mouthed to her, thank you. Amanda and I sat back down and as the group started chatting back and forth; about how interesting the filter was as the hoots were going around. When the conversation turned to casually talking about what everyone was up to tomorrow and winding down.

The fellows seemed to be talking about maintenance and us ladies got on the topic of our dresses for Christmas Eve we were all anxious to wear them. The only person that did not have theirs yet was Henry, which Elsie conveyed that with her being so focused on the filter she had not had time, then she gently took Henry's hand and said but we are going tomorrow for sure, right no excuses Elsie smiled.

Amanda spoke up and said I cannot wait the evening will be just perfect, I know it will be. Rosie agreed with Amanda that it would be a very special night. For now through Rosie says, looking over at Paul, I think it time to go home it has been a great day everyone. Paul took his cue knowing that he was the driver, got up, and started with his salutations as Amanda and I gave our hugs all around and told Jessie and Ryan that we looked forward to visiting tomorrow. When in the background we can here Rosie, yell out shotgun, as we say our good nights. Dustin was going back to the farm with Kevin and Jim and Janette were going to Jessie and Ryan's to play cards for a bit. While Henry and Elsie waved as they were walking arm and arm home.

We jumped onto Paul's cart and away we went back to the palace. While being chauffeured, Amanda and I watched the huge tree over the lake with the lights changing color and now we could see the full image of a fireplace in the background. As we moved, we could see that it really was four-dimensional. The glistening holographic tree that is set over the lake made the sky glow and dance in color.

Home at last Rosie says as Paul pull up to the patio, and starts to help us with the dresses. When Rosie says I will take those they need some work first as she takes the three garment bags back to her room. When Amanda asked Paul if he was going to have a coffee with us before he went home, you twisted my arm he says without hesitation and smiles at us saying, a coffee would be just perfect.

Rosie whisks back onto the patio and says well you all found the coffee as she went to grab the Baileys from the bar and bring it to Paul. Then we all had a seat around the hot tub Amanda and I having a smoke and gazed at the tree when Rosie has a big retiring shy, I am popped for some reason, if must be all the excitement of shopping she looked over at us and smiled. We had finished our smokes and I looked at Amanda and gave her a little wink, letting her know that was our cue to go to our room.

As we get up Rosie and Paul both gave us hugs said their good nights as we thanked them again for a wonderful day. As we get into our room although tired, we just wanted to chill for a while and have a smoke and finish our coffee before bed. The first thing I recalled once comfy, I said to Amanda was that we were not going to die a horrible death, isn't that amazing to know, unless of course we get taken out in a car accident or something like that, I looked right at Amanda and said, that is a huge for us. That means more than the wealth they are extending. When I realized that, she never said when, just that she was ready, Hum I guess Rosie will let us know when we are to go, Amanda oh yes Rosie will make sure we get there when we need to be.

Did you notice Amanda added, that Rosie seemed to be all over the idea of keeping an eye on us? I am kind of liking the feeling that they want and are going t be. Yes, it is comforting, even if we do not always remember that they are I chuckled quietly with Amanda joining in.

What a day she went onto say, the shopping the amazing tree and I really did enjoy the mild buffalo chicken strips they were tasty and not too hot. My thought was that the ships had more bite then the strips did, which made the slushy drinks go down quick. I had my share Amanda said as she got up to change into her housecoat. Yes between the wine and the slushy drinks, I had my fill, it is a good thing that they do not go excessive with the liquor when Rosie makes her punch and Elsie her slushy drinks. They do not knock you over; they just always taste so good and have a slow and easy rise about them.

We were joking around as we were getting ready for bed and when we finished our smoke we climbed up on the bed and snuggled in, said our I love you, before passing out.

Chapter Twenty-Two

Waking up on this day, felt different in a way I could not put my finger on as I lay there looking up at the beautiful hand carved designs of the ceiling. Amanda all sunk into the bed was awake and for a moment stared up at the ceiling the same. As we sat up and looked over at what we were wearing today, we smiled, this time it was a cotton skirt with pockets and Rosie flipped the hem to show that there were shorts underneath. So that we would be comfortable working at the farm and still look nice for visiting Jessie and Ryan. Our tops were satin and had little shoulder straps and a loose graceful flow. I would be wearing the green and beige outfit and Amanda's was a light and medium peach color. They were sweet we acknowledged and went over to have a smoke and coffee to start our day.

As Amanda is pouring coffee, I let her know that I felt something different about this day when I woke up but that I could not put my finger on it. Hum, Amanda looks at me and says, with eyes wide open hung over may be she smiles. No silly not that I grind, then totally veering away from what I was going to say, I do not think that I have felt hung-over since we got here, and we do drink more here than I ever did at home. I agree with that for sure, even baseball season I did not drink this much she replied.

What I meat about the day feeling different, do you feel anything I asked Amanda. She thought for a second and said the only thing that comes to mind is that with all the talk of the filter being ready and Christmas Eve right around the corner, we are getting much closer to the time of going home. That was it that was the sensation that I was feeling we are getting closer to being able to leave and take our journey home, wow you nailed it Amanda.

Momma did not raise a fool. I sat up very proud of myself and gave her a pat on the hand and a big smile. Well time to get mobile, we put our coffee's down and headed to the washroom to get ready. It has become routine to get ready at the same time in the huge double everything washroom spa, that we really do not even chat much when we are in there. We find that it has an echo in there so not the ideal place to carry on a conversation. We just do our thing and get out, and it does help move us along with our cloths always ready and waiting for us every morning. Having the cloths ready sure helps the day start right.

We come out to the patio where Rosie has us having breakfast by the pool, so that we had a perfect view of the Christmas tree. We both notice the patio even looking more Christmassy then the day before and we could smell the lilies and pine all around us.

Good morning, Rosie the place looks even more amazing then yesterday, even the Christmas store people would be jealous I said. Amanda added never mind the stores, even Santa would envious, we smiled all the way to the table. Oh thank you girls, it means a lot that you appreciate the little extras. Then Rosie changes her focus onto checking out our look and she says well don't you two look nice this morning, I came right back with yes, of course, we do, and it is all because of you.

Amanda comments on Rosie "little extras" what you have done around here is not called little extras you have transformed a tropical patio into a winter wonderland without the snow. Amanda went over, gave Rosie a big hug, and said quietly and with a straight face, Rosie doing anything in a little way is not in your vocabulary. We all got a rise out of Amanda's comment and Rosie appreciated the sentiment.

Rosie presented scrambled eggs and toast for breakfast she jokingly said they would ease the after effects of all the spicy food we ate last night; she smiled and patted her tummy. Breakfast is perfect Rosie I complimented her and then, remembered about the filter being ready and asked Rosie if a day had been set for us to have them placed, I am not fond or keen on the word injected or thought I said. Amanda concurred we do not like needles; Rosie says with a positive voice and bright face you will be fine girls, and Henry said she will be ready to "place" them she grinned, tomorrow sometime in the morning. I have already let Kevin know that you will not be there tomorrow. Wow, that was fast, when did you have time, Amanda asked.

Rose's reply, you have to get up early around here if you want to keep up, as she winks and takes a sip of coffee. I am good all good yes me too, all good here, I could not walk five seconds in your shoes Rosie, Amanda this time, making her blush a little. Rosie did adore the attention and recognition however sometimes it made her feel uncomfortable when receiving it.

Well it is time for you girls to be on your way and for me to get something done around here too. Rosie gets up to fill our go cups with coffee, when I asked her what she was doing for dinner this evening. I am having a quiet evening in Rosie says, we are not getting together at the café this afternoon because other then Ryan, the rest of the fellows are performing their monthly inspections today and will not be finished until this evening. My plan for this nice quiet evening is a bottle of wine a yummy grilled cheese sandwich and a chick flick, and she was looking forward to her time we could tell.

Ass Rosie hands us our cups and we grab our smokes I look at Amanda, all right I think we have everything sweetie and as we stood up and took our first couple steps towards our pink driving machine, I said loudly shotgun, mocking Rosie. We turned and waved see you later have a great day.

Wow, I say as we get into the cart the tree is still there and so huge, no kidding Amanda says and asks me to light her smoke as she takes off down the hill still admiring the tree on our way to the farm to see Kevin. Pulling up to the house Kevin is there to greet us and asked if Rosie had let us know that he will be working with Paul, Jim ad Dustin today and would not be around. Yes, she let us know so just show us what you want us to work on today and we will be fine. We will go to Jessie's when we are done.
As we follow Kevin to the backside of the greenhouse, he lets us know realizing that you girls were going for dinner after working here, I found a stand up job for you and that is our lattes wall of, vine berries that are picked standing up, so you do not have to crouch and sit on the stools. Kevin was please with his accommodation that was to convenient, making me ask him did Rosie let you know that we were dressed up today hum. Amanda chuckled when I asked as she caught on to just how convenient the timing was. I think that he was stunned at the question and thought it was funny I even asked, although he would not admit or deny just smile awkwardly. We both nodded at Kevin and new she had said something. Kevin then showed us the wall of barriers and explained that we were to only, pick the purple barriers any other color means they are not ripe.

If you are all, set here ladies I will leave you and see you tomorrow, thank you for all your help. Oh yes, and I left a special little package for you on the porch, for when you, he smiles and gives a wave. As Kevin walks away Amanda says that Rosie does not miss a trick does she. No kidding I reply I know she said something to him we had a sip of our coffee and started picking. As we were looking through the vines thinking aloud, I said that Rosie sure is protective of us; I think she is really going to miss us a lot when we are gone. Amanda knowing how attached Rosie has become, realized that what I had said was true and although we were extra work for her, she would miss it when we are gone.

Being at the back of the island, Amanda noticed that from where we stood we could still see the top of the Christmas tree and the twinkling star through the lush vegetation and the tall palm trees waving with the light breeze. We started chatting about Christmas Eve being such a big event what do they do on New Year's Eve, no one has even mentioned New Years at all, I find that interesting. Amanda said I wonder why we never thought to ask. We will ask Jessie and Ryan this afternoon when we are there.

Working at trying to find these purple barriers, which was not easy as they seemed to almost-hide behind the leaves, and we were not finding an abundance of the purple barriers like the ones Kevin, picked to show us.

Amanda holds up her bucket that is not even half-full and said that is about as I can do, I looked in mine and it was about the same. We looked at each other and agreed that was enough for today, it was time for a smoke break any way. Gathering up our pails and our go cups we start walking back to the porch, when Amanda says, I wonder what Kevin left us. Oh yes I forgot he said he left us a special package.

When we get to the porch, there is a big jug of ice tea up on the table by the porch swing and a little hand carved wooden box with a slide top with eight hoots rolled in Christmas rolling papers. I looked at Amanda with a smile and said well I guess we can sit here on the porch swing and have our smokes, and our first Christmas hoot I chuckled. Sounds good to me Amanda replied and then went over to the swing. She commented that I have seen the porch swing on TV all the time but I think this is the first time I have actually sat in a beautiful porch swing before. While she is pushing herself on the swing like a little kid, I poured us a glass of ice tea and went to sit with her and have our smoke before going to Jessie's. Being the shy people, we naturally were having a few puffs off a hoot before visiting was a good idea too; we were always on the same page when it came time for a coffee, smoke or a hoot.

Sitting there swinging slowly with tea and hoot in hand, this is perfect I said and passed the hoot to Amanda. When she said after looking around, and back at the twinkling tree, I feel like we are living in color here everything is so health, lush and vibrant. Not complaining, but it does not look like this at home. I replied it would when we do get home and are able to move anywhere tropical and have a lavish home. Holly crap Amanda turned at looked right at me and said, I have not thought of our going home like that. I suppose my brain thinks I am going home to the same life I left. You are so right mom, we are going to be wealthy when we get home and there will be no more work, wow. It is as if the light bulb just went on, the possibilities are endless. Dam, now time can start going faster, she whispered, then said only kidding. For now, it is just a fantasy and it will get real when we get home and check our bank account that is when we change our lives forever, I gave her a big smile.

By then we had finished our smokes and ice tea and discussed that we might as well venture over to Jessie ad Ryan's now even if we are a bit early. Kevin had the neatest item at the front door, instead of a mailbox on the wall beside the front door he had a small chock board so when we were getting ready leaving we wrote on it our thank you for the tea and the hoots with happy faces and we both signed. As we were walking to the cart, Amanda says Rosie needs one of those big porch swings with the cushions and the motion that was comfortable she says while looking back at the swing still swaying.

When we get to the cart sitting between the driver and passenger seats, there was a Christmas themed quilted cloth bag with three bottles of wine inside. We both look at each other and call out Rosie, at the exact same time. Amanda still a kid at heart instantly blurted out jinx, I looked at her and we chuckled, shaking my head, she says you are just lucky there are no punch buggies here, you would have a bruised arm, no one beats me at that game she gave me a look of confidence as she was getting into the cart. We were snickering as we were leaving and on our way to Jessie's.

Don't you get the feeling that everyone is always ten steps ahead of us I said to Amanda as we came around the bend to where the foliage opened and exposes the yard and house we could already see Jessie and Ryan sitting on their front patio waiting for us to arrive? As we pull our cart into the parking area, we could see water flowing over large stones and when we get out of the cart, to have a better look, we could see that the water flowed into a good-sized fishpond.

There were lilies and tall grass around half the pond and special lighting. Under the water was a maze of hiding and feeding spots for the colorful fish. Jessie and Ryan came up to us as we were admiring the pond and welcomed us to their home. Ryan seen that we liked the pond and felt we should know, he says with a straight face, that the pond is not only decoration some of these fish will be dinner one day, just saying, he chuckles as Jessie shakes her head at him smiling and motions us to come to the house.

Amanda grabbed the Christmas bag, of wine and presented it to Jessie as we were walking towards the house and confessed that it was actually Rosie, who put the wine in our cart. We cannot take the credit she grins at Jessie. Then I stopped abruptly, as I peered up at the home and realized the house was made of etched glass panels. This is incredible, I have never heard of such a thing, Amanda not seeing what I was talking abut say what. Jessie was very impressed that I noticed the etched glass paneling of the houses wall construction of the first level of the house. Two walls of the second floor had the same etched glass paneling. As I was babbling with Jessie, Amanda understood what I was going on about. When Amanda had to say to Jessie and Ryan, we sure would not have a glass house at home. Thirty below would feel chilly with only a pane of glass between you and all that snow, and forget running around naked she laughed with us joining in surprised with her comment. I am with Amanda on the chilly part, however I have not run around naked in my house for a while so that would not be my biggest issue, I winked at them.

Ryan said I was so hoping you would say all that stuff, we have something to show you when we get settled and open some of that wine Rosie sent along. We come up to the wraparound patio filled with plants and flowers, with Amanda noticing and pointing out to me the porch swing, I looked over and Jessie seen what we were looking at and she admitted after sitting in the one Kevin has she wanted one as part of the renovations. Ours is a little more high tech then his because it will rock itself once a person sits in it and you can regulate the pace of the rocking motion. Jessie went onto say that everything about this house is green, efficient and has all the comforts.

We here Ryan call out to us from inside the house, you will not get any wine if you cannot make it past the front door, he chuckled. Jessie waved us in and over to the kitchen that was copper and brass filled. The best way to describe their kitchen was IKEA on steroids. Every inch of space accounted for and all the cupboards had glass fronts. Jessie was showing us her favorite features of the kitchen such as the long black slate island that had bar stools on the one side and a large hanging copper range-hood at the far end over an open grill. There were two ovens and when she pointed out the sink having four tubs and two sets of taps, she looked at Ryan, then back at us, and said we enjoy cooking together and concluded we should designed our kitchen so that we can both be in here and not get in each other's way. Jessie could see we loved everything we were seeing and did not have much to say.

To the open side of the slate island was a dining table for twelve that was partly in the house and half way out onto the extended and wider portion of the wraparound patio that had a rattan gazebo with reams of beige cotton cloth weaved through the rattan frame. There were additional features of fire tables, water walls and ceramic pots filled with palms and lilies as we seen in the front when we came in. The fire tables are do not use and fuel, they produce four-dimensional images of dancing and colorful flames.

Ryan filled our wine glasses, was handing them out, and lifted his glass and says, here is to Rosie, she saves us from drinking all our own wine he smiled and then said only kidding, as he looked at Jessie. What I and we really want to say to you is thank you for dropping in on our island. We all have appreciated your breath innocence and excitement, you are genuine people and Jessie and I are honored and thrilled that we get to escort you home.
This will be quite the adventure for us and we wanted you to know that you brought a special something with you and we will all treasure these memories. Cheers Jessie says joyfully acknowledging Ryan's toast. We were moved by Ryan's toast and as we were thanking them for everything, Jessie was feeling a little emotional and said how about we get this tour moving, we have a wonderful dinner waiting for us when we are done. Ryan put his arm around Jessie and said lead the way, my sweetness he smiled.

Jessie lead us back to the entrance and on the other side of the kitchen was a great room with a black round stone fireplace with a mantel beam mantel made of glass. Ryan pointed to the fireplace mantel and explained the mantel is actually a twelve-foot long glass beam that is two feet by two feet square. He goes onto say and that is not the cool part. Ryan grabbed a remote control and the glass beam lit up at first it was blue, and then changed to green. He said that they could make stay any color they wanted or have it change with the music if we want. I had to go over and touch it because it looked so perfect, there were no flaws, cracks or chips. Amanda was right with me, and had to touch the glass mantel as well.

Jessie says to Ryan show them the panels, oh yes Ryan's face lit up and pushed another button and all of a sudden the etched glass panel walls went fully frosted, so you could not see out. Then the wall lit up first the bottom half of the panel was a blue wave, making the room feel like it was sitting beside a gleaming pool. Ryan then showed us that they could lower the frosting to any height and change the colors for mood and the patterns on the walls. When the glass is frosted, no one can see in even though we can still see the shadows of the outside. Jessie commented that even though we picked the glass, it did take us some getting used to, thinking that people could see in. Ryan throws in a chuckle and says, not that anyone is looking, mind you. Then Ryan demonstrates a few more of the wall designs to show us how the changes make the whole room and mood feel different.

The living room also boasted a Grand piano that was set on a raised octagon platform and under a mirrored dome and glass, panels formed to the octagon shaped of the platform. While I was busy taking the uniqueness of the teal and grey accented room in, Amanda asks so who plays the piano looking at Jessie. She smiles at Amanda and says; well neither of us is very good however, we really wanted the piano when we seen it and we figured we had lots of tie to learn. Jessie glances at Ryan who walks over to the glossy black Grand piano and without touching the keys like magic, the piano started playing on its own. We follow him up to the piano and see the keys moving and lovely music coming out of it but no hands. Jessie said Ryan you were supposed to pretend you were playing, he grind I did not get there quickly enough; I hit the start play too soon. We were all impressed with the sound and the music coming from the piano. Ryan left the piano playing softly while we continued our tour.

Jessie gives Amanda and I a nod and says, the upstairs first, then I will show you the bed rooms. The open stairs leading to the second floor were made of an aqua colored etched glass with handrail to match. I had to comment on the glass nowhere else would you ever see this, I was floored by what I was seeing and Amanda was just as impressed and as speechless as I.

When Jessie gets to the top of the steps, she moves out of the way so we can get the full panoramic look at the second floor that is an exercise area, dance studio and a two-seat beauty salon. The second floor is also glass panels and has a twelve-foot ceiling, although Jessie says they keep the upstairs half frosted all the time. The space is open with planters and a water wall creating some separation. We could feel the breeze flowing through the open windows and through the room. There was a beautiful sitting area by the beauty salon with a mini bar and all white wicker furniture that included an oversized white wicker hanging basket chair.

As we were walking further into the room, I asked Jessie if she did everyone's hair here, oh yes she replies without hesitation, I am the island resident beautician and Rosie already has you booked in the morning of our Christmas Eve party. Ryan was hanging back drinking his wine when he says hey what about me, Jessie looks at him and tilts her head as she says I will have you ready honey you don't worry your pretty little head. Ryan batted his eyes back at her, which had Amanda come out with a big awe that is so sweet.

Passing by the wicker sitting area and the beauty salon, we could see what looked to be an ice block tube, which was actually the casing of the elevator. The elevator can hold two people at a time so Amanda went with Jessie first and I went with Ryan. The round platform of the hydraulic lift was a perfect fit to the ice cube tube. The platform lift will only move up or down, when the passenger weight is stable. Before Ryan and I can get down, I can already hear Amanda speaking loudly you have to be kidding.

As I get off the platform and see that not only do they have a massive bed and padded headboard they have a open patio right into their own very privet pool with water fall and very romantic area around the hot tub, only a few feet from their bed. This is not what you would expect to see in a person's bedroom I gasped with excitement; I looked at Amanda Jessie and Ryan who I could see were beaming, as they watched our reactions.

Getting to the edge of the bedroom, flabbergasted at what I was seeing inside the plush plants and flowers, I blurted now that is cooking with gas and laughed. Startling Ryan, which had us all giggle when I got Amanda who was focused on the pool, to look over to see the full outdoor kitchen with BBQ, full bar, a red wicker sectional furniture with fire table, and picnic table along with a two-person hammock hanging between a huge grape vine looking archway. There was a fire pit and another covered swinging chair for two. Amanda and I went right over to the sectional to have a seat and take all of this in. Jessie came with us for a seat and a few sips of wine. We could hear the piano playing in the background while we were sitting back captivated by the view.

As we sat Jessie let us girls know that we had time for a smoke and pointed to the ashtray. We were so enthralled with the tour we had not even thought of having one until Jessie said we could. Amanda looked at me and said how about we share one mom. Sounds good I am anxious to see the rest I said as I smiled at Jessie and then looked back into the bedroom. When Ryan could see I was gearing up to ask a question, he piped up and said, one more awesome feature of this bedroom paradise, is that the glass panels slide back into the wall so that when we are having people over for a pool party we enter this part off the wraparound deck. Ryan had to point out to us, the wraparound deck access on the other side of the outdoor kitchen.

While looking back into the bedroom I pointed out what looked to be a cedar cove or nook area with orchids throughout the nook. Jessie says come I will show you the rest. We all got up from our spot on by the pool and as we walked back onto the bedroom, on the other side of the bed area, there was a colorful Tiffany glass water wall that provided the spa and massage area the feel of inclemency. There was a message table, sauna and stem shower and vanity. The area was dim lit and that had a tanning bed? Why do you need a tanning bed Amanda asked as we get closer and see the spa layout? Jessie chuckled and paused before saying, it was not a tanning bed, it is a collagen bed and what this bed has to offer is radiant skin reducing wrinkles and signs of ageing skin. It is the same idea as a tanning bed in that you lay in the bed for ten minutes a few times a week. The collagen and vitamin C light is a glow that helps with cell revitalization of the skin. I spoke up right away and asked if I could take one of them home with me! We all laughed when Ryan replied chuckling, sorry it will not fit. Crap I said, as I continued to look around. Amanda commented yes that would cut down on the costly creams. When Jessie said happily, what are you worried about, when you get home will be able to afford to buy your own plastic surgeon she reminded us. Oh yes, I guess we will have some money for a little nip and tuck if we want, when Amanda motioned with her hands to her chest, bigger boobs.

As we look around the corner of the cedar nook, we can see their master washroom had etched glass floor to ceiling sliding doors into their huge designer walk in closet. The washroom was black slate and glass fixtures with all the towels teal and gray. A raised two-person Jacuzzi tub had two glass columns at the steps that lit up and flickered like candles.

Still wowing at everything we come out of the bathroom and see at the end of the huge bed there was a hand carved wood chest that when Ryan touched another button on his remote a large screen TV came up from it. This is incredible, amazing, Amanda and I said to them and with Jessie standing right beside me I put my arm around her and gave her a squeeze, good job you two I really do not have all the right words to express how awesome your home really is.

Ryan looking quite proud made a point of holding up his empty wine glass and said, I believe that we all need a refill and dinner will be ready soon ladies. We were enjoying the tour immensely; however, when Ryan said that dinner would be ready soon I all the sudden feel myself being hungry when Amanda asks so who did the cooking and what are we having smiling brightly at Jessie and Ryan, as we were turning to go back to the kitchen.

It was a joint venture, and nothing as elaborate as Rosie puts on Jesse was saying as we come around the glass staircase and hear the piano still playing we are back into the open bright kitchen. Matter of fact we are having, she pauses and waits for Ryan to put on his oven mitts, and pull out a baking dish of bubbling, Jessie finally says … with Mac and Cheese. We thought that was perfect and as Ryan put the pan down to cool he said Jessie and thought you might like some comfort food and we wanted to make you something you probably have not had yet. Jessie looked at us and smiled when she saw that we were impressed with their selection. As Ryan was getting us, another bottle of wine Jessie was putting some last minute items on the table for dinner like a Cesar salad and garlic toast started setting the table. Amanda and I asked if we could help and as usual, we were told to have a seat and relax as Ryan brought us over a fresh glass of wine.

Once Jessie had the last item, the Mac and Cheese on the table, she signaled that we could, settle in and start filling our turquoise glass plates. The table was so large that it was easiest to stand and fill them with none of us talking other then Ryan asking Jessie to pass him a toast, as we are all digging into dinner.
Amanda was the first to speak up after a few bits saying how good everything was, and then turning to ask Jessie about our hair appointments, oh yes Rosie made sure that you are first in the morning so that we will have all

day to get ready. Elsie is also an excellent hair stylist and will be helping me with getting the rest of the ladies done. Amanda teasing mom, informed Jessie that mom has not sat in a chair for years; Amanda winked at me and embellished the statement by even saying that I had a phobia in going to a salon and that it is as difficult as going to the dentist. Jessie and Ryan both looked up at me, we chuckled, and I defended my phobia by replying, I have had some real bad hair scary experiences, trust me, I smiled and quickly said with confidence in my tone, but I trust you and Elsie.

As we continued eating, Ryan said to me that if I have any teeth issues that I should go see Henry and that she could take care of them pain free. Even that sounded good to Amanda, and I remembered we are seeing Henry tomorrow for the filters, I said I would ask her then.

Having the filters put in is a very smart move Ryan highly praised, and what Henry has designed and will be evolving so in time there is no telling what she can make them do, we may even be able to communicate to you through the device some day. Jessie was as supportive of the filter being most impressed with the potential long-term health benefits of being connected.

Ryan lifted his wine glass to propose a toast to Henry and her breakthrough filter we all joined in with cheers all around. On that wonderful note, I said to them the filters will be fantastic but they would not be a necessity if it were not for you two sailing us home. We want to thank you for that so, so much, Amanda was nodding and agreed that getting us home and you all back again will be a journey. Jessie wanted to reassure us that they are ecstatic to be going. Amanda looked over at Ryan then Jessie and immediately asks, is there any danger in getting us home and you all back? I looked up from my glass waiting for a response when Jessie spoke up and said the only risk would be when the sub surfaces in Alaska however, the timing of us surfacing will be synchronized with our satellite creating a mirror image of this area without any image of the sub visible by other satellites. When the sub is submerged, it is virtually undetectable Jessie says with confidence. Ryan followed by reassuring us and joking that they enjoy an adventure now and then but they are living proof by living their lives inside an island, that they do not have a death wish he laughed just the opposite in fact. That was good to hear, it was freaky enough thinking about traveling halfway around the word in a sub, and we did not need to add any element of danger to it too.

Once we all had our fill with Ryan eating three times as much as us girls,

Jessie gets up and pulls out of a smaller oven, and apple, caramel crumble that just looked scrumptious as Ryan and Amanda got up to remove a few things off the table to make room for desert. When Jessie put the yummy desert on the table, she confessed Janette made this for us. Yes, Ryan admitted there are certain things we can count on others to provide and between Rosie, Janette and Paul there are something's just never bother to learn, we raised his eyebrows and smile at Jessie and we all had a little chuckle, while Jessie started to serve up desert. Oh, my-goodness, I will burst if I eat that much looking at the portion Jessie laughing handed Amanda who looked at Jessie smiling back at her and then blew out her cheeks like a chipmunk.

We have lots and you can take what you do not eat home with you Jessie still chuckling over the oversized piece of desert she gave her. Rosie will eat what you do not; she loves Janette's apple crumble and will not care whose fork has been in it she laughed and I almost lost it. Jessie said it with such a dry humor that I almost spit out my mouth full of wine. For sure everyone on the island heard me laugh that time and I think the birds even went quiet for a second, wondering what that sound was. Ryan was laughing hardy when he blurted out; I wonder whom Dustin might have wounded this time. That comment had us all roaring again knowing that my laugh startles him.

After only having a few bits I was done, I was so full I could not eat any more, I had to sit back in my chair and concede, I had all I could. Amanda could not eat any more either. Jessie was done too, she was just picking at hers and Ryan finished his. Jessie stood up and asked us to come out to the patio and we can have our coffee out there. Ryan hung back to clean the table off a before coming out and sitting with us.

Amanda and I like little kids, went right for the large porch swing and Jessie took a seat in one of the armchairs. When Jessie looks over at me and said you look like you have something on your mind Colleen what is it she asked. I know there was something we were going to ask about but with the wine and excitement, it has slipped my mind, hum I smiled and look over at Amanda with a puzzled stare. Then Amanda's face lit up and she says I know what it was now. Jessie knew by the tone that it was going to be a quirky kind of question and responds, so the question is she smiled.

Then the light bulb went on for me, as Amanda started asking so what do you do for New Years Eve, if Christmas Eve is a formal event. Jessie sat back in her chair and started giggling. Just as Ryan came out with a hovers try of coffee and all the fixings. Before Jessie had a chance to respond I noticed that, the serving cart that Ryan was using did not have wheels. I quickly pointed that out to Amanda who had to bed down to see that there were no wheels. Wow, that is cool, I guess you do not have to worry about getting a flat I said and chuckled as I looked back at Ryan. What is up with the cart, Amanda asked.

Ryan replied it is a little something I created so that when you go from one floor surface to another like when going through the door, to avoid bumps the cart will maintain one hundred percent balance as the floor grades change. You will never spill again Ryan said proudly. That is quite the invention Amanda complemented Ryan, why does Rosie not have one she smiled. Ryan answered she loves that carts she has and would never change, and come to think of it she did blow a tire on the large cart one year, that Paul repaired for her, he looked at Jessie and smirked, while Amanda and I were smiling at each other. Once in position the cart lowered and sat flat on the deck. While Jessie started pouring coffee, she said now what were we chatting about before Mr. Show off came out, she winks at Ryan.

Oh yes, New Years Eve, with this night being the beginning prelude to a New Year, we have a pajama party to celebrate. We have no religious beliefs toward the holiday or any holiday for that matter, we recognize and know that as human beings we all need a reason to celebrate. Other then Christmas being a tradition of family and food coming together to make the all the other celebrations universal every month there is a themed holiday which for those not interested, can use as an extra rest day . The themed celebrations include a spring day party, summer day, fall day, and winter gatherings. We also celebrate by having an all sciences day party and so one. As Ryan was getting comfortable in his chair, we looked over at Amanda and I and said, we can also change our themes when take our annual vote.

That is interesting I replied as Amanda and I were swinging on the chair. Ryan had his remote control in his hand and with the sun going down he changed the lighting of the glass panels, which gave off a dancing hue of a combination of blue water and the flickering of candles. He had turned off the piano and had old Eagles music playing softly in the background.

Jessie sitting there content looks over at us, and asks if there were any other questions, that we might have. Catching us off guard, I looked back at her and swirled my face a bit, as I took a moment to think about her question with Amanda doing the same, hum. When it came to me to ask, is there anything else that we will need to do to prepare to leave. For you, other than the filter and packing no there is nothing I can think of, Jessie looked at Ryan he shook his head no, and commented that it will be us that will be performing all system checks and Rosie and Paul confirming inventory and schedules the days leading up to the departure.

Ryan speaking frankly said that really, when you think about it our departure is not that far off, not to get anxious about it, but in two days we have Christmas Eve and then after New Years, we start our opening count down. From then, the sub deployment departure is potentially only days away.

When you run down the time like that, it sounds quick when you say it I commented and for right now, I can honestly say I am not obsessing over the nearness or feel eagerness for time to pass quickly. Turning to Amanda I asked curiously are you feeling anxious about going home now that we know we will be leaving soon. Amanda answers with a yes and a no. I feel more comfortable when talking about leaving now, and I am not anxious or starting to wait for leaving which is good and I think it is because there is so much going on over the next while that I have a sense that we will get there when we get there, and enjoying every day I am here.
That is fantastic Jessie says and good to hear, with Ryan letting us know with a nod to Jessie, that Elsie and Henry would be please to know the sentiment, because as they would say, a calm state of mind is critical in living through any catastrophe. Although your story, as his voice raise in pitch, I must, say has a better ending then most catastrophes, Ryan smiles.

I happened to look over to the coffee cart and noticed to cardboard pastry boxes and smiled, Ryan saw that I had noticed that he had boxed up some apple crisp to take home with us. At that time I gave Amanda a pat on the leg and said okay kiddo, we had better be going; she was looking so comfortable as we were rocking slowly back and forth. As we struggled to get up, we began thanking them very much for the wonderful dinner and Janettes desert I said while giving Jessie a hug and praising their home.

Jessie and Ryan walk with us to our pink driving machine and hand us our apple crumble with Ryan giving us a third box, for Rosie he said, we cannot forget Rosie now. We wave as we start to pull out of their driveway and looking back, the glass house had a glow about it that was fixating. As soon as were out of the driveway, I pull out our smokes. We had only the one smoke each while we were there and were overdue. I lit us both a smoke and looking up see the large Christmas tree and feel a big smile come over my face as I hand Amanda her smoke.

What are you smiling about she asked, I am not sure really I saw the tree and smelt that apple crumble as I looked at you and felt a overwhelming feeling of happiness. Awe that is so cute mom, I love and adore you, I love you to sweetie more then you know. I do not think I could have survived this with anyone else, I finish saying as we are all most at the now, Christmas palace.

As we get up onto the patio, we see that Rosie is actually in the hot tub, listening to Christmas music and drinking wine. We head right over to her and give her a hardy good evening Rosie, I thought that hot tubs were not your thing. Hello ladies how was your visit, Rosie says and then switches to saying that hot tubs may not be my thing but every once in a while, we do things that are not our thing she smiled. Looking at us holding the pastry boxes, she eagerly asks is that Janettes apple caramel crumble, yes it is and Ryan boxed you up some. Oh sweet Rosie says and asks Amanda to fetch a spoon from the bar.

Girls I have your suites out ready for you, come for a soak and tell me all about your day. It was funny to see but by the way, she was talking, we could tell she had drunk more than the one bottle of wine sitting with her at the hot tub. We knew she wanted company and having a hoot and sitting in the hot tub was a good idea before calling it a night. We will be right back I said to Rosie who was immersed in her desert and loving every morsel, by the looks of it.

We get in our room and quickly change as we can hear Rosie turning the music up louder. She was getting right into the spirit I said to Amanda and who laughed yes it is some kind of spirits, implying it was not the season rather the wine that was getting to her. We had a little quiet chuckle before coming out and pouring ourselves a coffee and lining up our smokes and hoot to enjoy when we get into the hot tub. Amanda turned down the music just a tad and winked at Rosie saying we will disturb the neighbors; she smiled and got into the hot tub.

Before we even had our hoot lit Rosie said I heard your laugh earlier today and I was in the kitchen, the funny thing was when I heard the loud cackle I knew that it was you and it made me chuckle to myself. Yes, Ryan was wondering if Dustin wounded another one of his characters with it, I smiled big and Rosie snickered. We lay back and start enjoying the lights, music, and Christmas atmosphere. Along with our coffee and hoots, which Rosie did not pass on this time? Amanda and I glanced at each other, as Rosie was having a puff, like a pro I might add, indicating she did have a bit to drink.

Amanda asked Rosie as she passed the hoot what she did today and without hesitation Rosie starts running down the list of things that she had been fussing with in the kitchen and with a sly look at us both she says, I altered your dresses they will fit like gloves and a couple accessories to bring it all home. Rosie winked at us and did not say any more other then; you will see them in a couple days leaving us in suspense as to what she has done. I told Rosie and Amanda that the suspense of the dress is more intense then my anticipation of going home is, right now, I chuckled. Perfect Rosie replies that is what I was going for.

So how was your visit, what did you think of their home is it not the most unique house you have ever seen. Amanda said there is nothing like it anywhere I am sure, however if they are going to have children where are they going to stay, we did only see the one bedroom. I did not want to ask them just in case it was a thing of some kind and I did not want to provoke what could be an awkward situation.

Rosie thought that was nice of Amanda however not necessary. Rosie rolled her eyes and smiled as she was telling us that those crazy lovebirds are renovation wild and they do have the extra rooms, designed they just want to draw out the progress work on the home, and will start when Jessie is pregnant. So there is a plan, oh yes and I would think that when we are back from bring you home, that will be their mission.

I think I am feeling a little prune like, Rosie says smiling at us as she holds up her empty glass. Yes this has been nice but I am ready to get out too I said. Amanda agreed that was nice and will definitely help put me right to sleep, that and the hoot, of course she chuckled as she waited for Rosie and I to get out and grab our towels. Once out of the tub, Rosie was drying off and wrapped herself in her big towel, then poured a coffee as she looked over at us and said, I think I need one of these she grinned.

Well Rosie I think we are going to pack it in for tonight, we see Henry tomorrow, are you going to come with us. Of course I am, she replied, I want to know everything I can about the filters and I will be part of, and oversee every aspect of your journey home now. Thank you Rosie that means a lot to us and as Rosie stood to give us a hug, Amanda while getting ready to go to our room, remembered about our hair appointments and wanted to thank Rosie for making them for us, we had not thought about our hair. Oh yes I had forgotten about the hair appointments, you are so welcome ladies, I cannot wait to see you both all decked out. Amanda replied with a smile for Rosie as we were walking back to our room, we are all going to look amazing, and turned to blows Rosie a kiss.

In our room, we could smell the coffee and could see our two boxes of apple crumble that we instantly knew we were going to have some. While I got into my housecoat, Amanda went over to a hutch by our seating area to see if she could find a couple forks and when she pushed on the big cabinet doors that had no handles it opened up to show us the mini bar with sink and microwave. In the one large drawer Amanda opened, there was a full set of gold plated cutlery. Jackpot she says as she holds up the two shiny gold desert forks. I can honestly say I have never eaten with a gold fork before I told Amanda; this makes an already amazing desert taste even better I said and smiled. Amanda went to change and I poured us coffee to have with our yummy treat that we now had a little room for after digesting the thick and cheesy, Mac and Cheese we ate for dinner.

We were snuggled in our chairs and had our pastry boxes sitting on our lap eating with our gold forks when Amanda asked if I was going to have Henry look at my teeth tomorrow. You know I think I might, maybe she can repair some cracks in my back teeth that I think I got during the plane crash. Amanda's head shot up and she looked at me with total amazement. Mom I totally think I blanked that out in my mind hearing you now say it so casually, it is abruptly real that despite all odds we did survived a plane crash. I am sorry if I have upset you sweetie, I should have been more thoughtful before I come out with that. No mom, it is okay the thought was not upsetting it is just that it instantly became so real to me. Wow what a revelation, she mumbles as she has a forkful of her apple crumble, wide eyed recalling what she could with blacking out as the plane was breaking apart and regaining consciousness when we were already safe on the beach.

Absolutely it is incredible when you think of all the people on that plane we were the only two in the safest place when it all happened, the bathroom. I grinned and looked for Amanda's reaction that by her riffling back at me, yes, only my mom would be hung up in an airplane washroom, was positive.

We had a quiet little chuckle and one more fork full of desert, before having our smoke before bed.

Lighting up our smokes, sitting back, and gazing I quietly said what a house hey, that was something for sure but the glass walls would take some getting used to. Here they at least have their privacy and security is not an issue. We were once again drained and ready for bed. We had a few puffs and both made the climb onto the bed to say our good nights and love you.

Chapter Twenty-Two

When we woke up this morning, we see for the first time that we get to wear something twice, when Rosie had out T-shirt's, and shorts that we seemed to recall, although Amanda thought our tops were slightly different. As we walk over to our sitting area to start our day off with our coffee and surrounded by greenery and flowers and close to our open balcony, I say to Amanda with a good morning and a smile, it is another beautiful day out there, as she finished her stretch and was sitting down.

Every day is a beautiful day out there, she replied, and as she went for her smoke, added I think I am going to miss that, you know. Reminding her that we will be well enough off, that we can be where ever the weather is the nicest. Oh right, you are so right, I guess I do not believe it or think like that yet, she pauses and then she looked right at me and wiggled her eyebrows up and down and smiled, but I will get the hang of it, she said confidently.

Thinking that Rosie intended for us to be seeing Henry early in the say we figured we would not doddle and when we finished our smoke got up right away and went to get ready. Both of us going about our business in the washroom, Amanda thinking out loud said, I wonder how Rosie is feeling with the wine she had yesterday. Even though she said it in a normal voice, the words seem to echo in the room, we both smile but also cringed a little, hoping Rosie did not hear that.
Coming out to the extreme Christmas patio, first sets you back with all the decorations and flowers that are a wonderful displayed, we see Rosie sitting at the table with her sunglasses on. Oh my Rosie are you okay Amanda goes right up to her and puts her hand on Rosie shoulder, thinking Rosie was all

hung over. When Rosie whips her sunglasses off and blurted out, I thought you might have believed I drank too much yesterday when really the hot tub did me in, man did I ever sleep Rosie says. I put the glasses on to pull your leg. Amanda you are so sweet, you were genuinely concerned over what would have been a self-educed sickness. Paul or Kevin would have not been so kind she smiled.
Sit, sit ladies l made us French toast with fresh strawberries for breakfast today I had a hankering for them after watching a cooking show yesterday. They look so good I said, I am hungry and I am not sure why I thought the Mac and Cheese would have stayed with me longer. We even ate most all of our take home apple crumble I told Rosie. Amanda even said she was ready to eat as well and French toast is perfect.

As we got our plates ready, and start to eat, I asked Rosie if there was anything else that Henry was going to do to us today. Before she could answer, I relayed that Ryan told us that she is a pain free dentist as well, and that I should check that out. Are you having problems with your teeth girls, you should have said something we would have you in sooner. Amanda let Rosie know that it is not her that is having problems it is mom, and I said that it was to worry about or anything major I just had a few cracks I thought she could glue up, I chuckled. Admit it mom you want anything done that needs doing, as long as there is no pain she laughed. Yes, is that not what I just said, giving a big smile? You are one of those, are you Rosie said to me, with a little grin, only go when it hurts we know your type she chuckled.

Amanda says really Rosie seriously, is there was anything more we should know about before going. All kidding aside Rosie replied there is nothing to worry about ladies, the procedure is simple. Before Henry places the filter, she will scan you both and check, your vitals and internal systems for her baseline and then you will sit in her nice reclining chair. Henry will then freeze the injection area so you will not feel the needle and the secret to not feeling anything is not looking at the needle. To ensure you do not look at the needle I made my version of a sleep mask to cover your eyes so that you do not see the needle.

Holly crap, how big is this needle Amanda yelped. If you made masks to cover our eyes, it must be like an elephant tranquilizer gun. Rosie blurt out a huge laugh at Amanda and took a second to say oh no silly the needle is not that big, I just think you are that chicken she laughed again. Rosie was getting a kick out of scaring us a little; she knew that we felt we were safe, and for all our wellbeing, there is no changing our minds.

Rosie said when we are there, you can see what else she may have up her sleeve, Henry is a woman of many talents and access to a crazy amount of medical, clinical supplies, so ask away just in case. Henry designs and customizes her own creams and she makes a real mean old lady cream, you would love Colleen. Amanda, you do not need the old lady cream just yet, she smiled, Henry can make a skin type customized cream for you.

Well ladies, we should think about getting ready to go see Henry instead of just talking about her she smiled. Letting us know in her way that we will not be hanging around for coffee by the pool this morning. Seeing that we were done, Rosie started gathering up the dishes, put them in the tray, and went to grab our go cups to fill them with coffee.

I nodded to Amanda indicating we should have a smoke before we go, so we got up to gaze at the tree and lit up our smokes while Rosie was fussing about for a bit. We have not been in Henry's lab before I wonder what else she can do there, hum, I smirked at Amanda and said jokingly I wonder if I can get my boobs enlarge while we are here I laughed, and Amanda started right in, when Rosie asks so what is so funny over there. Amanda replied loudly on nothing mom was just wondering if she could get Henry to give her a boob enlargement while we are here. I was still laughing and tried to teasingly shush Amanda when Rosie started and we were all having a good chuckle. When we could catch our breath, Rosie says I am all ready if you girls are, let us go find out if you can get a boob job; she snickered and waved with go cups in hands us over to the cart. We butt out our smokes and walk behind her when I here Shotgun.

As we are getting into the cart I said to Rosie and Amanda come on I was only joking you guy's about the boob job, do not mention that Henry will think I am nuts. Worse, she will think I have no respect for her real talents, not that I know what they are but I do not think boob jobs is on any certificate she has I giggled. Both Amanda and Rosie were chuckling as we drove, when Rosie turned around and said I am curious myself, now that you have asked the question, I have no idea if that is possible here and if I say it is me who is enquiring would that make you feel better. I look at Rosie and say there is no way she is going to believe that it is you that wants a boob job. Look at you, Rosie you are perfectly proportioned and have an hourglass shape. Well thank you Colleen for noticing and it is true she will not believe it is for me, she laughed and gave Amanda a pat on the should leaving me in suspense of not knowing if my boob job comment will come up or how.

As we drove for the first time there was someone else coming our way and we wave as Paul passes driving to Dustin's birdcage. Rosie points to where she wanted Amanda to park as we see Henry and Elsie sitting on the front porch bench having an ice tea. Well hello ladies, Henry and Elsie come over to great us and welcome us to where Henry boasts all the real action takes place.

When we enter the reception area with Elsie all smiles and Henry taking the lead, we could see down the halls to glass cubed rooms and reclining dentist chairs examination tables. Come on Henry says I will give you the tour as she directs us past the examination tables there was a few large clinical looking pieces of equipment that Henry started to explain their purposes. The first machine we came to she described as a stand up MRI and that the internal scanning is horizontal. Our MRI provides advanced detailed information currently not available in the world today, and it is with the aid of our kinetic2 energy technology that make this machine superior however unrealistically costly in today's terms. I raised my hand a little to get Henry's attention to ask what if someone is not well enough to stand. Good question Colleen, we have special formed acrylic body boards that hold the body securely without having to strap a person in, we raise them and slide the person in horizontally. It is actually quite a feeling to be encased and hung that way, I know because I drew the short strew when it was time to test it Elsie said jokingly making us smile along with her.

The next piece of equipment is a rejuvenation tube; we would use this machine if one of us broke a bone or pulled tendons or muscles. Reconstruction configuration is determined by the type and nature of injury. Keeping it simple, the tube works with all the things that you cannot see toil to put whatever that is broken back to the way it is supposed to be. We believe that if knowing prior to appendices removal being a surgical necessity the machine may help to repair the damage. We have not been in any position to try it and Elsie's appendices are perfect she said with a straight face and gave Elsie a little nudge, humorlessly implying to us that Elsie is her test subject.

The other large piece of equipment is a pod that we hope never to have to use. The pod is a life preserver in the case of critical illness or disease. There is nothing our equipment, technologies and I cannot fix however sometimes all we need is more time. The pod will provide precious time and can sustain the human life for an extended time. However, if the failing outcome will be total organ shutdown, and if we still need more time for a cure. As the body, lies in the coma like state that it is in the pod gives an estimated time of organ failure and if we are not able to administer what I would call the miracle cure the pod systems will start sequencing for a cryogenics type of process. We do not freeze the person like an ice cube although we do have them safe and comfortable while we find a cure. Elsie commented that the pod is a marvel and certainly one she hopes we never have to use, but I am glad it is here.

Looking around there were separated workstations with lots of unique equipment and glass rooms that sealed for containment, to be able to quarantine if needed. As we walk to the back of the lab, there is a long stainless steel trough like sink against the wall with a huge window that we can see the surgical room. Just like you see on TV and the movies the room was large, tile lights trays tables, man I could not believe what I was seeing. I looked over at Amanda and we went right up close so we could see it all when Henry turned on another bank of lights that turned the room bright white.

We were all standing at the sink looking at all the surgical equipment inside the room built into the walls and hanging from the ceiling. Amanda asked Henry what the seal on the door meant and she explained that confirmed the theater was one hundred percent sterile. Of course, as we were all in awe gazing through the window for a second, Rosie for sure saw this as her opportunity to have fun with my earlier comment she coughed to get attention and, blurted out with a straight face, for sure Colleen you could get a boob job done here. I let out a cackle right off the bat, it had slipped y mind but knew she was not going to let it go.

Of course, Henry and Elsie look right at me and Amanda had to hang onto the sink she was laughing so hard. No, no I replied once I could, I was kidding around. Rosie said you make wonderful skin creams and Ryan said you are a painless dentist, so I was being funny and said I wondered what else you could do and I threw out that I should check on a boob job, Amanda and Rosie just thought that was hilarious.

Looking back at Henry and Elsie I paused and with an innocent look on my face I asked so, well, can you? They all lost it, before I had the chance to clarify and say, fix my teeth I mean. Oh right, Rosie gave me a nudge and a wink. Oh, my goodness Henry says that was fun as she wiped the corners of her eyes.

Well let us go back out to the reception area and we can see the office and lounge area. There is coffee, fruit, and pastries and we can answer more questions there Elsie said. Henry takes the lead and we follow them back to the lounge where we took a seat at a boardroom table. Elsie poured coffee, when Henry asked if we had any questions about the filter, I jumped in yes, who goes first? Amanda shot a look at me of surprise and smiles while she says back you big chicken. All I could do was grin because she was right although I pretended to be brave and waved my hand in the air only kidding, I will go first.

Okay then, first we get you into the body scan, and informed us that we can keep your cloths on but all no metal allowed. The scanner will not operate if it detects any metal. Then you sit in my reclining chair we clean and freeze the injection area and position your head based on the projection from above that marks the exact location and configures depth of the implant. Then minutes in the chair and done how does that sound, you ready. I asked if I could have a sip of coffee before we start, for sure no rush Henry replies I think I want one of those raisin tarts before starting too.

Elsie let me know that she can have a look at my teeth while Amanda is getting her filter implanted if you would like, Henry gave the two thumbs up and thanked Elsie, you are in good hands . That would be awesome if you would not mind, I have a few cracks and if you could through some white to them that would be great I smiled and gave a little chuckle.

Then Henry circled back and said to us, you know we could perform breast enlargements here; however, I am not sure how well that would fit with the story of being stranded on an island that supposedly does not have communications and limited power if any, she tilted her head and shrugged her shoulders, just saying. Oh yes, you are so right about that, I never thought that far ahead I snickered, and Amanda smiled, and then directed her comment at Rosie by saying at least when you start to get droopy Henry can give you a pick me up she laughed changing the boob focus onto her. Rosie had a surprised look saying back to her, these babies are not going anywhere, making us all chuckle.

When I said okay, I am as ready as I will ever be looking over at Henry. When Henry stands up right away and agrees let us get this done. We go to the back and I first stand in the scanner with my hands by my side when I hear Henry say just hold your position for a minute and I will have what I need. We are good you can come out now as I see her keying in some information into the computer. Now if you could come sit down here we will get you in line, when I see Rosie by the door watching what was happening. Amanda stayed back chatting with Elsie who was explaining more of what they can do in the lab.

Henry had me sit in the reclining chair and turns my head, and moves my hair out of the way. Henry rubbed a cold cloth on my neck and within seconds, I could not feel that she was touching my neck at all. Then I feel her reposition my head and says okay Colleen do not move. Closing my eye's I could feel my grip on the armrests tighten anticipating the pain of a needle. When all the sudden I hear Henry say, wonderful we are done. Just let me confirm the placement and we should be good. Yes we got it, how do you feel Henry asks, fine I replied, I feel fine, matter of fact, I did not feel anything thing, even I could hear my amazement in my voice.

Okay, now we monitor you and the filter's interaction for the next few days and we will activate the imbedded program once you land in Alaska. Rosie was listening carefully and asked Henry, is there anything we needed to do or watch out for over the next day or so. Henry answered Rosie with saying no nothing really, although I believe the girls are going to feel tired this afternoon as their bodies accept the foreign object. Rosie wanted to confirm with Henry that with our big Christmas Eve party tomorrow there will not be any side effects. All right Colleen we are done and you will feel the freezing coming out shortly. Henry looks over at Rosie and says okay now if we can get Amanda back here you girls can go rest for the day. Rosie went to get Amanda while I got up out of the chair feeling no different.

Rosie comes with Amanda when Henry says Colleen you go see Elsie now and she will check your teeth over. Amanda and I pass each other in the hall and she looks at me and quietly says well… It is all good, I did not feel a thing but I did close my eyes, I said in passing.

Elsie brings me to another reclining chair in a cubical that was set up as a dental facility. She sits me in the chair and says this is dentistry like you have never seen before she smiled. Without x-rays or any checking Elsie squirts some jell into a rubber mouth guard and inserts it into my mouth and says okay now bight down and hold that for one minute. I was please that the jell did not make me feel like I was going to gage and did not have a horrid taste. While my mouth was shut tight Elsie looked at me and said are you excited for tomorrow, all I could do was nod and I gave her a thumbs up. Elsie smiled, and let me know that she is thrilled that we get to dress up, that is not something we do around here much.

We hear a little bell ring when Elsie says you are done. Let us get those trays out of your mouth and give a rinse and then you tell me if you can feel any more cracks in your teeth. If this does not completely fix the damage you were feeling, we will have you back for a better check up before you go. After I rinse my mouth out I am feeling around my teeth with my tongue and I could not feel any of them, my teeth were smooth and when I looked in the merrier I was super happy with how white they were. Wow, all that in just one minute and no pain, I jokingly said to Elsie you are my hero.

As I was coming out of the dental cubicle and Henry done with Amanda as we meet in the reception area, I give a big smile to Amanda and Rosie so they could see my teeth that looked brighter. When I let them know that all the little cracks are filled in too and they feel great. Thank you so much for the no pain and white teeth. Amanda commented that she did not know that she even got a needle.

Henry put her arm around Elsie and boasted that we are specialists at not inflicting pain, saying proudly. I am ecstatic that you have the filters, and for now we can monitor your health and tract you for life.
We will work at evolving the capabilities of the filter and hope to someday, be able to communicate with your subconscious. If you do get to the point of being able to do that how will we know I asked Henry? I cannot say for sure how you would know, although I believe that our communications will come though to you as a dream. Once we do get there, we will make sure that any messages are simple and clear to not confuse you or mess with the suppressed memories of the island. Amanda says with commitment, when mom and I are at home and together we will make a point of checking in on and chatting about our dreams.

Few, I said and started to fan myself with suddenly feeling a hot flash come over me, Rosie says it is time to get you girls home to relax Henry says the implants will make you tired and you want to be ready for tomorrow. Jessie and I are planning facials and manicures for you this afternoon. Are we going to Jessie's beauty salon Amanda asked Rosie? No, we are just going to do them on the patio. You will love the facemask it is amazing and makes the skin feel new again.

As we give our thanks and hugs to Henry and Elsie, Rosie asks Amanda if she is okay to drive, with Amanda replying I feel fine and the freezing is already gone. Okay, let us get you girls home and take it easy Rosie says as she gives Henry another hug on her way out.

Just as I went to open my mouth I here Rosie, shotgun! Amanda chuckled and looked back at me and said mom, face it you just cannot beat Rosie at that game. Yes, I guess you are right I replied and looked at Rosie who was sitting in the front and turned to just winked and smile, you know it girl.

We wave good-bye at Henry and Elsie as Amanda drives away. As we head back to the palace I said from the back well that was sure easy and I love how my teeth and look. Amanda commented that they do look whiter mom I smiled proudly.

Pulling up to the palace we See Jessie and Janette fussing about with tables and chairs making the patio look like a Christmas themed makeshift beauty salon party. We say our hellos; Rosie goes right over to Janette, and thanking her for coming. After our greetings and seeing Jessie mixing up a bowl of pink goop, I felt I needed to sit, have a hoot and a coffee. I walked over to the hot tub sitting area with Amanda following and asking if I was okay. I am fine sweetie; I just want to have a hoot and a smoke before they put pink goop all over my face I chuckled. Yummy, it did look like melted pink marshmallow Amanda gave her visual impression, which made me think the pink goop was going to be sticky.

We light up a hoot, and were sitting back watching the ladies getting everything ready when Rosie brings us over a fresh coffee and takes our go cups back to the bar. Jessie comes over and sits with us and says any time you are ready we can get started. Hey, your teeth look great Colleen Jessie noticed right away was Henry able to fix them too, Elsie was the one who worked on my teeth, they feel perfect, and let Ryan know that there was no pain, I smiled.

So what is the pink goop Amanda asked Jessie, who smiled at what Amanda called it. The pink goop as you call it is the most amazing skin cleanser and skin rejuvenates, that you could imagine. The facemask as we call it does the same thing as our revitalization bed however the mask is more intense with instant results where the bed is an ongoing whole body maintenance process. Is it sticky I asked, Jessie looked at me with a grin and repeated, sticky why do you think it is sticky she asked. I answered well, Amanda referred to the pink goop as looking like melted marshmallows and I instantly thought of sticky, I am not sure why. Jessie thought that was cute and then said actually it is more like fluffy silly putty.

That will feel different on the face I am sure, oh you will love it and we put it on the face warm and leave it for thirty minutes, you will be asleep in five, it is so relaxing Jessie says with shy.Rosie called over to let us know that there were finger sandwiches and snakes here for us to nibble on and wine if anyone was ready. Jessie told Rosie I will have one of those as she got up to get her wine and a little sandwich. We finished our smokes and I could go for a sandwich so as we got up to join them I was contemplating wine and asked Amanda what she was going to have, hum, I just had a hoot, we are going to have a mask on that is going to make us go to sleep, wine sounds perfect.

As we take our seats in the reclining bar stools with pull out headrests and brass foot bars, Rosie brings us a glass of white wine. I can hear the Christmas music playing in the background and I let her know that it sounded so pretty Rosie. I love listening to the music of this season Rosie replied as Jessie and Rosie approached Amanda and I to start to wrap our hair in towels to keep it out of the way of the mask.

Warm support pillows supported our head and neck as Jessie was making sure we were comfortable, as she said earlier; we will be in the position for about thirty minutes. I am all-good, bring on the pink goop Me too Amanda says after we both take a good sip of wine.

With latex gloves on Rosie and Jessie pinch off a glob of the pink goo, roll in balls, and then lightly pressed onto the skin until the face is fully covered. It only took a couple minutes to apply the masks with Janette observing making sure, they were going on evenly. What a weird feeling, wow Amanda and I were not expecting such a sensation from a facial. Jessie says now do not wiggle the mask will find every crevice and will start to rise like bread, Jessie, Janette and Rosie chuckled, they knew we were not expecting that to be part of the process and we knew we were supposed to be still.

As we lay back and can feel the mask doing something, we could hear the ladies talking about starting manicures when I just closed my eyes and like that I was gone, out like a light I did not hear anything after that.

When I awoke an hour later, the pink goo was off my face and there was a light blanket covering me. I feeling groggy when I woke, I slowly opened my eyes wondering what was going on, I see Rosie, Amanda but no Jessie or Janette. I asked right away how long I was asleep for, Amanda smiles at me and answers about an hour, really wow and Jessie and Janette have already gone home. Rosie replied yes we got your face and your nails done with you sleeping through it all. I look at my fingernails that were now long and black with tiny white buttons and little bowties, to match my tuxedo dress.

Focusing in on Amanda, she held up her fingernails that were a match to her dress with gold strips and her face glowed, it was radiant. Amanda you look beautiful I said softly still feeling sluggish, then asked for a merrier to check me out. Rosie was beaming and had a large merrier for me to have a look when I noticed that they both got up closer, obviously to see my reaction. When took a good look in the mirror I almost wanted to cry, my face looked better than it did ten years ago and Amanda let me know that she was proud to have such a beautiful mom inside and out. Rosie gave Amanda a pat on the shoulder letting her know that was so sweet. I complemented Rosie's fingernails that were painted white with gems embedded.

I am exhausted for some reason; wow Amanda could you grab me a smoke please Rosie brings me a coffee and reminds us that Henry did say the filter could make us tired, replying well between the filter and the facial, I just want a smoke a coffee and maybe go to bed. Amanda spoke up and said that she was not feeling like no ball of fire but she is okay. Amanda trying to liven me up says, I just want to look in the mirror and gaze at my amazing face she said jokingly.

Rosie lets us know that she is bringing out a little dinner for us first and then we can both toddle off to bed. Tomorrow will be a long day and I want you both to enjoy every minute of it she says and then give us both a big smile. Rosie was just as excited to get all dressed up and we could tell.
I did not move I was so comfortable in my chair when Rosie got up to get dinner, I took this time to quietly ask Amanda what did I miss, was I snoring

I giggled. No, you were fine mom; I fell asleep to but woke up when Jessie was pealing the mask off my face. It tickled and tingled all at the same time as she pulled it off in one piece. The pink goo formed to our exact facial features and was supposed to peel off like a rubber mold. Jessie likes pealing the mold off the best, as you can see instant results as you lift the mask off the face. Cool I replied, only I cannot believe I slept through that and my nails being done.

Rosie rolls out with her serving cart, signaling for me to take my seat at the table with Amanda. The chatting and coffee was helping to bring me back to life and when Rosie lifted the covers off the food, we see that she has made soft tacos and cheese fries. No sooner, did Rosie lift the covers, Paul, Kevin and Dustin pulled up and as we are saying our hellos from a distance, as they stayed in their cart with Rosie dodging into the kitchen and right back out again with two bags of food for the fellows. Rosie walked the two full bags of dinner over to them, and as we hear them all thanking her for the tacos and cheese fries, she reminded them in a stern tone, that tomorrow they are to be spit shined and polished when she sees them. We heard then chuckle a bit and mumble, as they called back to us to have a great evening as they were pulling away.

When Rosie came back to the table, I asked her why they did not come in. Rosie looks over at me and says we will be having dinner with them tomorrow and you girls have had a big day. Dig in she says while she seats herself. I want you to know girls that the filter is new technology that I trust although to ensure success we do not disrupt its success. We all need our rest for tomorrow, and they wanted to watch some space movie at Dustin's place and they love when I make tacos, they are all too lazy I am sure she giggled. I have to say my face sure does feel amazing that is for certain, Amanda was just as impressed with not a blemish or pore to be seen.

The tacos were good, a bit on the spicy side and were juice; I let the girls know that for me the mission was to eat without getting any of the firry orange hot sauce in my fingernails. That stuff can stain you know, as Rosie and Amanda watch me hold my taco awkwardly and shake their heads smiling. Yes, mom you do need to go to bed soon, I smiled back at here and chuckled, yes I think you might be right sweetie.

We are all going to call it an early one tonight Rosie asserts, I am existed for tomorrow and everyone knows how much this does mean to me, they will do everything in their power to make it the best they can and I love that, about them all. What about dinner, who is helping with the cooking and setting up the dining area, I all the sudden thought to ask Rosie. Looking up from her plate Rosie replies that is the best part of having an evening affair, is that I have so much time to work on the food and my dress will take seconds to get on, she smiled at us and confessed she has tried it on several times already. She continues with saying that she will only be away for about an hour when getting her hair done.

After breakfast you, ladies can take off to Jessie's to get your hair done and then come back here and I will have your dresses and accessories out for you when you get back. Amanda and I smiled at Rosie.

Although the food was very good, after having a few bits I did not feel like eating anymore and I could see that Amanda was only picking at her fries. I looked at Rosie and with a big shy I said I think I just want some coffee and a smoke, I am just whipped. Rosie smiled and said you girls go and relax in your room. I have coffee and sweets there and trust me you will feel energized tomorrow she winks.
We get up to go and hang out in our room for a bit before I was going to crash, when Rosie gave us each a big hug and thanked us for the day. As we said our thanks and goodnights, we look out to the large beautifully decorated glowing tree when Amanda smiled at Rosie as we turned to go to our room.

I walk straight to my housecoat, went behind the carved dressing screen changed, went to the washroom and then walked to my spot in our tropical sitting area, and plunk myself down. Amanda was not far behind and when she sat down she took my hand and said are you okay mom, I have not seen you this drained before. Oh, sweetie I am fine, nothing a coffee, hoot and a smoke will not cure I smiled and put my other hand on hers and reassured her that I was fine just pooped. Amanda then poured our coffees and brought over the tray of sweets that Rosie had left. My eyes lit up then when I saw my Christmas favorites; I had to take a mincemeat tart and a shortbread cookie. Amanda took gingerbread and a shortbread cookie too, they looked so picture perfect, my mouth watered as I put them on my napkin.

Well that brought you back to life Amanda said as I had the mincemeat tart gone in two bits. That was so good I let her know, as I went for the shortbread that melted in your mouth, oh my goodness I gush these are exactly how I remember the best to taste. Wow those were yummy, as I sat up more alert and said to Amanda now let us have our hoot and keep the tray right here I smirked at Amanda and took a sip off my coffee before lighting our hoot.

Sitting there not saying anything passing the hoot Amanda looks right into my eyes and says mom you know that your face does look at least ten years younger with no lines. I am sure you have not looked close enough to really notice but you are look radiant mom. Tomorrow when you get your hair done I will hardly recognize you I am sure. Thank you sweetie I love you, and you are right I really have not taken a good look yet. Yes, I am pumped for tomorrow and you did get Kevin to take care of our little present for Rosie, yes, he left a little not on the seat of our cart letting me know that he took care of it. I think she is going to love what we created for her and it is all thanks to Kevin spilling some concrete mix on the path. She wanted something from us and I do not think you can get any more personal than this. We are geniuses in our own right I proclaimed to Amanda.

As we are finishing the hoot, I had to have more shortbread and then a few sips of coffee before having our smoke before bed. When Amanda commented I wonder what Rosie has done with our dresses and what accessories she is taking about. That will be exciting but we will not even see them until we get back from getting our hair done. I know they will fit perfectly however I have a feeling that she has changed my dress a bit and then added that I confess I hope the accessories are big and shinny I chuckled.

Sitting back relaxing having our smoke and finishing our coffee I said quietly, tomorrow is Christmas Eve sweetie and with the filters in place now, that does mean we are getting closer to going home. I feel nervous about that in some way although I cannot put my finger on what exactly it is. Then with a straight face looked at her and said I sure hope our partners are genuinely happy to see us when we do come home and before they find out, that we are wealthy, I quietly snickered. Then quickly let her know that I was only joking and kidding around. They are going to explode when they see I said and winked at her as I got up to give her a big hug good night and then hauled my butt to bed.

As crawled in bed Amanda tidied up a bit and I think I was as sleep before she was finished in the washroom.

Chapter Twenty-Three

Waking up this Christmas Eve morning, I did lay there for a minute and could already feel that body and I my mind were refreshed and energized. I roll over on my side to see if Amanda was awake and say my good morning. Amanda looks over at me and starts to stretch and asks how I felt, when I surprised her by sitting right up and saying fantastic, I feel great this morning. How about you sweetie, well I have not had coffee so it is hard to tell yet, she smiles and says, just joshing mom I feel great too.
I look over at what Rosie did have out for us to wear today and I had to smile, when I see that they were flowing poncho dresses that were obviously chosen because they will be easy to take off once our hair is done. Amanda sat up to see what I was smiling about and said those are pretty and comfortable. Yes, Rosie just thinks of everything. As we go to sit in our balcony lounge for coffee, we can hear the Christmas music broadcast throughout the island and the acoustics were amazing, playing was a children's choir softly singing in a foreign language and music we did not recognize, nonetheless the singing and music gave me goose bumps, it was so perfect.

As we are having our coffee and smoke, I said to Amanda I guess we better not doddle this morning and get out for breakfast. I am hunger I told Amanda, and then noted that with the way I have been eating I would have thought I would have put on weight but I really do not think I have. Have you stepped on the scale in the bathroom yet I asked Amanda, she says yes I have weighed myself and I have actually gained five pounds and all in the right places, I might add, letting me know she is pleased with the gain and points to her boobs, we both snickered.

Okay I said to Amanda as I stood up, let us get this day on the way, I cannot wait to put my dress on I looked at Amanda as we walked out to the patio. Rosie was there to greet us with a hug Christmas Eve day, hug and good morning and handed us each a little red flower, a type I was not familiar with although had a very similar smell to freesia. You look radiant ladies, how are you feeling today Colleen Rosie asked, perfect I replied I think it was the shortbread that fixed me right up I chuckled. You look comfortable in the dresses; they look so nice on you both.

Come have breakfast before the fellows come to remove a majority of the furniture off the patio to make way for the formal dining gallery. Amanda looked a bit surprised as she was being seated what are you talking about, a dinning gallery. We could see Rosie light up knowing that she was about to wow us again with her explanation of what a dinning gallery was.

Rosie begins by pointing out that the design patterns on the floor that change and that from the bar to the hot tub lounge area the floor will raise to a height of fifteen feet, which exposes the formal dining area with a large wood carved dining table with seating for sixteen. All the china is of the finest and has twenty-four karat gold rims on every piece. The utensils are stainless and twenty-four karat gold as well. This dinner setting is as over the top as you can get. The linens are silk and the chairs you melt into ensuring comfort while dining through several courses. Rosie adding that with the decorations once the dining area comes up you will see how this whole patio can change into an elite formal setting. This was one of Sires designs and the attention to detail is amazing.

Wholly crap Amanda blurts out the floor is going to raise and inside this cube is a full dining room with dishes even on the table. The room was sterilized and vacuumed sealed prior to being lowered it has not been used since It was set up, so we all get to enjoy it as a first together. Wow, I cannot wait to see that I said to Rosie, who replied it should be up by the time you get back.

Have your breakfast girls and we will get you off to Jessie's place.
This morning we have juice and French toast and I hope it will hold you over. Rosie shows us the thick, fluffy platter of French toast. Rosie goes onto to say that we will be having hors d'oeuvres; Amanda skewers her face at Rosie who then says with a smile, you know appetizers and light finger foods in the afternoon later.

Our guest will start arriving around five and dinner is at seven. So the countdown has started Rosie looked at us with a big grin, and then had a bite of her toast that was smothered in strawberries and gazed out towards the tree. As we were finishing our breakfast, we listened to the festive music that Dustin was broadcasting throughout the island and we just enjoyed a quiet and peaceful moment.
That has to be the best French toast that I have ever eaten I announce to them as I put my napkin down and fill my coffee. Then I said I have to have a hoot and a smoke before I sit in the chair, Rosie turned her head and said now that sounds serious. Amanda laughed and reminded Rosie that mom going to get her hair done is as scary as going to a dentist, other than Elsie of course, she giggled. Oh right, well then you just have your hoot, smoke and coffee. You are going to love it once you get there, I can promise you that, and you are going to love what Jessie will do.

With us all done our food, I lit the hoot right at the table saying I am both excited and anxious about going. I do need a new hairstyle and the grey is so grown out that I look like a skunk. With wearing my hair in a ponytail all the time that hides how bad it really does look, I smiled. Yes, mom I must say that is the most grey I have ever seen. Looking over at Rosie I said I normally color my hair once every six weeks or so, and she blinked and said now why have we not done that sooner she exclaimed, Jessie could have colored your hair any time. I guess with not mentioning it, and always seeing you with your hair in a ponytail, I never thought about that being something to do and with not seeing Jessie's salon until just the other day, it just never came up. Huh! I cannot believe I missed that she says to us with a puzzled look on her face.

We smiled and finished our smokes while Rosie got up and got our go cups ready and this time she put a good shot of Baileys in each one of them, as we hear her say tis the season, as she turns to hand us our go cups.

All right Rosie we will get out of your way for now and go get our hair all beautified. Rosie says I will have your baths ready when you get here. Amanda and I let Rosie know that we had our baths before we came out this morning, we did not want our hair to get wet or go flat if we bathe after is has been done. Well are you two on the ball this morning, and here I was going to set up your baths all so nice for you. Amanda replied to Rosie you have enough done so much already, you have other things you wanted to do today besides baby us, and you need your time too. We love you Rosie, you are simply amazing, and we give her a hug then turn to go to our pink driving machine to go to Jessie to get our hair done. For Rosie's benefit a yell out shotgun, and laughed as we got in the cart and waved good-bye.

Amanda was focused on driving and asked me to light her smoke, as she turns and says, to me you know we will be in the chair for at least a couple of hours implying I should have one too, I snickered and took heed and lit us both a smoke. I took a sip of coffee to realize it was straight Baileys, I did not say a word.

Pulling up to the glass house that was all in Christmas theme now with garland and ornaments and two red and white stockings hanging on the patio banister. We could see Elsie Jessie and Janette sitting up on the porch chatting as we pulled in. Walking towards them, I hear Janette and Elsie both commenting on our faces and how clear and fresh they looked. Amanda and I gave big smiles as we approached, showing that we felt as good about the transformation as they thought we looked.

Well ladies are you ready to go all Hollywood Jessie says giving her two thumbs up with Elsie smiling, and saying never mind Hollywood we can do better than that she quipped. Janette said her hellos and then her, good buys, you girls have a great time and enjoy. I will see you later, Jim and I are heading up to help Rosie for just a bit and then I will be back for my turn, she waves as Jim pulls up he gives us a big wave and yells out a happy Christmas Eve ladies, I am here to pick up my woman. Janette jumped into the cart with Jim and took off to the palace.

Amanda went to take a sip of her coffee and I could see her face wrinkle up as she was not expecting straight Baileys in her go cup. I blurted out a laugh as I was waiting for her to take a sip knowing she was unaware of the contents. Amanda yelps, that is not coffee it is even cold, I chuckled more and said Rosie made our go cup's Baileys on ice not coffee. I was surprised too but I wanted to see your reactions and did to say anything when I had my sip during the drive here.

Just then, Jessie said forget the coffee and Baileys we have champagne and cranberry juice for our morning as Jessie and Elsie pour us each a large wine glass full. Jessie wanted to make a toast, raised her glass, and said to good hair days, as we all agreed and brought our glasses together.

Okay let us get this show on the road as Jessie leads us upstairs to the salon. We get seated and the capes go on when Jessie who was doing my hair and Elsie who was doing Amanda's says you ladies just sit and relax we have our styles and colors picked out already. We do not need product to color hair any more we have new technology that is the new hair hoods. We can digitally created colors then programmed into the hood that uses strobe-luminescence to embed the colors throughout the hair. How long it takes to color the hair, is determined by the length of the person's hair. Colleen yours will take ten minutes and Amanda fifteen minutes to color and have the highlights we are looking for.

That sounds wonderful Amanda says, that should make you feel better mom she smiles. Yes, I am all-good I trust you ladies one hundred and ten percent-I gleamed. As the hoods were going on they looked and felt more like a foot ball helmet then something you would see in a beauty salon. There was a key pad on the side of each helmet and once Jessie and Elsie finished entering in the information I could hear a slight ticking noise in the helmet and my scalp felt warm. Elsie had to raise her voice to let us know that we would hear the ticking noise and warmth and that it will be hard to talk while the coloring is happening. We caught what she was saying and smiled and took a big sip of our champagne as we see them both take a seat close by, while they wait. We could see that they were chatting and enjoying their drinks but could not hear what they were going on about.

Then all the sudden I hear a ding, my helmet was done. I was so excited to see how this was going to turn out. I sat right up as Jessie was taking off the helmet and could see my hair fall out of the helmet like it was silk and was the most wonderful rich auburn with some faint gold highlights. I almost wanted to cry my hair looked and felt so different already and that took only ten minutes. Wow, I am flabbergasted I exclaimed to Jessie and Elsie.

As I was still gushing over my hair Amanda's helmet gave a ding letting Elsie know that she was done as well. Before Elsie even started lifting Amanda's helmet off her head, her hair was already sliding out of the hood it was so soft and straight and silky, that is incredible I said as Amanda was speechless and in awe of her hair. Amanda had streaks of many colors in her hair and the color just popped, she was so happy too.

Jessie let me know that she was going to give me a cut and then put a little

style in the hair but with the color the way, it came out and with what you are wearing this evening, we will keep the do simple, she smiled at me. Sounds perfect, you know best is all I said.
Not that it mattered, but I did think it was funny that I was not given a change to make any requests, then I figured Rosie had already made them for me I chuckled to myself.

I gasped at Amanda, your hair it is incredible she was looking in the large merrier as she rocked her head back and forth and watched her hair just flow. Jessie was snipping away at my hair, like no bodies business and was still in the conversation.

Amanda asked Elsie, so what was the plan for doing up my hair she follows with a hum … as Elsie was running her fingers through Amanda's silky long hair; she tilts her head and says. I was going to put it up in a Celtic styled weave, however now your hair is to silky to stay in a weave without using a can of spray and that is just yucky Elsie expresses. Elsie looks over at Jessie and they concur that all her hair needed was a loose curl with some hair from each side pinned up in the back. Elsie went to one of the drawers and brought out a gold leaf barrette that was so delicate and dazzling that she could use to pin up the back of Amanda's hair.

I was so busy paying attention to what was going on with Amanda and Elsie that I did not notice that Jessie had finished my haircut and was starting to curl and style it. When I did get a glance at the cut I was so impressed it was so age perfect with keeping the wispiness and some length to the style.

We were not much longer when Jessie and Elsie took our capes off. Elsie then says well, have a look, as they brought us over to the full-length mirrors. We all started beaming, you have done such a wonderful job you two, Amanda and I were stumbling over each other's words trying complement and thank them for the work that they had done. Wow, Rosie will be so impressed I commented which had Amanda saying that is so sweet mom, to think of Rosie. Elsie says everybody is happy then that calls for another glass of champagne, and have a good look at your new knockout looks.

Getting ready to leave, Jessie makes sure that we have all our stuff and Elsie brings the empty bottle of champagne with her. I could feel my hair bounce while I walked down the stairs and I could see the color change in the reflection of the glass.

As we get to the porch, we give both of them huge hugs and thank you for everything. The hair coloring and styling was such an uplifting feeling and we made sure to let them know how awesome we felt. We will see you in a while ladies, I said back to them as Amanda and I walked to our cart. Elsie says, I cannot wait to see everyone all gussied up. Have a great afternoon, as we all wave.

Pulling out of the driveway, first things first I said as I pull out our smokes I jokingly say to Amanda slowly now, so we do not mess our hair, I smiled sat back and took a puff off my smoke. Coming up the hill to the palace, we could see that there were a few people there. Not wanting to show everyone just our big transformation just yet, Amanda looks at me and says hoot at the beach, and before I could answer, she pulls a U-turn and heads us towards the beach.

Amanda parks and says I want to just go up there see what it looks like when it is all done and go get ready. I want to show off the whole package today and not just the half that is done now she smiles at me, I totally understand and agree sweetie I love the suggestion. We would only get in the way and we can see from here as they leave I chuckled. Right on, we look amazing; we have our Bailey's on ice we can have a hoot and a smoke and then go up how does that sound. Like a plan mom, like a good plan she smiles as I light up the hoot.

You know this is the first time in at least fifteen years that I have liked my hair, I am so happy with how it turned out I said to Amanda.
For sure, her face lit up when she replied I do not know how that hood works all I know is that my hair has never felt this healthy before. As we have the first puffs off the hoot, we see Rosie leaving to get her hair done, when we hear a faint do not break anything as she drives away. Amanda said I can see Paul, Kevin and Dustin there but I am not sure if Jim is there or not. He is probably getting ready with Janette. Well the only other two not accounted for is Henry and Ryan; I wonder what those two are up to I said, trying to remember if Rosie had said anything earlier about who was going to be doing what when. We will find out later I smirked at Amanda and had another puff, I am really enjoying this, and it is helping to settle me down with all the hype of the evening. Amanda agreed, me too mom.

While we were having our smoke, we see Kevin leave first and then a minute later Dustin was getting in his cart to leave. Even though he has to drive right past us to get to his birdcage, Amanda parked our cart in behind the trees so he should not have seen us as he drove by, not that it mattered. We did not think that we had been sitting there that long when unexpected we see Rosie driving back up to the palace, that was quick Amanda said and I added I think we should be going as soon as we finish our smoke, knowing she will be looking of. We ponder over the massive tree and all its lights and tune into the music in the background as we butt out our smokes. I look at Amanda and said are you ready to do this kiddo, making going to a party sound a whole lot more difficult than it will be.

Come on Amanda gestures to me, I want to see this pop up dining area I can tell that something looks different up there. We get in our cart and make the quick drive up the hill where we see that Paul is just leaving. Howdy, ladies I have not seen you around although I have heard you so I know that you are doing good. Might I say you are looking lovely, I am going to get spit shined and polished myself and will return shortly. He jumps into his cart and gives us a wave.

As we take the few steps up onto the patio where Rosie was standing at the landing, we stopped in our tracks when we saw the four huge marble pillars holding the stone ceiling embedded with starlight's that twinkled. The dining table and chairs looked to be for royalty with the heavy wood carved table and armchairs with thick gold striped cushions. The table was set perfectly with every gold-rimmed plate and gold plated fork in its proper place and order.

Rosie looking at the dining area says to us, head up girls the napkin rings are fourteen karat gold and are heavy so do not be startled and drop yours. I will be watching to see how everyone reacts when they go to grab theirs because no one will be expecting them to be so heavy. Then she turns to us and gasps, your hair is amazing wow turn around show me she says. Rosie was beaming she was so happy with how we looked.

We started focusing on the details of the formal dining room and then to the changes to the whole patio. Rosie was ready the bar was all lit up and well stocked. There were four-foot tall pillar tables spread out that we can set our drinks on and server up appetizers. Each pillar table will have something different on them and for your easy drinking pleasure; I have made a vodka cranberry punch that you can stick with for the evening that should not get you loaded Rosie winked at us. Then she said no guaranties though, making it clear that it all depends on how much you consume, as she was kidding around.

Okay ladies, I have your dresses out and ready and a couple extras she grind. I have also pulled out some make up for you that I thought you would like to try. If you need any help with getting your makeup right, give me a yell, I may not use the stuff but I do like to put it on other people.

As we walk towards our room we, were both excited to see what we were going to be wearing?
Knowing that Rosie had made some changes to our dresses and not sure what the extras, were we picked up the pace into our room to see what awaits us? As I walk in and see the first change being that my dress was now an emerald green backless tuxedo jump suite I could see the wide flowing pant legs with the satin band down the side of the leg that were slight to above the knee. Oh my goodness Rosie I yelped wow this is incredible, she hears me call out. Rosie shuffles into the room and says I hope you do not mind I liked this color much more and I thought making it a halter style with the emerald green satin collar and lapels gave it class. The gold and crystal buttons just added that much more and your shoes match perfectly. So what do you think, I love it Rosie, I went over to her and gave her a huge. I could see she was a bit worried about mine because she totally changed my outfit.

Then she asked Amanda so what do you think, Amanda looked at her dress and realized that Rosie had turned her dress into a one shoulder outfit and added more gold trim to her hem. I love it Amanda says to Rosie but what bras do we wear she asked oh, I have them on the bed here for you she clapped her hands together I am so glad you like them girls, that means a lot. Now get ready so I can see you. We will get ready if you go get ready too, we want to see you, and without the kerchief or scarf over your head, we chuckled not wanting to say anything to her earlier.

As she leaves, I quickly change and put my cool, low back halter bra on and slip into my dress. Amanda helps zip me up in the back and the jumpsuit fit like a glove once I had my shoes on I was blown away at how I looked. The halter tuxedo top was cut low but the amazing bra gave me cleavage and made my boobs look perky. With my hair done and the dress on, I did feel red carpet ready and that was even without makeup on. Wow mom you look out of this world and as I look over to Amanda I see two large blue velvet and gold trimmed boxes on the dresser and pointed to Amanda to open the box. Amanda took the blue velvet boxes off the dresser and brought them over to me and we each open a box that had a necklace earrings and bracelet in each box.

It was easy to see whose was who's with the one that I opened being all emeralds and diamonds. Interesting the designers theme of the emerald and diamond set was snakes. The emeralds were begets throughout the diamonds and gold settings integrating the form of the snake. When Amanda opened, her box there was a gold chain and diamond necklace with matching chain and diamond earrings along with matching gold and diamond tennis bracelet. Holly crap said quietly for some reason, Wow these are like the crown jewels Amanda snickered. When I said jokingly, I wonder if we have to give them back, Amanda could tell I did not want to.

We hear a knock on the door and hear Rosie asking if she can come in, of course you can come in and let us see what a polished Rosie looks like. When Rosie opened, the door and we got a look at her all dressed up with even a touch of makeup, and her hair in the Celtic weave. Wow, I could feel my eyes fill up with happy tears she looked amazing as she walked in and twirled around for us.

Rosie saw that I was in my outfit and her mouth dropped open, and then she turns me around and comments now that is what I call a perfect fit. I love the color on you, and the jewelry brings out the twinkle in your eyes she says to me with a smile. Rosie, knowing how much I love my shinny things, she brought in with her another large blue velvet box and motioned for us to come see what was inside. We followed her over to our sitting area and Rosie opened the box to show us an assortment of diamond and precious stone rings that she said we could wear what every and as many as we wanted for this evening, she chuckled. My face lit up and of course I had to try them all on, as Rosie and I were fooling around with trying all the rings on and her explaining them to me. Amanda went and sipped into her dress and put her shoes on then came over and cleared her throat getting our attention. As we look up and in awe of how marvelous she looked seeing Amanda standing there with her had on her hip and her head cocked to the side like a runway model I was so proud. Rosie simply said, your perfect girl.

I motioned for Amanda to come sit with us when Rosie said now pick yourselves out a ring or two as the cherry on top. After trying them all on we both chose two for the evening, I found a chocolate diamond beget band for my thumb and a three-karat yellow diamond. Amanda liked one of the diamond bands and then picked the five-karat solitaire with diamonds around the whole band. It was huge but fit her perfectly. Rose picked a diamond and blue sapphire ring and a blue sapphire and diamond band. Once we had picked out our rings, Rosie was tickled, by the way, we reacted and as we were wiggling our hands in the air showing off the rings, Rosie said that she had a couple last minute things to do yet and with these shoes on everything takes longer she giggled. Rosie let us know as she was leaving that she had been wearing our apron today and that she loved it. That is good to hear Amanda says you cannot get anything on you now.

We just have to put some makeup on and we will be right out Rosie, no worries you have a bit of time yet, have a smoke and finish up, then come out and bedazzle me! Feeling beautiful just as we were, we felt we were not going to need much makeup. We decided that we would get our makeup done and have a smoke; I said to Amanda jokingly that I think we need the practice of walking in high shoes again and the washroom and back is a good start.

We get up to walk to the washroom, and can see ourselves in the full mirrors and cannot stop looking at the reflection we were seeing. It was like there were two younger, classy versions of us looking back we looked incredible. Amanda nudges me to move along. As we get in the washroom, we see the makeup that Rosie has brought out from the drawers of stuff, which she thought would work. Of course, she picked the right colors and products. It was only ten minutes and we had our makeup on and were ready to make rock our entrance. As we were beaming looking at ourselves, Amanda looks over and says… smoke?

We picked a perfume from the line up on the vanity and started walking back towards our balcony sitting area. When we get to the table, we see that Rosie must have snuck in a left us two beautiful crystal steamed glasses full of punch to sip on while we have our smoke. We did okay with the shoes on our short walk to the table. I am happy that the shoes are comfortable for a high-heeled fancy shoe; I told to Amanda as we go to seat ourselves carefully. However, I think we could still use some more practice. It has been a while since I have worn a shoe like this even at home; I have not had a reason to really wear them. Amanda replies as she smiles, only Christmas parties and Weddings. We hold up our beautiful glasses of punch as I toast to us, for always surviving and being able to live out this fairytale together.

Amanda's eyes swollen up with tears could only get out a quiet bravo mom as she reached for a tissue. I grabbed us a smoke each, gave Amanda hers to get her mind off her tears, and as she composed herself she said I love you mom and I could not have done any of this without you. I smiled back at her and to not get too emotional I winked and said ditto sweetie.

The way we looked and the ambiance we could feel we were ready to get the party started. We only had a few puffs and then grabbed our glasses and took one last goggle at ourselves and strutted out to the now formal and beautifully lit banquet room.

As we come out Rosie had her back to us, and we could see the loose bun and weave in her hair and her white dress was a perfect hourglass. When Rosie heard us and turned around, she had her hands out to her sides, her face lit up and she called out oh my thundering, you ladies look exquisite. Us, Amanda gushed Rosie look at you, the group will be floored when they lay their eyes on you and Paul might just have a heart attack Amanda said just kidding around with Rosie.

We were all twirling around, putting on a bit of a runway walk, and showing off our shiny rings, when Rosie sees Paul pulling up the driveway.
Okay ladies, Rosie says these is it, all excited let us pull ourselves together and go over to the bar and fill our glasses. Then she says with a whisper, I will take a glass of punch over to Paul as he comes in and girls you follow me. Following Rosie, we could see Paul all decked out in a western high collar long coat tuxedo, with shiny black boots with gold toecaps. Moreover, then how good he looked was that we could almost see his knees buckle when he got a good look at Rosie.

As he approached her, he bowed to her and gently took her hand to give it a kiss when he said softly Rosie you are a pure vision of beauty. There eye locked onto each other as she handed him his glass of punch as we stood there in the awkward silence. Paul clears his throat, and slowly letting go of Rosie hand, looks over at us expressing how elegant we all looked, compared to this cowboy he snickers.

Amanda compliments Paul and says you clean up not too bad, what do you think Rosie, looking for a response Rosie says not bad for an old guy she grind and gave Paul a desecrate little wink. Now that we were in the middle of the banquet area, there were the pillar tables with different h'orderves on

them the symphony music playing in the background and lights were all winkling and the space felt elegant.
While gazing around and complimenting Rosie on what she had done with her giving some credit to the fellows, we see a sting of carts coming up the lane. Instantly I was excited and Amanda looked as happy to see everyone, as we move up closer to the landing to greet our friends as they come in. First in is, Janette and Jim and oh my goodness they were a perfect match. Janette was wearing a royal blue off the shoulder satin slim line gown with the added striking feature off long white gloves with small blue sapphires in a delicate design on the top of the hand and rim of the glove. Jim wore a black tuxedo with a royal blue bow tie, matching cover bun. Right behind them was Jessie and Ryan who wearing royal purple silk, with Jessie's dress was strapless with a full skirt and packets. Ryan's tuxedo was mirror image of Jims only with purple accessories.

Rosie was handing out glasses of punch as we got past all of our blubbering and gawking over how everyone looked. As Jessie and Ryan make their way in, Rosie gives them a glass of punch, and Amanda stops to chat with them, while I am still front and center checking out what everyone is wearing.

Behind Jessie and Ryan there were Henry and Elsie who were wearing leather dresses Henry was wearing black and Elsie red. Their kit leather gowns had corset tie in the back tops with Henry's being slim lined skirt with a slit up the left leg and Elsie had a fuller scalped skirt, longer in the back and shorter in the front, showing off her legs and shoes. The dresses were unique and I loved them, mostly because of the material they were made of. Amanda came over to say hello to Henry and Elsie as I take Amanda arm and said are those not the most amazing dresses. Henry and Elsie gave us all a bit of a pose as we admire their gowns, hair and jewelry. With kind of being in a bunch I said all you women look out of this world beautify, someone has to get a picture.

Not without us you will not, I hear Kevin laughing and call out as he and Dustin step onto the landing and take the stance like top notch formal models of the year. We all clapped as we see their over the top old styled ruffled high-collared shirts and short black tuxedo jackets which showing their burgundy cumber buns with pants pressed and perfect length right to the shiny black leather shoes, they knew they looked yummy. As the two come down the stairs Rosie hands them a glass and says I could eat you both, you look so handsome. Kevin wiggles his eyebrows and Dustin gives the two thumbs up, nailed it!

With everyone there, Rosie was pointing out where everyone's favorite snakes were placed and making sure at the same time that we all had full glasses. We gathered more into the center of the room in and around the pillars of food when by request.
Elsie asked if all of us men included would show off a bit more and do a runway walk past the group. A little parade showing off our evening attire, we will never have this again and I want to have you all engrained in my mind they way you look this evening.

Paul responds to Elsie's request with saying so everyone one can hear, I will go last, that will give me time to get a few glasses of Rosie's punches in me before I get up there and strut my stuff for you all he smiles. Kevin and Dustin started chuckling strut your stuff that we have to see.

Okay then Rosie says Colleen you can go first. My head turns to her me, why me first, I asked Rosie replies someone has to start and I pick you, come on show us what you got. Amanda loved that I was picked first and said to me, you can do it as words of encouragement.

Feeling amazing anyway, I did not need to be asked again. I got out in the open and as I walked by the group, I pointed out my matching jewelry and hair. Adding in a couple slow turns so that everyone could see all around the dress, I did feel like I belonged on the red carpet. Getting back to my drink, everyone clapped and was complementing me when I motioned with a wave over to Rosie, Elsie and Jessie thanking them for the way I look and feel. Rosie then gave Amanda the nod that it was her turn.

Amanda had everything going for her that night and looked like a model out of a magazine. I could feel my pride and emotion swell giving me a lump in my throat as she walked by so sultry, that is my little girl; I thought to myself, I had to take a couple good drinks of my punch to compose when I felt Rosie put her arm around me and give me a squeeze. When Kevin sees the rock on Amanda's finger and says wow missy, do you get to keep that, as she makes sure that we all get a good look at the diamond on her finger as she was beaming walking back to where I was standing. Amanda jokes position is nine tenths of the law you know, as she made a fist, as if no one was getting it off her finger. We all laughed at her expression of rightful ownership. She said to the group, hey I am just glad it did not pull me over while walking in these shoes, as we were laughing Kevin cautioned her yes you need to stay away from any ledges the ring could tip you off, Dustin and Kevin were joking around.

Next up was Jima and Janette who went up together when Jim twirled her around showing off how well they fit together. Ryan and Jessie followed suite and tried to mimic the same motions made my Jim and Janette mocking their grace and elegance and just fooling around. Jessie wore an exquisite wide band deep garnet choker with an eye catching garnet teardrop. They too look wonderful and over the top with Rosie and Amanda both piping up one saying well done and the other bravo.

Henry and Elsie are next with both of them wearing the finest and softest leather both Kevin and Dustin wanted to feel their dresses as they went by. Henry's dress was sexy and fit in all the right places and Elsie's gown with the shorter front had a classy and sassy look going on all at the same time. We all applauded, and complement them as they strut over to the bar to fill up their glasses. Then it is Kevin and Dustin's turn and after seeing everyone else prance around they got right up and put on quite a show. As they were starting to walk through all of us putting on their swagger when Rosie says to them jokingly you boys really did miss your true calling. Dustin and Kevin burst out laughing by the way Rosie had said it that got us all chuckling as they sauntered back to their drinks.

Then I said, okay it is Paul and Rosie's turn and without hesitation Paul walks across the floor to Rosie and put's out his hand for her to take. They walk side by side with her hand resting on top of his as he shifts her slowly side-to-side showing off her dress and her hair. Then looking in each other's eyes as if none of us were even there, as he guides her with his hand on her lower back, to where she was standing. He lowers his hand and bows to her and she returns the gesture with a slight curtsy and whispered thank you to him as he turned and went back to his pillar of snakes and his drink.
I turned to Amanda and I whispered wow, did you just see that. Rosie, who was right beside me, gives a bit of a cough and gets all of our attention by ringing a large brass hand bell that was sitting on a corner of one of the dining room hutches. Thank you all that was fun and I am thrilled by the attention to detail that you all went to, this all means so much to me and I want to thank you all for making this night perfect for me.

I want you all to know that even though our island systems have us under constant surveillance, Dustin is capturing this evening for us with special screening and you will all be receiving a digital picture frame with three sixty picks and snippets of video of this evening, loaded into them. The gesture was old school and impressed the group with the thought that went into it all. Rosie and Dustin received cheers all around for the thanking them for the present. When Rosie looks over at Amanda and I and says, you will have the same upload to the filters and when you are together, you will be able to view in your minds the same shots and clips that the picture frames will have here. It will not be quite the same, but may be when the dust settles in a few years, no pun intended; one of us will be able to send you one.

If the pictures are accidently ever seen by anyone other than your partners they will be explained away as a privet party you were at when you were in china together. We have thought of everything ladies, Dustin says proudly and Henry boasts my little filters are such marvels as Elsie smiles proudly. Rosie rings the bell again, it is getting close to dinner ladies and gentlemen, so the smokers have time for a smoke and Elsie, if I could ask you to come help me in the kitchen for a moment. When Paul walks right up to Rosie and says what can I do, and looking like he was not going to take no for an answer. Rosie motions for both Elsie and Paul to follow her while she told the rest of her guests to fill their glasses and please relax and take a seat at the table. Our feast will be out in just a few minutes.

Amanda and I drifted towards the pool that was reflecting the large twinkling Christmas tree lights and the flickering flame of the fireplace, to have our smoke. The rest of the fellows and Henry came over to with us, for their smoking pleasure with Kevin and Dustin having a hoot and Jim, Ryan and Henry lighting up a sweet smelling cigar while Janette and Jessie were over at the bar chatting.

I love Janettes gloves I said to Henry and Amanda they are just stunning and fit without even a wrinkle. Henry had a smirk on her face when she said I have a few pare of them in different colors, I think we all have a few pare of the long evening gloves after we were playing around in the lab one day and realized we could make seamless gloves that look like they were made of the finest leather. A 3D printer made those gloves and they fit to every crevice in her hand, I love the stones Janette has put in them Henry smiled and said maybe we can sneak you a pare home she whispered to us and winked.

All the sudden we hear the dinner bell ring again and we hear Rosie announce, dinner is served, would you please come and take your seats. We were all hungry even with the snakes that we had been nibbling on and as we approach the table, you really get a sense of the elegance of the setting.

Rosie proceeds to tell the group how the table works as Sire designed the table with a conveyor. The table is so large that the bowls and platters of food and condiments are put on an oval conveyor that turns within the table so that each item passes in front of each place setting and will continue to rotate until each serving has passed by once. If you want more of something or seconds, you tap the impeded brass rail in front of your service and the conveyor will turn until a serving utensil is touched the conveyor will stop. This is not like any dinner table I have ever sat at before Kevin says; this takes buffet to a completely new level he joked. Rosie smiled and said that the conveyor acts like a hot plate and knows which dishes to keep warm. The conveyor is set inside the table so the dishes do not sit up to high and disrupt or get in the way of any conversations.
Everyone was comfortable when Rosie asked Paul and Jim who were at the opposite ends of the table, to open the champagne chilling in the buckets near them. I leaned over to Amanda and said I am glad we did not sit there I suck at opening champagne, we smiled. Then nonchalantly with Rosie still standing said abracadabra, we all looked over at her when Ryan blurts out, what did you just say? When just like magic the covers all slid back and the platters of food slowly started to move.

Rosie asked that we start serving and I will list off the dishes for this evening. With everyone reaching for their napkin resting on the plates in the gold napkin rings, Amanda and I noticed her slight pause watching for reaction. We pretended to not even notice the weight as we watched to see who was going to say something about the heavy rings. When we see Ryan have to put a little extra effort into picking his napkin up, he was the first person, to mumble wow as Ryan gave Jessie a nod to pick hers up. Then it was Paul, who let out the holy crap lady, are you afraid the napkins were going to blow away or what. Rosie burst out laughing with everyone now holding their napkin ring as if they are lifting weights.

Once we composed ourselves, Rosie wanted to pass on the history of the heavy gold napkin rings, that she was not sure if the group was aware of the extent of the gold. As we were all dishing up our food, Rosie proceeds to tell us that Sires had a fancy for changing his cash for gold. Sires has so much of it that he decided he would have decretive items molded so he could see and hold his gold and not just have it in a vault somewhere hidden away. There are designs and art work like the dining room gold napkin rings spread throughout the island we just do not notice them anymore. Kevin looks up with a serving spoon in one hand and his fork in the other and replied to Rosie, I know where they are he said, I have to move them statues and things you call art around now and then he gave a little chuckle and went back to filling his plate and eating at the same time.

With the conveyor going around Rosie did want to announce the selections for the evening. She pointed out the dishes quite quickly as we were filling our plates. We have a shrimp and ice berg lettuce salad, along with lobster skewers. The main course is turkey, stuffing mashed potatoes, gravy and asparagus. We also have, ham sweat potatoes, porgies and cabbage rolls to make sure there is something for everyone she finishes. We all cheer Rosie on, and complement her on her party and amazing dinner as the conveyor kept moving and would stop at each setting, and then carry on, it was a phenomenal circle of food. Kevin and Dustin while eating were fascinated by the table and were chatting all technical and wanted to check it out better later.

We were all, taken back by the presentation of the food the amount and verity, with all the compliments and accolades Rosie started to blush. Our dinner plates were of fine china with gold plated designs rims that were oddly shaped and supersized. There was a lot of room on the plates without having to heap the food on top of each other, mind you by the time Kevin and Dustin were finished loading up you could not see much separation. It was so fun serving from one dish and then another dish of food would be right behind it.

For the next few minutes, we were all quiet and enjoying every bite of food, with music playing in the background and the lights twinkling above us the ambiance was amazing. Then Paul put his napkin down and got up to refresh everyone's champagne. With all our glasses full, Paul remained standing and he raised his glass to Rosie, thank you for a wonderful evening and first class dinner. You bring us all together Rosie and we all wanted to thank you and although we do not normally give gifts, to commemorate this time with our welcome guests, Paul glances over at us and smiles. Rosie, we had a painting done up of the evening we were all on the lake on the water boards for you.

Just then, Jim comes up from behind Rosie and presents the oil painting of us all floating in a circle with the reflections off the water and the colors of the evening sky the painting was marvelous. The artist was Janette. Rosie stood up right away and did start to tear up she was so moved by the gesture and went right over to Janette and gave her a hug. You have no idea how much this means to me she says to us all, while she whips her eyes. Dustin screeches oh yes I do, I even have a bruise to prove it when I almost accidently gave it away Henry kicked me under the table. Henry sat up and said whom me, I would not do that she batted her eyes and mischievously smiles.

Then Kevin says well seeing as you are all sappy now, he gets up and Rosie tilts her head as we see him go to his cart and bring back something wrapped in a cloth that looked heavy even though it was smaller than the painting. Kevin looked at Amanda and I and said you are up.

They all looked at us, and I looked at Amanda who jabbed me to start talking. I looked back at Rosie and reminded her that she once upon a time told us that anything we were going to give her, as a present had to be made by us. Well one day, when Kevin was forming some stepping-stones for the farm we saw the slabs setting when we decided to put our handprints in the one slab and initialed it. Kevin pulled back the cloth covering the stepping-stone and to our astonishment Kevin had done some carving and etching to the stone to make it look more delicate and presentable.

Rosie brought her hands to her face and the tears started to flow as she walked over to the stone, to put her hand in our imprints. Oh my goodness, these are priceless, I love them both it what perfect pieces to always remember this time. Rosie said to the group, this night could not get any better she exclaimed. Rosie came over, gave us hugs and kisses, and then gave Janette another squeeze while still whipping her eyes a bit.

To lift the mood, Rosie motions everyone back to their seats and boasts there is still a lot more food people, please have more. The food was hot in the trays and Ryan wanted, more stuffing so he tapped the rail and the conveyor started moving and when the stuffing came around and he grabbed the serving spoon the conveyor stopped. Kevin loved the table and as soon as it would stop Kevin would tap the rail to make it go around. Rosie just kidding around finally asked Kevin to stop messing with the table, you will break it, and she chuckles. Not wanting to disappoint Rosie, we all ate as much as we could with Ryan, Dustin and Kevin cleaning up, reducing the feast to mere leftovers.

Amanda and I were enjoying the watching and listening of the group as they interacted and joked around as we were, one at a time finishing our meals. Janette was sitting on the other side of Amanda and saw the opportunity to ask if she could have a look at her gloves and that she had to feel them. Janette tickled that we loved her added touch of the gloves handed them to Amanda confiding, that when she did put them on it made her and her dress feel royal and joked with Jim when they were getting ready that she should have went the extra mile and put a tiara in her hair. Rosie overheard Janette say about the tiara and leans forward, looking past me sitting right beside her and Amanda sitting next to me and gasped, oh you so should have, Janette you look exquisite Rosie gushed. Janette was flattered and Jim looking so proud, when Janette replied thank you so much, next time I will, she smiled at Rosie and us. Jessie and Ryan sitting across the table were chatting themselves and kidding about how good ma and pa looked this evening.

We can see that Rosie was taking a good look around the table to see if everyone was finished dinner and when seeing that we were, she stood up and then said again so we could all hear, abracadabra and holly crap, if the conveyor did not separate. We all watch in amazement as the open-end of the conveyor started a one-way drive into the base of the table going underground. As the platters of food went down, the end of the track pulled a covered hiding the track and seamlessly making the table a complete flat surface. Jessie was most impressed and asked so where does it all come out. Rosie beaming said they pull up into the kitchen where the dishwasher is, I will show you next time you are in there she says. Jessie motioned with two thumbs up, I said jokingly, I do not think you will ever get to see it Jessie, Rosie never lets anyone in there I laughed.

This time it was Kevin coming around to fill glasses with Henry and Elsie only having eyes for each other and so full I needed to stand, I glanced over at Amanda and signaled time for a smoke. Paul got up to stretch his legs with Jim getting up to join Paul. While Dustin and Kevin were coming for a smoke, Paul broke out the cigars. We were not feeling any pain this many glasses of punch and champagne later, and we felt we were walking okay in our shoes. Although, feeling so good about how we looked, how we walked, was not as important. Giggling with Amanda as we found a pillar we could brace ourselves against so we did not wobble while having our smoke.

Once Rosie had finished chatting it up with the ladies around the table, they all came over to join us. Henry, Rosie and Elsie had one of the long, slender cigars with a wooden tip, while Jessie and Ryan each had two shooters on their table. When I saw the shooters, I instantly got goose bumps and knew I could not do those, I nudged Amanda pointed at the drinks and shook my head no, when Jim went over to the music panel to switch the mood up, and put on an old Elvis country song to start. As Jim walks by Amanda and I he says quietly, if Paul and Kevin have had enough to drink the country music selections I have made will get them dancing, he winked and then walked over to Janette and asked her cordially to dance. Ryan instantly followed suit and asked Jessie to dance as well.

We watched as Paul casually put down his cigar and while Rosie standing closer to Henry and Elsie, he walks tall and with confidence over to Rosie, extend his hand out to hers, and then bows slightly to ask her to dance. Rosie spellbound by Paul's approach immediately accepted. Amanda and I clinked our glasses together and enjoyed watching them all dancing. While they were all dancing Kevin motions, he is lighting a hoot so we shuffle closer to them, making sure we could lean against something. Dustin notices our glasses getting low and asks what we would like. When I asked for punch, Amanda said that sounds good I will have some two. The music is playing so nice and the lights are amazing I was saying to Kevin as he was lighting the hoot, when suddenly I stopped and sniffed the air and utter wow that smells different. Dustin jumps in saying; this is our holiday special we like to call it, as he gave us our drinks. Dustin making sure that Kevin did not all the credit he explains that he created the strain that I call cures all and Kevin is the master grower that brought our baby to life, just so we could cut it down and smoke it Kevin and Dustin started laughing. When Dustin grips, I am so full it actually hurts to laugh. As we passed the hoot around, Kevin relayed to us again, how great the hand print idea was, and that the slab will be with Rosie forever. Dustin added that the painting that Janette did was taken from a still shot we took from the surveillance system and enhanced the colors which Janette reproduced with such detail in the oil painting. Dustin let us know that he had his own smaller version print copy, you can come see when you spend an afternoon with us on the water slide. You have been avoiding it and you have to try it once before you leave or you will regret it, he raises the pitch of his voice and proclaims, forever. Kevin right there agreeing with Dustin, you just have to give it a whirl; the fellows raised their glasses to Amanda and I and said that is a yes then, with big smiles. Amanda was fearless however, I on the other hand, not so much. I went along with the idea not wanting to be a party pooper, but somehow in my gut I knew I was going to do everything I could to get out of it, thinking to myself.

Trying not to be obvious we could all see Paul and Rosie dancing close and looking deep into each other's eyes and we could all feel their connection, not only see it. Henry and Elsie were so cozy together always seemingly having something to be chatting about. After a few dances, the couples stopped for refreshments with Rosie coming over to us and giving a big hug to both of us. I love you; this night would not have been as special for me and awesome, without you both here.

Rosie speaking louder, can I have your attention please? As we all turn to Rosie and she had out attention she proclaims that you cannot have an amazing dinner as we had without an over the top desert. Just as she spoken the word desert, Elsie came out of the kitchen pushing a serving cart that had a very large and tall white cake. As Elsie drew closer to the group, we could see that it was a white angel food cake with fresh strawberries and a glaze with whip cream or vanilla ice cream.

I see Kevin and Dustin light right up when they see what is for desert, Amanda jokingly scoffed at them, I thought you were so full. Kevin answered first with saying, full of food. This is desert and I have a different spot for that he chuckled and motioned to move to the food. Dustin looked at us as we were looking for his answer when he grind and replied, what he said. With the hoot done and finished our smoke, Kevin and Dustin were staring at the desert cart intently, and could not hold out any longer and both excused themselves.

Amanda said I am full, but I do want to try some and asked if I wanted to share a piece with her. Rosie was serving so realizing that was not going to happen, we grind at each other and ended up with each a very large piece of cake with all the fixings the same as everyone did. We all went back to the dining table to have our desert and with the walking in the high heels, carrying the large dish I was happy I made it without a fumble and giggled to myself because I did. Amanda could tell that I was pleased about something and surmised it was my walking in the shoes.

Once we were all seated Henry stood up, wanting to give her thanks for the evening, and jokingly said as much as I bucked Elsie on getting this dressed up, she looks down at Elsie and says, I am so glad she stuck to her inclination. I want you all to know that there is no one else in the world I would want to have shared this experience with, other than the people at this table now and I will cherish this evening forever. Without a second of silence, there is applause, and Elsie stands to give Henry a hug and softly puts her hands on Henrys cheeks, giving her a gentle kiss on the lips. Sitting back down, holding hands.

Kevin and Paul were coming around filling glasses as Rosie responded by kidding around and thanking Henry and Elsie for looking so hot. That got the group chuckling with Henry and Elsie sitting up and agreeing with Rosie, as we all supported the comment. The leather dresses were sexy and fit them as good Janettes long gloves did. We all felt elegant and special in our own way, including the men.

We were all chatting back and forth while eating our desert that we all thought we were too full to eat however, the angel food cake was so light and fluffy we found some room. Dustin exclaims, Rosie you are the best chief in the world, and I mean in the whole world and then goes right back to his dish to finish it off. We thought there was more but no, that was it. Dustin just randomly blurted out the comment to Rosie, which made us all laugh with Kevin picking on and insisting Dustin has had too many wobbly pops.

Once we settled, Rosie glanced at Paul who nodded to Jessie and Ryan to explain what they have analyzed out of the recent digital messing. For starters, Jessie says Sires wished us all a happy holiday season and joked that we could take an extra day off. By all accounts and measures the world and atmosphere is recovering much better than anticipated however this will only advance the submersible departure by a one or two days. Ryan then speaks up and informs Amanda and I that our bank accounts have been established under our new identities which are all in order with the best credentials to go forward with.

Ryan stopped and with the pause, we all had the same question on our minds. It was Amanda that spoke up first and said so you know what our names are Ryan looks at Rosie, Paul and Jessie and responds yes we do.
Would you like to know he asked? Of course, you boob; she said jokingly we want to know Henry blurted out, catching Ryan and the rest of us by surprise. Do not leave us hanging here, what are their new names are going

to be. I know once the filters are activated and confirmed it will be automatic but for now, she holds up her glass, I am being snoopy and want to know. Do their new names fit the two people we have grown to love when I let out awe and Amanda adding that is so sweet.

Well what are they I was now anxious to know and asked, when Ryan looked at me and said Colleen your new name will be Emma Watson. I tilted my head, said, it sure could have been worse, and chuckled, when Rosie and Janette agreed that they liked it. While Henry pondered as she looked at me then smirked and said that will work, not a bad choice.

Amanda, what is her new name Henry prompted Ryan. Amanda's new name will be Dawn Watson with mothers name listed as a last name on the birth certificate. Remember that everyone will call you the same; it is only when dealing with the government that you have to use the new identities. With the money, you will have that will not be a problem. Yours and your family's lives will change in an instant when you go home Ryan was getting excited leading up to letting us all know just how much money we were being given when he paused again making Kevin quip, out with it man, how much is Sires giving them. I promise, I will not tell anyone he looks at Dustin and high five. Ryan was thrilled to be the one to announce that we were each going to receive, ten million dollars.

Oh my crap, I sat back in my chair while I heard the gasps of happiness. The people here did not need money however; they knew what ten million would mean for us when we do get home. Everyone was so happy to hear that we would be, set for life. Rosie already knew the amount, and turned to gesture the two thumbs up with a bit smile. When Jessie yells out, I know where we are taking our next vacation she chuckled, as she winked at her mom and gave Ryan a nudge, to wherever you are! Amanda exclaimed back; you would be treated no less then royalty, she grins and raised her glass in the air. I second that promise, I agreed with Amanda. Anywhere any time, we will be there for you all, Amanda and I nodded to the group.

Henry motioned like a light bulb go on I think to make sure we did not get all sappy, and blurted out, loud enough to get all our attention and said with a bright face, people do you not get it. When we do take a break from the island we actually have friends to see as part of our journey. What a wonderful contemplation Rosie then thanked Henry for planting the happy thought. Then Rosie gets up and says to the group carry on people, I just have to get our coffee from the kitchen.

Then Paul sits up to the table, looks at us all, and proceeds with saying, if we think the money is cool. He had all of our attention, Paul looking right at me then paused, so took the cue and I responded, yes cool we do think the money is cool, I smiled and tilted my head a bit confused with how he started the conversation. Then Jim piped up and said Colleen you are going to love the next part he winked which had us all curious as to what it was Paul was holding back. When just as Paul was going tell us Rosie, comes out from the kitchen pushing the serving cart with a large silver coffee urn and a variety of teas.

Once Rosie notices we are waiting for her to stop fussing around so Paul could finish what he was saying, when she could sense the silence and looked over at Paul and then smiled and said, me bad and giggled then grabbed her glass and came over and stood at her chair that was beside Paul.

Okay, the cool thing is that the one suite case each that you will be taking is a specially designed case that is military spec and for your enjoyment can conceal the jewelry that you have been given. Both Amanda and I shoot a shocked look up to Rosie … you mean we really get to keep some of these trying to contain my excitement, I asked Rosie and Paul to confirm.
When Kevin stands then Dustin with Kevin saying to us takes them, and run, Kevin laughed, pointed to a hoot he had rolled, and the group chuckled. When Rosie did confirm that yes we did get to keep whatever we could stash, she winked. We got up and gave Rosie, Paul, and hug before going to join the fellows for a hoot. As we were walking over to Kevin and Dustin I had to nudge Amanda a couple times, I was so excited about getting to take a few shiny things home with us. I even whispered I wonder if you get to keep the little five-karat number on your finger now, I snickered. Amanda nonchalantly, looked down at her hand, hum I wonder, she smiles.

Just then, we see that the couples are taking to the dance floor and this time even Henry and Elsie were up slow dancing. The four of us, were just fine with having a hoot and watching. When Dustin asked quietly if we were starting to get excited about going home, when Kevin cuts Dustin off excited, how about the anxiety of being in the sub for them days, Kevin shuttered. Dustin smirks at Kevin and then looks at us and says do not listen to him, you will be fine, it is only weenies like us that do not do well in closed spaces. Amanda says closed spaces what do mean the sub is bigger then either of our homes she chuckled, Kevin replies yes but you will sometimes be miles under the ocean and you cannot just go out for a breath of fresh air anytime he chuckled. Dustin pipes up again and confirms that we have nothing to worry about, and Kevin gives a big grin and says I am only joshing you ladies, it may not be my thing but you will have a blast for sure. We never really did answer Dustin question of being excited about going home other then the positive expression and nod we gave before Kevin interrupted.

With finishing the hoot and my drink done, I nudged Amanda and Dustin and Kevin know that I was going for a coffee and asked if anyone would like one. Kevin and Dustin said we are find, there is more punch we have to drink up yet they joked as Amanda said I am with you mom, I will come with you and fix my own. We give the fellows a little wave and thank them for the after desert, desert and walk around the dancers as we carefully walk to the coffee.

I cannot believe this night, it is amazing and everything is really happening for us, wow. I am feeling a bit overwhelmed sweetie I revealed to Amanda. What emotion should I be feeling or expressing, is it anxiety, for leaving or excitement for going home. I am also feeling guilty about what we are being given even though we are not supposed to. Mom, you are fine Amanda gives her voice of confidence.
It is natural for us to feel bad about leaving these wonderful people and this amazing place and a the same time be excited to be going home. I know all at least all the women; will understand our mixed emotions, as we get closer to leaving. Amanda says with confidence mom, I have concluded that the money and jewels are nonessential stuff to them and giving it to us gives, all of them pleasure. You are right sweetie nothing to be riled up about now, I love you sweetie I am so proud of you.

I take a sip of coffee and calm down as we watch the dancers float across the floor. We see Rosie and Paul not taking their eyes off each other and Jim and Janette looking so comfortable and dancing as one while Jessie and Ryan being the flamboyant ones on the floor were carrying on like they were on dancing with the stars Amanda and I giggled. Then there was Henry and Elsie that you could not slide a piece of paper between they were holding each other so close. They all looked so happy and content.

Once the slow song ended, the couples wanted to refresh their drinks, and to relax for a bit. Rosie had us all move over to the hot tub area where the seats were comfortable, with the fire tables lit and the lights twinkling, this was a cozy spot to wind down the evening. Before coming over to sit with the group, both Dustin and Kevin were getting themselves another helping of desert. Rosie had a big grin when she seen that they were going for more food.

Before Rosie sits down she thanked us all for a wonderful evening I will remember this forever, she put her hand over her heart and said thank you all again, before being seated.
As we, all get comfortable and seated Kevin pipes up and asks what the plan is for tomorrow. Rosie will you be having leftovers for us or do you just want me, to come by and pick up my care package he laughed as he put another fork full of cake in his mouth. Not at all surprised by Kevin's question Rosie responds by saying with a straight face, asks the man with two hollow legs, only kidding my precious, she smiles and says to him.

Then Rosie blurts out with an upbeat and positive hey folks, seeing that tomorrow is a no workday, I thought that we could have a mini golf, tournament in the morning. I have teams made up and prizes for special holes on the course. Paul chuckled at Rosie's preparedness as the thought of a mini golf tournament sounded like a lot of fun to us all; we agreed that a tournament was a great idea for tomorrow. Rosie commented that she even took into consideration not wanting to do anything to early or strenuous after these evenings' events of drinks, feast and late night and that is why she came up with mini golf as being the perfect event for the day.

Then answering Kevin's question about the food, Rosie relay's to the group, that she thought that after our tournament we could have what our leftovers at the café tomorrow. How does that sound, as Rosie proceeds to look around at us all giving the nod yes when she came to Ryan when he confirms that he can sleep in, Rosie smiled at Ryan and replied yes you can sleep in, we won't meet up until eleven thirty giving us lots of time to enjoy our Christmas morning. Ryan winked at Rosie and says count me in it to win it, he laughs and showed everyone the two thumbs up as if the challenge is on. Which Kevin and Dustin jumped all over Ryan's confidence, with uttering not chance man, we hear the banter when Paul calls out, without a doubt people, I have you all beat. Rosie looks at Paul and says, we will just see about that, as she looked at all the ladies, and says no worries gentlemen, we know what we have to do.

Amanda who is not the best golfer and looking to get a bit of a rise out of the group, says to Rosie so what is that… show off our boob's, she smiles, if you are counting on me to pull us through we better show some skin she laughs. The group roared not expecting Amanda to come out with anything like that at all. Paul was shocked and almost spit out his drink when she said it, he laughed uncontrollably for more than a few seconds. Which kept the obvious subconscious visions and chuckle going?

Man that is good coffee Paul says to Rosie once he composed himself trying to change the subject of the challenge. Thank you Paul, Rosie says politely knowing he was trying to divert from Amanda's boob comment when Rosie adds we will all be on teams and we have to count so many balls from each person so it is all fair. No worries Amanda you can keep your boobies covered.

Rosie continues to explain that there are four people on each team and if we would like to know, she can tell us our team's now. With us all relaxing and having our evening nightcap, and smoke Kevin said for sure, tell us now and maybe we can come up with team names for tomorrow. Rosie lit up when Kevin said that, and said, I never thought of team a name, that is a smashing idea. Okay then, the three teams. Jessie, Ryan, Henry, Elsie then Colleen, Kevin, Amanda, Dust then Rosie, Paul, Jim, Janette.

All right gang let us take a few minutes have a refill and think about some team names and, we can have them silkscreened on t-shirts for us all in the morning. We all went into our own little huddles and started throwing out some good team names and chuckled over some of the ridiculous names thought of. After a few minutes of silly suggestions and poking fun at each other and us all implying others do not stand a chance and talking a tough, when Paul's says okay everyone times up, you have one more minute to agree on your team name or this could go on all night. We could tell Rosie liked the take charge Paul as she gave him a nod for setting a time limit.

Okay we are ready Henry exclaims, as she looks at their team, thrilled at their choice she did not want anyone else to take it, blurted out we are the Hole in Ones! We all clapped that was a great team name. Next Kevin spoke up for our team and, says with a gruff deep voice … Err Billy we are the Putting Pirates another applause for keeping it clean and then Janette pipes up and says we weapons of grass destruction and you all better bring you're A game tomorrow she chuckled with a group applause and Rosie had all the names.

Realizing that it was getting late Henry and Elsie were the first to make the move to get up and give their many thanks and hugs all around with complements and best wishes gushing. As we were walking them out to the patio landing and looking out to the tree hovering over the lake Henry took Elsie's hand and said to the group we will always cherish and remember this evening forever then blowing Rosie a kiss as they got in their cart and then waved as they drove away. Elsie yelling back we will see you on the course yaw all.

Then it was Jim, Janette, Ryan and Jessie sharing the hugs and best wishes. Janette made sure Rosie knew what a wonderful job she had done with the party and that no one could have done better. When Rosie thanked Janette for the painting, it is perfect Rosie's eye started to tear up as Janette says I loved painting it for you, my friend, they hugged tightly while the fellows shook hands and patted shoulders.

The evening was suddenly ending with Dustin asking if we want to have hoot before they leave. Yes, another coffee and a hoot would be perfect I replied to Dustin. Amanda said you must have read my mind she smiles, as we walk over to fill our cups and see Rosie and Paul back fusing around the bar.

Once we have our hoot and coffee I think I will be done Amanda says to me, oh me too sweetie, I am pooped now. To liven her up a bit, I ran my hand up and down my side very sultry like and said I just do not want to take any of this off yet I laughed she thought that was funny too, knowing that I was partly telling the truth.

We get back over to Kevin and Dustin who had lit the hoot and were finishing their brandy; yuck, I do not know how you can drink that stuff Amanda cringed her face up. Paul hears Amanda's comment when he proclaims that for the best smooth sipping, you are right Amanda they should be drinking scotch that will cure whatever ails he smiles. Oh nasty Amanda says to Paul and cringes her face again, that is as bad as the brandy. I was chuckling because I felt the same but it was Amanda who Paul joking called cup cake, which she was fine with, when it came to drinking that fire water as she called it.

Finishing the hoot Dustin and Kevin let Rosie know that they were leaving to and they came to give her a big hug and thanked her for feeding them and a wonderful night. Kevin and Dustin bowed so nicely to Amanda and Kevin, then said see you on the course mates, no pun intended he smiles. With Dustin, being a gentleman, and letting us know that we both looked beautiful this evening. They gave Paul a bear hug and a handshake and headed towards their carts.

As they drive away, Rosie sits down and gives out a big shy and a few sound, then said I loved it, I loved every moment of the night as she looked up into the sky. Paul, Amanda and I knew that Rosie was happy and pleased with how the whole party went off without a hitch. With presents and golf tomorrow, being the icing on her evening's cake. Paul was as happy for Rosie as Rosie was and it was obvious to Amanda and I that it was time for us to call it a night and go to our room.

Well Rosie, Paul I said as Amanda and I stood to call it a night, when Rosie shot up from her chair and came for a group hug. I will cherish forever your gift and I know that when I put my hand in your impressions I will be able to feel you in my heart. Thank you girls, you mean so much to me.
Paul came to give us hugs too and thanked us for inspiring the evening that has put Rosie in such high spirits and has meant so much to her. He was so pleased to see her happy and content and looking as elegant as she did. Rosie standing there could see her reflection and knew that she owned her look and that Paul was smitten. As we poise and start our exit I joked that we managed to keep our shoes on all night as Amanda and I turned towards our room, whishing them both a good night as we walked carefully, to not fall over now, after doing so well all evening.

As soon as we get into our room, we plunk ourselves down on the bed and take off our shoes. We both felt relieved to get the shoes off and then I asked Amanda if she could undo my dress so I could get into my housecoat. Me to mom, I have been looking forward to curling up and unwinding in here for a bit.

Once changed and move over to our balcony sitting area we see a pot of coffee and two pieces of angel food cake with a bowl of strawberries and whip cream on the side. Oh my goodness, when does she find time to do all of these little things, I looked at Amanda. I think it is when we think she is going to the washroom she does other little things on the way so we never really notice, Amanda smiled gave a little chuckle, think about it that is the only time she is out of eyesight. Kudos sweetie, I think you are right.

With coffee in hand and sitting back in our chairs just gazing around in awe of the night, not even knowing what to say first, we lit our smokes. What popped in my mind first are Rosie and Paul, I looked over at Amanda and said in a quiet voice not knowing if they were still out there or not, did you see the connection between the two of them tonight. They were on fire those two, I am sure everyone seen it and felt it I said. Amanda comments I wonder if this evening will take their relationship to the next level for them, whatever that is she smirked. It might, but I am sure they would keep it a secret even if they did. Rosie is very independent and privet so her love life is something I believe she would keep under wraps.

What do you think of our new names Amanda asked me. The new names seem to only matter on paper and will use our original names in our privet world. Therefore, I think I am okay because at least we are not named Helgastine or something freaky like that. Even the filter might not be able to make me remember a name like that, we snickered quietly. I wanted to reassure Amanda that when she does get married she could put her first name back to Amanda as you take your partner's last name and make it legal. I will have to re-marry LB to get my last name back, and with the bank account that comes with the name, I am all-good with being called Emma, I smiled. No kidding Amanda's eyes open wide, I keep forgetting that part unbelievably, and then claims I love my new name too.

I am pumped about being able to take some pieces of jewelry home with us. Yes me too although if we have our own money to buy jewelry why is taking some home with us important to you mom. That s a good question and I think my best answer is that the jewelry is something very special to us being given to us here and that we will treasure for our lifetimes and that can be passed down for generations. We cannot do that with Paul's ribs I blurted out a laugh. I am not sure why I said that but it was funny, bizarre and made Amanda roller her eyes at me and chuckle too.

Settling back we having our coffee, I stuck my fork in the cake and had to have one last bit before going to bed. When I mentioned the dinner and how many dishes there were, and they all tasted outstanding. Rosie even makes her stuffing just like I do and I think I ate more than my share of the lobster, I wonder if anyone noticed I grind. Amanda asked me how it was possible to cook all of that when we hardly saw her in the kitchen. I shook my head and

offered the explanation that it was, magic! Only kidding sweetie, she must of had the prep work done days in advance so all she had to do was transfer the cooked dishes into the conveyor covered platters as they were ready and where they kept warm until ready to eat. I still do not know how she pulled the whole dinner; desert and evening off, really.
Well sweetie, you looked amazing this evening and I am so proud of you. Going through this together is huge for both of us. Right now sweetie my heart can feel the grief that our families are feeling and the pain of us not being there this Christmas. It must be horrible for them what they are going through, then thinking more of what I just said, I quickly answered myself with I hope that money can fix all that; I tilted my head and smiled at her. I did not want to bring us down over something we can only fix by coming home.

Motioning that I was ready to go to bed, Amanda said well I guess this will be a Christmas that we may only remember when we are together or as a party, we went to in China, so true sweetie that is weird hey. After getting our markup off, we climb onto the bed, we give each other a big hug, wish each other a Merry Christmas, and snuggled in for a good sleep, it had been a long day.

Chapter Twenty-Four

Amanda waking up before me she sits up quietly and as she is stretching I open one eye and with the covers all around me in a muffled voice I say Marry Christmas sweetie. Yes, it is Christmas day although I am not feeling it the same as when we are at home. It is the same as when you were little, and we went to Panorama skiing over a Christmas you were not happy. Even paying extra for a condominium with a fireplace and decorated tree did sit well with you or feel like Christmas. We brought your gifts and had stockings to open but that was not Christmas for you, I grind. This being a tropical Christmas away from home, setting aside of course the disastrous reason we are even here, I can imagine would be close to the same.

I sit up to great the day and see our golf shirts all silk-screened and ready to rock. Rosie even put a skull and cross bones behind our team name. Our shirts were black with a white skull and cross bones and red lettering the Putting Pirates. Rosie had out knee length black shorts and matching red sneakers.

We got up to have our coffee when we thought we could hear some slight noise coming from the patio when I hear Paul's deep voice. Right away, I jump to conclusions and whispered to Amanda that he must have stayed the night with Rosie, when Amanda says mom don't be silly, he is probably here helping Rosie get ready for the tournament. Oh, you are probably right sweetie but my thought, was juicer then yours. Then she looks right at me and says like a real busy body, I bet he did stay and then chuckled implying that I was not the only one thinking it.

As we finish our coffee and smoke, we go to get ready to get out to the patio to see if Rosie needed any help. Amanda said, as we were getting ready, after all the food I ate last night I feel hungry this morning, what is up with that she smiles. Yes, I am hungry too and I can smell that Rosie has bacon out there yum.

We did not take long getting ready with our hair still looking great from last night, all that was needed was to run a comb through our hair brush our teeth dress and out the door we went, to see what the commotion was that we could hear going on, and find out what was for breakfast. Coming out of our room, thinking we were calling out to Rosie and maybe Paul, with some pep in our steps out and saying loudly Merry Christmas, we see everyone.

When we get out to the patio to our surprise everyone was there with Rosie rolling out her hot serving carts full of eggs Benedict, bacon, sausage, hash browns and toast. There were also pasties and a fruit platter. Amanda points out that Henry was making a smoothie over at the bar. We hear coming from the unexpected crowd good morning sleepy heads. Wow, we wave to the group that were all mulling about getting their shirts on or standing at the buffet when I say good morning Rosie, I said as we walk over to the breakfast buffet carts where she was standing, and I got in her face and asked her, did you even sleep last night. Then deliberately looking around to see that, everyone has his or her team shirts already and pointing to the wonderful breakfast she has prepared. Rosie looks in my eyes trying not to smile and says I slept enough and winked and gives a big smile to Amanda and I as we get our coffee.

Come on girls load up, you are going to need your strength and wits with you today. Really, Amanda says, she smirks it is only mini golf. When Dustin exclaims, just mini golf, girl this is the battle of the decade, we have going on here. As Paul comes to the buffet table and says his good morning, he comments to Amanda, never mind Dustin he just thinks he is better then he really is, Paul chuckled and looked over at Dustin. When Janette of all people chimed in saying, Rosie you should just give us the trophy now it is inevitable that we will be taking it home. Janette took everyone by surprise with her comment and even Jim took a step back and jokingly said who are you woman, my Janette is not competitive, then he cozies up to her and says slowly, what you doing later smiling Jim gives her a kiss on the cheek. Jessie and Ryan were just as taken back by her comment and Jessie made sure her mother knew that the trophy does not have your name on it yet, and blows Janette a kiss and gives Ryan a high five.

Wow, this is sounding hilariously serious, Amanda said while she was filling her plate, this I have to see she grinds. When I said with my plate full, and before sitting down no worries Amanda we got this, we brought our "A" game today, and the secret is in our red sneakers. Right on girl, Kevin says the win is in the bag. The mockery went on as the group was filling their plates; we could tell they all loved it.

With plates full and settled down, I had to ask Rosie. How did everyone know to be here this morning, did I miss something, I chuckled. Rosie looked over and said once we had the shirts done, Paul went home and I guess with being so pumped I had a bit of a nap and when I woke up all I wanted to do was cook and I enjoy cooking for a crowd. I sent off my Merry Christmas early morning message letting everyone know shirts were ready and breakfast was being served. Rosie looks over at Ryan and apologizes for interrupting his sleep in, but I was sure breakfast would make up for the early rise and shine. Ryan replies to Rosie that it is all good, you were right I would much rather eat your food then sleep any day; he raises his fork to her and smiles. Amanda and I listen intently and just enjoy the fun.

When Elsie brings over a large jug of strawberry smoothies, saying these ones have a little kick people and smiles. Dustin and Kevin were all up for a glass when Paul says do you not see what she is doing, What, Kevin looks up at Paul what is our sweet Elsie doing. She is trying to get you tipsy and take you off your game, he chuckles. The fellows turn and look at Elsie standing there so innocent, who me, I would not do that she bats her eyes, besides we do not need to get you tipsy to win, she high fives Henry.

Rosie stands up and says welcome teams, then proceeds to hand out scorecards and explain that our round of mini golf is best ball, and that each team member has to count a minimum of four balls.
The rules are on the back of the cards Rosie shows us the card and what holes are marked as prize holes with obstacles. Dustin has all the lights and nativities' operating on the course and our Las Vegas Strip is alive and ready for us. We could all tell she was pumped and ready for a great day of mini golf and applauded her for the instructions and for putting the golf tournament together and breakfast.

Rosie packed a bunch of goodies into totes that she wanted taken to the course, with Paul and Jim finished their breakfast she asked them if they would mind taking the totes to the course when they go as she points to the bar. With us, all finished breakfast; I think we could feel Rosie's growing excitement and we were tickled when Rosie asked for all us girls to pitch in and help her to clean up so we could get the tournament started. There was very little chitchat going on the fellows moved the serving carts to the bar and put the chairs back in place and the totes in the carts. Rosie was very impressed at how quickly we had everything cleaned up and put away. Before leaving, the last stop was to fill up our coffees or smoothies before we left.

Amanda and I gather our stuff and start walking towards our pink driving machine with Jessie and Ryan behind us and Henry and Elsie following. We will see you all down there as we wave at Rosie before leaving. Amanda says I need a smoke; way ahead of you as I was holding her smoke and just going to light it, she smirks. Well this should be fun and interesting all at the same time I relayed to Amanda who concurred yes, this will be a great day giving a big smile as we are turning into the parking area. We could hear the music playing and lights flashing. It looked a little different from when we played the last time. We take our time walking up finishing our smoke as everyone is pulling in. When Dustin parked I complemented him on the added features, he replies I will not take all the credit Jim and Paul did all the physical work, I only had to wire the features and program them to work as we play the course.

Rosie had Kevin and Paul bring the totes to the patio lounge and as Rosie was fussing about Dustin looks at Amanda and I and says hoot, we have to have hoot before tackling this course. Kevin sees the hoot in Dustin's hand and makes a beeline over to us leaving Paul with Rosie.

Jim and Janette went over to help to chat with their teammates and help unpack the extras that Rosie had brought. While Henry, Elsie, Ryan and Jessie seemed to be strategizing their game, or at least giving the impression that is what they were up to, with serious review of the courses new challenges.

While we were having our hoot, I confessed to our team that I was not too worried about how well we score as long as we have fun. Kevin looked at us with hoot in hand, leans in, and says quietly that is good because honestly girls, he takes a hoot, we do not stand a chance against most of them. When I blurted out a laugh that startled everyone and got the whole group laughing.

Once done our smokes, we all go to the lounge area and see what goodies Rosie had brought. Right away Amanda points out the little trophies, and then says holy smokes there are gold, silver and bronze metals Amanda nudges me and says loud enough for everyone around to hear, I could not do as much as Rosie has done in the last twenty-four hours, in two weeks she chuckles. Rosie, Paul how did you have time for all of this, Dustin and Kevin were smiling over what Amanda said when she said really did you two sleep at all last night she chuckled. For some reason Rosie started to blush and quickly brushed it off by saying, what can I say kids when you are as good as I am things come together like magic she winks.

Henry and the rest make their way into the lounge and Henry says so what is all the commotion over here. Oh not much I tell her, Amanda just thinks that Rosie has super powers I said jokingly. Amanda taunts hey, mom thinks so too. Henry looking seriously at Amanda, Rosie does have super powers. As the rest of the group was, quiet and waiting to hear what Henry was going to say, when Henry proclaims, Rosie's super powers are that she has mastered planning and organization. Henry gave Amanda a pat on the shoulder and said there is no magic she is just that good. The rest of them waited to see our expressions once Henry gave the no thrills answer. Then everyone chuckled seeing our obvious disenchantment with her response. Henry gives Rosie a wink as she moves to grab her and Elsie's putters. Now if we are all ready, let us get our tournament started, Rosie calls out to us all.

Paul has the master card and calls out the Hole in One team is up first and then second is the Putting Pirates and saving the best to last we have weapons of grass destruction, he smiles and holds up his fancy club that had a carved wood handle and gold inlayed club head. Holly doodle I said when I saw Paul's custom club and I pointed the club out to Amanda who then looked at Kevin and Dustin and said you were right about not having a chance we all giggled amongst ourselves.

The games started and from start to finish, we laughed all day, drank too much and played some real bad golf. There were actual sand traps and water obstacles along with tall grass and thick rough to deal with. With the much resent upgrades completed to the course no one had actually played a full round so it was very funny to watch the island keeners struggling with their games. There were even prize holes with like the third, if you got a hole in one on the third hole, the prize was a putter very similar to the one Paul has with wood and gold inlay only not as fancy. There were a few holes Rosie had it set up that we could win funny prizes on, which the most fun. When you come to a hole and see that the prize for the longest putt may be a haircut or a cooked meal, we all really got a kick out of the creative prizes that were priceless. Amanda and I joked with Dustin and Kevin throughout the game as we noticed that they actually tried harder on the holes that they could win meals.

When done, we all thanked Rosie for her idea and that we had a fantastic time. As we, all take a seat in the lounge Paul proceeds to get all our attention and announces sounding official, as anticipated it was Rosie's team, grass destruction that was the wining team as gives Rosie, Janette and Jim a thumbs up. Ryan blurts out teasing that it was only because you made that freakish putt on the tenth hole that got you the win. Paul smiling proudly then cleared his throat, continuing by saying our hole in one team came in second with one shot behind. Henry and her team all stood up and took a bow with us cheering them on.

Well people Rosie says loud enough so that we all heard, I want to thank you all very much this was another amazing day and my stomach hurts from laughing so hard. She looks over at Jessie, as we all do who was still wet from falling in the water. Rosie lets us know that the food is at the café so if anyone wants to change, as I am sure Jessie does she nods, do that and then head right over. Rosie points to Amanda and I and comes over to us to say that she did lay out something for this evening if we wanted to change. That would be great Rosie, are you coming up with us. Not right now girls, I want to check on the food and have everything out, and then I will dash up and change. You go ahead she says, and do not doddle she grins and says just joshing you, take your time I will be a few minutes getting things ready anyway. Amanda blurts out a laugh, a few minutes is like a mini second, not that there is such a thing but your time is calibrated different than others magic or not, Amanda bumped Rosie's elbow, implying she may not believe what Henry said.

We were all chatting about the day, the game, and our performances while packing up and getting ready to leave when we all started shaking hands and giving hugs, and thanked each other for the game. When I came over to give Rosie her hug she started to tear up, which made me tear up the same, sensing her enjoyment and happiness of her past couple of days.

Once the fellows had all the stuff packed in the carts it was time for a quick change and then to the café. As we all head off in our own directions, I lit Amanda and I a smoke when I confided that I needed a wee coffee and a sit down before going to the café. Looking over, Amanda says I am running out of steam. Then thinking aloud, how about once we change, we will go to the café have dinner and call it an early evening. We can come back and go to bed, when I replied without hesitation that sounds like a perfect idea. We are not the only ones that are feeling a little tired and will be calling it and early night sweetie.

As Amanda turned to go up the hill, I said to her that Rosie must have been getting close to running on empty by now too. I believe that it is only adrenalin she is operating on now I chuckled. Amanda was smiling and said yes but when she does crash, she will be out for a while I agreed with a nod.

One we park and as we are getting out of the cart, I made growing sounds looking for sympathy from Amanda who looks at me as we start walking towards our room and says; oh no, you are not getting out of going. I smiled and batted my eyes at her, she replies jokingly, and that will not work either mom. We will go have something to eat and be back soon. Okay yes, I know you are right; I am just ready for a hot bath and bed sweetie, but I will get my second wind I smile.

As we walk into the room and see the outfits Rosie has out for us, Amanda blurts out, not what I was expecting but all right, these will work she giggled. When seeing the two flowing long floral dresses one with straps and one without I knew what Amanda meant by not expecting. These fancier girlish outfits were not typical of what Rosie normally picked out for us. The floral patterns and delicate material was beautiful however not only beautiful, once we had them on, we realized just how comfortable they were to wear. Bonus, I smile and gesture to Amanda with my hands by my sides, that the dresses even have pockets. Amanda chuckles at, the way I am waving my hands around while in my pockets.

We take one last look at ourselves in the big mirror, complement each other as we do and deicide that we better get moving, Rosie will be looking for us soon. Walking out to the patio our dresses seemed to flow and glide behind us. By this time, we were feeling refreshed and hungry and as we get out to the cart, I noticed that the holographic tree over the lake was gone, although now the lake had a pink hue, which looked cool Amanda, commented. We will have to ask Dustin what else he can do with the lights and pictures she says, as she is getting ready to drive off. Smoke sweetie, I asked with Amanda replying what took you so long and chuckled.

Pulling up to the café, we could see that most of the group was already there, with Kevin and Dustin still wearing their team shirts and drinking beer. When we got out of our pink driving machine, Rosie quickly came right to us to get a good look at our dresses and let us know how lovely we looked in them.

Rosie getting between Amanda and I and walking in with us arm and arm taking us right to the bar and asks what we would like to have to drink this evening. Hum, Rosie I think I will have a beer of all things, when Amanda says you know that does sound good, make that two please. The fellow's frosty cold beer looked, refreshing. Janette was standing with us at the bar and Paul was leading up the winner's conversation with the fellows and joking around when Jessie and Ryan arrive. Amanda calls out to Jessie, I bet that feels better than the wet shorts, you look so nice too, with her floral body hugging halter dress and her hair all done up in a lose bun.

Ryan came over to let the group know that Henry and Elsie would be here in just a bit. He looks at Rosie and says I believe they are bringing desert, I could smell something yummy waft by on our way here and the smell was not coming from the café. Although it smells wonderful in here, it is not the same smell. Jim heard what Ryan was telling us about the smell, and then casually Jim sticks his nose up in the air and then looks over at as standing at the bar, says with a big grin, I know what they are bringing and pauses.
Kevin and Dustin tune into the conversation so what are they bringing, Jim responds without question they are bring crapes, so mater a fact that Rosie speaks up and cheerily says right on folks we are having crapes for desert. Girls you are going to love their crapes Rosie says to us as Janette says jokingly that Elsie and Henry's signature crapes are almost as good as my, signature apple crumble. Rosie chuckled yeah you all have your specialties, I am just the master as she toasts herself and we all laugh and of course agree with her.

As we were all having a good chuckle, Henry and Elsie drove up with a large silver serving try in the back of their cart. Right away Kevin and Dustin went to help carry the covered serving tray in with Henry looking at the rest of us looking at Paul to put him on the spot and say's okay what's up, you are all acting weird. You just drove up how can you say we are acting weird Jessie's asks, well Rosie is blushing and the boys rushed to help get the tray out of the cart and when they peaked to see what was inside Dustin gave Jim a thumbs up. Holly crap you caught all that in four and half seconds, Jessie chuckled as she put her hand on Ryan's shoulder for support.

Well then, Paul says, I guess we are busted. We were guessing what you were bringing for desert because Ryan commented that he thought he caught a waft of a sweet smell on their way here and Jim nailed it right off the bat. Rosie jumps in with a thank you ladies, these are wonderful and we all know that you two make the best and Amanda and Colleen are about to, Rosie nodded at Henry who looked over at Elsie and winked and then asked what's your pleasure darling. Elsie looked around at what everyone was drinking and said you know what I will have a beer, that will wash down the sweet drinks I have had she smiles. Amanda and I were standing back having a smoke while everyone was mulling about the buffet and the bar when finally we hear… All righty then, I believe we are ready for dinner Rosie announces. With the long day of fun, drinking and not much food, we were all hungry and as Kevin said, there is nothing better than a holiday feast of leftovers yum.

As Amanda and I get to the buffet and take our plates and utensils, we see a swell of food that looked equal to the meal we had the night before. We all dug into filling our plates and we did a good job of emptying the trays. Amanda and I watched as Dustin and Kevin were walking with their full plates to the table as they watched to makes sure none feel off.

Once we settle into our seats and start, eating Paul raises his beer and says not just, because we won the tournament, this was a great day and I want you all to know that with never spending this kind of time together in the past I have to admit the time is well spent.

Perfect, Dustin says to Paul, I am so glad you said that old man; Dustin wipes his mouth and declares to the group that he is having a water park and scary old move party. I want to have us all at the birdcage for a day before the girls have to leave; Dustin knowing full well, that by mentioning us leaving would make Paul happily say yes to the party. Rosie says the party sounds great but you are not getting me on the waterslide of yours that is for sure, Janette ditto with the rest of us ladies, all opting out of the slide action.

Oh, you girls just do not know how to have fun Kevin smiled then looking down at his plate not wanting acknowledge all us women looking at him. When Dustin kicked him under the table and said you are not helping dude.

Jim repeats Dustin's party plan, Water Park and old scary movie, so what did you have in mind for the movie. I am sure that you have all heard of it and most likely have seen it however I bet that it has been years for everyone so I thought we would watch The Shining. Now that is a good movie Amanda chimes in first with Jim agreeing yes, that is one of the original out there kind of scary movies. Cool that sounds good and what are you planning to feed people at this all day party event, Jim questions Dustin who looks up from his plate, huh oh well, I have not thought that far ahead yet.
So when did you come up with the idea of the party, Jim lifts his one eyebrow and smiles. Dustin with a sheepish look replies, well the party came to mind the instant Paul state about time well spent, we all laughed.

This dinner is great, passing on the praise to Rosie I said, However as I look over to Elsie and Henry I am leaving room for these crapes I just know they are going to be delightful. I was surprised that Amanda was still eating and actually went up for seconds of whipped potatoes and dressing. I lean over to Amanda and let her know that I was impressed but where was she putting it all, she smiled and shrugged her shoulders, I have no idea but this is just hitting the spot.

Rosie finished first and then went over to grab the coffee pot and a big bottle of Baileys and bring them over. Oh, a coffee Rosie that would be perfect Janette says us too Amanda and I both agree. Elsie got up to bring out our desert of rolled crapes filled with cream cheese and a wild berry mixture with whip cream on the side. When we get up to the large tray of desert, I could not resist and had to take two even though I felt full my eyes thought I could do it. Amanda only took one but loaded up on the whip cream. Ryan Dustin and Kevin waited until we had all served ours up and then they counted the rest of the crepes in the tray and divided them up giving them four each. Wow, you fellows are going to explode if you eat all that I said kidding around. Jessie says Ryan will belly ache for a while but he will be fine she giggled and nudged him with her elbow. Ryan looks at Jessie with a sweet look on his face and says to here you know me so well, I love you. Rosie commented awe that is so cute Ryan, but we all know that is your routine, you eat too much and then suffer and complain for next couple of hours. You are lucky she takes such good care of you as she does; Rosie glances over at Janette who was smiling and Jessie sitting up proudly and leaning over to give Ryan a kiss on the cheek replies to him I love you too sweetie. We all rumbled around the table with the gushy show of affection, Jessie and Ryan were inflating for our entertainment.

Eating as much as I possibly could, I put my napkin down and thanked Rosie, Henry and Elsie for the wonderful food and amazing desert. Elsie responding with I loved the leftovers as much as our first meal looking over at Rosie and we love making our crapes because they are enjoyed so much. Then looking over to Amanda and glancing at Kevin who was still working on finishing off his crapes, I said smoke then smiled and got up with Amanda.

As we get up and move away from the table Rosie comes over and says that whenever you girls are ready to leave you can go. You do not have to stick around here, I know that you are both tired and when I snuck away to change I got your Jacuzzi tub and suites out for a relaxing soak when you get home. That is so sweet Rosie, we are good for a bit, I think, and Amanda nods agreeing that we were good for now. Kevin and Dustin were finally finished eating and came over for a smoke and a hoot while Paul Jim and Ryan were having a brandy, and chatting about the day.

The rest of the ladies were mulling about tidying up a little and chatting up a storm about Dustin's party. Which by the sounds of it, will only be his party by location. We could hear the ladies were planning everything else, we snickered while standing back catching snippets of what they were discussing.

Dustin looked at us and tilted his head and winked, then said softly mission accomplished. Dustin began to chuckle then Kevin followed knowing that the ladies would not trust him to plan a party which he was all good with. Amanda agreed the only thing you will have to do is make the popcorn and that is if Rosie lets you. Dustin, says to us you know I think that is the one thing I do make that she loves, so that may be my contribution to the party.

Paul says if they decide to have it at the beach BBQ and picnic area at the bottom of the slide, I can make my ribs again. As full as we all were, Paul's ribs sounded like a real good plan for Dustin's party.

The ladies were finished doing what they needed to and came over to join us before calling it a night. Amanda and I were running on empty now and started with our hugs and thanking each of them for an amazing couple of days. Kevin hands me a refill to our special smokes, says as he smiles you will like this batch, and wiggles his eyebrows.

I put my arm around Amanda and pointed to our wheels, it is time to get mommabear home sweetie. Amanda grins at me and as we turn to walk to the cart we wave back at everyone and I blow a kiss to Rosie as we leave. Driving away we were smiling and waving and once we were out of sight I let sat back in my seat and let Amanda know that the last couple days have been an overload and that I was not planning on doing anything tomorrow. Amanda quickly suggesting a TV day and may be we can watch a program series they must have a good portion of them all archived, we can ask she finishes.

Hey, Amanda blurts, we forgot to ask Dustin about the lake having a pink hue that she remembered as we see the lake again driving up the hill. Oh yeah we did, we can ask Rosie in the morning.

When Amanda parks and we step onto the patio, I could feel myself being anxious to get into our room and relax, unwind from our couple of very interactive days. Once we get into the room the first thing I do is change into my house coat and get seated in our balcony lounge area and pour myself a coffee.

Amanda did to say anything until she had changed into her bathing suit to go into the Jacuzzi and then came to have a smoke with me. What is up mom, something is going on I can tell, oh it is nothing sweetie, I think I am just tired and starting to feel restless, is the best way to describe my feeling about leaving, I reply. I cannot put my finger on one thing I said to Amanda, it was as if a wallop of reality hit me when I stepped onto the patio and I was overcome with thoughts of us leaving. We are talking actually being merrier days away from leaving and not months any more. Along with an instant replay in my mind of our close nit relationships and activities, we have shared with some wonderful people that we will never see again, a rush of uncertainty or something like that came over me. Hum, Amanda thought for a second and then asked and how are you feeling now. Actually, sweetie I am feeling much better already, thank you. Mom you are fine and it was a bit of a panic or anxiety attach all you needed was some quiet time and relax with your coffee and smoke. I am going in the tub for a few minutes, I am sure it will bubble away what little life I have left and man am I going to sleep tonight she smiles and gets into the tub.

I sat back in my chair, looking out to the night sky, and randomly thought about how awesome my dress was the other night and how amazing and vibrant I felt and with thinking about the jewelry I was wearing, and even in my hazy relaxed state, I could feel myself outwardly smiling. When Amanda says so what is tickling your funny bone, might I ask. Shaking off my daze, I replied oddly enough I am sure I was thinking of the jewelry I was wearing with my dress and your ring of course, that is a bedazzled for sure sweetie. Do you think that you will take it when we leave I asked. What do you think can I and if I can should I? The best thing for us to do is talk to Rosie and let her know that we do not want to take items of such value. I raise my coffee cup to Amanda and say, I guess if we are rich when we get home, we can purchase and have our own shiny things made. Oh yeah Amanda exclaims I keep forgetting that part she chuckles and says that is enough for me, I am out. Grabbing her big towel and wrapping it around her, she comes over and sits down beside me. Like magic, as Amanda steps away from the tub lights above dim and flickering bulb candles light up our balcony sitting area. I filled our coffees, took out one of Kevin's new smokes, and said a couple puffs before bed, sound like a plan. Amanda smiled and nodded yeah, that sounds like a great way to finish off our evening I love you so much she says.

Chapter Twenty-Five

When I woke up the next morning I sensed that I had a long sleep and looking at the clock I could see that we had slept in an extra two hours. Plopping my head back on the pillow, Amanda rustled a little saying I have to pee so bad I should have got up a long time ago. She quickly lifts herself out of bed and darts off to the washroom. I sat up and smiled then focused in on our out fits for the day and they were so fitting for the day that we had already slept an extra two hours of.

I call out to Amanda and let her know that we are wearing men's silk pajamas today, what are you talking about Amanda says as she come out of the washroom and sees our silk two-piece men's pajamas with button front and pockets with drawstring wide leg pants. Our pajamas were custom fit so they were loose but not baggy fitting. The one for mom was chocolate brown with beige trim and Amanda's was beige with chocolate brown trim. They even had our initials embroidered on our breast pocket.

We went over to have our coffee and our smoke starting our day off on our favorite foot. I said to Amanda that after our hoot, everything was a blur, I do not remember getting myself to bed, I smiled at her and concluded that the end of the evening seems rather fuzzy. We were that tired mom but you were still with it enough to go to the bathroom before you went to bed she grind. Hum, I am sure it will come back to me; I cannot believe that we slept an extra two hours. Really, Amanda gasped, I did not think of the time she replied with an aha, that is why I had to pee so bad she chuckled.

I wonder what Rosie is doing we must have missed breakfast Amanda commented. I wonder how many times she came in here to check on us to make sure that we were okay, we giggled. Want to make a bet that Rosie has food ready for us whenever we get out there, Amanda looks at me, ah no, because you are probably right. Amanda says now that we mention food; I am getting hungry how about you. You bet sweetie, let us get our butts moving and see what Rosie has on the agenda for today. I am guessing not too much seeing, as we will be in our pajamas all day I smiled.

We take our time getting ready and emerge from our room to see Rosie in the same silk pajamas but hers were gold in color. Rosie's pajamas had additional embroidering of dragons on the back and on her pant legs. Rosie turns and throws out her arms and says you girls look fantastic and ready for a leisurely day. With us both smiling walking towards her Amanda asks so what is the plan for our pajama day she snickered. Rosie hit the mutton on the remote she had in her hand, the lounge area lit up, and the country music started playing softly. It is slot machine day; Rosie's face was lit up as she is pointing to the lounge that looks ready for the day.

That is an awesome plan for the day Rosie I complemented her on the idea. Then she says come we will have brunch first and then go over and play. Sounds great Amanda replies, and then sorry we are late. No worries Rosie says as she walks us over to the table she has set and then opens the serving tray to show us that she had made quiche. Rosie also had fruit, cheese, and pastries to choose from as well.
Pouring our coffee as Amanda and I sit Rosie asks so how was your sleep. Amazing for me, sleeping in two hours, with Amanda yeah mine was great too until I was rudely awaken with having to go pee so bad. Rosie pipes up, that does suck and is so disruptive she smiles.

Getting our breakfast, Rosie was surprised that we both had more food than normal on our plates when Amanda looked at Rosie and said that for some reason after all the food we have eaten, I am hungry this morning. The individual quiche looked so good as I asked Rosie how her evening was. Paul and I had a great time after everyone left we sat out on the patio for hours chatting about the last couple of days and we have grown closer then we have ever been girls and I have you to thank for that.

We look right at her and I say first cool, why thank us though. Well Rosie drags out, I believe that for some reason I always felt I had to keep Paul and my relationship strictly professional and keep my feelings at bay. However, with you both here and with the fun you have somehow reignited here, I realize once you are gone, I do not want to spend the rest of my life missing you. When I have someone here that really does care about me here. We are going to take it slow and everyone already thinks we have been having a secret affair going for a long time so no one will think anything of it she chuckled.

Amanda said yes, they do all think there is something more than just work going one between you two and that is wonderful to hear that you are taking your relationship to the next level. I am even more thrilled that you think it was us that had something to do with the connection she smiles and both Rosie and I. That is awesome Rosie, we are so happy for you. It would be terrible to think of you without a partner in this tropical paradise once we are gone. Now you will have two homes to reside in Amanda says with a grin and then I jumped in saying, and do not forget, two to clean I chuckled.

Rosie we noticed that the tree is gone now and that yesterday the lake water had a pink hue, Amanda commented. I have not checked today to see if it was different but yesterday it was pink, right looking for confirmation that we were not just seeing things. Rosie chuckled, no, you were not seeing things, and it was Dustin that has made some additional lighting alterations and can now mirror almost anything over the lake and manipulate colors reflecting off it. Images over the lake and changing colors sounds like it will be fun, I replied.

If you girls are finished eating how about we take ourselves over to the lounge, have coffee, and get the machines warmed up Rosie smiles and stands up and grabbing the coffee pot. Amanda and I get up and follow right behind her when I complemented Rosie on her pajamas and the designs of the dragons. I have had these for a while and they are so comfortable and I thought that you might like to have a pare. Today just seemed like the right day for them and they will be comfy while on the sub, as pajamas will be all you need for a few days she chuckled.

Rosie setting down the coffee pot on a close table, and Amanda and I cozy up to our machines. I asked her how we explain some of the items that we have been told we will be allowed to take home with us. Fortunately, for us Rosie replies, you were coming home from a trip in China. If ever having to explain any items purchased or events you will recall them from your trip.

As we log onto our games and all settled, Rosie looks side-to-side looking at both of us one at a time. Which we stopped as she exclaimed now the jewelry on the other hand, I could feel my face drop thinking the worst that I was not going to get to keep my favorite piece. Not wanting to show any disappointment, I said what about the jewelry, Rosie hesitates knowing we were anxious to hear what she was going to say. Relax, Rosie smiles, all the jewelry you take with you, at first you will proclaim as being zirconium crystals just fake, and once you have your new wealthy lives established then you can have them properly apprised under the radar and by then it will not matter.

Few, I said to Rosie and Amanda jokingly as I wiped my forehead. Rosie laughs, knowing that I have grown quite attached to my shinny things. As I see Amanda looking down at her rock on her finger knowing she is happy she gets to keep hers too because she has not taken off since she wore it with her evening dress. Trust me when I say girls, that you are not being selfish by taking anything from here including the bank accounts.

Now that you're new identities have been established and your bank accounts opened, I have a special surprise for you. More Amanda exclaims, what more could there possibly be she asks. Well this is the fun part of playing today; Rosie beams everything you win on your machine you get to keep. When you cash out today, all your winnings will go into your new accounts. No way, you are joking, both Amanda and I spoke at the same time. I am not kidding what you win is yours to keep. You will not need more money, but playing with real money makes the game more interesting.

Looking at the machines, we see that what was showing as points in now showing in dollars and Amanda sees that she has three hundred thousand dollars on her machine and I have two hundred and fifty thousand. There is now way this is ours, oh yes it most certainly is Rosie says so have fun we have all day, she hits the button with her machine reading two million dollars, I asked her when she is going to cash in her wad of cash. I had never thought of it before but lately I think there may be a trip in my future and I would cash it in then she smiles and winks at me.

As we really started playing our games, I thought to ask how the finances work for the people of the island. Is the group paid for being here or is it free room and board, I laughed jokingly, thinking what I said was funny and Amanda snickered? Oh, no silly, that was a good one but no, actually, we all have more money then we could ever spend. If I cashed out it would be to commemorate a trip off the island and when I came back, I could start fresh again.

Well that is great to hear that everyone is comfortable I say to Rosie, she replies, and that is why we want to make sure you girls are going to be okay when you get home. You have been through enough and after a taste of this life she smiles, we want you to be able to enjoy the rest of your lives as you so choose and enjoy your time. That is so amazing Amanda says to Rosie and I agree, for an experience that was so bad, we sure landed on our feet and are the lucky ones. We cannot thank you enough Rosie, this has truly been the most inconceivable thing that could have happened, I say as I lean over towards Rosie and nudge her shoulder. Rosie appreciated the thought although not get mushy she kept playing and jokingly said to Amanda, I noticed that since you found out that you are playing with real cash and that it is yours, you have taken your bet off max don't be chicken, it's only money kiddo, Rosie chuckles.

As soon as Amanda puts her, game back to a max bet sure as crap if she did not win another fifty thousand dollars. Wow, I exclaimed as I look over at Amanda and her machine that was flashing the lights around the screen, as it was adding up. We all laughed, Amanda's shocked face was hilarious and she was giddy over the win, especially because it was real money and not just points in a video game.

Boy do I feel like I want a smoke and a hoot I smiled and looked over at Amanda, hey yeah me too. We had been having so much fun and were distracted that we had not thought about having a smoke. Rosie smiles and turns her chair and gets down and says, I am getting my Baileys and will grab us a fresh pot of coffee, and off she went.

Amanda and I were joking around back and forth, as we had our hoot, about who was going to be the big winner today and that pushing the button is more intense when it is not just a game, and the stakes are real. We realized that we were playing just as cautious with someone else's money as would be our own, which this really was our own, it just had not totally sunk in yet. Rosie had been gone longer then just getting coffee so we knew she was up to something, most likely food of some kind, Amanda and I naturally assumed. We were having a great time and I was getting up there in cash too but no big wins for me yet. Being in our silk pajamas, at the machines and enjoying our hoot was awesome when Rosie comes out of the kitchen-pushing one of her serving carts just smiling away as she approached.

I made us some finger sandwiches to nibble on and as she pulls open the hood covering the food we see a feast of food, much more than just finger sandwiches and Amanda and I instantly start to laugh, who in the heck is that all for I was able to utter out.

Oh I thought after your hoot you would be hungry she said with such a straight face, and we just roared, I am only kidding you girls Rosie confirms, but your expressions were priceless she says smiling. No, no, girls this is not all for us, Paul informed me that Dustin and Paul would be coming up soon, as they have new information for us. That sounds good, right. Leaving no room for Rosie to answer I added do the others know. Rosie replies I am sure that by now everyone has received the up-date, that means you have too Rosie Amanda realizes and says so what is it Rosie, tell us what is the news. Rosie smiles at us and says we will wait for the fellows to get here they can explain everything much better and that will be a good time to break for lunch.

Kidding around Rosie says saved by the bell as Paul and Dustin pull up. Amanda and I save our games and let Rosie know jokingly that we would have squeezed the info out of her if Paul had not shown up just when he did, I chuckle and Amanda smiles yeah, you are lucky. Yes, I was worried; Rosie winked back at us, we shrugged our shoulders smiling and we all went to great the fellows on the patio.

Paul says with a big grin well good day pajama girls. Dustin, I like the pajamas they are perfect for activities of today he looks over at the machines all lit up and smiles. You have an up-date for us Rosie says to them. We do but without food, we cannot remember all of the information he chuckles. Implying they were not talking until they were fed. Amanda takes Paul and Dustin's hands, and says as she pulls them over to the lounge area, well then you just come this way. Rosie was obviously expecting you as she has prepared enough food for an island I joked as we walked over to the table.

Dustin noticed the dollars on the machines and smiled, saying to us as he started filling his plate I see the machines have converted points to cash that is sweet. Paul adds that the machines are more challenging with you are playing for cash and not points. Yeah that is for sure Amanda pipes up but it is a game of chance and I have a number in mind that I will not go below, she smiles and taps at her temple keeping her number a secret.

As we all fill our plates and have a seat at one of the lounge tables, Rosie nudges Paul and says well the girls are waiting to hear what the news is. Paul had just taken a bite of his sandwich and nodded to Dustin to start. Well people, the big news is that the countdown has begun; and your journey home will actually start in the next few days. All the sudden I could feel my stomach drop and my heart started pounding when I grabbed Amanda's hand and squeezed. Amanda turned to me with her mouth open and both speechless for a second. Really oh my, my, my I felt a hot flush come over me. Rosie could tell I was overwhelmed and excited at the same time, by the news. Amanda's face looked rosy while still in quiet surprise, as if not believing this day would come, then I could see her face start to light up as she absorbed and accepted the news.

Paul went onto to say that the atmospheric conditions have vastly improved and the world is starting to work together on restoration and displacement of the people. For us here the first thing that will happen is the core plug will implode, then we will have a least one day for the rock to settle and then ladies, down and away we go.

Jessie and Ryan will start all systems checks, plotting and programming cloaking navigation systems and Jim and I will be working on submarine inventory, and then says jokingly any special requests. Rosie jumps in with saying to Paul I will take care of all the food ordering. You do not worry about that I will have our grocery list to you tomorrow she perked up from her thoughts of us leaving.

At least you are coming with us Rosie that will make the trip. Then I looked over at Dustin and I said what about your party. When Rosie piped up and said, we decided we will have Dustin party as our New Years Eve party because we will be leaving right after that. Sadly, Rosie says, Dustin's party will be our last groups get together but it will be one to remember she exclaimed and with Paul adding, you bet, we will make it the second party, of a life time to remember, looking over at Rosie and giving her a nod as we chuckled. Making sure Rosie knew that nothing could have topped her elegant event.

Wow, this seems to be happening so fast all of a sudden, Amanda says as we all dug into our lunch gripping the news as it did meant different things to us all. When finished nibbling I was ready for a refill of coffee and a smoke, and Amanda was right behind me as I motioned to get up. Rosie, Paul and Dustin carried on talking about departure preparation that did not really mean much to us so we went back to our machines for our coffee and smoke.

Almost sweetie, almost home I say as I am trying to contain my excitement, I know Amanda replies quietly, I almost cannot believe it. Everything will start to happen fast now, with them all starting on departure now, crap we are going to be in that sub soon.

Once they were all finished, their lunches the three of them come to the machines and watch us play for a bit, when Rosie pours herself a Baileys on ice and says this is a straight up, kind of day and smiles as she is getting back into her machine chair. Amanda and I ask Dustin if he wanted a hoot before he left and with a hardy of course, Paul went and sat with Rosie at her machine.

As I light, the hoot Dustin starts talking about how cool the news was and that it did come as a huge surprise to them as well. This information means so much to our systems data and research, I know for you it is all about getting home, but for the science behind it all, it is miraculous. The changes that had to occur in such a short time are incredible and our statistical data is suggesting that by ending all war and uniting the world, human can clean up their act pretty darn fast, he proclaims.

Finishing our hoot and coming back to the machines Paul get's up and says to us that he will be bring our suite cases tomorrow so that we can pack a few things. Remember girls your luggage was not with you and supposedly stranded on a primitive island and not this island paradise, he smirks. Not that luggage and contents really matters because of the imbedded story and planned stages of getting you home and the allusive story depending on the reason for having to tell it. Paul goes onto say once the family hears the imbedded story of the primitive island and them giving you all the money. When they realize they are wealthy, you just have to say you would prefer not to discuss the time, and they will drop it.

Rosie looks at us and then asks Paul if he would mind walking us through the projections again, seeing as we do not have as much time as we thought we would have to casually get the conversations started. Paul looks at Dustin who smiles and takes that as a signal to have a Baileys on ice with Rosie and he came back to the table and sat down filling his glass and sitting back.

Paul began by saying; yes, it is important to have a conscious understanding of the fundamentals of the plan and projections. Having that information locked in your minds will help when faced with scenarios not foreseen in the initial coding. With having the background locked in, you will be better prepared to navigate the best answer, having to rely on the filter less. The filter feeds back the unanticipated event and prepares the correct response so a slip does not happen twice.

Okay then, Paul grabs his coffee and says that with dropping you off at your door with a person that confirms you are safe and collaborates are aware of their new destiny. We avoid all the hype and explanations of your return.

Frankly, girls your partners would have had to obtain and produce death certificates for you to be able to claim any insurance benefits, which presumably they have obtained. That is why the changing of our names to avoids any insurance problems. Colleen you will remarry your husband under your new name and Amanda we are thinking your name will be changing very shortly after you get home; Paul wiggles his eyebrows and smirks at Amanda. When you are settled may be donating the money to a charity that was paid out to your partners well, it is not as if you can pay them back he laughed. We chuckle thinking that what he said was true.

Once your waiting partners are, read in so to speak, you assume your new identities. The immediate plan is that you gather a few things from the house and then there will be a quick stop at Amanda's place, which from what I understand is on the way to the international airport. Amanda nods at Paul impressed that he knew that. Paul went onto to say that you four would be the only ones at this point that know the situation at this time and know you are going to be jumping on a privet jet that is taking you to Costa Rica. Once in your new condominium subdivision, with its own golf course with privet dwellings with the luxuries of a beach resort with pools and staff to take care of your every need.

You notify the rest of your immediate family of your miraculous survival giving a quick summary and that it is imperative they do not let anyone else know specifically social media. Letting them know, that all their questions will be answered when they arrive. To ensure your immediate family follows direction you will confirm that they no longer have to worry about their futures and that they are to do as the assistant's instructs. The assistant will be calling them immediately after your call. They will all be instructed, to pack lightly even for the children as everything they will need will be available on arrival.

A privet car will pick them up and take them to a privet jet that will fly them right to you. There will be one jet picking up the family in Saskatchewan and the rest will travel together out of Edmonton. I believe there may be one daughter that we are going to have to retrieve from rural Alberta so we are working on that obstacle now. The ideal scenario is that we have your family in the air within one hundred and thirty-five minutes to avoid detection and reduce stress on everyone at home. There will be explaining to do and sweeping them away and showing them their new lives is the best way to do that.

Holly smackers, I said with a smile and big wide eyes, that was a lot of information. Dustin says yeah, this is the coolest rouse to be part of I love it all he grins, and takes a sip of his drink. While Rosie agrees, it is a bit to take in although you have to know that it is a perfect plan, she nods to Paul and Dustin.

There are more details Paul says but that is what we have up our sleeves and how we anticipate events to follow through. Now that I have talked your ears off, Dustin and I will leave you to enjoy the rest of your pajama day. Paul puts down his coffee cup and thanks, Rosie for the lunch and coffee then nudges Dustin who was taking his last sip, to get up. Dustin salutes us as we smile and they turn to leave, Rosie walks them out to their cart.
Amanda and I sit back and look at each other, flabbergasted and she starts to smile and it got bigger when she says, can you imagine it, once Jen gets the news life is good and she will be flying on a privet jet to Costa Rica, she could be on the plane in thirty minutes. That girl is going to go bat crap crazy the minute she gets the news, oh goodness yes, not only are we alive, we will all be rich and in a tropical place. As Rosie comes back to the machines she asks so what is all the chatter about. Amanda spoke first and told Rosie that Jen my sister who thought she lost her mother and sister in a plan crash, will need to be sedated, once she gets the news. Jen has two little girls that will need to be attended she chuckles; hubby will have his hands full with Jen. Amanda and I both, knowing all too well how her sister will react to something this enormous.

Rosie replies I am glad you expressed her reactions so dramatically I will let Dustin and Paul know so that they can incorporate the accommodation into the plan and ensure that there is a nanny for the girls. You may not be far off in thinking that she may have to be relaxed, just saying but she will be fine Rosie grind, no worries. If there is anything else like that you can think of you let me know so that we are be prepared. I found myself thinking of Jen and her likely reaction and yeah as soon as her hubby gets home, she may have to be put out, I could feel myself smile.

Amanda looking up to the sky and then to me, I think everyone else is going to be cool about the news and will follow the plan getting them all to Costa Rica to get the answers. That part should be okay with having everything pre-arranged, all they have to do is pack a small bag, jump into a car and then a plane.

Rosie lets us know that the subdivision has houses for each of the five girls, which can be theirs when they visit or if they decide to stay. You never know what any of them will do Rosie comments, once they have money some may choose to go back home. You could also go back and rebuild your lives there or just go for visits.

While sitting and slowly playing our machines, we joked about Jen and her possible reactions, when Amanda had a brain fart and gasped what about Molly and Moo. Rosie says, now who, the heck is Molly and Moo you have not talked about them. They are my cats and mom has Buddy, what happens with them. Way to make things complicated ladies, Rosie replies as we start to feel guilty about being a bother and making this more difficult than anticipated. Then Rosie smiles and says I am only joshing you girls, only kidding, and no worries. With flying on a privet jet we can get the pets to the subdivision but they be quarantined for a bit. What a relief, Amanda says I and adds I cannot believe that I have not thought about my cats much at all. Rosie was fast to say that to save our emotions our subconscious has tucked things away for you, and now that we are able to talk about home more comfortably your mind is opening up to you.

I on the other hand have enjoyed my time without Buddy I laughed, Amanda looks over at me and says mom that is mean, and you do not mean that. Oh Rosie, if you new Buddy and we joke about Jen getting excited, Buddy may have a heart attack when he sees us. That is, if he did not pass with being gone. Our dog Buddy is a nerves Nelly and used to follow my every footstep, so the time away from him, has been pleasant I smile and wink at Amanda, who replies awe you love Buddy.

The assistant will make sure that every detail is addressed including sending out all applicable notices of the abrupt absence. Which after a couple of days will be all clear and they can do what they choose from there. A couple days of missing in action is not a big deal and if the money changes their direction or desires in life they can all make the changes they want, and carry on their lives knowing that mom and sis are alive and doing well, and a matter a fact exceptionally well, Rosie proudly smiles.
When all the sudden my machine lit right up and the words, mega winner popped on my screen and it started adding up. Wahoo, I said pointing to my machine that was showing I just won a million dollars. Holy crap, Amanda are you seeing this, you bet Rosie drinks are on mom she chuckled.

Drinks, now that sounds like a great idea Amanda, how about we have Caesars, doesn't that sound zippy. Sounds great Rosie, I will have a smoke while I boast that I have to let my machine add up as I smile at Amanda who stops to have a smoke with me.

Rosie is at the bar mixing like a pro and said we will have to let Paul and Dustin know about your big win they love to hear about the wins. Rosie put our drinks in jars with handles and put in spicy pickled asparagus as a garnish. With rims seasoned the drinks looked great, ad as Rosie hands them to us we cheers. The drinks tasted better then they looked we raise our jars and cheers before we have a big sip. When Amanda asked Rosie if we could save our games or do, we have to cash out today. You can save them; we will cash them out and transform the money before you leave.

Moving over to the table, I grab a couple finger sandwiches at the serving tray before sitting down while Rosie and Amanda were settling back in their chairs. Rosie turned up the music a little and we started wiggling in our chairs and lip sinking to a very old country song named, stand by your man. We were actually not doing too badly with the words when Rosie hit another button on the remote and of course, a karaoke screen came down at the end of the pool table. Rosie pointed to the narrow cupboard where the pool cues were standing and nodded her head at Amanda the microphone is in the cabinet if you want to give it a go Rosie smiles very big, but did not move to go get it. When I say to Rosie, come on show us what you have in you, I bet you are just awesome.

Rosie says there is no way I am getting up there unless I have a jug of these she says lifting her drink in the air. I am with you Rosie, love singing but not in the habit of getting up in front of an audience to perform. There are some things that I know that I am okay at but singing is one I admit, I am not that good at or confident with. Amanda agreed we had definitely not had enough alcohol to get her up to sing either, as we chuckle at each other for being chickens. We were all good with just sitting in our chairs, singing like country stars and armchair dancing.

It was not long when Amanda decided it was time for a hoot, which I said to her, you read my mind sweetie. As we, were passing our hoot around and asking Rosie if she wanted a puff and her smiling, I will stick to my wet habit thanks. Then Rosie lowers the music and asks if we are hungry yet, there is a stew and dumplings ready for us, when we are. Now that sound really good Rosie, what made you think of a stew. You know I am not sure, it has to be forever since I made one. My favorite part of stew is the dumplings Rosie says looking at Amanda who did not seem too impressed. Amanda you will love my stew as she jumps up and says, give me a minute and I will bring out the best stew and dumplings you have ever had she boasts as she leaves the lounge and goes into the kitchen.

Just as we are finishing our hoot, Rosie comes out of the kitchen pushing a smaller serving cart that had a large crock-pot of stew and steamer full of dumplings on it. Once she parked the cart, she even filled our plates for us and gave us each one dumpling to start with. Trust me ladies you are going to love this as she fills up her own plate and take two dumplings.

As we started to eat, Rosie watched Amanda to see her reaction and, to Amanda's surprise, she actually did like the stew and really was impressed with the dumplings, she nods to Rosie and comments that honestly I have never had anything like this before. I agreed with Amanda, I had not had or made many stews in my past and this was not like the stew I had ever eaten. So good Rosie, the best, we gave her the thumbs up. While we ate and drift off in our own daydreams, Dustin's party came to mind and I asked Rosie so what is the plan for New Years Eve, did everyone like the idea of Dustin's water park and movie night party. Actually yes, and we are going to have the water park portion of the party on the beach. At the bottom of the water slide, the fellows can take the elevator up if they want to go repeatedly, yuck

Rosie smiles. They will not get into a submarine if they do not have to, yet they will shoot through tubes that tunnel through a mountain, I do not get those two, she goes onto to say. That the move idea is great and we must be a messed up group because we even like the twisted movie he chose. We can see any movie or show and we can take breaks at any time so we will see how it goes.

Amanda says back it up a second Rosie, what did you say about elevator to the waterslide. Oh yes, the worst confined space ever she grins. The elevator is a clear fiberglass tube that fits one person at a time. When you step on the platform, it takes you to the top of the water slide, so a person does not have to go through the house and up to the second level to take the slide. The elevator will take a person down as well of course although; none of us has ever used it that I can recall. I am surprised that we have not seen it. Rosie comments, the elevator shaft is for the most part, hidden and covered by the trees yeah and with being, half slammed all the time why would you notice, Rosie blurt out a huge laugh. This gets Amanda and I both chuckling as well, knowing that she has half-bit right. I am sure Dustin said something about that when we were there but right now, I cannot remember for sure Amanda replied. I was having the same laps in memory, but seem to recall Dustin saying something about access to the slide. All I can really remember is how much everyone laughed when they talked about you Rosie taking the slide that broke me right up. The fellows loved that you at least tried, and how much you howled going down it.

Dustin's New Years Eve celebration will be an awesome send off party, as we will be leaving somewhere around thirty two to six hours after. I can say that calmly now because I am going with you on most of your journey home and I know that the party will not be our last good buy, Rosie smiles and tilts her head glancing at us both and says that makes having the party easier for her to talk, and think about. We will not think about our good buys just yet and girls I know in my heart that when everything is all said and done, I am going to be able to see you again and that is what will hold me together. I lunge forward and say what you talking about Rosie; we will get to see you again that is fantastic, Amanda smiles big at Rosie and asks when can that happen? Oh, it will be at least a year or two but I will only be able to come to see you in Costa Rica and from what Henry says that if only one of you is there, my presence will act as the same conduit as if you were together, bring back the true reality and secrets.

This is the best news Rosie, I said seeing the relief as well in Amanda's reactions we were both thrilled. Knowing we will see each other again will make leaving and good buys a little less painful. On that note, it is time for another drink. What is your pleasure ladies Rosie gets up waiting for an answer, looking at me I replied, I will have a glass of wine, Amanda hum, I think I will have a glass of wine as well please Rosie, I better not have any more spicy drinks or I will be burping casers all night she chuckled. I tapped Amanda on the arm and said that is better than farting them, we all howled, we thought it was funny. When Rosie exclaimed okay, wine it is then, excellent choice girls, I will join you Rosie grabbed the glasses, put two bottles in a cooler of ice, and brought them over.

Setting the wine and glasses down Rosie looks at our plates and asks if we are done. I can tell that you must have liked the stew and dumplings because you ate everything I put on your plates. On the other hand, Rosie gazes at us and says, or did you eat it all, out of not wanting to hurt, my feelings because I served up your plates. Rosie smiling away quips, I am only pulling your legs and joshing you, would you like more though? Amanda replies I am full and you gave me just the right amount and I loved the dumplings. I have to agree with Amanda, portion and yummiest I have ever had, I smiled.

Lets toast Rosie says to us, okay what are we toasting we ask. We are toasting our friendship, the bond we will share forever, without getting all mushy though and winked, Rosie raised her glass, as we clink our glasses together and repeat, to friendship and our bond forever.

Relaxing back into our chairs sipping our wine Rosie asks how we like the wine, we both reply that it is good, Rosie starts to chuckle, you know you are drinking a thousand dollar bottle of wine as she grabs the bottle and empties it and fills our glasses. Oh dear, I would not have ever known I confessed to Rosie, Amanda shrugged her shoulders, do not look at me, I without a doubt would not be able to tell the difference that is for sure, smiling back at us.

Well then, a wine this expensive deserves a hoot to go with it I say to Amanda, when Rosie says why not.

I am home, in my pajamas drinking wine with my friends, a hoot is just what this special evening calls for she smiles and says spark that hoot. Cool, I reply as we settle in and watch the words appear on the karaoke screen as the music was playing.

When Amanda, turns to Rosie and asks, so when does the plug blow out of the submarine shaft. That is a good question Rosie all the sudden wide eye, I am not sure now. Let me chat with Paul, and we will find out, I know it is soon. It is not important Rosie do not rush Amanda let her know that the thought was random and had just crossed her mind, nothing that we needed to bother Paul about. Bother him Rosie replies, are you kidding me he is probably just sitting on the beach doing nothing, and wondering what we are doing more then anything, I would bet on it.

Rosie grabs her glasses and sets them on her nose for a second, when she said he will get right back to us one the time. Rosie takes her glasses off and both Amanda and I are wondering what she did that got that message to Paul when all we saw her do, was put the glasses on? That is when I said to Rosie, it is stuff like communicating through glasses that does make us wonder, you know that right, I chuckled. Then a second later Paul was pulling in, Rosie snickers, awe he must have been lonely and felt he had to deliver the message in person all smiles as Paul walks across the patio over to us.

Amanda and I look at each other as if we did not just fall off the turnip truck, we knew she was looking for any excuse to chat with him and he was looking for any justification to come see her. We grind at each other and look a sip of wine while we finished our hoot that Rosie was no longer interested in, with Paul there.

After Rosie poured Paul a glass of wine, he sat down and said so your question was when the shaft core would blow. Well ladies, the countdown has started and in eighteen and a half hours it will implode so it will happen during Dustin's party. Oh my that sounds scary Amanda says to Paul. No worries Amanda the plug is almost a mile beneath us and was designed to fall away. Once the core plug implodes, it will be a couple hours after the blast before we will have any visual of the opening. However, our sonar will show us how well the core plug disperses, and depths of any protruding rocks. We are not anticipating any problems, although I admit I am glad that Jessie and Ryan will be at the helm Paul smiles, there could be some tight spots to navigate through and they are skilled. Rosie lights up and says it will be one heck of a voyage and other then dropping you girls off in Alaska, which I cannot deny that part will suck, not giving any time for gloom, she quickly adds, on the upside; I am excited for the expedition Rosie confirms and smiles.

Is there anything else about us leaving that we need to know I asked Paul and then looking over at Rosie, everything seems to be happening so quickly? Do you not feel the same, I ask Amanda. We get our suit cases tomorrow and then Dustin's party, the shaft opens and we are days away from leaving, Yes but Rosie says, we still have a ways to go to actually get you home safe and sound and have follow the plan to through as designed. From then on, you can decide for yourselves where you want to travel and call home. I just have a funny feeling that the residence in Costa Rica will not be a place you will want to be away from, for long.

Paul explains that we will all be at Dustin's at the proposed time of implosion and we will stop what we are doing at the time to monitor and make sure that everything goes off without a hitch. Jim and Ryan will be at the sub entrance in the operations bunker where they can safely oversee the shaft reaction to the core blowing. If needed they can make any water level adjustments, if for any reason the reaction is more intense than anticipated. There should be no more than a burp noticed in the submarine pool. The rest of us will be able to watch above and below from the birdcage operations panels. Wow that is crazy I said to Paul and Rosie then looked over to Amanda and said wow again, feeling speechless.

Well that is about all I have for you ladies Paul takes the last sip of his wine, when both Amanda and I thank Paul for coming and explaining and giving us the update. Rosie then looks around and says to us all well let us have a Baileys and coffee to cap off our visit, how does that sound, she asks. Sounds good to me, Paul answers immediately and almost before Rosie could finish asking. Yeah, that does sound good Rosie I replied with Amanda, giving a two thumbs up, as she was reaching for a smoke.

While Paul got up to help Rosie, Amanda and I looked at each other and I whispered and joked that Paul did not want to go home and that he wanted to spend more time with Rosie. Amanda snickered maybe we should give them some time and go to our rooms, we could say we are going to have a Jacuzzi in our room. Will that not sound a bit obvious I replied quietly, there is a hot tub and pool out here? Yeah, but I think once we get our coffee and just let Rosie and Paul know that we are turning in early they will understand, and if they do want to be alone she will not try and convince us to stay. You are right sweetie and your idea is a good one, I am ready for some alone time.

Then Rosie and Paul walked flirtatiously back to the table with four supersized coffee with whip cream even. Both Amanda and I chuckled as they handed us our drinks and I commented now that is what I call a coffee and Baileys. Rosie said and the mugs will keep your coffee at perfect drinking temperature right to the last sip. Dustin being Dustin had these made and they are not like theorems and do not cool down, if there is liquid in them. You dial in the preferred temperature and the mug will keep it, to the last drop. Now that is incredible I mutter as I take a mouthful of whip cream, with Amanda chuckling now that is something mom is going to want to pack with her that is for sure she chuckled more. How do they work Amanda asked, Rosie went and got an empty mug and brought it over to show us that screwed into the base of the mug was a batter and temperature gauge. The battery will last eight hours and the mug can detect if it has been, left with only drops in the bottom the sensors will turn off the mug. That is too cool I replied to Rosie I love them, hats off to Dustin. Paul agrees that is impressive.

I look over at Amanda with tired glazed eyes, Amanda smiles back, then turn to Rosie, and let her know that we have had another amazing day Rosie. Then she smiles at both Paul and Rosie but by the looks of mom, this will be an early evening. I did not contest Amanda's remark about the way I looked, because, she was right and turning in early sounded like a good idea. I smiled at Rosie who nods and replies certainly girls if you want to call it a day by all means, you take your coffee's and if you are up to it, I have your stuff out if you wanted to have a Jacuzzi. I instantly smile and sinker to myself and then say softly that is so sweet Rosie and Amanda comments you are always two steps ahead of everyone lady, you are amazing then gets up and goes over to give Rosie a big hug before leaving. As I get up out of my chair, making old person groaning sounds, with coffee in hand I pat Rosie on the shoulder and give Paul a wink as we say our good nights and head off to our room.

As we close the door, I said to Amanda that I think Rosie and Paul wanted time together, you think Amanda replies smiling, and Paul was fixated on Rosie this evening.

The only reason he kept talking was to spend more time with her she chuckles. Walking over to our balcony lounging area we pass by our bathing suites and towels laid out on the bed and smile. Getting all comfortable and hashing out the information Paul had communicated when Amanda admits, that she is starting to get very excited about going home and that now she is afraid that time will just drag. Agreeing with her on the time dragging part, I let he know that at least we have a few things to keep us busy before we leave.

Yes but that is not the time dragging that I am concerned with. It is the days of our journey home that I think are going to just drag and I am dreading. Well sweetie, maybe we can stay high enough that time just flies by I chuckle softly, trying to take the weight off the comment.

We will be fine; sweetie the plan to help time pass while we are on the sub is sleeping a lot. Other then wanting to spend as much time with Rosie and the crew as possible, sleep is the best.

Amanda, sounds good in theory, but how do you plan to sleep when you are anxious and excited, oh well our supply of hoots should do it and whatever Henry will give us to help with our rest, I smile and wiggle my eyebrows up and down. I finish with saying that I was sure our nervousness has been anticipated and have readied a clinical sedative as an alternative, when our hoots no longer have affect as we get closer to the last leg of our journey. You are so right mom, hoots can only do so much and with how excited we are going to be, we will need to be put out, Amanda raised her coffee and we both chuckle.

Are we going in the Jacuzzi I asked Amanda, as we both look over at how beautifully lit the area is and how inviting it was when I said how about we go in for a bit, have a hoot and a coffee and then call it a night. That sounds good, Amanda replies I could go for a relax in the tub. Yeah I know that it is going to feel great but I am having a hard time getting out of my chair, when Amanda blurts, oh get up. We have a pot of coffee hoots, smokes and look Rosie even left us a cheese, fruit and pastry platter we do not want to let go to waste. Fine time for you to start thinking about not wasting, I mumble and smile, come on mom you know you wanted to come to our room to give Rosie and Paul more time together. I have seen you smoke and drink a heck of a lot more and it was the lighting that made your eyes so glossy, she snickers, so get up and get your bathing suit on and get in the tub Amanda says jokingly. You are right sweetie that tub sounds great and as I hone in on the platter, I could nibble a little too I guess, the tray actually looks yummy. Amanda smiling says, now you are just getting the munchies you are so funny mom, I love you so much.

We get up and start to change out of our beautiful pajamas and put on our bathing suits and grab our towels and take them over to the tub. We gather our smokes and coffee pot so that we have everything accessible while we are in the tub relaxing. Sinking into the formed lounge seats of the Jacuzzi all could think to say was oh my gosh, make sure I do not go to sleep in here this is so wonderful I look over at Amanda who is all laid back and looking up, replies I will watch you if you watch me she giggles.

Lighting a hoot and passing it back and forth we thought about our winnings of the day and why we were never as lucky at home playing the machines as we are here. When I figured that when you are betting ten thousand dollars a pull instead of our two dollar bets the machine better be nicer, we chuckle with Amanda adding yeah, and this is real money and ours wow that is crazy and still hard for me to wrap my head around. Me too sweetie, me too although I am getting more at ease with the thought of being well off and I am so curious to see our Costa Rica resort that we are not going to want to leave.

The resort does sound comforting and once we get there we can plan our new lives, looking right at Amanda I said very seriously, once we are in Costa Rica and we have our immediate family there that is when I will actually be able to relax and believe our ordeal is over.

I smile big at her and blurt, then sweetie you look out, we will be able to do all the things we could not before. I think our thing will be a big ranch with horses and a beautiful log home Amanda says, as she is daydreams aloud. Hum I thought for a second and said, well once we are tired of the resort I wink, for us off the top of my head would be owning a customized motor home and drive across Canada. Wow, that sounds cool mom, good plan. Yeah it is, although for some reason I think with the resort being homes and a privet subdivision on the beach, with a golf course and so many amenities that it will take at least a year before LB would even think of doing that. Amanda only takes a second to come back and say well then, that will give you time to have one built exactly the way you want. You are so right there, but after a year of being, waited on hand and foot; I find it hard to believe that LB will want to go anywhere or do anything where he has to fend for himself; I laugh and let her know that I was only kidding. By then he will be ready to get out and do something different.

With chatting, smoking, and sipping on our coffee we were starting to fade fast and with a bit of a jolt and splashing startling Amanda, I motion that it is time to get out and go to bed.

I am right behind you mom that just did me in I am whooped now. We grab our towels and wrap ourselves all up then shuffle over to the bed; I just needed to lie down for a minute before I had the energy to change. The minute of rest I needed turned into all night, I never even said good night to Amanda who woke up the same as me, still wrapped in our large soft towels. It was almost as if we had not even moved all night.

Chapter Twenty-Six

Waking with such a feeling of relief and not really knowing why, I rolled over closer to Amanda and with a cheery voice; I said good morning sunshine, how was your sleep. You look like a burrito the way you are all rolled up in there, I giggle. Amanda pokes her face out of the towel and then her arms come out to stretch and says quite frankly I slept great last night, how about you. I would compare how I slept to unconscious, and yes what an awesome sleep.

So what is on the agenda for today anyway, Amanda asks. You know other than Paul bringing our suitcases I am not sure and add that, it am not sure what the big deal is anyway, it will only take a few minutes to hid my shiny things I chuckle and Amanda smirks. Getting up we see, that Rosie has out for us to wear. Colorful stretchy sleeveless tops and black three quarter length leggings, that looked very comfortable. Changing into our housecoats, we then walk over to our balcony lounge to have our coffee and smoke.

As we pour our coffee and go to take our seats, we hear a knock on our door, which was strange because if Rosie wants in the room she just walks in and calls out Rosie, is here. Amanda calls out come on in, we are decent in here. When the door opens, there was Rosie and Paul rolling in our suitcases. As we stood up to great them, they turn around and roll, right back out of our room with Rosie exclaiming if we want to know all the secrets of our luggage we have to come out to see them, as the door closes behind them. Amanda and I look at each other and shrug our shoulders, now what was that all about Amanda smirks. Then I gasp, and said do you think that Paul stayed over with Rosie last night, I mean they are acting quite giddy for this early in the morning are they not I chuckled.

Well we had better get our butts out there or they may come back we agreed and went to get ready and check out these special cases. Coming out to the patio there was Rosie, Paul and to our surprise Jessie and Ryan were also sitting around the table having coffee. We extend our good mornings to the group and I ask our surprise guests, so what brings you here this morning. Then joking around I exclaimed, are you two the master minds behind the suitcases and is this like a Bond movie where you are going to show us that our cases are bullet proof and can do tricks, I sinker. Ryan gives a smile, and then pans the table and replies proudly; yes, we did develop the cases unique qualities. Ryan winks, and says and yeah the cases are bulletproof, that is a given but I hate to disappoint you though, they do not do tricks, we all chuckle.

Rosie says come on everyone have some breakfast and we can chat about this all morning, sit down girls and eat, Rosie says as she pours Amanda and I coffee. Paul then says with all the work that Jessie and Ryan have put into making the cases special, we might not need any of them especially the bulletproofing Paul grins, when Rosie clarifies that their entire luggage line is made to be indestructible.

Now girls you have nothing to worry about Rosie cut in, you are being escorted and flown in a privet jet to Costa Rica, the security of the cases is not as critical. That is good to know I reply but what is it that makes them so special. Jessie beams and starts to list off some of the things the cases do. Starting with they are indestructible and when the cases are x-rayed, the projection viewed, is a programmed image, so that the reading is of an image and not of the actual contents. If the case is to be inspected the shapes and items will resemble projected view and appear as being laid out correctly. The case has GPS and cameras to photograph handlers while in transit.

Ryan gets up to open one of the cases to show us that the interior does have hidden compartments that I guarantee will never be discovered through any source of inspection. The only way the interior side panels will or can open is with the owners fingerprint on the silver nameplate inside of the case. The side panels are where you will keep your passports and all your new personal paperwork and banking information. Of course this is also where Colleen is going to stash all her shinny things, everyone looks right over at me and we sinker as I nod yes with a big smile.

Jessie adds that when one of us travels and has to go through airports and cross borders, security and privacy is vital. Amanda asks Jessie if everyone will be able to come see us when we settle in Costa Rica. With Henrys new filter and the setup of the privet subdivision, for sure, we can, although not all at the same time, she clarified and smiles saying someone has to stay behind and hold down the island.

I have to admit that just knowing our paths will cross again someday is making leaving you all easier. Well, we four will be with you all the way to Alaska, then sadly handed over to, and directed by what are seemingly drivers and pilots however, they are the elite and handpicked by Sire so you will be safe. These handpicked individuals will also ensure that the plan progresses as prescribed.

Wow, all of this is so amazing, you are all so amazing I said while Rosie was making sure that everyone was eating and filling up our coffees. Paul replied we know and chuckled and Ryan gave the two thumbs up, and Jessie just smiled and winked. With the open case sitting close to me I had to check out the hidden compartments, and then looked over at Jessie and asked naively, so how does the case know my fingerprint hum? We uploaded your information into the cases earlier and if someone was to try to steal the case away from you, as soon as they got ten feet away, the handle of the case will give them one hell of a zap that will knock them on their asses.
There was dead silence, when I look over at Amanda and I blurt out laughing, we had never heard one curse word out of Jessie and she meant what she said. As we were still chuckling Amanda says, what about the poor baggage handler wont they get zapped? Oh dear no Jessie smiles and shakes her head. The bag understands regular travel processes and can actually detect if they are in proximity of a potential threat, and if separated from your bag at the time of the detected threat, your phone will receive a message, alerting you of the identified danger.

Once all luggage is loaded in the aircraft or train, your case will scan and let you know before departing if there is the potential of a boom being onboard. That is how cool the case is she smiles proudly.

I look at Amanda who looked puzzled with a squirreled up face and says to Jessie, you mean that you uploaded our fingerprints, you have them, too cool how and why do you have them just out of curiosity Amanda smiles. Fingerprints were part of the information Henry gathered when you first came here along with the medical information received when the filters were implanted. Oh yeah right, I totally forgot about that, so what else does the suitcase know about me, looking for more details on the cases.

Once all luggage is loaded in the aircraft, or train, your case will scan and let you know before departing if there is the potential of a threat onboard. That is how cool, the case is she smiles proudly.

Well Jessie replies, the case rally only has basic owners' personal information however what makes them so special is their ability to worn and protect and conceal with leading edge technology that makes it indestructible.

Rosie sits up and says well that should be enough talk about the cases, what do you think are you good now girls. Rosie looks right at Amanda and I, rolling her eye and smiling, letting us know that she had heard enough. We both agreed, yes we are good, all that is left to so is pack them I let everyone see my big wink towards Rosie and then a laugh. Only kidding I quickly said to them, just fill mine with shiny things and Kevin's special batch and I will be good, I chuckle again and nod implying I was only pulling their leg.

What is up Rosie Amanda asked so what is the plan as she looks around the table. We are all meeting at the café later for happy hour, to finish our plans on Dustin's party. Paul pipes up and excited says, that he is bringing a treat this afternoon and I think it will be a twisted lemonade or beer day to go with my surprise appetizer.

Rosie obviously knowing what Paul was planning to bring she makes a yummy sound. When Ryan stands up and says to Jessie with a smile wanting to make his exit. Happy hour sounds wonderful; he looks at Jessie, and extends his hand to help her from her chair. Then says to Jessie you had better get us home my love, so you have plenty of time to take advantage of me before happy hour. Ryan standing there puts his hands on his hips as we all chuckle when Jessie who was not at all jolted by what he had said and exposed the truth by elbowing Ryan and said, be honest you just want to go have a nap before happy hour. Ryan smiles and looks at Jessie so adorably, you know me so well my love and smirked as they moved away from the table and thanked Rosie for the wonderful food and express gratitude towards Paul and us for our delightful company.

As the two of them were heading out, we gave a wave and thanked them

for all the information and then turned to Rosie and asked, if there was anything that we could be doing, before going to the café.
Rosie lets us know that by the time, we take the cases in our room and freshen up; we should be ready to go. We will be early, and make the twisted lemonade and get some beer on ice before anyone arrives. Paul gets up and says well ladies this has been a slice but I had better get going so that I can get my scrumptious surprise ready, then he looks right in Rosie's eyes, smiles and says, later alligator then swaggers back to his cart.

Hum, what is up with that Amanda chips at Rosie, who attempts to down play the obvious look and bounce in his step. Oh silly, that is just Paul being over confident in his cooking. So what are we having that has him skipping like a little girl I asked, Amanda looked at me smiling I commented what, that is what he looked like to me I laughed. He did not skip like a little girl, which is a bit of an overstatement Amanda replies, but that is what the rest of them are going to hear, later she blurted out a laugh. Rosie and I were surprised with her finish, and started to chuckle with her.

Rosie takes a deep breath and says, anyway… Paul has been smoking salmon and some other fish that were ready for harvest so we are having a wonderful fresh and smoked fish treat this afternoon. Amanda curls up her nose when Rosie says oh no girl; you do not get to curl up your nose until you have tried the spread that will be out. I laughed, as Amanda looks so shocked by Rosie's quick response to Amanda's slight body, facial language that she noticed in a flash. Amanda did not think she was that obvious but did not deny that her idea of eating good fish was the frozen fish sticks from a box. Rosie and I thought that was hilarious and started laughing again when Rosie stopped long enough to let her know that she will enjoy it all and with a beer, the smoked salmon will become your new favorite, trust me she says still smiling. It will not all be fish, there will be other stuff as well reassuring Amanda that she will not starve.

Now you go freshen up girls, and we will head down to the cafe and see what Paul and the others are doing. Rosie up and fussing around the table says to us that she has a few things to do in the kitchen while we freshen up and then we can be on our way.

As we toodle off to our room and follow instructions with a smile we were not long getting ready and even put on our boots with the bows to be comfortable this evening. As we come out to the large area we could see that

Rosie had already gotten things ready and in the carts and as soon as she saw, us yelled out "Shot Gun" and laughed out loud. Rosie did not have our go cups ready for the drive and when I gestured what no go cup .... Rosie replied that we will enjoy the lemon aid once we get there and winked at us. Let us be on our way ladies Rosie says as we follow behind her to our little pink power machine! It was a nice drive down the hill and Amanda noticed that the water looked almost purple today and got me to look over to see the change. That is so amazing that we see the water as being purple but is really is not!

As we pull up to the café there is Paul and Jim mulling around the bar and getting the platters of smoked fish on ice. There was a big large glass urn filled with sliced lemons and a pink lemonade with a gold tap and spout. Rosie saw that I was looking over at the pink lemonade when she caught my eye and indicated with the waving of her hand that is was good and just a little spiked as she winked at me. Both Amanda and I head for a large glass of the lemonade and then moved over to the couch area to get out of the way and have our smokes. With taking big swig out of my lemonade I see that the rest of them are driving down their paths with Elsie and Henry walking in as usual.

I called out to Elsie and Henry asking why we're walking in, when knowing full well they were planning on having a few drinks and the that they felt the short walk home is always refreshing. Henry calls back as they get closer, letting me know that after the last few days ... they needed the exercise and chuckled.

At that time Amanda and were lighting up a special smoke as we see Dustin and Kevin parking with Kevin coming in first taking a deep breath, saying I do not know what smells better Paul's smoked salmon or my special blend the girls are smoking he chuckled as he goes to the bar and grabs a beer for himself and Dustin who had already joined us on the couch. Finally yet importantly, we see Janette with Ryan and Jessy entering the café with the ladies both carrying a big lemon meringue pie each! Bravo, we hear Rosie say as she sees what they have brought with them then says loudly that will be perfect after our dinner. Amanda and I could see that Rosie was genuinely impressed and was unaware they were bringing them.

With everyone getting there drinks and snaking a bit Dustin lets out a big puff of smoke and gets up from the couch then walks towards the side of the café and pulls over a white board on wheels. Then he lets out a caught to get everyone's attention to say here, here, people this party is going to be all done old school and laughed as he could have easily used the computer and projection system in the lounging area of the café.

As we are all looking over at Dustin's white board we can see that duties and responsibilities have been assigned to everyone in preparation of and during what he is, proclaiming will be a great sendoff party. Keeping in mind the time that will be needed by certain individuals, as the core is to implode at 17:00 hours right smack dab in the middle of the party however, Dustin goes onto to say it is also accidently fitting for this party.

Paul and Rosie are standing up at the buffet and were starting to fill their plates when she motioned for everyone to follow suite so we could review Dustin's plans. We were done our smokes and the rest all had full drinks so we started for the table when I could see the relief in Amanda's face when she saw the crock of brown beans and macaroni salad along with buns and veggies, so she did not have to eat the fish.

The smoked salmon was amazing with cream cheese and there was all the fresh veggies from the garden. The white fish was also even tasty but I preferred the salmon and loaded up. Rosie saw that Amada did have a plate full so she did not press her to take some fish. With full plates and Dustin anxiously sitting there waiting for everyone to be seated as he lifts his beer he clears his throat and proceeds with … may I bring our attention back to my white board for your feedback if you can lift your faces from your plates he snickers. Then all of a sudden, I hear Paul say so where is your name on this chart hum! Dustin reply's with a big smile well I am the Forman and will oversee everything. I am providing the theater and making the popcorn doesn't that count for anything, he raises his eyebrows to Paul. I look over to see Rosie and Janette shaking their heads while we could see the smiles on the others.

Paul spoke up again and said that it is probably best that the rest of us take of everything else because it is critical that everything with the core goes exactly as planned or everything that is to follow that will be delayed. We could hear the seriousness in Paul's tone however, he did not intend on dampening the mood. Having said that, I know everything will go as according to plan with the core that I am sure. It is more that you take the time to get your place cleaned up and with a very brief pause, Paul let out a big laugh breaking the silence.

Rosie let the chuckles settle and then agreed with Paul by adding that she has not had any time to go over there and clean it up either as she does on occasion.

Eating away and looking at the day as it is on the board I noticed that under Amanda and Colleen all it says was to shop up on the beach at 10:00 am and bring the special smokes with a little drawn happy face beside the request.

The plan is to start the party off by hanging out on the beach, playing some volleyball and have BBQ hamburgers. From there we will have to disband while preparations for the remaining steps of the process for the core implosion are completed. When that is about to take place everyone not involved in the process will be in the bride cage with Dustin and can oversee the production from his operations panels. Like I said before it will be like a big burp in the submarine bunker and it will take on some water and the sub will go for a bit of a rise but have no fear that is exactly what is supposed to happen. Dustin adds that from the birdcage we may not even hear or feel the implosion that we are not sure.

As Amanda and I look around the table we see that everyone is good with the plan so far. And then we hear Rosie pipe up continuing with the chart and clearly says once we are all good with the core thing she smirked at Dustin and Jim down playing the event with a smile. Then she proceeds to address the group with, then we will all be gathering in Dustin's theater room and get comfy for our, Rosie's voice goes deep and slowly says our scary movie night! Kevin just screams out BOOO! Which startled and scared the hell out of us all. Even Rosie jumped and then abruptly threw her napkin across the table at Kevin and started to give him heck while we all howled. Jessie spilt her drink and Elsie said I think I peed myself a little and that just broke us all up again. It took a minute to gather our composer but as we calmed down. I suggested to the group, how about a comedy then? Janette Amanda and Elsie clinked their glasses agreeing with my suggestion so the choice of move went for a vote to see what we were going to be watching. Jim then piped up by say with a show of hands people who wants the comedy and with everyone's hands going up but Kevin and Dustin we knew what kind of movie we were watching both the fellows put on the pouty faces but they were fine with a comedy too.

Henry put her hand up and said that she wanted to be the one to pick the movie and with Henry being a trusted movie picker I guess, the group agreed that she could. Although Dustin did not have it on his white board, Rosie suggested to the group that after the movie that we go back to the beach for our night cap. We could have fireworks tomorrow evening too while we are at the beach in the evening Dustin said out load. We have a fireworks program that will blow your minds ladies as he smiles and wipes his mouth and fingers on his napkin then gets up to get another beer while he saunters over to the lounge area so proud of his presentation and last minute thought of the fireworks.

As were we were finishing our dinner that Dustin inhaled, Amanda asked if there was a theme to the party. There was a second of silence when Janette blurted out, it is a beach party already so how about hats! We all were our favorite hat! I hear Kevin laugh out and point at Paul saying well it will not be a surprise hat party that is for sure, when we all look at Paul, smile, and chuckle with him already wearing his favorite cowboy hat he loves so much.

Rosie and Elsie chimed in saying that they love the idea and Amanda then questioned the ladies … so other than a ball cap, what kind of hat goes with a tee shirt and shorts and then giggled a little.

As I get up from the table to go fill my lemonade up again I motion to Amanda letting her know I was going over for a smoke where Dustin was sitting finishing his beer. As Amanda was making her way over I lit up a big fat special smoke and I here Kevin say now we are talking that smells yummy as he takes a couple long strides to the couch.

Jim Paul and Ryan were hovering around the bar and the huge lemon meringue pies listening to the gals chat about the hats they have and could possibly wear tomorrow while joking amongst each other. Then I over hear Rosie chatting with Kevin about bringing some fresh fruit for the BBQ. Everyone seemed to be comfortable and all set for tomorrow's activities.

Then Rosie chimes out that she is cutting the pie if anyone wants a piece and I have coffee and tea out as well. We all hear Rosie's call and take heed as we mobilize over to the desert table that was so nicely set up. As we all gather in and around to get our piece of pie, Amada pointed out that the meringue was as high as she has ever seen and perfectly browned on top. I look over to see Ryan taking his first bit and then notice him give Janette a big wink as he passes her going for the coffee.

Kevin and Dustin shot up from the couch when Rosie called and both put a big scoop of whip cream on their pie, if a six in meringue wasn't enough I thought to myself. Man those fellows can eat! As I looked up at Amanda who was just as surprised as we were gazing at their heap of white fluffy whip cream on their plats. As I raised my eyebrows, which the group just happen to, noticed the look of amazement, and we all stated to chuckle with Kevin and Dustin both oblivious to the fact that what was being made fun, of was the excessiveness of the whipped cream.

As we were winding down for the evening Paul moved beside Rosie and then did get everyone's attention to let us know that we would-be having one last general meeting before the girls leave so that we are all current with Sires messages and instructions so that we confirm all outside contacts have been made. Some of the final details about family accommodations and such we can review while we are in the sub making our way to Alaska. Paul goes onto say that he does not know of the day or time the meeting will scheduled at this time but that he should know sometime tomorrow.

Amanda was the first to speak up and say that she is glade to hear that because she says she is still putting some of the pieces together in her mind and that will help clear up and questions. Then she said seriously … the real problem is that I do not know what I do not know so I do not know what to ask! Then Amanda let out a good chuckle as she let them know that is one of my favorite sayings. The group agreed what a simple concept but so true Ryan commented back.

It was not long and everyone was pitching in to wrap and clean up so that we could all get home and relax for a bit, as I am sure they want to get their hats ready for tomorrow I was thinking as Rosie had no problem with letting us all help.

With the café area all cleaned up, we did not even stop for a smoke before we all started for our carts and Elsie and Henry arm and arm started walking home. We sounded like the Walton's saying good night as everyone went off in their own directions. As Rosie was heading to our cart, Amanda and I hear the blast of Rosie's bello "shot gun". I chuckled and Amanda shrugged her shoulders and looked at me as if I should have expected that! When I hear Paul, behind me say to Rosie oh let the girls go I will give you a ride back.

Amanda and I did not want to make a fuss over Pauls gesture so we just kept walking to our pink cart as I said loudly shot gun startling Amanda. I could hear Rosie chuckling behind me.

As Amanda starts to drive I lit Amanda and I a smoke for the road, which she thanked me for and said wow we have not had a smoke for a while and I need more coffee I said to Amanda. It was only minutes and we were pulling up to the amazing palace that was lite up so nice and as you walk up into the lounge area more lights turn on as you walk further into the open area. Amanda and I had a couple puffs off our smoke and then went up to the bar where there was always coffee on.

Just then, we hear Paul pulling up with Rosie and they seemed to be joking around and having a laugh as they come up to the bar with a couple plastic containers. We get our coffees and head over to the lounge by the hot tub so we can have a hoot and chat about the day. Paul and Rosie were saying there good nights then Paul gives us girls a big wave and says I will see you ladies in the morning. Rosie lets us know that she will put the containers away and then be right back to discuss our hats for tomorrow. We watch and see that Rosie looks like she is almost skip to the kitchen; Amanda looks right at me with a huge smile and says well someone is in a good mood! We pass the hoot back and forth and then Rosie comes out of the kitchen and goes over to get her coffee at the bar and of course adds a shot of Baileys in hers. As Rosie saunters over to us with the remote control in hand we hear the music come on softly and see the color lights start to twinkle in the lounge area. Rosie plunks herself down puts her feet up and says … hats ladies any ideas she asks? I pipe up with other then the hats you have given to match outfits we have worn what other hats can we choose from. We could see Rosie's face light up as she wiggles her eyebrows and says there are hats galore in the massive closet in the back of your room. I do not think that you have spent much time in there since I first showed you when you came here. Amanda was quick to reply that with her taking care of our daily attire we have no need and I said with as busy and captivated you all have seemed to keep us we have not had much time or reason to check it out more. Amanda and Rosie could see the surprise in my face as I said that as even I was shocked I have not been snoopier in there. That closet is the envy of all I am sure of that I smiled and took a sip of coffee and butt my smoke.

Well then, girls Rosie says let us get a fill up on our coffees and go have us a look. Amanda was the first one up leading the way to our room. The stone doors to this space are something in themselves and once open the closet looks like a mini department store. All our faces light up as we walk in and Rosie takes the lead passing by the glass cases loaded shelves to of course the hat section of the closet. Rosie draws back a big Curtin exposing all the hats that were hung on hooks on the wall as high as 12'. There was a telescopic hook to use to get the ones at the top. Even the telescopic hook was cool because all Rosie did was point at the hat at the top she wanted and the stick extended exactly to it. When Rosie demonstrated how it worked, I had a big smile and took the hook from Rosie before Amada could. I immediately saw a white fedora with a red band at the top that I thought just looked awesome and small. I looked over at Amanda winked said, If that hat fits that was going to be mine. Rosie was so pleased that I found one so quickly and when I tried it on it fit like it was made for me and I looked awesome with it on … if I don't say myself I told the girls and smirked. Rose looked at Amanda to see what she was eyeing and Amanda did not need a hook to get her hat which when she went to grab it from the cubby Rosie and I just agreed right away ooh yeah that is you Amanda that's you! She had picked a black ball cap that was cover with shinny crystals. It looked amazing on her we all had a good laugh while Amanda I posed in several positions with our hats. When we asked Rosie so, what hat are you going to wear? We stop to have a sip of coffee and look around more when Rosie says with a bit of a surprise sound to her tone; as if the light bulb just went on, I know what hat I am going to wear as she snapped her fingers. Both Amanda and I were looking at her to spit it out but she just said I will surprise you in the morning she winked. Okay ladies I think it is time to shut her down for the evening grab your coffees we have another big day in front of us and as she guides us out of the closet the light dim as we walk out as she says things are going to start to happen quickly now so you need your rest.

Once in our main bedroom Amanda and I take off our hats and put them on the large dresser and then give Rosie a hug as she leaves the room softly saying as she closes the door behind her, have a good sleep ladies.

Amanda I mosey over to our couches by our Jacuzzi tub and agree that we will have a smoke and finish our coffees and then head to bed. Reminiscing over the day, Amanda commented that I can feel that I am starting to get a little anxious for going home now with the expression of concern on her face. I patted he hand and said that as long as we stay focused and try not to get too far ahead of ourselves we will be fine. I agreed that I do not want my cranky to come out and have them all see me at me worst right at the end of our stay, we had a quiet little chuckle as Amanda points to her temple remembering how short fused I can be at times. Recalling, while we were sitting in a drive through to get a coffee years ago the line was taking so long that I actually called to complain while actually idling in line. Amanda pipes up and quotes "it is only coffee people" which is exactly what I was saying while waiting in the long line up of cars… too funny mom!

We finish our smoke and coffee's and pull ourselves out of our comfortable chairs and shuffle over to our big beautiful bed and say our good nights.

Chapter Twenty-Seven

This morning Amanda was up and sitting in the lounge looking out over the island daydreaming when I opened my eyes to see her sitting there not smoking or even have her coffee poured. I sit up and say hey my little precious what's up today? Amanda looks over to me and says she is glade that we will not remember much of the island when we are at home because I really think I would miss this place a lot. As I get up out of bed and head her direction I looked over to see that we have the cutes little beach outfits to wear and Amanda's even has shinny colorful crystals on hers to go with her hat.

When I point to the outfits Amanda smiled and said so when did Rosie get them in here, did you hear her come in, I looked at Amanda and said me, no I was sound asleep all night I never even got up for a pee I smiled big. We pour our coffee when we can both hear the beach boy's song playing in the background the music was being broadcast throughout the island. We both look at each other and smile knowing that meant that Dustin was already up and getting the mood on. We figured with hearing the music so loud and clear that also meant that Rosie would be waiting for us. We quickly have our smoke and start to get ready for the day that seems to take us no time at all. We are all dressed in our pock-a-dot shorts and halter top out fits and our sweet sandals. Amanda was black and white and I was red and white and they both looked awesome with our hats on!

Coming out to the lounge area thinking Rosie would be right there all we saw was the coffee pot ready and fruit to nibble on at the breakfast table when all of a sudden we hear a squeal as Dustin comes up the hill at full

speed with Rosie hanging on for dear life. When Dustin comes to his abrupt halt Rosie slaps Dustin on the arm and says I told you before, not to drive like that when I am in the cart with you she huffs and says as she is coming up the stairs … I will never drive with him again he cannot be trusted she shows us a big smile and tells Dustin in a stern voice to go see Paul he wanted him for some set up. Dustin yells back you know you love my driving Rosie don't deny it!
Dustin looks right at Amanda and I shrugged his shoulders laughing then pulls a U-turn to go back down the hill. As Rosie settles down and grabs a coffee she looks over at us and says how awesome we look, and that we definitely look ready for the beach today and that the hats are the topper for sure she smiles at us. I said so where is your hat Rosie she pats the top of her head and says oh yeah, I will be right back you are going to love this one. She jumps up and walks to the bar and pulls out from behind it, a big tall white chef's hat. We both laughed when she plunked it on her head and gave it a pat making fall to one side. Amanda blurts out perfect! And claps her hands.

Rosie starts to dance a little on her way back towards us going with the music with us following with a little armchair dance too. We were enjoying the moment for sure. Once we get back on track Rosie says it is almost time for us to head down to the beach girls. We will be early but we can hang out there and enjoy ourselves while we wait e for the others to arrive.

Amanda says how about we have our hoot and meet you down there unless you want to wait she asks Rosie. We could tell Rosie wanted to be where the action was, and Paul so she did not hesitate to say okay girls you have your hooty and I will bring some stuff down to them. She gets up from her chair heads to the kitchen and brings out two wicker baskets and a red and white picnic tablecloth. While she sees us enjoying our smoke and watching her with hands full she winks and says I will see you girls in just a bit.

We were not long finishing our hoot as we chat about how cute Paul and Rosie are then we both motion to get up and tootle over to our go cups that Rosie had ready and we start to dance our way to our pink driving machine as we are complementing each other on our hats.

We could hear the music so clear and it was upbeat and beachy so we grooved our way swaying and bouncing in our seats with go cups in the air during the short drive. We were just joking around as we pull up to the Lake Front and beautiful turquoise blue water and white sandy beach. I looked over at Amanda when we were getting out of the cart and I said I am sorry I will not always have this memory to keep. She reply's you will always have it as long as we are together and winked. Oh yeah cool I said and Dustin was dancing by himself over to us with a big drink in one hand that had umbrellas and fresh fruit sticking out all over the top. Amanda laughed and pointed to his drink and said a little much? Dustin shakes his head no and starts dancing back towards Rosie. Dustin makes a quick turn and says I love the hats girls as he brings his hands up to his head and poses showing off his not so surprising Mexican sombrero! I gave him the two thumbs up and a big smile.

While Dustin was still dancing around in the sand Rosie and Paul were fussing around the food and booze table chatting away as if no one else was even there. Amanda and I make it over to the table to see the spread and get ourselves a drink. The feature drink of the day was strawberry Dakari. Kevin was coming up the path with another large basket of strawberries and said to Rosie this should last us a while. Rosie laughed saying with this group you really think so Kevin. Paul standing tall in his rattan cowboy hat took a big sip out of his drink and agreed with Rosie saying yup, I can see another trip back to the farm to get more in your future Paul chuckled.

Then out of the rustling bushes comes Henry and Elsie making their sneaky entrance. Rosie puts her hand up to her cheeks and gasps when she sees Elsie wearing a parrot's hat and Henry wearing a black leather bickers hat with silver spikes in the band. We all were so impressed with their choices with Henry saying first that she was keeping her Christmas theme going with the black leather. We were all cosigning up to the bar, admiring all our hats, and filling our big glasses with the drink of the day when all the sudden we hear the honking of a horn through the music and it was Jim and Janette with Ryan and Jessing right on their tail.
Paul let out a loud yippy, which caught us all off guard so we all were staring at Paul when Janette started making her entrance and modeling her purple felt bowler when I blurted out now where did you get that hat it is amazing I love the color. Elsie was just as impressed as I was with Amanda saying now that is a hat. By this time we were all lined up at the bar to watch as Jim, Ryan and Jessie were making their way in to see Jim wearing a sailors cap lilted to look cool we all give a little clap as we see Ryan dawning a boaters captains hat with a red and blue head band. Very pouch Kevin says and gives a nod. Ryan takes a bow and extends his arm behind him bring in

Jessie who was wearing a pink pillow box hat that just looked fantastic with her long flowing hair. Once the hat parading was over, Rosie pipped up to let, everyone know that for the young at heart we have volleyball set up or we have badminton if you prefer. I chuckled and said to the group, I don't know about the rest of you but I sure would need a few more drinks and a big puff before I could even think of volley ball but I could probably handle some badminton. I hear Jim and Janette give out a here, here seconding the motion. With Dustin and Kevin chuckling to each other, Kevin saying I told you so buddy no one want to play that today. Well it was worth a try he replied. Rosie pats Dustin on the shoulder with words of encouragement saying you always have your ladies on your viewer to watch. Dustin's face went a bit flushed not wanting to admit that he likes watch the girls fumbling his words and shooting back with they are professionals and great at their sport. Paul cracks up and says yes Dustin we know as we all joined in on the ribbing.

We are all chatting is up and nibbling on the munchies that Rosie and Paul set up when all the sudden Kevin looks at Amanda and I with a big smile and say hoot? It feels like we have not had one in a while he scratches his nose and winks. As Kevin lights up the hoot Dustin is right behind him sparking another one saying hey man this is a beach party what a beautiful beach without a great aroma to go with it. Paul pipes up and says the aroma we should be smelling at the beach is BBQ burgers and hot dogs and I will get them started shortly.

Elsie and Henry walked into the water with drinks in hand and Janette was enjoying the lounge chair swaying to the music. Jessie and Ryan picked up the badminton rackets and threw one to Amanda and Kevin each to come join them. Amanda looked at Rosie and said but I don't want to put my drink down and made a sad face when Rosie came up to her and took her drink out of her hand and said so sweetly the she would make sure that it was okay and full when she got back. I smirked as Amanda looked back at me because I knew that Amanda just did not want to look like an idiot playing a game she was not great at on a sandy beach with everyone watching her. With Amanda walking over to the net I smile and gesture to Rosie and Paul, no worries the drink of the day will have her playing like a pro I let out a good laugh.

Henry started splashing Rosie and I could see that I had better get out of the way as this could get serious. Just then Paul hustles over to the BBQ and

Kevin runs to the water to help Henry with the splashing when I hear Rosie say loudly if you get my food all wet and mess up the table I will get even. Yicks Henry says with a pouty bottom lip like a little kid, okay I will stop with Kevin still splashing Henry said to him while laughing, do you really want to feel the wrath of her getting even man. Kevin stopped very quickly when he realized the consequences could mean no cooking for him.

It was not going to take long for the rest of the food to cook so we were all just chatting about the day our hats and Rosie was making sure that everyone's drinks were topped right up. With Amada, still farting around at the badminton court with Kevin, Ryan and Jessie. I looked over at Janette and asked so what is the movie that you picked for this evening? I could see all heads turn to hear the answer as it was a secret. Right then Janette lit right up and announced that the comedy that we will be seeing is an old one called it's a Mad, Mad, Mad World which I thought was fitting for today and of course this group she laughed and slapped her knee. I lifted my head and looked right at her saying I cannot believe that, I actually have seen that movie a few times and it is hilarious. Janette was pleased that I knew of the movie and all the others had no idea.

Amanda comes towards Rosie with her tongue hanging out of her mouth letting Rosie know she needed her drink after all the jumping around. Jim bumps my arm and says I have the game for you and he motions for me to follow him to the horseshoe pit and when I saw that, I said now there is a game I can get into. I yell to Amanda I need a smoke sweetie mommas going to whoop some butt Jim looked at me surprised as I let out a big chuckle knowing that it was all the liquid encouragement talking and all the ladies howled the fellows let Jim know that he better be sharp or else you heard the lady Kevin belted out.

Paul was cooking and everyone started watching us play horseshoes when Dustin lit a special hoot as he called and walked it over to me as he said quite clearly that it would help improve my aim. After taking my puffs and as Dustin was going to turn to walk away and share with Amanda, if holly crap I did not get a ringer, well we all exploded with laughter. The timing was perfect and then just at that moment Paul rings a big cowbell scaring the heck out of all of us but Rosie who was obviously aware of Paul's calling to the picnic. Rosie was going around with a big pitcher filling everyone's drinks as we gather around the huge picnic table filled with all the fixings for a beach side BBQ.

The talking seemed to subside as everyone started to eat with the fun summertime music playing in the background. Amanda and I were not feeling any pain and not all that hungry just happy seeing Rosie in her chef's hat enjoying herself. The chatting went on about my ringer and they could all see I was so proud of myself. Amanda tilted her head onto my shoulder acknowledging my lucky accomplishment.

Oddly enough, Paul was the first one finished and the group could see after his large display of wiping his mouth and hands with his napkin that he was starting to think about preparations. When he with a grin and one eyebrow lifted looked right over at Dustin and said so are you ready for this, when Dustin looks back at him and says what why aren't you talking to Jim and Ryan as well acting surprised. Really, Paul joking says to Dustin, do you really think I need to ask Jim or Ryan that question with a paus Dustin winks at Paul and says No! Rayna nudges Jessie's arm and looks at us to show his hand and makes a waving motion with his and smiles, as Dustin says in a forced sobering voice I am fine no worries old man I am pumped and ready to make this happen. No amount of alcohol or weed could impede my ability to do this. Rosie chimes in by saying now you are just trying to show off you.

After that, all being said we jumped up almost at the same time and started to help clean up as Rosie was saying fill you drinks people while Henry, Elsie and Janette were wrapping up the food. When Amanda and I back out of the way to have a smoke as the rest of the dinner area was being cleared away.

We knew and could tell by their change in domineer that the group was starting to focus and put their attention towards the Core implosion. Although the mood was great and the gang was, all joking around With Rosie directing the clean up production while Paul was talking to the fellows to make sure that they had completed their preparations we assumed. At this point, Amanda and I felt a little invisible, which we were all good with as we smiled at each other while we stood back had our smoke and watched.

As we were putting out our smoke Dustin announces that we can all head up to the cage where we can get ourselves set up to see the core implosion in all its glory he says with pride and then bumps into Jim taking away from his projected sober behavior. That got everyone looking and snickering, when Dustin says okay let's get this show on the road. Kevin jabbed Dustin in the shoulder as he follows him to the cart and says lets go bud lets show them your stuff.

Paul was going to give Henry and Elsie a ride to the cage when I hear a yell out from Rosie "Shot Gun" Amada looks over at me and says you had your chance mom and grabbed her drink and with a big smile started waking to our pink driving machine. It is tight with all the carts and there was no logic to parking so we get out carefully. While walking to the entrance of the bird cage and in my own little haze, I realized that the fellows did not go down the water slide while we were at the beach like they went on about before. So I asked them what was up with not using the slide, with Ryan quickly coming to the defense and saying it was because after eating you are supposed to wait a half hour before going in the water. Amanda says good save Ryan however not so true … there was plenty of time for the brave to take the plunge. Amanda raised her drink looking for a cheer from Rosie and I who were right behind Ryan.

We hear Jim call to Ryan hey there you come with me we need to get to the bunker operations booth and check on the program to make sure all systems are a go. Jim gives Janette a little kiss on the cheek and pats the top of her hat as the two take off to the submarine bunker. Paul was going to oversee operations with Dustin in the birdcage. We all hustle into the open structured living space and island main operations controls area with the amazing gliding chair. The ladies convers to the kitchen area and set out the leftovers from the picnic and drink supplies. Rosie gets Kevin's attention and lets him know that he needs to make a quick trip to the farm to get another basket of strawberries.

Elsie sees Rosie's gesture and says she will go because she wanted to pick up some fresh butter for the popcorn anyway then we hear Henry yell out "Shot Gun" and let out a real good laugh saying I have wanted to say that ever since you girls got here. I have never heard that before and I think it is so cute. Elsie had a big smile as they turned and both headed back out for groceries. I wanted to be close to the action and stayed close to Dustin where Amanda and Kevin hung back and lit a hoot watching the action. Rosie Jessie and Janette were getting ready to make another jug of daiquiris when Elsie brings back the fresh strawberries and getting coffee ready for later. Without trying to be obvious I could see them peeking through the greenery keeping an eye on Paul and Dustin waiting for the que to come over to see the production.

Dustin and Paul were watching monitors and digital counters, graphs and charts all over the large panel when Dustin called out and got on the key board and started entering a stream of numbers with Paul going through the final steps manual ensuring Dustin goes through the checklist. Dustin has Jim and Ryan on speaker so we can hear them talking in the bunker operations booth.

Just then, Elsie and Henry walk in with the strawberries and butter when Rosie with a pitched voice says to the group lets fill up the drinks people, I believe count down has commenced. Dustin and Paul confirm we have ten minutes to implosion. Amanda comes up behind me and puts her arm around me as we watch all the monitors that do not mean anything to us.

As everyone huddles in Paul points to the large monitor in the middle of the panel that is showing a dark blurry blackish but bubbly view. Letting us know that when it happens we should see the rock blow away to expose the ocean floor, which is about the depth of a football field.
Dustin plunking away at the key board looks up and says that with the explosion the water will be obscure, cloudy and blurry for a while. Paul takes over by saying once detonated, and all system check out we will have a few hours to let things settle and plenty of time for our move and for the brave a slide on the wild side so to speak, he laughed at his own little joke. Rosie who was standing right beside Paul snickered.

Not realizing how much time had passed, gather together when all the sudden we hear Jim over the speaker counting down, Paul and Dustin say hang onto your hats people … 10,9,8,7,6,5,4,2,1!

We were all watching the computer monitor of the interior of the submarine bunker wanting to see how it reacted to the explosion. At the end of the count, we all felt a slight vibration in the floor and with all that we had to drink, we were not sure if it was the island or just us being slightly impaired?

Amanda and I let out a big woo was that it, we could see that the submarine raised up about eight feet and descended right back down in its rock water tube. The bunker floor filled with water about two feet high and then drained right back into the opening. Paul and Dustin were intensely watching the monitors and gauges when we hear both Jim and Ryan yell out all systems are good in the bunker and with the submarine. How are things with you people Ryan asks? Paul's even sounds relieved and says all systems are showing good here as well. Jim says that they will perform a quick inspection of the bunker and the submarine and be right back.

All the sudden there were high fives and hugs all around right on it worked Dustin proclaims while Paul was all smiles and turned to Rosie and gave her a big hug and a kiss, not caring about anyone else at that moment. Rosie was hanging onto her hat when Paul put her down and we could all see her blushing as if she was on fire. She could see all of us girls just loving the spontaneous show of affection, which they both suddenly tried to down play.

Paul then put both his hands in the air making the brushing motion and saying to us all okay, okay the show is over people you can all go about your business now.

Kevin piped up with hoot anyone and nodded his head towards the outdoor balcony; I smiled thinking who has an outdoor balcony in an open cage. We all went our desired directions with Elsie and Henry being the first to pick their seat when we hear Dustin say oh but that is my chair, Elsie looks over at him and say you snooze you lose sweetie they chuckled together and made no motion to change their selected seats. .The rest of the group was mulling over the appetizers that were out and Rosie was getting Dustin and new drink, patting him on the shoulder you deserve this one and gives him a little nudge.

Jim and Ryan giving Paul the two thumbs up on their way in and go right over to Janette and Jessie to give them a little hug and order up a drink from Rosie. Amanda, Kevin and I work our way over to the group and I ask Dustin so when we starting this movie, I seem to remember it is a long one. Dustin smiles and says ask Henry she is sitting in the chair of control he chuckled as she wiggles her bum into the chair. Okay take your seats everyone Henry clearly says, the movie feature that Janette has selected is about to start. Janette spoke up with you are all going to love this movie, trust me.

We all shuffle into our seats that are the most comfortable theater chairs I have ever sat in and the room looks so amazing when the lights start to dim and the large screen come to life with complete surround sound. I had seen the movie a few time in the past and after the day we had and the drinking done, I am sure I was a sleep within the first fifteen minutes of the movie starting.

Too funny, as the lights were coming back on I hear clapping and a whistle while Amanda was shaking my arm to wake me up. Wow, that was a great nap I smiled and then said as I stretched in my chair. Elsie was standing in front of me and said with a sad face, you missed the buttery popcorn. Amanda quickly saying it's okay Elsie, I ate enough for both of us and smiled with wide eyes. The whole place smelt of popcorn, I was surprised that did not wake me up.

We were all stretching when Rosie says coffee before we shut her down for the evening folks. She got a yes from us all. Amanda looks over at me while she is yawning, and says smoke mom, you bet kiddo we get up and move out of the way while food was being picked at and we heard the laughing at spots in the movie that they liked. Kevin comes over to us and says quietly, I have seen better but don't tell Janette I do not want to hurt her feelings he smiled and proceeded to light a night cap hoot he called it. After having a couple puffs we go over to get a cup of coffee to help wake me up, we see Jim, Ryan, Paul and Dustin go back to the control panel to see if there were condition improvements. There was so much of a change in the three hours unattended that Paul called everyone over to come have a look and see how clear it was under and around the bottom opening.

Paul and the fellows were all smiles with Jessie being the most vocally impressed with the conditions as she admitted to us that she was concerned that navigating out to the open ocean was causing a dollop of uneasiness if the rock had not blown away accurately would have posed obstacles they would have to navigate.

Ryan was just as please to see Jessie happy after seeing the exposed area and no obstacles meaning the dive and sailing out was not going to be a problem. Even Janette gave a quiet sigh of relief.

It was getting on and Henry and Elsie were tired and started giving their congratulations tipping their hats and bidding us all a due. As they walked out Kevin heard his cart start up, he looks over to see Henry driving when he yells out to her that's my ride lady … she yells back to him not now it isn't she laughs and waves back at as she speeds down the lane where we can hear Elsie just wailing.

Paul looks over at Kevin with a big smile and says no worries man; I will give you a ride back to the farm. That is when Rosie jets out with her "Shot Gun" realizing she was going to be coming home with us. It was then that Jim and Ryan reminded us all that tomorrow is our final meeting and that we will have all the details of the girl's departure and family accommodations to go over.

Rosie says we will be ready and lunch is on me she chuckled with Ryan replying lunch is always on you Rosie. Rosie smiled and tips her hat and says you are all welcome. Well that is our que, Jim gestured to Janette with Ryan nodding and putting his arm around Jessie as they say there well wishes for the evening and wave as they get to their carts. I flop down in Dustin's gliding captain's chair and let Amanda and Rosie know, I was done and could someone please take me home. Amanda says okay come on mom I will get you home Rosie had our go cups and a bag then said let us get this one home. Rosie winked at Paul as we walked by and she thanked the fellows for a great day as Rosie grabbed my arm to walk with me to the cart, as if I needed the help.

It was a short drive back to the palace and once I was at the top of landing I gave Rosie, a big hug and I kept right on walking to our room with Amanda chuckling behind me. Then I hear Amanda say to Rosie, see you in the morning, sweet dreams.

Once in the room I was undressed hat off and on the couch for a smoke and sip of coffee before Amanda even got out of the washroom. Once she came over to sit down Amanda commented how glad she was that all went well with the core today that was a big part of us leaving as scheduled which I believe now is in two days. When Amanda said that I felt my stomach drop and rush of panic come over me. My face said it all and Amanda came over for a hug with softly saying mom we are going home. We both started to tear up as we held our hug for a moment. After wiping away the tears, I asked Amanda in a positive voice, smoke sweetie. She replays sure and then bed, I think tomorrow will have all the detailed information we have been waiting on. Not even smoking a whole cigarette, we headed off to bed.

Chapter Twenty-Eight

I could tell when I was waking up that I had slept in longer than normal but I sure felt great. Amanda was already awake just sitting up in bed day dreaming for sure. I greeted her by saying good morning sunshine she looked over and smiled at me asking how I was feeling. I look up at her and say … surprisingly sweetie, I feel great!

I lift my head up to see what we are wearing today and look over at jean shorts and tee shirts for both of us. I motion for Amanda lets have our smoke and coffee I know that we are bit poky today but we are spending our last couple of days here and I want to take in every part of this room. Amanda smiled big and replies yeah even with the money we will have when we leave we could not afford this kind of space she winked.

As we go to get ready I hear Amanda blast out a laugh so I come darting out of the bathroom to see that our tee shirts actually were silk screened with the big block letters with the wording… Rosie Queen of the Island! We could hear Rosie in the lounge loudly snickering knowing we had just discovered our shirts.

We make a big jump out to the breakfast lounge with arms spread wide showing off our shirts and Rosie clapped her hands and complimented us on the look. Rosie motions for us to come sit down as she is asking how I was feeling this morning. All good Rosie all I needed was a good night sleep. Before we even started breakfast, Paul drove up with a big smile and carrying the chef's hat Rosie was wearing. Rosie gets up to get Paul a coffee, grabs her hat from him, and throws it behind the bar as she blushes. I nudge Amanda and say that is odd … I know I was out of it last night but I am sure that when Rosie came home with us she was wearing her hat so why does Paul have it now hum I wiggle my eyebrows up and down and giggle. Amanda has a bit of toast and Paul sits down beside her and leans in to ask so what is so funny girls. Oh nothing I reply sheepishly. That is when Paul reads Amanda's tee shirt and gasps, oh my crap girl now you are parading these pour girls around like billboards for you. Dam woman you know you are loved by all, he blurted out a loud laugh that I am sure Dustin could hear. Oh the group is going to love them he says and takes a drink of his coffee

You know they all love it when I remind them she says with a very straight face. Once Rosie sits down Paul proceeds to tell us that between all the talent here and all the help that Seri was able to provide from his end we have gone through everything with a fine tooth comb and worked out every angle possible so we believe you are going to be ecstatic as you here the plan unfold today.

Amanda and I both look right at Paul, I sit up straight and without interpretation of thought ask so when do we leave, not realizing how selfish it sounded at first. Then quickly I back peddled by letting them know I do not know how to measure the overload of information other than in days to departure and that I meant no disrespect, not letting in any time for feedback until I finished my spiel. Rosie was very quick to respond with no worries sweetie we love having you hear like crazy but you girls were not meant to be here a lifetime. Rosie pats me on the shoulder and tilts her head letting me know my abruptness was not offensive.

Paul then looked over at Rosie and said that Kevin will be late for the meeting and that we can start without him. Paul proceeds to explain by saying them darn pigs again, if I did not love pork so much I would say we should be rid of the feisty little critters, he chuckled and shrugged his shoulders at us letting us know he was not going to be made to feel guilty because he love his BBQ pork ribs.

Rosie stood to tidy up a bit and let us girls know to move over to the lounge and have our smokes out of the way as Paul and Rosie start to set everything up for the meeting. Amanda and I mosey over and sit down and lite a smoke and watch Rosie and Paul chatting softly and working together they were both grinning a lot and we were not sure what that meant. Amanda turns and says you know Paul never did give you and exact answer to your question oh yeah your right, I guess he wants to tell us all the details together. Makes sense and then I said to Amada hooty! She smiled big and said perfect!

Amanda had barely lit the hoot and low and behold, Dustin makes his entrance so of course, we have a little chuckle and Amanda lifts her hand in the air as he was sniffing the air. Rosie tells Dustin to get himself a coffee and they would come join us in a bit. Dustin comes over and says what a great time he had yesterday and that everything was looking real good as far as our deep-sea departure from what we viewed yesterday and the footage he has to show us today. Dustin takes a big puff and says while holding his hoot in you are really going to love today and I am not talking about the food either he blows out his smoke and giggles and coughs at the same time. I look at Amanda and we can both see the excitement in our faces when I said well then let us get this meeting started.

Rosie and Paul come to sit with us just as the hoot was put out, with Rosie letting us know that the gang is all on their way now and we will start when everyone is here. Other than Kevin of course, yeah I heard that Dustin butts in saying its really too bad I heard about his pigs Dustin smiles thinking it was funny and better yet that he did not have to help.

Just then, we see three carts coming up the drive like a train with the group coming as couples two by two. Rosie gets up right away to show them the fixings she had out and make sure they all got their refreshments. Ryan was still wearing his hat from yesterday and told the group that his wife thought is looked sexy on him, Jessie's head turns fast and with a smile said I did not say that I said if you put an ascot on you would look like the captain off Gilligan's Island. Jessie was laughing at what she had just said and even slapped her leg thinking she was so funny. Ryan said well I could not let them know that I really liked the hat he shrugged his shoulders and snickered.

When Amanda and I stood up and they all saw our tee shirts Janette burst out laughing first, which had everyone pointing, and letting Rosie know that yes you are the Queen, which of course it was a highlight for Rosie, who always liked to make people laugh and feel good.

Jim asked if he could have all of our attention and please be seated in the meeting area so we could see the big screen. Paul gets up and says yes people we have a lot of information today and this will be our last meeting with the girls here. We will be sorry to see you go ladies, but at least we have an amazing plan to get you home safely and be able to enjoy the rest of your lives in comfort. Rosie pipes up and asks how everyone's drinks are doing before we sit down.

To start with, Dustin is sitting at the controls and welcomes us then brings up a holographic world glob showing a large X in the middle of an ocean then a dotted line to Alaska. With Paul standing up and addressing the group saying to start girls, as Paul looks right at us we have, it confirmed that we are leaving tomorrow evening at 11:00 PM. The space went silent for a moment and then I gasped looking at Amanda, Rosie then back at Paul … that is so soon I could feel my voice quiver. I could see Amanda's nose start to go red like did when she was little and about to cry.

I looked around at everyone there and all I could think to do was mouth the words thank you so much. Paul got my attention again as said now there is a lot that is going into this time line and that is what we intend to explained now.

Jim spoke next saying that our travel home is not going to be the issue at all. Our family dynamic is what needed meticulous planning as far as having the details of reconnection as discussed. It is to be made clear ladies, just because we are now able to open up the island and get you on your way home does not mean that the world you are going back to will be the same. To be frank there are parts of the world that may never be inhabited again and the world leaders have had to make some drastic changes to bring it back to what it is now as they were forced to work together for the survival of all humanity.

Having said that gloomy bit onto the family dynamics. Jim looks at the groups and says with Sires now decoded and more frequent communications Sire realized that the headrest was to get it so that your family would follow our instructions blindly so the best way to motivate people is with money. Jim carries on, confirmed is that we will both be receiving 10 million dollars as promised. Amanda grabs my hand and then Rosie jumps in her chair and interrupts with saying add your machine winnings to that she smiled and gave us her thumb up. Amanda and I were listening intently with the others looking just as intrigued.

Jim then said that you girls getting money would do little to motivate your family to just up and leave. So he carries on by saying, it was decided that each person will receive 2 million dollars when they are first approached by what we call Seri's attendants who are in place to ensure of their attendance at the reunion. Your family members will all be more then assured that their homes and animals would be cared for, beyond all expectations for the expected week they could be gone.

Going through the list of effected members we will explain their individual plans to get them to you next.
Amanda and I hanging on Jims every word when just then Kevin pulls up interrupting Jims speech which he stopped talking to look over and see Kevin looking at Henry with a big smile and said hey you know I had to hoof it to get my cart seeing as you ladies abended it at the café. Henry had a huge smile so proud of herself well Elsie was letting Kevin know that it was all Henry's idea I had nothing to do with it she says waiving her hands innocently. Henry looks at Elsie and winks they thought it was too funny.

Amanda and I appreciated the break in the mood as we smiled at each other relieving our intense focus. Kevin goes over to the bar and gets himself a beer saying as he is walking through, after all his hard work this morning I deserve this as he opens the bottle and motions cheers to the group. After total disruption Kevin acting completely oblivious sits down and looks at Jim and Paul then scans the group again with a boyish look, speaks up, and says so well people, what have I missed. With a second of silence the group all looking right at Kevin the breaks out in a bit of a laugh, with Rosie saying oh Kevin you really know how to make an entrance don't you, she said as she motioned to Jim to start up again.

Jim clears his throat and starts again, with how we are were going to manage each family members plan to get you all to Costa Rica to reunite and plan for all your futures.

Going through the list as the timeline for departure for each member is different. Colleen your husband and Amanda's fiancé will be receiving a hand delivered message by their assigned assistant. Once together the assistant is to provide confirmation of you both being alive and that all is good. The assistant will explain that due to reasons out of their scope, that not all details can be divulged at this time however soon all will be clear.

Jim continues with … The assistant assures that the homes and pets will be well cared for in their absence. Explaining that they are part of an elite and privet group that has access to all and the finances to manage any scenario. For instance, there will be a big limo waiting to take them to a privet airstrip where they will embark on a privet jet that will be taking them to Costa Rica to see their partners.

After hearing, that much I sat right up raised my hand and said I really think I need a break and a smoke this is getting very heavy. I bring my hands to the side of my head and make the mind-blowing motion with my fingers and Smile at Amanda as I stand. Rosie was quick to ask is everything okay sweetie? Going for a refill on my coffee, I said oh I am all-good for sure Rosie I am fine. I think I just wanted a smoke with a little smirk. I hear Dustin and Kevin say cool let us have a little hoot before they get going again.

Amanda follows behind me and says loud enough for everyone to hear … so what is going to make them believe the assistant. As Paul was at the food table, he pipes up to answer Amanda's question by saying that the assistant will have official crepitation and carrying our pictures and provide them both with a pouch holding $500.000.00 dollars for each of them. The assistant will proceed to let them know of the arrangements to get the rest of the immediate family there but that the assistant will need their help in convincing the others so that they cooperate with their specific plans for departure.

When finished explaining that part of the plan, I said out to the group that were all up and moving about the bar and food table. That sounds like it should not be that hard at all and with my little pause I finished by saying once you have our men convinced. I could feel I had a big smile and that Amanda was looking at me when she said are you kidding mom once they get the money they will do exactly what they are told she gave a hardy laugh and then said only kidding people only kidding. Once they have proof that we are alive they will follow instructions. Henry and Elsie liked Amanda's comment, looked at each other, and said at the same time… men! That had the group's attention with the ladies all laughing more so then the men.

Dustin and Kevin finish passing the hoot around when Dustin says let's get back at it people we have a lot of cool information yet. We can see Rosie is fussing around making sure that everyone is comfortable with full drinks and snakes at the ready as we start back to our seats.

Jim is back at the controls and with everyone's attention front and center, again he says Okay so once the assistant has your partners convinced then they will be given the exact instructions that they are to relayed to the rest of the family.

Letting everyone know the exact course of actions that will get them picked up and in the air. The family members will be instructed that employers will be compensated for all absence from work in the case of on their return that they have an interest in carrying on with their current path; they will have no problem without consequence from their employers. Just then, we hear Janette pipe up and get our attention saying with a smile yeah as if they are going to want to go back to a working life once they have their newfound fortunes. Amanda surprised the heck out of us all with her blurted big laugh when she tried to speak out to let us know that all the sudden she had a flash envisioning Jennifer her sister just going crazy! Not only with the news that her mommabear is alive but that she also has money!

Once we finished with our giggle, It was then that Paul started talking again giving Jim a break saying that the timing is important for getting the limo pickup in rule Alberta and Saskatchewan where they will be picked up and taken to a privet stipe close to their homes. From there then flown to the privet jet at the privet-landing strip just outside of Edmonton where Lawrence and Aaron will be waiting. This is where all of the family will converge and then fly together to your paradise destination.

The family will have verbal confirmation from your husband through a skype call to each of them. Your husband will be letting them know that this is not optional and that when the limo arrives to pick them up will be accompanied with a person to assist that will be able to stick handle any unforeseen situations of the day and answer their many questions as they make their way to the jet.

They will all have varying pick up times giving Lawrence and Aaron two days at home prior to the scheduled meet with the rest of the family and the privet jet. The Edmonton based family members will have a bit more time to gather with Lawrence and Aaron and prepare. With each family member having their own limo, and assigned personal assistant to help navigate their departures. Being aware of the coming connection your family members will be greeted and confirmed by the assistant, who will first provide the evidence of you lovely ladies being alive and then receiving proof of the money transfer of 2,000.000 dollars going into each of their accounts.

The firs assistant connection will be Kimberly whom lives in rule Alberta he says and points up to the quadrants on the monitor. The reason she is first is that she lives on and acreage with horses and other animals that will need care while she and her partner are away. The assistant will have a veterinarian stay at Kimberly's in a mobile veterinary clinic along with help to care for the animals and manage the place in her absence.

With all the family having pets the assistant will give them, the option of putting their pets up in a high-end kennel of their choosing or the assistant will offer to stage themselves in a motorhomes outside of the homes and provide the pets with daily care in the comfort of their own households.

The assistants will gain your families trust quickly as trained liaisons so that everyone is comfortable asking questions and that there is no surprises to make them any more nerves as they would already be. Paul lets out a big breath when Rosie, Janette, Jessie and Henry start clapping. I look over at Amanda and mouth oh my god, and they say aloud this is happening sweetie.

Rosie stands up, and heads to the bar as she asks how everyone is doing can I get anyone anything. You have time for a washroom break or a smoke if needed. Amanda jumps up and says you don't have to ask me twice smiling at Rosie. Kevin said I am with you girls and was right behind us with Dustin grabbing a beer and then coming over for a puff.

Ryan was sitting back in his chair taking in all the information along with Jessie was whispering to Ryan who themselves were starting to get excited to be the ones sailing us home.

Paul clinks his glass to get our attention again and said that when we are already we have more. We were all getting into hearing the intricacies of the plan and timing of the string of events to get us all together in Costa Rica so we finished our smokes and toped up our drinks to be ready to hear the next stage.
Before Paul started talking to the group again for some reason without thought, the question popped out of my mouth so what is the significance of us leaving tomorrow at 11:00 PM exactly. Paul looked back at me and

Amanda poked my shoulder saying good one mom. Paul replied good question Colleen I will get to that part right away. As he continues he says outside of all the drama that will happen once your family are all aware that you are alive and that there is money you will not have to concern your selves with. I am sure that once you are all together the stories of how they all got to you will be the talk for a while. Paul wanted to let us know that we should not focus on that component of the journey home and the reuniting.

Now ladies for the reason why we are specifically leaving at 11:00 PM is because at the point all program information, data and conditions line up and are predicted to be perfect for a safe and undetected start to our under water portion of the way home. I admit that the timing did come as a bit of a shock to me as well, I honestly thought we would have another day as he turns his head to look at our crew Ryan, Jessie and Rosie.

We now know, that Sire is and has been keeping an eye on us here and have lined up all the assistance at their end to manage the above water to ground to flight last legs of your journey to Costa Rica. Paul expressed how pleased he was with the amazing detail. Carrying on Paul looking around the group adds that once we reach a specific longitude and latitude in the submarine, miles away from the island. Sire will be able to lock onto our submarine signature that will help them calculate travel time to complete the process of booking transportation. With having exact times this will ensure that, the transfer boat and icebreaker are at the exact coordinates when the sub surfaces. The Alaskan team will be picking up the four of you once the sub surfaces off shore of Anchorage. For your girls safety yes Ryan and Jessie will escort you and stay with you right to the point of you boarding the privet jet in Alaska. Once the jet is off the ground Ryan and Jessie will repeat their steps back to the submarine where Rosie and I will be waiting to go directly back to the island.

It was then that Dustin stood up, turned to the group, and let us know that we have received another video message from Sire, which I believe is to be a parting message to Colleen and Amanda along with updated data for our systems. Just then, Henry spoke out as if the light bulb went on … saying so that is what was happening this morning? I could tell before we came her that her lab computer systems had allowed new data and it was working to process, what was obviously clean data or Dustin's operating systems would have quarantined the data and stopped the processing. Knowing if there was a problem, Dustin would have let me know.

Getting back to Paul, he says on that note ... I believe we have gotten through the bulk of the journey information so we will have a question period after we see what Sire has to say. So how about we all break. Rosie is up like a shot and nods her head to Janette then both of them headed for the kitchen.

It was apparent that we all had the same break time thought of having something a bit more serious to drink then coffee and beer as we all line up. Jim and Ryan took up a spot behind the bar while Rosie was in the kitchen and asked what we all wanted to drink. Paul jokingly butted his way to be the first by saying to Jim I did most of the presenting so I am parched and deserving he chuckled then said to Jim I will have a creaser kind sir, if you please. Ryan went right to pouring Jessie a glass of white wine. When Henry and Elsie let, Ryan know, they would have a glass of white wine as well. Amanda and I were standing back a bit and still processing information looking at each other when Amanda asked so what are you having mom. I felt zoned out but came back as Amanda said I am having a creaser like Paul. Yum that does sound good sweetie. Creasers and a smoke that will bring me back as I smiled and let Jim see that Amanda and I would have what Paul had. Jim winks at us and grabs two glasses at a time and fills them with ice and doing the bar tender thing like a pro.
As we all had our drinks and started walking to the lounge area Rosie and Janette come out to the kitchen pushing a large serving cart that they parked up by the bar and opened the big stainless lid to show us all that we are having mac and cheese and corn dogs. When everyone's head turns and sees the food that was being brought out there was a great surprise reaction with instantaneous applause. Our reaction was a bit over the top however, Janette and Rosie both curtsied the crowd with a big smile. As Janette swoops over to the bar to see Jim, he handed her what looked like a martini. I asked Henry who was standing by me if that was a martini that Janette was sipping on, I have never seen her have one of those before. Henry lets me know that Jim has been practicing his mixology skills and she was saying that she has taken a shine to them, Henry smiles and continues, but mostly for the two big olives, she laughs as she takes Elsie's hand and a sip of wine. Elsie lifted her glass, said I think I will stick with my wine, and smiled.

We take our place in the lounge to have our smokes when Kevin says to me ... so girl how you holding up? Is this all getting to be too much? I replied I am okay, just absorbing information, a little subdued may be, realizing how close we are to leaving and never coming back here. I took a panoramic look overhead holding back my tears. In an instant the music comes on playing some Queen tunes, Ryan was making sure to lighten up the mood of our cocktail hour while we mulled about enjoying our drinks.

It was not long before Amanda and I are hearing conversations turning to the receiving of a Sire's video message. With the group all having different interests are all hoping to garner specific information to each of them. With us all chatting in the lounge we hear Rosie call out to us come get dinner people. Kevin lifts his face up from his plate, and looked at Rosie as she snickered. I know I do not have to tell you twice. We could tell that Rosie was getting anxious to see the video and Paul with an empty glass went right over to Rosie to get her a drink and keep her occupied. Two by two, we all head over to the serving cart to fill our plates with some good old fashion mac and cheese and corn dogs.

Dustin caught that Rosie was getting restless we watch Dustin leaning over to Paul and made the suggestion how about we take our plates back to the meeting area and show the video while we have dinner. Paul turns his head, sees Rosie through the corner of his eye, and gives Dustin the nod.

Dustin stands up, claps his hands, and says how about a bit of a show while we eat. Let us see what Sire has to say I am chopping at the bit to know, as I am sure you all are.

Amanda and I were just going through the motions and following the group as we are taking in the day trying to remain somewhat normal. Once plates were loaded and drinks filled, we took our places so we could see the monitor when Dustin says is everyone settled and ready. We let out a few loud readies, and Ryan blurts out roll-em already.

Dustin clicks the controller and we see a grainy screen filled with colorful lines when suddenly we could see Sire face on the monitor. Kevin whistles and says loudly hey their friend! Rosie lets out a big shush, as she looks right at Kevin who blushingly made the motion to Rosie that he would be good.

Sire sitting up straight with a majestic looking background started talking, Amanda took my hand looking like she was sitting on pins we both turned to look at the monitor. Greetings my friends, my sweet Rosie I hope you are still cooking up a storm. Paul I miss our chess games and cohiba's, Jim my old friend I hope you are taking good care of your lovely artistic wife

Janette. Henry and Elsie our medical wonders, of the world I am sure you noticed that your systems at the lab were receiving data today as I have sent you some research that we have been working on here that we hope you can help us with. Actually, Henry, we are counting on you to analyze and confirm the information of the files and report to us your findings so we can further advance our extrasensory perceptions program that could take your filters to the next level. As Seri was greeting the group and as individuals, after hearing that, we all clearly turn to see Henry and Elsie who were visibly excited about the news, which lit them up with enthusiasm. Not knowing why I could feel their excitement with Amanda's grip tightening. I look at Amanda and quietly say well that has got to be cool, we smiled at each other as Sire continued By saying my good pay Kevin, how does your garden grow man, we could see that Sire thought that he was being funny with his slight grimes. Ryan, Jessie I am thrilled that you get to take the submarine out for a spin. I would trust her with no others you are both top shelf captains. Dustin my good man, you keep the island afloat so to speak and we owe much of our existence to you sir. Looking over at Dustin, he was shining his knuckles on his chest and mouthed to us all … you are welcome!

As Seri then addresses Amanda and myself. It was not as if he was seeing us in real time however, we still sat up and took notice that all eyes were on us now when Sire had said our names. I hope that your short stretch on the island has been days of pure fantasy with getting to spend this unfortunate time of world devastation, with the best people that humanity has to offer. I have all confidence and faith in the amazing people of the island who I knew would get you through this very difficult time of family separation and displacement. By his tone, we could hear his sincere and empathetic reflection of our situation.

Sire continues by saying … on a lighter note ladies I am sure you are clear on the substantial funds that will be distributed amongst you and your family members. I would like say that we are buying your silence however, the money has nothing to do with that at all. It just that I am immensely rich and just that I can, he gave out a bit of a belly laugh. He sat back in his chair and we could see by his body language gripping both his lapels about chest height that he was proud of his wealth and unapologetic for having money and came across to us, as if he was thrilled to be able to change our lives forever.

As Sire composes himself he looks, back into the camera says so now for the facts, as I understand them to be at this time. We could tell that he was looking over at another monitor and reading to us that the submarine captained by Jessie and Ryan with Rosie and Paul as crew carrying our two very special passengers will be descending the submarine shaft at precisely 11:00 PM tomorrow evening. He looks into view and says that does not give you girls much time for packing he snickered, only kidding he throws in for Amanda and my benefits, speaking from experience you know smiling … I have four daughters, sire winked into the camera.

Sire looks back at the other monitor and proceeds to say that Paul and Jim will complete their stability analysis in the morning 10:00AM to 12:00PM and stock the sub accordingly based on days at sea and people on board for total days of the journey. Rosie will have her fresh food supplies ordered with Kevin having them to the sub ready to load at 11:00 AM. Henry and Elsie will have completed their medical assessments and inventory of the sub replenished by 1:00 PM. Jessie and Ryan will start their sub operations checks at 2:00 PM with Dustin's assistance monitoring and confirming all systems responding to specifications from the birdcage.

I believe you will make the cocktail hour right on schedule he let out a little chuckle it will be margarita night wont it? Then says I wish I could be there with you. I am sure that the sendoff will be momentous and emotional knowing that the future is bright for us all will help to ease the lost feelings that I know will be felt.

In closing people, I would like to thank you all for taking such good care of our little invisible island and our precious guests that we were blessed to receive. It was just then Kevin actually broke our silence by saying loud enough for us all to hear … I would not go so far as saying we were blessed, he has not been scared out of his seat from Colleens laugh! Instantly all eyes were on me and we all started to howl. Kevin's timing and what he said was perfect and exactly what was needed at the moment.
Sire continued speaking as we lowered the volume of our laugher as Sire carried on to confirm that we will be monitoring all steps of the journey and will connect with the group once our captains bring her crew and submarine home. Good luck everyone and to Colleen and Amanda our paths may cross in the future. He ends with Sire Signing off and holds up his fingers as if he was smoking a hooty. I looked at Amanda, pointed to the monitor, and said in a soft voice now that is one cool bazilionair and smiled.

All the sudden the monitor went all fuzzy ending the connection so Dustin turned off the monitor while we all looked around at each other and started a quiet applause. I could feel myself take a big breath and let out a huff a little overwhelmed to say the least. I compose myself, lean over to give Amanda a hug, and whispered in her ear … I think I need a hoot sweetie! I see out of the corner of my eye that my suggestion lightened her thoughts of the moment. Rosie sees our hug and hustles right over to wrap her arms around both of us and gave a big squeeze. All the sudden our mom and daughter hug turned into a large group embrace as the rest of them came to surround us with arms wrapping and holding us up as we both started to cry and this time there was no holding back the tears. After a few seconds, Henry says it will all be okay girls this is overwhelming and reality is starting to set in. The group embrace slowly detached and Elsie and Janette hand Amanda and I tissues to wipe our tears. We take another minute with Rosie by our side to compose ourselves before re-engaging in conversation.

Rosie was very keen to quickly change the mood and must have motioned to Dustin to get some music playing as I unexcitingly hear Dolly Parton singing coat of many colors and the evening twinkling lights come on. Coming from the bar, we hear Kevin speak up loudly directing at Amanda and I … Hoot anyone? As hit toasts with a beer in one hand and a hoot in the other. Kevin raises his arm and waves us over to the pool area. Rosie with her hands on our backs gives us a soft nudge knowing that we needed the distraction. Henry was close behind us and as we reach Kevin, she hands us a glass of white wine saying this will go good with Kevin's special blend as she smiles so sweetly at us. We both thank Henry for bringing the glasses over as I have a big puff.

Knowing our eyes were probably red and puffy from having our little break down however we were put more at ease as we looked around and could see that so was everyone else's. I was thinking while Amanda was having her puff, that this was the only emotional episode we have had with the whole group during our time in the island.

The fellows were at the bar getting drinks and talking softly with the ladies mulling around the food cart. When Rosie takes charge and invites everyone to the lounge come on people let's sit back and reflect on the day's events. Rosie had her coffee and Bailies and waves everyone in. The three of us put out our smokes s Amanda nudges me and directs my attention over to Dustin and Ryan coming from the serving cart with each a bowl of Rosie's cheesy mac and chees with a corn dog stuck in it. That made us smile as we went to find our comfy seat. Henry, Elsie and Janette had full glasses of wine with Jim and Paul last to join the group as they were filling up with scotch. Amanda noticed that Ryan and Jessie were drinking none alcoholic fruit punch and asked so what is up with the no gas in your punch she chuckled at her word change. Jessie pipes up and proudly says we are driving tomorrow and we what to be at the top of our game for our departure. Ryne and Jessie clinked their glasses when the rest of us almost simultaneously followed with a here, here!

A wow comes from Dustin it is hard to believe you girls will be gone tomorrow night wow; this all seems to have happened so fast. Feeling brave enough I spoke up and said it been one hell of an experience that I wish I could say I will remember forever but no I will not. All good though I do know that I will remember when I am with Amanda and that is all I need now. I pat Amanda on the hand and she gives me a nod. Were all good mom we are good. We were a bit of a somber bunch but could not help ourselves from talking about Sire more then what he said but the way he looked and the background of only seeing Open Ocean like Sire was in a huge bubble which caused a hullabaloo with the group as they all hypothesize one his location. Amanda and found it quite humorous to listen to them banter back and forth.

After deliberations got nowhere Henry and Elsie who had finished their big glasses of wine were ready to go home. Although the reason for leaving may have only been so Henry could start combing over the information sent specifically to her. I see Rosie give Kevin the eye brows letting him know to drive the ladies home, which he picked up on her signal immediately and starts to get up from his chair and says I think I will grab myself a little care package and drive these nice lady home.

Kevin is up doing his thing when Henry and Elsie both say their good-byes and come over to give us a big hug when Elsie says in a cheerful voice we will see you girls in the morning then they follow Kevin to the cart.

In minutes it seemed that everyone else had finished their drinks and Ryan saying tomorrow is going to be a big day I need to get my beauty sleep, he leans towards Jessie and says right my little precious. Jessie laughs and responds by pinching both his cheers. Okay let's get you home. Jim and Janette stand at the same time letting us know that they were going to be on their way as well. We all look over to see Dustin gathering himself a care package so with his food in one hand Dustin waved and pointed to the door only footsteps behind the others as they head out home.

Paul and Rosie looked very relaxed in their chairs when Rosie looks over at both of us as we were sitting quietly and asks so how are you girls doing? Amanda and I look at each other and I know I could not find the words to actually describe what I was feeling but I did come out with … I am just flabbergasted. Both Rosie and Paul snickered over my chosen word and you Amanda, how are you holding up Rosie asked again. I am doing okay, as Henry said just overwhelmed. I am now realizing how very excited I am for what is going to happen next.

Well I am glad you girls are holding up okay we figured you would be find once everything sunk in, which Rosie looks over at Paul and pats his hand … it has for us all now. Rosie perks up and declares there is no room for sadness during your last hours in the island so we have decided that our sendoff party tomorrow will be Hawaiian luau. Paul making light of the discussion, and as he groaned getting out of his chair, looking at each of us. I know, you all just want to see me in some flowered shorts, I know. Paul laughs and turns to take his glass back to the bar as Rosie with her empty cup gets up to go with him.

A Hawaiian sendoff sounds fun I said to Amanda, I wonder what Rosie will have us wearing for our maiden voyage I giggled. Amanda well that is something to look forward too. I sensed Amanda was out of sorts and realized at this point there were no words that were going to help so I winked at her and said... hoot sweetie. She replies with a grin, now you're talking mom. I open our shinny case and grab one of Kevin special blends hoping it would take the edge off the angst we were obviously experiencing.

Rosie and Paul slowly work at cleaning up the serving cart that was almost empty putting things away and chatting quietly. As we pass the hooty back and forth, we can feel our edginess subside.

We can see that the palace is all back in order, as we put out our smokes. We hear Rosie say so who is up for some casino time before we call it a night. Although drained Amanda and I both lit up, and sprang out of our chairs surprising each other and Rosie. It is did not take much to get us out of our frump that was for sure. Paul was still at the bar and we heard him say right on I think will pour myself another, this should be fun he exclaims as he starts walking over to all the lit up machines. Rosie comes out with a fresh pot of coffee and some pastries to nibble. Amanda was first to place her bet and hit the button she looks over at me and says come on, momma needs a new pair of shoes and then laughs while Rosie squeals her face what's that? Amanda looks at Rosie I have no idea what that means, I just remember hearing it from a horse racing movie years ago and shrugs her shoulders and hits the button again. I was getting myself all set up and comfortable with smokes and coffee close and then I placed my bet and hit the button, to mimic Amanda I said giddily come on baby needs a new pair of shoes. We were all smiles as the machines dazzled us with lights and some small wins. Paul was hanging with Rosie at her machine where they were taking turns hitting the button and messing with the bets when Paul unintentionally hit a max on a game that was one hundred thousand dollars a hit on a max bet and low and behold if they did not get and big win. Paul hit the jackpot and the win was million dollars! We all just lost it, first because we could not believe that he hit max bet and then because he actually won the jackpot on it, wow high fives all around that was incredible. I am sure that everyone heard us carrying on over the huge win.

Once we had settled down Amanda and I got a bit brevier and started upping our bets a little however after about fifteen minutes of playing a large bet then it was Amanda that let out a aloud yippy! I got the bonus she says. We stopped playing our games so we could watch Amanda play her bonus round that was going to triple all wins. We were cheering here on as the game kept spinning. Holly crap Amanda you got extra spins you are so going to do this. Paul with a big smile and rosy cheeks reminds Amanda remember chicklet whatever you win you actually get to take with you. Oh, yes wow that is crazy I said with excitement. As Amanda's game kept playing her bonus spins the dollars were just adding up. With my machine not being so cooperative I watched the others play while I lit a special smoke. Amanda turned recognizing the waft and said I will have some of that mom; she smiled just as she won another three extra spins. Holly crap I shouted look at you go sweetie, too awesome.

After all the excitement, Amanda won another five hundred thousand dollars to add to her kitty. We both had to us, huge dollars in our bank. After our hoot and the big wins, we were all starting to deflate slumping in our chairs and Paul hanging on Rosie's machine when Rosie says okay girls how about we cash out now and see where you are.

We were ready to call it quits now not realizing that this was the last time we would ever play the machines with Rosie. Amanda and I hit our collet buttons to finds out that we were close in wins however, Amanda did come out ahead of me in the wins. Amanda was able to add eight hundred thousand dollars to her ten million dollar account and I received seven hundred and fifty thousand. We were beaming for sure not even comprehending at the time how much money that really was.

Once cashed out we were so done. The adrenalin we had was wearing down and our body language was letting Rosie and us know that it was time to shut her down for our last night. Rosie coming down from her high stool Paul helps her down and then gave her a big bear hug saying to her, you and I are going on a journey of a lifetime tomorrow how wonderful is that. Confirming that he was more than just smitten with Rosie, I don't think he even felt our presence as he looked deeply into Rosie's eyes takes her hand and give the top of it a sweet kiss and says until tomorrow my lady. Then in his regular cowboy Paul, voice he states to Amanda and I that I will see you ladies in the morning. It is going to be a very special, special day. Rosie still entranced with how Paul spoke to her or in what he had said, she did not move or speak and had a gaze in her eyes as Paul started walking away giving us all a big wave. It was then that as we were leaving the machines, Amanda and I were funning with Rosie about how obvious their feelings for each other was to us and for sure the others.
Rosie tries to down play and divert by abruptly changing the subject over to asking us if we had enough energy to have a Jacuzzi in our room or were we just showering and heading to bed. Rosie was filling our coffees and so cute, gave us three little bottles of Baileys each. Without too much thought, I replied I think once I have a seat in our so comfortable tropical parades lounge chair in our room I may not have the energy to get in the tub. I may even jus shower in the morning I smiled at them both. Amanda says yeah I think a coffee and a smoke will do me in too.

At that moment before saying our good nights we all realized that this would be our last night here, when Rosie got between Amanda and me and put her arms around our waists and starts walking us to our room and says I am sure going to miss you two. At the door, she gives us both a hug and a kiss on the cheek then holding our hands she lets us know that we are one of the best chapters in her life and she will cherish forever. Looking at us seeing our eyes start to fill, she sternly says to herself mostly, I am not going to cry as lets go of our hands she turns to walk away and says sweetly good night girls sleep well.

As predicted we get into our room got our housecoats on sat in our lounge had a smoke and for a moment just looked at each other. I was finally able to verbalize my thoughts and the only thing I could come out with was … Wow we really are leaving tomorrow sweetie. Amanda sits up and says I almost do not believe it you know. Like it is too good to be true. Well we got it right from the horse mouth so to speak that everything is good to go. Then unexpectedly she says I wonder what it is going to be like being in a submarine for that length of time. I was so quick to say thank the creators for our two smoking chairs. They might have had to sedate me otherwise for our underwater journey I started to laugh. We finish our coffee and smoke and both make the motion of trying to pull ourselves up from our chairs. Once up we slowly head over to the big beautiful bed that we have had the pleasure of sleeping in for a while. Before settling in, we share a big hug, I let Amanda know how proud I am of her, and the way she has handled all of this, you have grown up my precious. Mom I could not have survived any of this without you. We exchange our I love you's and say our good nights.

Chapter Twenty Nine

Waking up this morning, late I did feel very different. My eyes were open and I laid on my back just staring up to the amazing ceiling when I hear Amanda quietly say are you awake mom. I replied softly yes I sure am then roll over on my side facing her. How long have you been awake I asked her. May be ten minutes she replies. Man did I ever sleep how about you, like a rock she smiles.

Its then I think to look up to see what might be hanging for us to wear for our Hawaiian sendoff. As I sit up, I had to nudge Amanda for her to see first that at the end of our bed were our two large packed suite cases and second to see two of the cutest hibiscus floral long fitted sleeveless dresses with slits up both sides. Now those look sweet Amanda says. Yeah but look at the flip-flops they have embedded shinny pink rhinestones. Rosie knows us so well I said as I slide myself out of bed. Amada then pipes up so when did Rosie have time to pack our suitcases, who knows I have just decided she is magic because no human I have ever come across could hold a candle to what that woman can do in a day.

We decide to have a quick coffee a smoke then have our showers and get ready. Keeping with the routine that we had develop over the time we had been here. Once already, we wasted no time to get out to Rosie who we knew would be waiting for us with breakfast ready. As we come out of our room, we can see that Rosie is wearing a beautiful peach flowing crape dress that was longer in the back and shorter in the front that had a maze of flowers in varying peach tones.

When she sees us, she is once again impressed with her own work and how we look in her creations. She likes when we walk and pose as models would, we think you are so cute Rosie Amanda says as she wiggles her hips like a hula dancer. Yum breakfast smells wonderful I smell bacon as we were walking over to the perfectly arranged breakfast table Rosie had set. I let Rosie know that once again you have out done yourself the table looks beautiful with the fresh flowers and fruit arranged together. With coffee pot in hand, she says thank you but I cannot take the credit; Janette brought it over this morning with her little grin, she winked at me. Amanda says Janette was already here this morning, looking surprised. Oh yes Rosie responded. Kevin was here earlier with Paul to finalize our meat and produce order for the trip too. Rosie gives a big smile pouring our coffees, wow you girls really slept well, I am glad to hear that. Wow we sure must of, we did not hear any commotion out here or know that you had wheeled two large suitcases into our room. Yes, I brought them in just in case there was something you wanted to add that I might have missed.

Rosie opens a silver domed tray and show me that she had made us eggs benedict and extra bacon on the side for Amanda. With wide eyes, I let Rosie know that breakfast looks amazing. Amanda joking said I think this is almost lunch mom the morning is almost gone. Oh dear I feel my tummy turn, time was starting to feel like it was going by fast. Yeah sweetie you are so right. I raise my eyebrows, look at both of them, and say yes the countdown has begun … Eek!

No worries girls it is just like you are going on vacation and you will half the island with you for most of the journey. Rosie says to us once you girls are on the jet, land in Costa Rica and escorted to your new and very exclusive privet ranch you can defuse and explore your new surroundings. It is when you are all together that your family madness starts she laughed it may be a very special time reuniting, however the drama and craziness that will come with it I would be dreading more than the journey she said with a straight face with pause then gave us a big smile. Rosie could see the shock on Amanda's face and the contemplation in mine when she burst out with … only kidding ladies! We had a little chuckle while we continued to nibble on our breakfast.

Knowing Amanda and I did not have much to do today and the others are all taking care of business I suggested that Amanda I grab our go cups and do a couple cart runs around the island one last time having a few puffs along the way. I proposed my idea to Rosie and Amanda, with Rosie quickly agreeing that was a good idea. Amanda right over at Rosie and says you just want to get rid of us for a couple hours so we are out of your way and you can get your stuff done. There is no denying it Amanda smiled knowing she was right. Rosie had a little blush on and responded yes girls there are a few things on my, to do list yet and I feel I am running out of time.

With all that, Paul is doing to have the submarine ready he is also cooking a roast pig the traditional way. In a pit for our Hawaiian luau at the café, this evening and I nowhere are a few things to down there. I pipe up and say is there anything that we can help with? We do not have to go on a boondoggle if there is stuff we can be helping with. Rosie sinkers at the word I used and repeats boondoggle what the heck s that she asks. Amanda and I chuckled back and I said it is what you call … getting out of the way and out of work. Rosie liked that one and said she will have to use that on Kevin, as he is the best at that she winked.

You girls can go on your boondoggle and get in some visiting along the way and if there is, more you want in your suitcases have that put in before we all meet at the café. I will have a change of comfortable clothes out for you on the submarine to start our journey in comfort and style she smiles proudly.

We could see that Rosie was somewhat distracted keeping an eye on her tablet on the table which she does not typically have with her. We had finished our breakfast and could see that the sooner we got out of her hair the better so Amanda and push ourselves away from the table as we went over to fill our go cups. Rosie springs out of her chair and says let me do that, you gather your smokes and I will have these ready in a second. We both move out of Rosie's way as she gets our coffees, saying you girls don't know how to mix your coffee in the go cups, it a special mix that makes them taste so good. We were not about to argue as we see her pour in about three ounces of baileys in each one. As she hands us our go cups she says now that is how it is done girls, then she gives us the nod to get on our way.

Amanda and I were snickering to ourselves as we get to our pink driving machine knowing she was in a hurry to get rid of us. Amanda gets in her driver's seat, looks over at me, and says smoke! Seeing that I was already getting them out she smiles and away we go slowly this time down the hill taking in all the sights and smells. Amanda says I will be taking all the scenic trails and thought we would stop at the picnic area for a hoot. That sound good sweetie as sip our coffee when all the sudden we hear Hawaiian music softly playing throughout the island so everyone could hear. That is so cool I said to Amanda, yeah that takes surround sound to the next level for sure. I let out a laugh as what she said stuck a funny note with me. I see her look over at me with the expression on her face, like what she had said, was not that funny. Oh well to me it was funny and I still had my chuckle.

We pull up to the picnic area where we see the waterfall magnificently flowing out to the rock face and into the lake with its aqua blue sparkling water and white beach. Amanda parks and we both jump out with me prepared with hoot and coffee in hand. I light the hooty as we gaze out and pass it back and forth not getting into any deep conversation we recalling Rosie wanting us out of her way and smiled as the plum of smoke seem to hang around us. Then out of the blue, I give Amanda a jab in the arm and say look who is coming up the path. Of course, it was Kevin barreling towards us as we hear him say I smelt a little piece of my haven wafting and figured I had better come check it out. Kevin was laughing as he jumps out of his cart and says so how are you girls doing today. As I pass him the hoot he has a big smile and says so did Rosie kick you out? Amanda let out a laugh and responded with how did you know? Kevin continues, are you kidding me, when Rosie is on a mission we get her what she needs and then we all know to stay out of her way. Kevin takes another big puff and starts to turn back to his cart letting us know that he still had a few things to take care of on Rosie's to do list and I do not want to be the one to piss her off today he snickers as he gets in his cart. I will see you girls at the cafe later as he waves and zooms away.

It is funny that Kevin always seems to show up when a hoot is lit Amanda comments with a grin. Yeah something, like when you were younger sweetie. You always seems to know when I was having my hooty I bumped her with my hip and she shrugged her shoulders and motioned back at me a one thumb up. Feeling relaxed we sip our coffee and have a smoke. I get that tummy drop feeling again and said to Amanda wow I guess the clock is ticking we will be leaving soon wow! Amanda says yes we are leaving this evening but we will not be on dry land for days. Silence came over us for a second realizing what we have in front of us and that leaving today is only the first leg of our journey. I did not mean to say that to be a poo; it was just the thought that crossed my mind when you mentioned us leaving today. Well sweetie I think we have time and there are a few more spots to cruise by before meeting at the café. Amanda looked at me and questioned if there was anything else I could think of to put in our suitcases. I replied I have no idea what is in them in the first place and nothing here is ours to take.

I think I am good with whatever Rosie packed for us I am sure she would have done a much better job than I would have any way. I beg to differ mom Amanda says without hesitation, you are one of the best suitcase packers I know. Awa thank you sweetie, but that is with my own stuff I laughed. True she agreed.

From where we were standing, we could see Jim, Paul and Ryan in the distance going in and out of the submarine bunker, there was definitely action there. As Amanda, points to the cart as she is ready to move on she says how about we stay away from them so we do not get in the way, I agreed I do not want to upset the process. So then … where to sweetie I looked at Amanda. Hum how about we drive by everyone's homes for a last look, sounds good to me as long as they do not think we are spying on them I grinned. We jump into our cart and headed down the path to the far end of the island taking the greenery covered back paths that Amanda has come to know well with all her driving. Coming up to Jim and Janet's place we see at the driveway entrance they had a banner hung wishing us all safe travels and best wishes to Amanda and I. It did not look like anyone was at home. With Amanda stopped I jumped out of the cart and grabbed a stick then etched in the dirt a big heart with the words we will miss you! All our love, Amanda thought that was such a sweet gesture. We both had a lump in our throats when I get back in the cart and lit a smoke for us when Amanda puts us in gear and away we went to Ryan and Jessie place that looked very quit but with them coming with us, it was expected. When we get to Henry and Elsie's place, we can see that Elsie sees us and waves us to come in. We pull up to the house to meet Elsie that is all dressed in in her Hawaiian attire with a flower in her hair. I am so glad you girls are out taking your last spin around the place. Amanda laughs we had to get out of Rosie's way, Elsie's expression on her face went to a big smile as she says oh yeah that! We all snickered.

Elsie proceeds to let us know that Henry did receive some very interesting information yesterday so she has been absorbed with that today but I was going to get her in a bit and get some booze into her so she will relax for our luau Elsie let out a good laugh. Then Elsie stuck out her right wrist shows us that she had put a temporary tattoo around that looked like scrolling swirls intertwining with the words written … Live life like Colleen laughs! Awe Elsie that is so amazingly sweet I said as I could feel the tears come to my eyes knowing that Amanda would be feeling the same overwhelming emotion she gives us both a hug and says no, no girls no crying now let's save all our tears for your sendoff.

Amanda and I compose ourselves and whip our eyes when Elsie lets us know that she is going to pick up Henry and they are to start mixing up some slushy drinks and Rosie wants a punch made too. Elsie winked at us and says by the drinks Rosie has put on the menu, we may be pouring you two girls into the sub she giggled again shaking her head. Amanda and I take our Q, get back into our cart, and wave as we hear Elsie confirm that she will see us at the café shortly.

When we are out of ear short of Elsie, I grab Amanda's arm, and say awe her tattoo was so cute I was so emotionally moved when I read her inscription. Wow what a thoughtful gesture, Amanda looks over at me and says mom your laugh is indescribable and so infectious. Mom you can light up a whole

Living a good Alberta life enjoying a career first in floral design and credited for being very involved in Wayne Gretzy's wedding. Then my big jump into construction progressing into the oil and gas industry as a health and safety professional auditing and traveling throughout Canada and the U.S all while rising two beautiful girls. Remarried to a wonderful man later in life past making babies and now have five intelligent, beautiful girls and four amazing granddaughters.

Being asked to go to China to facilitate a safety-training program to fourteen of their best pipeline engineers was my career highlight in the safety world.

I have an imagination that keeps me occupied, this story was one that was running through my mind, and the only way to stop it from replaying in my head was to write it down. Oh and there is so much more!

CPSIA information can be obtained
at www.ICGtesting.com
Printed in the USA
LVHW041415120120
643337LV00001B/118/P

9 781951 653019